Royal treatment

Duke William's lip curled. He turned the quirt in his hands. "Your little stallion has a terrible temper."

Lark thrust her chin out. "He does not," she said. "What he has is a good memory."

The Duke scowled. "You would be wise, brat, to mind your own memory. Remember to whom you're speaking."

A retort sprang to Lark's lips, but she thought of the Duke's threat to her family, and she bit it back.

"Yes," William said, with a cold smile. "I see you understand." He slapped the quirt into his palm. "You may have passed your first Ribbon Day, but you have other tests facing you. And with an unruly stallion."

He took a single step closer.

"One failure," William murmured. His eyes were like black ice. "Just one, Miss Hamley, and he's gone."

AIRS
AND
GRACES

TOBY BISHOP

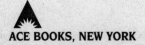

ACE BOOKS, NEW YORK

THE BERKLEY PUBLISHING GROUP
Published by the Penguin Group
Penguin Group (USA) Inc.
375 Hudson Street, New York, New York 10014, USA

Penguin Group (Canada), 90 Eglinton Avenue East, Suite 700, Toronto, Ontario M4P 2Y3, Canada
(a division of Pearson Penguin Canada Inc.)
Penguin Books Ltd., 80 Strand, London WC2R 0RL, England
Penguin Group Ireland, 25 St. Stephen's Green, Dublin 2, Ireland (a division of Penguin Books Ltd.)
Penguin Group (Australia), 250 Camberwell Road, Camberwell, Victoria 3124, Australia
(a division of Pearson Australia Group Pty. Ltd.)
Penguin Books India Pvt. Ltd., 11 Community Centre, Panchsheel Park, New Delhi—110 017, India
Penguin Group (NZ), 67 Apollo Drive, Rosedale, North Shore 0632, New Zealand
(a division of Pearson New Zealand Ltd.)
Penguin Books (South Africa) (Pty.) Ltd., 24 Sturdee Avenue, Rosebank, Johannesburg 2196,
South Africa

Penguin Books Ltd., Registered Offices: 80 Strand, London WC2R 0RL, England

This is a work of fiction. Names, characters, places, and incidents either are the product of the author's imagination or are used fictitiously, and any resemblance to actual persons, living or dead, business establishments, events, or locales is entirely coincidental. The publisher does not have any control over and does not assume any responsibility for author or third-party websites or their content.

AIRS AND GRACES

An Ace Book / published by arrangement with the author

PRINTING HISTORY
Ace mass-market edition / January 2008

Copyright © 2008 by Louise Marley.
Cover art by Allen Douglas.
Cover design by Judith Lagerman.
Interior text design by Kristin del Rosario.

ISBN: 978-0-441-01556-6

ACE
Ace Books are published by The Berkley Publishing Group,
a division of Penguin Group (USA) Inc.,
375 Hudson Street, New York, New York 10014.
ACE and the "A" design are trademarks belonging to Penguin Group (USA) Inc.

PRINTED IN THE UNITED STATES OF AMERICA

10 9 8 7 6 5 4 3 2 1

PROLOGUE

THEY came across the water in the early morning, emerging from the fogbank like figures from a nightmare. The warboats pierced the rolling mist, long, narrow shapes of bloodred and midnight black against the gray. Huge dogs with metal collars snarled and slavered in the bows, but the warriors themselves, squat, bearded men in leather helmets and jerkins, stood in ominous silence, swaying with the rocking of the boats. The long oars dipped again and again into the cold green sea. Every boat bristled with spears, and in each stern an archer was poised, ready to send a covering barrage of obsidian-tipped death.

The men of Onmarin, which meant every male above the age of ten, were out in their own small boats, fishing for the cod and plaice that swam beneath the glacier. The village was empty except for the old men who stayed behind to work on the drying racks ranged along the docks, women and girls mending nets in their thatched cottages, and little children. There was no one to protect them, but there was no reason to believe protection was needed. Old Duke Frederick had put an end to the raids from across the Strait, and the fishing villages of the Angles had lived in peace for more than twenty years.

The first shout from the docks brought only raised eyebrows and curiosity.

But the shout was too much for one of the dogs. He roared, and then leaped, huge and black and terrifying, over the bow of the warboat, crashing into the water with a great splash, swimming with powerful strokes toward the land. Moments later the first boat ground into the sand of the beach, and its ugly warriors swarmed over the sides, no longer silent, but yelling in their brutish language.

The fisher-folk of innocent Onmarin understood then. Women began to scream and children to wail. Mothers clutched babies to their breasts and herded toddlers and young boys ahead of them as they dashed inland, seeking the dubious safety of the dunes. The old men on the docks stood their ground, shakily, but bravely, wielding their filleting knives against the spears of the raiders.

The awful dogs bounded up the narrow lanes between the cottages, howling. Spears rose and fell, and the filleting knives slashed. Blood began to spill over the weathered boards of the docks and drip through into the icy water below.

And behind the farthest cottage, where a corridor of packed and rutted sand ran between the dunes, two winged horses rose, one shining black, one pale gold. Their powerful wings drove against the cold air, and their riders bent low over their necks.

One of the barbarians caught sight of them and gave a gleeful shriek. A volley of arrows spewed into the air, but by Kalla's grace, the winged horses were too far away, their ascent too swift and steep.

They flew as high and as fast as they dared, leaving the coastline behind, banking above the dunes and into the morning sunshine, escaping from the carnage on the ground, fleeing to the safety of Lady Beeth's protection.

ONE

Aᴛ the summer home of Lord and Lady Beeth, Larkyn Hamley reined her horse into the salt-scented wind. Tup broke into an eager trot, then a canter. His ears pricked forward, and his black hooves drummed on the grass of the park, faster and faster, blazing toward the grass-covered dunes that formed the northern boundary of the estate. Lark snugged her right hand into the handgrip of the breast strap, and held the reins loosely in her left. She gripped Tup's ribs with her calves, and he sped to the hand gallop.

His long, narrow wings opened, rippling in the breeze. The ribbed membranes caught the cool morning light in their ebony folds as they stretched to catch the air.

"Hup!" Lark cried, and Tup sprang upward. The wind rushed above and beneath his wings as he lifted above the narrow beach and out over the green sea. His hooves curled tightly beneath his body, and he ascended steadily. A fogbank obscured the horizon, hiding the glacier from view. Lark glanced over her shoulder to see Hester Beeth and her palomino, Golden Morning, launch above the dunes behind them. Goldie, a Foundation filly, was heavier and slower than Tup, but her flight was as elegant and deliberate as an eagle's.

Beneath the winged horses the cold green waves splashed

against the land, edging the beach with amber foam. Tup's wings stroked harder, and they rose high into the misty morning, banking to the west along the coast. Hester and Goldie flew close behind. Gulls darted above and below the winged horses as they carved an arc above the gentle inlets of the district known as the Angles. The Ocmarins rose in jagged splendor ahead, already white with snow. At home in the Uplands, Lark thought, the autumn fires would be set to burn the bloodbeet husks, sending ribbons of char drifting above the fields. Here in the Angles, the season brought fog in the morning and chill sunshine in the afternoon.

She glanced to her right, marveling at the nearness of Aeskland, the forbidden country. The girls of the Academy of the Air whispered midnight tales to each other about the barbarians who lived beneath the glacier. The stories said they were savage men and fierce women who lived in dirt houses, obeyed no law, and disdained all gods. With a shiver, she turned her eyes forward again.

It was tempting to fly on all morning, for the sheer joy of fresh air and freedom, but they had promised Hester's mamá to obey the Academy rules. Unsupervised flights could last no more than an hour. They would soon come to ground on a sandy spit near the fishing village of Onmarin where Rosellen, the Academy's stable-girl, lived with her family. The girls carried gifts, a tiny pot of fresh honey from the Beeth hives, a skein of dyed wool, twists of silk ribbon.

Their brief holiday was almost at an end. In two short days they must return to their studies, but until then, Lark luxuriated in Lady Beeth's indulgence. Lark could not remember her own mother, and she had worked hard on her brothers' farm since she was a tiny girl. She loved being petted and spoiled by Hester's mamá.

The chill of the sea air made Tup's flying seem effortless. Lark felt the brush of his wings over her calves, the warmth of his muscles beneath her legs. He swerved a little, flicking his tail to tease Golden Morning. Goldie ignored him, flying steadily onward in her dignified way.

Hester pointed, and Lark saw the jumbled roofs of the village ahead. They clustered around a little bay created by a narrow spit of sand. Docks and mooring posts edged the water. The fishing boats had already gone out, but gentle smoke curled from fires beneath racks of drying fish. A few figures moved between the racks.

Lark moved her right knee against Tup's shoulder, and he slowed, stilling his wings to glide on the air currents rising from the land. Hester and Golden Morning hovered to their right, as if they were flying Points, and the flyers circled, twice, three times, each pass a little lower, giving them a chance to find a landing place, look for obstacles. They came to ground neatly, first Tup, then Goldie, the horses' hind feet thumping lightly on the strip of sand, forefeet reaching, wings fluttering as they balanced.

By the time they trotted to the end of the spit, a band of small boys appeared between the cottages, pointing and calling. Before the girls had dismounted, and the horses had folded their wings, Rosellen herself appeared. She came running, the crowd of ragged boys at her heels.

She slowed to a walk as she came near the winged horses, saying to the children, "You lot stay back. Winged horses don't like men, and are not overmuch fond of boys, neither." The urchins exclaimed in disappointment, but they stopped where they were, goggling at the flyers. Rosellen gave the girls her gap-toothed grin. "What a gammon my mam is! Didn't believe two Academy girls would visit the likes of us."

Lark laughed. "Hello, Rosellen. What a pretty village!"

Hester stood with one hand on Goldie's neck, looking about her. It was possible, Lark thought, that she had never stood on her own feet in such a place. She would be accustomed to passing through rural villages in the comfort of her mother's carriage. Every Academy girl, except for Lark herself, had been brought up in wealth and comfort.

Rosellen came to Tup, and he nuzzled her shoulder and made the little whimpering sound that was his and his alone. Rosellen chuckled, rubbing his forelock, then dropped an awkward curtsy to Hester. "Thank you for coming, Miss."

"It's good to see you, Rosellen," Hester said. If she felt at all uncomfortable, she didn't show it. But then Hester, like her mother, was a born leader, and Lark imagined that included making herself fit into all kinds of situations. Hester held out the little bag of gifts. "My mamá sent these for your mamá."

As Rosellen thanked her and accepted the bag, one of the

little boys dared to move a step closer to Tup. Lark smiled down at him. "Would you like to pet him?"

His mouth opened, round as his awestruck eyes. "Really? Even though I'm a boy?"

"Aye," Lark said. "You won't be a man for quite some time, I'm thinking."

"Soon enough!" the boy said stoutly, puffing out his chest.

Lark laughed. "Well, if it's as soon as all that—maybe you'd best keep your distance after all."

The urchin's face fell, and with it, his thin chest. "Oh," he said. "Oh, but—but maybe not just yet, Miss."

"Nay, I think you're right, lad. Come now. Walk up slowly, and let's see how Tup feels about you."

The boy crept slowly toward the horse, one skinny hand extended. Lark felt certain there was nothing to worry about. This lad would see many more summers before he became a man. Tup only flicked an ear toward him and didn't budge. A blissful smile spread over the child's face as he stroked the glossy black coat and touched one silky wingpoint with a tentative finger.

"What's your name?" Lark asked.

He said softly, "Peter, Miss. Your horse is so beautiful!"

"Aye, Peter. You'll get no argument from me."

A straggling line of children formed, each waiting for their chance to touch a winged horse. Rosellen shrugged apologetically. "Them's never seen such," she said to the girls. "I hope you don't mind."

Hester stepped forward, leading Goldie. "Of course we don't mind," she said. "Come along, children. Goldie loves to be stroked."

By the time the children had each had their turn, patting first Tup, then Goldie, Rosellen's mam had come out of her cottage and walked down to the beach. She wore a shawl around her shoulders and a scarf covering her sandy hair. Lark and Hester inclined their heads to her at Rosellen's introduction, and Lark marveled at how much Rosellen looked like her mother, freckled, sturdy of figure. The gifts were bestowed, and greetings passed along from Lady Beeth, which made the fisherwoman blush furiously. She whispered in Rosellen's ear, and Rosellen turned to Hester.

"Mam wants to send some dried fish to her ladyship," she said. "If she'd like it."

"Of course she would," Hester said warmly. "Mamá loves fish." She smiled at Rosellen's mother, and the woman seemed to gather a little courage. She nodded, and curtsied, and spoke to the scrawny boy who had first approached Tup. "Peter, do you run to the docks and fetch a packet of fish for Lady Beeth."

He grinned at Lark and touched his forelock with two fingers before dashing away.

"My father and most of the men are out fishing, but my sisters want to meet you," Rosellen told the girls. "Will you come to the cottage?"

Soon girls, horses, and the gaggle of youngsters, shoving and shushing each other, trailed through the crooked sandy lanes of the village to Rosellen's tiny cottage. It was a ramshackle affair, thatched and sun-bleached, the walls leaning inland as if giving way before the incessant wind from the sea. Rosellen called, and two sturdy girls, as freckled and square-faced as Rosellen herself, emerged. A third hung back in the doorway. She was small, and painfully thin, with pale hair and only a scattering of freckles across her delicate face.

Rosellen pointed to her sisters. "Annalee, and Ginetta. Yon shy one is Lissie."

The girls stared as if frozen at the Academy students in their black riding habits, until their mother hissed at them, "Manners, you girls! We may be fisher-folk, but we know how to greet our betters!"

Lark dropped her eyes, embarrassed, as Rosellen's sisters curtsied. She wanted to explain that she was no higher in her station than any of them, but she knew they would never accept it. Now that she flew a winged horse, and kept company with the daughter of Lord and Lady Beeth, things were different. Already she was called Black by the other flyers, after her horse's proper name of Black Seraph. Only in her heart was she still Larkyn Hamley of Deeping Farm, the Uplands.

Hester spoke a courteous greeting to the girls, and Lark did her best to imitate her. In a few moments, Annalee and Ginetta relaxed and began plying them with questions. Only Lissie hung back, disappearing into the cottage the moment introductions were complete. Their mother brought out a simple breakfast, and an assortment of rickety chairs appeared so that everyone could sit down in the lee of the house, away from the wind. One of the urchins brought a few morsels of grain for the horses, who accepted them as graciously as Hester Beeth accepted the heavy dark bread and smoked fish presented by Rosellen's mother.

"Where's your saddle?" the boy named Peter demanded of Lark. "The big horse has one."

Lark cast Hester a look, and her friend grinned wickedly. "Yes, Black," she purred. "Where *is* your saddle?"

Lark tossed her head, and said to the child, "I like riding bareback, Peter. The saddle gets in my way, and Tup's, too."

"Them horsemistresses don't like it, though." Rosellen said.

"No," Lark admitted. "They don't."

"Black got through Ribbon Day by the skin of her teeth," Hester said. "And now she has to learn to ride like a grown-up."

Lark's tart response was interrupted by a shout from the docks. Rosellen's mother glanced at her daughters. "Annalee, do you go and see . . ."

Before she finished her request, a terrible sound, like the roar of some great beast, came to their ears. Annalee dashed around the side of the cottage.

What she saw made her cry out, and press her hands to her cheeks. Another shout followed, and then a cacophony of howling, human and animal, setting all the girls and children on their feet. The horses threw their heads up, and Tup began a nervous whickering.

"What is it?" Lark asked. She seized Tup's rein, afraid he, too, would dash to see what was happening.

Rosellen had followed her sister, but now she ran back to Lark and Hester. Her face had gone pale, her freckles standing out like flyspecks. She cried faintly, "It's—it's barbarians! I think they're Aesks—they're on the beach!"

Lark thought she could not have heard right. Barbarians? Surely there had not been an attack from Aeskland for . . . well, not in her lifetime. She moved to see for herself. "How do you know, Rosellen? How would you—"

Hester strode past her, Goldie close behind. As she stepped out into the wind, strands of her long hair escaped her rider's knot and whipped around her shoulders. "She's right, Black,"

Hester snapped. "Kalla's teeth, the Council will be furious! Rosellen, can your family get away? Get inland?"

Lark hurried around the cottage, and gazed out to sea. What she saw stunned her.

In school, she had seen the books with pictures of barbarians coming to Oc in their warboats, but those were old books, old like the stories the girls whispered on the sleeping porch. Lark had never expected to see barbarians for herself. Every book claimed that the Duchy had ended their raids forever. All her life she had believed that Klee was Oc's only enemy, and that a subtle one, marked by intrigues and deceptions and endless diplomatic maneuvering. Danger came from the east, not sailing across the Strait from the north.

But here, in fact, it was, in the shape of red and black boats, quivering spears, archers with bows poised, and great, awful dogs even now bounding up from the beach.

Lark clutched Tup's mane, and her heart pounded in her ears. He stamped his feet and snorted and switched his tail.

And then Rosellen's mother ordered, "You two girls, Lark and Hester! Get away from Onmarin, now!"

Hester and Lark stared at her. She looked utterly different at this moment, as if she stood taller, straighter, her freckled features gone hard.

"But—" Hester stammered, poise gone for once. "But—but what about you, Mistress? What about your girls, the children—your village? Your men are out to sea—"

"Don't know" was the abrupt answer. "But we don't want the devils to capture two flying horses! Go!"

When the girls still hesitated, Rosellen snapped, "Go, Lark! And Hester, get you to Lady Beeth and tell her—that's all you can do for us!" Without waiting to see if they obeyed, she turned back to her mother. "Come on, Mam, let's take the children—try for the dunes!"

Screams rose from the docks. A few women with babies in their arms fled past the cottage, wailing. Rosellen's sisters and the little gang of boys dashed away toward the dunes, but Rosellen, with a cry of "Lissie!" turned back to the house and disappeared inside.

Lark and Hester leaped aboard their horses and reined them

in a half circle, looking for a place to launch. Lark, though her heart rebelled against abandoning the village, knew Rosellen had been right. It was her duty to protect Tup, her bondmate, even if it meant her own life.

They found a relatively flat place between the winding dunes, a path of packed sand, ridged and rutted. Hester led the way, grim-faced and pale. Lark and Tup followed.

Sensing their riders' intensity, the horses fairly leaped into the air. It was hard, because they had to canter away from the pre-vailing wind. The ground was uneven and the launching space cramped, but they made a gallant effort. Their ascent was wobbly and uneven, but they succeeded. They were aloft.

As they rose above the dunes, the barbarians caught sight of them, and a great shout rose, words in some guttural language Lark couldn't understand. A cloud of arrows flew from the lanes of the village, but they fell short by many rods.

Lark took one agonized look back at the village. The battle on the docks was already over, the old men slumping beneath their racks of fish. One of the barbarians also lay still, short, thick legs dangling absurdly into the water. The wardogs had the run of the village, and Lark heard a hoarse screaming from one of the cot-tages that made her blood run cold.

Kalla's heels, what could they want? What could Onmarin have that barbarians desired?

She turned her face away and called to Tup. "Faster, Tup, fly faster!"

He responded, driving his wings harder against the wind, his neck stretching forward.

Lark tried to concentrate on her balance, on gripping Tup's barrel with her calves. She breathed in great gulps of sweet cold air, fighting nausea at the thought of the terrible things happen-ing behind her. How fragile a thing was peace! The safety she had taken for granted an hour before had been shattered in a heartbeat.

She gritted her teeth against despair, and prayed to Erd, the warrior god of the north, to defend Rosellen and the villagers of Onmarin.

TWO

PHILIPPA Winter pleated her gloves between her fingers as she gazed across the Rotunda. The thirty-eight Council Lords sat in tiered rows of elaborately carved chairs. Each had a secretary at his elbow and a page standing behind him. Their ladies filled the balcony with the glitter of jeweled caps and tabards girdled with gold. The autumn sun glared on the windows, and the air inside the Rotunda was close, heavy with too many perfumes.

Philippa was glad not to be forced to sit. She paced the outer aisle, looking down over the heads of the lords to the dais. There Duke William lounged in his high-backed chair, lifting one languid hand to smooth his white-blond hair. His timid wife, the Duchess Constance, huddled in the chair next to him, looking lost in her heavily brocaded tabard. A great rope of pearls twisted about her neck and hung to her waist. It looked as if it might strangle the poor woman.

"Your Grace," intoned one of the lords. Philippa stopped pacing, and leaned forward to see who it was. As she did so, William's gaze lifted, and found her. His eyes, dark and glittering, held hers with a look that made her skin go cold. The animosity between them had grown more bitter with each passing year. She supposed now, since the Academy was opposed to him in the present complaint, it would intensify even more.

It was Lord Carden speaking, his secretary holding his notes for him. "Your Grace," he said again, forcing the Duke to turn his attention to him. "The former Master Breeder has lodged a protest against the Palace regarding his removal from office."

William lifted one pale eyebrow. "Indeed?" he said. "And on what grounds does he object to our decision?"

Lord Carden was an old man, a veteran of many Councils. Another man might have hemmed and stammered under the dark regard of a Duke known for vengefulness, but Lord Carden was long past the point that William could hurt him or his family. He stood as straight as a man of his years could do and lifted a letter from his secretary's hands. "Eduard Crisp writes that the new Master Breeder is unsuited to his position, and that he himself was unfairly removed from a post in which he had served honorably, as had his father before him, and his grandfather before that."

Philippa watched William's face during this recitation but could see no flicker of anger, no sign of indignation. William looked, as he had during this entire Council session, indifferent.

Lord Carden's voice dropped a tone. "Your Grace, Eduard Crisp has brought a serious allegation against the Palace."

"Because he lost his job?" drawled the Duke. "I hardly think that justifies troubling a Lord of the Council."

"No, Your Grace," the old lord said. "He accuses you of violating the bloodlines."

Philippa drew a swift breath, and she was not the only one. The chamber vibrated briefly with gasps and with shock. Even the ladies in the balcony froze, sensing a confrontation.

"Surely, Lord Carden," William began. He came slowly, almost indolently, to his feet, and tugged at the embroidered vest he wore beneath his coat. "Surely you, of all people, would not give serious consideration to such a charge."

"Duke William, as your father so often reminded us, your great-great-grandfather Francis was a wise man, and a prescient one. When he codified the bloodlines, he made any violation of them treason, and he did it for all of the Duchy of Oc, not only for the Academy and the Palace."

"We need no lecture, my lord," William said silkily. "And we take offense at the very mention of treason in this Council."

"We are a small duchy, Your Grace, and easily overrun. The winged horses are our greatest treasure."

William lifted both hands, palms up, and cast a quizzical look around the chamber. Some lords were shaking their heads with disapproval—Philippa's brother Meredith was one of these—but there were a few who sat gazing at the Duke with their arms folded, their eyes hard. Frederick, William's father, had earned the respect and even the admiration of his Council Lords and his people. The new Duke enjoyed no such popularity.

Philippa drew back as she saw anger kindle in William's face. She could see him assessing those lords who looked defiantly at him, could guess that he was already estimating which of them were vulnerable. "The Palace," he said, with a curl of disdain on his lips, "takes the preservation of the winged horses seriously. We work closely with the Academy. Master Crisp—" William sniffed dismissively. "Master Crisp is in error. We shall address this with him personally."

Lord Carden was not put off by this veiled threat. Philippa knew he had no young granddaughters, no debts or family crises, nothing with which William could manipulate him. He said, with the stubbornness he was known for, "Nevertheless, I propose an investigation, Your Grace."

On the opposite side of the chamber, Lord Beeth stood also. Lord Beeth's daughter was a second-level student at the Academy, and would in due course become a horsemistress. Like Lord Carden, Lord Beeth was immune to William's anger. He was a small, stout man, guided by his wife in everything he did in the Council. He spoke loudly and clearly. "I second Lord Carden's proposal."

A tense silence stretched over the Rotunda. The two lords looked about at their colleagues in search of support. When none came, William began to smile. "I believe, my lords," he said, with deceptive lightness, "that three voices are required to initiate such a process. It appears that the majority of you are wiser than my lords Carden and Beeth." He spoke the names with slight emphasis, and Philippa heard it as the warning it was meant to be.

She spun on her heel and strode from the chamber, her black riding habit whipping about her boots. Someone must warn Eduard.

IN the ordinary way of things, Philippa would not be required to attend meetings of the Council. But Margareth Morgan, Headmistress of the Academy, had not been well for some time. She relied on Philippa to be her eyes and ears on days like this one, and though Philippa had planned to spend part of this brief holiday at her family's home, she had willingly given it up to help her friend. Now, as she hurried to the stables on the outskirts of the White City, she was glad it had been she and not Margareth. Margareth was too ill and tired to deal with the posturing of the Duke and the Council Lords. Philippa loathed politics, but when they concerned the winged horses, her personal feelings didn't matter.

She retrieved her mare and hurried to the long, narrow flight paddock beyond the stables. As Winter Sunset lifted her into the cloudless sky, Philippa looked back at the white turrets and towers, the tidy green parks and neatly cobbled streets of Osham. She had always loved the White City, and never more so than when she had flown for old Duke Frederick. Now, with Frederick gone and William in the Ducal Palace, the city seemed tarnished somehow, as if the new Duke's dark nature had dimmed its beauty.

Sunny's wings beat strongly and steadily, carrying them toward the Academy. The flight was swift, with the wind at their backs, the slanting rays of the lowering sun in their eyes. Sunny soared above the gambrel roofs of the Academy stables, aligning herself with the return paddock without guidance from Philippa. She sensed, of course, Philippa's feelings of urgency. She touched down, her wings wide and still, and cantered easily toward the stables. Philippa leaped down from her saddle and turned for a brief moment to lay her cheek against Sunny's red mane. "Have a rest, my girl," she said. "I'll see you later, and we'll have a good brushing."

The interim stable-girl, a rather dull, thickset woman, came out to take Sunny's reins, and Philippa said absently, "Rosellen not back yet?"

"No, Mistress."

"Ah. Well, see to it you cool Sunny down. She feels warm to me." When the woman didn't answer, Philippa said, frowning, "Did you hear me, Erna?"

Erna sighed as if responding took too much energy. "Yes, Mistress."

"Answer me, then, when I speak to you," Philippa said with asperity. "Walk Sunny about, then rub her down."

Erna nodded and turned to plod heavily toward the dry paddock, with Sunny at her heels.

Philippa pursed her lips, but she left her to it. She stripped off her gloves as she hurried across the circular courtyard toward the Hall. Bramble, the oc-hound, came to trot at her side, and Philippa touched her silky gray head with her hand. Most of the Academy was deserted, the girls and instructors not yet returned from their holiday. She left Bramble in the courtyard and took the broad steps of the Hall two at a time. She removed her riding cap and smoothed her hair in its rider's knot as she strode past the painted portraits of winged horses that lined the foyer. She knocked once on the Headmistress's door, and went into her office.

"Margareth," she began. "Do you know where we can reach Eduard—" She broke off, seeing that Margareth had a visitor. "Why—Lady Beeth—I thought—were you not in the north, at your estate—with Hester and Larkyn?"

Amanda Beeth, a tall, broad-shouldered woman, turned at Philippa's entrance, and the grim expression on her face made Philippa put a hand to her throat. "Are the girls all right?" she demanded, sudden anxiety making her voice harsh.

"They are," Lady Beeth said, with the directness Philippa had always admired. Amanda Beeth's strength of character was reflected in her daughter.

Margareth Morgan nodded to Philippa. "Our girls are well," she said. "I sent them to take care of their horses, and then to the Dormitory."

"What's happened?" Philippa asked sharply.

"There has been a raid."

"A raid? Where, and by whom?"

"Onmarin, a fishing village near our northern estate," Lady Beeth said briskly. "Warboats, the girls tell me, sailing across the Strait."

"The girls!" Philippa exclaimed. "Surely they weren't there?"

"They were," Lady Beeth affirmed. "They had gone to visit Rosellen, your stable-girl, and meet her family. The raiders came while they were there, and Rosellen's mother—who must be a very smart woman—sent the girls off immediately. We've come back as quickly as we could. My phaeton makes good time. The girls wanted to fly, but I thought it was too risky. I made them ride with me and lead their horses."

"But then—but what happened?"

"We don't know yet," Margareth said.

Lady Beeth's strong features were drawn in hard lines. "I can hardly believe it, even now. There has been no trouble from across the Strait since I was a very small girl."

"The horsemistress in the Angles didn't see the warboats coming?" Philippa asked.

Margareth said bleakly, "There is no horsemistress in the Angles, Philippa. Duke William reassigned her to Isamar."

"Isamar," Philippa said sourly. "Our new Duke is uncommonly fond of the Prince, it seems." A familiar pain lanced up the back of Philippa's neck. She winced and rubbed at it. This was terrible news, for Oc and for the horsemistresses. There had been years of peace for Oc, ensured by the careful husbandry of old Duke Frederick. She had hoped that her own battle, and its attending tragedy, had been the last in her lifetime.

Amanda Beeth stood up. "I must reach my husband," she said, "before the Council closes, and while the Duke is still there."

Philippa got to her feet as well and pulled her cap from her belt. "I will go with you, Lady Beeth. Duke William must act in this matter."

"You will need fresh horses," Margareth began, but Lady Beeth shook her head.

"Thank you, but we changed them on our way. This pair is rested enough."

Margareth stood behind her desk, bracing herself on her hands. "Philippa—have a care."

Philippa paused in the act of putting on her riding cap. "What do you mean?"

"It won't help the cause of Onmarin to make the Duke defensive."

Philippa gave her a mirthless smile. "I'm not alone in criticizing William these days."

"Nevertheless."

"I'll do my best, Margareth." Philippa turned toward the door, already pulling on her gloves. "We must make certain the Lords of the Council understand how serious this is."

Amanda Beeth opened the door and held it for her. "I know my husband won't let the matter pass, and not only because it happened in our district. It is too much an admission of Oc's weakness, or its negligence."

"I hope the Council agrees with his lordship. Oh!" Philippa touched her forehead with her gloved fingers. "Margareth, I almost forgot. We must get word to Eduard . . . the Council refused to investigate his case, and the Duke is furious. Eduard should be warned."

Margareth had followed her to the door. "I'll go myself, Philippa."

As Philippa and Lady Beeth hurried down the steps to the courtyard and the waiting phaeton, Hester and Larkyn emerged from the stables, and dashed across to them.

"Mamá," Hester said urgently. "Make Papá do something for Rosellen and her family!"

"We'll try, Hester."

The driver clucked to the horses, and the phaeton rolled smartly out of the courtyard toward the road to Osham. Philippa looked back over her shoulder at the two girls in the courtyard, tall Hester, with her fair hair smoothed into the rider's knot, Larkyn small and vivid, with violet eyes, her dark curls cut short. Their innocence made Philippa's heart ache. It had been easy to believe, when Oc and Klee made their uneasy peace, that the times of war were past. She hated to face the knowledge that such times would come again and weigh on these young flyers. She knew all too well how heavy the memories of war could be.

THREE

LARK brushed Tup's coat until it shone like the blackstone of her native Uplands. She combed his tail, and clipped his mane. She used the hoof pick to remove tiny pebbles and bits of bracken wedged around the frog of each hoof, and then polished his hooves with pine tree oil until they glistened. Tup loved to be groomed, and would usually groan with pleasure under the currycomb, or nibble at her hair, giving his little whickering cry as she brushed his mane. Today, though, he was quiet, though his ears followed her every movement. Even Molly, the long-haired Uplands goat who kept Tup company, seemed to have caught Lark's bitter mood. Molly pressed close to Lark as she worked, and Lark stopped from time to time to rub her poll.

When Tup's grooming was done, she rested her cheek against his shoulder, feeling his warmth and strength, not caring that she was covered in horsehair and probably smelled as much like horse as he did. Molly pushed between them, and Lark closed her eyes, drinking in the comfort of her bonded companion and the little brown goat. They made her feel as if she were home again on Deeping Farm, as if she could walk out of the stables and go into her own comfortable, ancient kitchen, with its slanting floor and scarred table, the rue-tree just now shedding its leaves beside the door.

She was still there when Hester came along from Goldie's stall. Lark sighed, and straightened as Hester leaned over the gate. "I hear the carriages on the road," she said. "The others are coming back."

"I wonder who will tell them," Lark said.

Hester shook her head. "I don't want to be the one. Do you?"

"Nay. I can barely stand to think of it, much less speak of it." Lark gave Tup one last pat and crossed to the gate. She and Hester went out into the sunshine, to stand in the cobbled courtyard and wait for the carriages to arrive.

"Poor Lissie," Lark said softly. "Poor little lass. She must be frightened half out of her mind. I hope they won't hurt her."

"They're Aesks," Hester said grimly. "Barbarians. She may not survive either."

"DOES it mean war?" asked Isobel softly. She and the other second-level girls clustered around Hester and Lark on the sleeping porch, on the upper level of the Dormitory. Word of the tragedy had spread like running flames at dinner, and those girls who, like Isobel, flew Foundation horses, looked especially grave.

Hester also flew a Foundation, and Lark knew she had always expected to be assigned to the Angles, or Eastreach, or the South Tower of Isamar. Foundation flyers were the first to be called upon in times of war; they were the strongest and the heaviest of the winged horses, used to patrol the coastlines, to escort armies, sometimes even to fight. Isamar and Klee, once a united kingdom, had fought a brief, bloody war more than dozen years before, but a truce had been reached between the Klee and Prince Nicolas. Though at times uneasy, the truce had held, and all of Oc clung to the hope of peace. They had believed the barbarians to the north vanquished long ago.

"It depends," Hester answered Isobel. "on how the Council decides to respond."

"But there can't be any question! This have to send a force to Aeskland!" This was from Grace, a girl who flew an Ocmarin filly. "Those poor children!"

"Don't be such a weakling," a voice sneered. It came from the far end of the sleeping porch, where most of the third-level girls had their cots. Lark knew this voice well, with its forced accent. "There's nothing to be done for them now. They should have taken steps to protect themselves, my father says, instead of expecting the Duke to do it for them!"

Hester's gray eyes met Lark's with a flash of warning, but Lark didn't care. She snapped, "They're citizens, Petra! They pay the tithe-man like everyone else. It's Oc's duty to protect them."

"Why don't you go after them, then, Goat-girl? If you care so much?" Petra Sweet stalked between the cots and came to stand before Lark, hands on hips, her features looking knife-blade sharp in the flickering light of the oil lamps.

"I do care," Lark said, lifting her chin. "And I would go in a minute."

"No doubt," Petra said. "You probably feel more at home with fisher-folk than with us!"

"Have a care, Sweet," Hester began, but Petra ignored her.

"Learned to use a proper saddle yet, Black?" she said to Lark. "Or are we going to have to ship you back to the Uplands with your little crybaby and that filthy goat?"

Isobel stamped her foot. "Petra Sweet, you just leave Black alone. She flew her Airs on Ribbon Day, just as we all did. No first-level class has ever done better."

"First-level!" Petra said. "What will you do about the second-level? Just wait for your Grand Reverses, to say nothing of Arrows!" She smiled, showing small, sharp teeth. "Without a flying saddle, your goat-girl will be tumbling through treetops, and likely bring you all down with her."

"Petra," Hester began, but Lark put up a hand.

"Never mind," she said. "She doesn't bother me. I'm an Up-lander. I don't need to argue with yon shoemaker."

Anabel sniffed loudly, then pinched her nose. "What is that *smell*?" she said. "Is that bootblack?"

Grace giggled. One or two others laughed, too. Petra glared at Lark, her eyes narrowed.

Until Lark arrived at the Academy, Petra had been the only girl there who did not come from titled aristocracy. Her father was a wealthy businessman, a manufacturer of shoes, and Petra felt her status keenly among the daughters of Oc's barons and earls. She had seized on Lark's country origins with fierce joy.

Lark had repaid her by blacking her eye shortly before Ribbon Day.

Petra looked down her nose. "I only warn you, girls," she said, "for your own good."

She turned and stalked away. Beatrice, who Lark had always thought the quietest and most demure of all their class, stuck out her tongue at Petra's retreating back. Everyone laughed.

Lark clamped her hands over her mouth. In her emotional state, she feared a burst of laughter would disintegrate into tears of grief. Rosellen had been her friend, her faithful support through her difficult first months at the Academy. She couldn't rid herself of the image of thick-bodied Aesks in their leather jerkins, swarming through the lanes of Onmarin. The wardogs' ghastly howling haunted her dreams. And poor Lissie, and small Peter, kidnapped, carried away by barbarians in those black and scarlet warboats . . .

She pressed the heels of her hands to her eyes, and the laughter around her died. No one spoke, though Anabel Chance put an arm across Lark's shoulders and squeezed her gently.

The other girls turned to their cots. One by one they blew out their lamps, and the sleeping porch quieted. Lark lay awake for a long time, worrying about what lay ahead for all who flew the winged horses, horsemistresses and students alike. She watched drifts of cloud blur the stars, and a pale sliver of moon rise behind them. She must write to her brothers in the morning and tell them the bad news. She would not want them to hear it from someone else.

PHILIPPA, too, lay wakeful in her bed. She had spent extra time rubbing down Winter Sunset after her long flight from the Angles, then blanketing her against the night chill. As she crossed the courtyard to the Domicile, the pallid moon barely pierced the thin cover of cloud. Winter's hand would soon be closing over the Duchy of Oc.

By the time she had reached the ruined village of Onmarin, other folk from the Angles were there, gathering up the dead, beginning the burials, comforting the fishermen who had come home with their day's catch to find their cottages afire, their families slaughtered. By the time the bodies had been counted and identified, everyone knew that two children were missing, abducted by the barbarians.

Rosellen, the Academy's stable-girl, had not survived the attack. Her body had been found in her cottage, where she had run back for her little sister. It was that sister, young Lissie, who was nowhere to be found. A small boy, Peter, was also unaccounted for. As in the old stories, the Aesks had taken children, and if the tales were true, poor Lissie and little Peter were doomed to lives of slavery—if they survived.

The news from the Council was tragic. Duke William was disinclined to war, and so, it seemed, were most of the Council Lords. Philippa tossed in her bed, fretting over this failure. Duke Frederick would never have tolerated the abandonment of any of his people, however poor or insignificant. When the South Tower of Isamar had been attacked, he had ordered his soldiers to war, and his horsemistresses into the air, without hesitation.

How many years ago had that been? Philippa counted back, startled to find that thirteen years had passed since that awful day. The memory, the awful sight of Alana Rose falling, was as fresh as if it had happened the week before.

And now, with Frederick in his grave less than a year, William spent his energies spying on his own people, fawning on Prince Nicolas, manipulating anyone who stood in his way.

Philippa, who had studied statecraft with the old Duke himself, agreed with Lord and Lady Beeth. If Oc did not move to protect its own, there could be more incursions, more offenses against the people. It boded ill for the Duchy that the Council felt otherwise.

At last Philippa gave up trying to sleep. As she often did, she gathered her bed quilt around her and sat in the comfortable armchair beside her window. She gazed out across the courtyard at the clean lines of the stables, the well-groomed paddocks. Tomorrow the new term would begin, with the arrival of a new class of first-level girls and their colts. Like the cycle of the year, the cycle of the Academy would go on, war or no war. So it had been for centuries.

She found the thought comforting. History had not recorded the name of the first brave woman to bond with a winged horse, to mount it, to launch into the sky in defiance of every natural law. And what man was the first to understand that no winged horse would abide him near?

Philippa's eyelids drooped, and sleep began to steal over her, there in her soft armchair. No one would ever know those names. Philippa was too pragmatic to believe the old fables about winged horses descending from the Old Ones, but for years she had turned to pondering the mystery as an escape from hard times, as on the day Alana Rose fell to her death, or when Irina Strong also fell, through her own fault, but with just as final a result.

Philippa yawned. Her muscles released, and her eyelids drooped. Who had been the progenitress of the horsemistresses? How far back, layered under recorded and unrecorded history . . .

Odd, that an unanswerable question should be her meditation, her repose. But it was. Philippa yawned again and forced herself to get up. She would be stiff in the morning if she fell asleep in the armchair.

She wrapped the quilt around her shoulders and was on the point of turning to her bed when she caught sight of a dark figure trudging up the lane from the road, just now coming into the courtyard. Sleepiness vanished.

Everyone else was abed. Every light had been extinguished in the stables, in the Dormitory, in the Residence. Philippa leaned toward the window, squinting through the darkness. The person was not tall, wrapped in a shapeless cloak and wearing a hat with a drooping brim. Whoever it was stood staring up at the darkened windows, looking at each building in turn.

Philippa reached for a coat to pull over her nightdress. She could hardly leave someone out in the cold and dark.

She slipped as quietly as she could down the staircase and across the foyer. She opened the front door and stepped outside. At the clicking of the latch, the stranger whirled to face her.

"Hello?" Philippa said.

"Oh!" It was a woman's voice, and a woman's plump face Philippa saw as the visitor jerked off her hat and bobbed a clumsy curtsy. "Oh, thank ye for coming down, Mistress. I know the hour is late, but I've walked so far . . . and I have nowhere else to go."

"The hour is indeed late," Philippa said. "But you had best come in. Quietly, please." Everyone is sleeping."

"Oh, aye," the woman said softly. She held her hat before

her in her two hands and climbed the steps, walking as if her feet hurt her. Philippa stood back to let her pass and saw that it was not a cloak the woman wore, but a long, rather ragged shawl, wrapped several times around her stooped shoulders. She carried a satchel in one hand.

When they were in the foyer of the Residence, the woman set down the satchel and stood awkwardly in the center of the tiled floor. Philippa struck a match and turned up two oil lamps on a breakfront. When they were burning steadily, she faced the woman, her brows raised.

The woman was past middle age, red-cheeked, with gray hair scraped into a braid that hung down her back. Her eyes were red and swollen, her face haggard and full of misery. She said, in a choking voice, "I'm Evalee Brown. Rosellen was my daughter."

Philippa put a hand to her throat. "Kalla's heels," she breathed. "Mistress Brown—I'm so sorry—" She crossed the floor swiftly and put out her hands to take the other woman's. The hat fell to the floor unheeded. "Don't tell me you walked all this way!" she said.

From the apartment beneath the stairs, she heard a door open and close. She was sorry to have wakened Matron, but it couldn't be helped. She put an arm around the grieving mother's shoulders. "Come to the kitchen, Mistress Brown," she said. "You must have something to eat."

"Perhaps—I could do with a cup of tea, if 'tis not too much trouble." Her voice broke on the last word, coming out as a little, exhausted sob. Philippa urged her toward the back of the Residence, where Matron kept a small kitchen supplied with tea and coffee, bread, a few simple things for making off-hour meals. When she pushed the door open, she found Matron already had the kettle on the boil and cups set out.

"Matron, you're a wonder," Philippa said. She introduced the two women, then urged Evalee Brown into a chair. Rosellen's mother accepted a cup of tea, circling it with her work-worn hands, and looked up into Philippa's eyes.

"He won't do nothing," she blurted.

Philippa was on the point of asking what Mistress Brown meant, but then, with an impatient gesture at her own slowness, she said, "Ah. You mean the Duke."

"Aye, Mistress. My man heard the Duke said there wasn't nothing to be done."

"Many of the Council Lords disagreed, Mistress Brown."

"That don't help," the woman answered. Her eyes were as bleak as the windswept coast that was her home. "That don't bring my poor Lissie back, or pay them demons for what they did to Rosellen."

"I'm so very sorry about Rosellen," Philippa said in a low tone. "We all are. She was a fine, hardworking girl, and we miss her." Matron set a plate of buttered bread on the table and withdrew from the little kitchen. Philippa pushed the plate nearer her guest.

"You know what they did to her?" Evalee Brown said in a tone of dull horror.

Philippa didn't want to know. She had been told Rosellen was dead, and had asked for no details. She could hardly say that to the girl's mother, though. Mutely, she shook her head.

"They savaged her, that's what they did," Mistress Brown said. "Rape is hardly the word for it. Rape, then . . ." She hung her head, and was silent for a long time. At last, she whispered, "My poor girl. All she ever wanted was to be near the winged horses." Her head began to move, side to side, trembling on her neck. "It's my fault. I wanted to see her once more, just wanted her to come for a visit. If I'd let her be, she would still be safe, out there in yon stables, mucking stalls and mending tack."

Philippa stretched her arm across the table and covered the woman's rough hand with her own smooth one. "It's not your fault," she said. "You couldn't have foreseen—"

Evalee Brown suddenly sucked in a noisy breath. Her head came up, and her hand turned to seize Philippa's with an iron grip. "They have my Lissie! Those animals, those beasts—my little Lissie, what's afraid of her own shadow! And he says—he says—"

"I know," Philippa said grimly. "I know what he says."

"You have to help me." It was not a plea, but a statement.

"I don't know what I can do," Philippa began, but Evalee Brown interrupted her.

"You know what them barbarians are like, Mistress. They make slaves of the children they take, they use them however they please, as if they was animals. It's been a long time, but we all know the stories, and we can't leave my Lissie and poor little Peter to them! We can't!"

And Philippa, with grim resignation growing in her breast, knew she was right.

WHEN the new girls and their foals began to arrive, Lark and the other second-levels were in a classroom that fronted the courtyard. Mistress Star, their instructor, gave up trying to keep order and allowed the girls to crowd into the windows to watch. Anabel and Hester were on either side of Lark, with the others kneeling or standing on tiptoe to see.

It was the first time Lark had seen a new class arrive. The girls of her own class, Beryl and Beatrice and Lillian and the others, had all come to the Academy in the usual way, their spring foals in tow, just as the warm days of autumn folded into the chill days of early winter. Tup had been a winter foal, a surprise to everyone. It was true, as Petra Sweet never tired of reminding everyone, that Lark was never intended to bond with a winged horse. But Lark believed firmly that Kalla, the horse goddess, had made her own choice in bringing Tup's dam to Deeping Farm for her foaling. Lark and Tup had not arrived at the Academy until the following summer, and everything about them was different.

Below, in the courtyard, she now saw how it was supposed to be. Colts filed wide-eyed and light-footed into the stables, their bonded companions at their sides. The oc-hounds who had fostered the colts paced alongside, feathery tails waving. The girls were no less wide-eyed than their colts, gazing around them at the emerald paddocks, at the long, whitewashed stables, at the majestic Hall flanked by the Dormitory on one side, the Domicile on the other. Some came in carriages, their winged colts trotting alongside. Others came in phaetons, or even, in one case, a girl rode a wingless horse with her foal on a lead beside her. None arrived, as Lark had, in an oxcart, her colt accompanied by a little brown Uplands goat.

Hester nodded to Lark as if she could hear her thoughts. Anabel exclaimed over the colts as they paraded across the courtyard in a palette of equine colors.

"Noble," Anabel proclaimed, as a roan filly trotted into the stables with her bondmate.

"There's a Foundation," Isobel said, pointing. The colt was a dapple gray, almost white. "And there's an Ocmarin."

Lark leaned closer to the glass to get a look at the little dun creature following a girl and the first-level instructor. "Get a blink at him," she said. "Those little pins—he looks a bit like Tup, doesn't he?"

"If by that bit of Uplands dialect you mean his legs," Hester said dryly, "I can't agree. That colt's legs are thinner than Tup's. Look how his croup slopes, too, where Tup's is so flat. And by the way, Black, I thought you were going to start calling your horse by his proper name!"

"I keep meaning to, but I'm so used to Tup. And he's used to it, too."

"No saddle and no name," Anabel said mildly. "You might have to try a little harder."

Lark sighed. "Aye," she said. "I suppose I could try calling him Black Seraph—or Seraph—though it's a mouthful. But the saddle still troubles me."

"You have to give it a chance." This came from Beatrice, surprising Lark once again. In fact, all her classmates surprised her, except for Hester and Anabel. All during her first long months at the Academy, she had felt as friendless as a bummer lamb. Only Hester and Anabel had treated her as one of their own. But since their triumphant Ribbon Day, her classmates had behaved differently, teasing her as friends might, going on about her country accent and her Uplands dialect. The last step of her true belonging would be to learn to use the flying saddle.

"Aye," Lark said again. "We have work to do, right enough."

Beatrice gave her a shy smile. "You're so good, Black. You have a beautiful seat. I know you can do it."

Lark blushed. "Thank you, Beatrice—Dark, I mean." She turned back to the window, warmed by the camaraderie. It was a quirk of Academy life that girls were called by the names of their horses. The moment Tup had received his proper name, she had become Larkyn Black instead of Larkyn Hamley. Sometimes, she still forgot to answer.

As they watched the last of the newcomers being sorted out,

Horsemistress Winter came out of the Hall and crossed the courtyard with her long-legged stride. She stood, pulling on her gloves, her bony face pale in the sunlight, waiting for Winter Sunset. The stable-girl who had taken Rosellen's job appeared with the sorrel mare, and the girls all leaned forward to watch Mistress Winter's standing mount, a lithe, swift leap into the saddle, and her brisk trot toward the flight paddock.

"Do you suppose she's off to the Palace?" Anabel asked.

"I don't think so," Isobel said. "She and the new Duke hate each other."

Hester and Lark exchanged glances. They knew the true depth of the conflict between Philippa Winter and Duke William, but they had sworn not to speak of it.

Lillian said, "They say she wanted to marry him when she was young."

"Oh, surely not!" Beryl put in. "She would never have wanted to marry!"

"Why not?" asked Anabel.

"She's—why, she's a *horsemistress*!" Beryl exclaimed.

"She wasn't a horsemistress when she was sixteen," Lillian said pertly. "She was a girl, the daughter of an earl. And her family was very close to the Duke's."

Hester interrupted. "There they go," she said. All eyes turned back to the window to watch Philippa Winter and her glorious Noble, Winter Sunset, launch into the mists of the autumn morning. Sunny's coat was a splash of red against the grayness, Mistress Winter's slender, erect figure a slash of black, barely moving as Winter Sunset drove them up and away.

"She's perfect!" Beatrice breathed.

"None better," Isobel agreed. "Too bad she's so sharp-tongued."

Lark restrained a protest. It was true enough, Mistress Winter was abrupt in her ways. But surely, she was the best flyer in all the Duchy. Lark watched her wing away to the south, the opposite direction from the Ducal Palace. She leaned into the window, gazing after the slender rider and the sorrel mare until they disappeared into the distant sky, and she wondered.

The antagonism between Mistress Winter and the Duke was no worse than that Duke William felt for Lark herself. He had wanted Tup for breeding, that secret breeding only she and

Hester and Mistress Winter knew of. They kept his secret in hopes that knowledge would give them some power over him. But the Duke had never forgiven Lark for keeping Tup from him.

Even now, safe in the Hall, the memory of Duke William's icy dark gaze gave her a shiver. She hoped Mistress Winter, her protector, would return soon.

FOUR

"FRANCIS, you have the best eye for horses in Isamar."

Lord Francis Fleckham, second son of Duke Frederick of Oc, bowed slightly to his prince. "Your Highness," he said mildly. "I think you exaggerate. But no one who grew up with my late father could help learning about horses, winged or not."

Isamar's prince, Nicolas, gave the younger man a lazy smile. "My own father had little interest in them, except for the prestige they brought him." Like all the Gelmonds, Nicolas had brown eyes and brown hair. Isamar's royals looked more like the Klee than they did like Isamarians, harking back to the days when Klee and Isamar were one single, albeit troubled, land.

"Well, in this case, Prince Nicolas," Francis said, nodding toward the tall stallion in the paddock, "given the color, the long backbone, and the depth of his chest, I would judge your stud has Foundation blood."

Nicolas eyed the horse. "A pity he throws no winged foals."

"I wasn't aware," Francis said, "that you aspired to breeding winged horses." He kept his tone deliberately light, but a prickle crept over his shoulders. The winged horses were Oc's province. His father had devoted his life to ensuring that they remained that way.

Nicolas gave a brief, noncommittal laugh. "I am no breeder," he said. "I barely ride."

Nicolas was a fat man, and only a horse the size of the stallion in the paddock would be able to carry his weight. Francis was not a diplomat, but to state such a fact would be an obvious political error. And Francis, though he preferred books and numbers to statecraft, had no wish to offend the Prince.

Nicolas waved a beringed hand at his stable-boy. "We won't ride today. Too tired."

The stable-boy bowed and led the horse away. It was a chilly morning. The cold saddle leather creaked against its fittings as the stallion pranced and pulled at his lead. The stable-boy set his heels to keep from being tossed off his feet. Francis suspected the Prince was simply too lazy to deal with such energy.

"Come, Francis. Coffee and breakfast." Prince Nicolas strolled past the open stable doors without pausing, and Francis was forced to follow him. He would have preferred to walk through them again, to smell the familiar odors of horseflesh and sawdust, saddle soap and grain. Those powerful scents reminded him of his father. They had never been close—indeed, Frederick had been close to only two people Francis knew of, and both were women—but Francis had admired and respected him. It was, he thought, a poorer world since the loss of the old Duke.

He glanced into the stables as they passed. At the far end, in the largest stalls, were the six winged horses of Oc, assigned here for ceremonial purposes, at great expense to Isamar. Francis often stood in the window of the library and watched the horsemistresses drilling in the air above the Palace. That, too, reminded him of home.

But there were no horsemistresses about now, on this cold morning. A few stable-boys came and went, and the one stable-girl who cared for the winged horses. There had been an elaborate party in the Palace last night, and the Prince's reddened eyes and general scent of old wine and tobacco attested to that. Francis had been forced to attend, for appearances' sake, but he had made his excuses early, and gone to bed. He had risen early this morning, as he usually did, to enjoy an hour's ride on his own dun gelding. The last of the leaves had fallen from the birches and vine maples. Snow covered the distant mountaintops, and bare tree limbs stretched into the sky like some dark script written across silver parchment.

Francis, with other second and third sons of the duchies of Isamar, had served in the Prince's Palace for three years. For some, it was preferable to being ruled at home by elder brothers, but Francis chafed under the artificiality and the excesses of the Prince's court. His love of books did not extend to account books, although he did his best to fulfill his duties. He often thought, had he been simply a Lord of the Council, he would have founded a great library in Oc, one to rival Isamar's. Unlike many of the other young lords, he had never coveted William's position. He had no wish at all to live in the Ducal Palace, or to rule. He wished, in truth, that he had been born a commoner, free to choose his own path.

He thrust such thoughts aside now. He could not change the circumstances of his birth. His father could perhaps have arranged something different for him, had he requested it, but Frederick had died all too early. And now Francis, like every other citizen of Oc, was subject to his brother's orders. William had made it clear he expected his brother to stay in Isamar, to be his liaison with the Prince.

The cooks had seen the Prince's approach through the windows of the Palace's great kitchens, and by the time Francis followed Nicolas into the morning room, a table had been set with a silver coffee service and covered dishes that emitted fragrant steam from beneath their lids. The Prince settled himself, with a groan, into a sturdy chair and waved Francis into one opposite. "Eat, Francis!" he said jovially. "You need meat on those bones of yours."

Francis sat down and took a cup of coffee, but he gave a rueful laugh. "Your Highness, I would think you had given up fattening me by now," he said. "My lord brother and I both have these long bones that resist all our efforts to cushion them."

"Lucky," Nicolas said, his mouth already full of a great rasher of bacon. "But you would make me look better if you were not so skinny."

Francis took a modest plate of bacon, with a boiled egg, and a helping of steamed and buttered bloodbeets. "These could be from our own fields of Oc," he said, spearing a slice of bloodbeet and holding it up for Nicolas to see. "From the Uplands."

Nicolas wrinkled his fleshy nose, and waved a dismissive

hand. "Can't stand the things," he said. "Give me bacon and bread, thanks."

Francis was saved from further conversation by the arrival of two other young lords, each with a question for the Prince. Francis ate his breakfast and left the men talking. He carried his coffee to one of the tall, many-paned windows that faced out over the city of Arlton.

Unlike Osham, Arlton was a city of colors. Its builders had borrowed from the blackstone of Oc's Uplands, from the gray granite that came from Eastreach, and the pink marble from Crossmount. It sprawled along the Arl River, circling the Palace with broad avenues, spilling out in twisting lanes and terraced gardens. The party the evening before had begun with a demonstration by the winged horses of Oc, flying above the parks and plazas, circling the pink and gray towers of the Palace. Nicolas had preened with pride, as if the horsemistresses belonged to him. They did not. Francis didn't bother mentioning it, because everyone knew the winged horses were Oc's pride, not Isamar's, and Prince Nicolas paid for their services with taxes wrung from the banking and shipping that made Isamar famous.

Francis had excused himself early from the banquet of imported wines and exotic meats, the platters of elaborate pastries. He was thoroughly tired of princely affectation. He longed, in truth, to go home.

He was about to turn away from the window, to turn back to his fat prince and the company of young lords gathered around him, when he saw a flash of red against the cold blue of the sky. He leaned closer to the glass, and peered into the distance. Yes, there it was . . . the unmistakable outline of a winged horse, with its slender black-habited horsemistress astride. As he watched, the pair came closer, growing larger and more distinct with each wingbeat. They banked around a tall spire and soared above the wide stone bridge that arched over the river.

Francis drained his coffee. This was not one of the horsemistresses residing here at the Palace. In fact, Francis recognized both horse and horsemistress. He set his cup on the nearest table and turned to bow to the Prince.

"If Your Highness will excuse me," he said.

Nicolas, his mouth full, waved a negligent hand. Francis hurried from the room.

He went down the stairs at twice the speed he and Nicolas had come up. When he came out into the fresh air, he took a deep draught of it, tasting the tang of rain in the wind. By afternoon the clouds that hovered on the northern horizon would blow south, and by evening the autumn rains would begin falling on the city. The horsemistress must have been watching the sky with some anxiety, fearful of being caught by the storm. But then, this particular horsemistress no doubt knew exactly when the rain would come, precisely how much time she had to make her journey from Osham.

Francis buttoned his greatcoat up to his chin, and thrust his cold hands deep in his pockets. In moments the magnificent sorrel Noble came up from the park at a posting trot, wings rippling in scarlet folds, drops of white lather flying from the jointure of wing and chest. Her rider was slender and tall, her riding cap pulled low over her rather long face. Francis stepped out into the return paddock and waited for them to reach him. When they were close enough, he called, "Mistress Winter! What a pleasure!"

She lifted a gloved hand, and a moment later, leaped as lightly to the ground as any girl, though he knew she was thirty-eight years old. She was the same age as William, ten years older than he himself. Only the weathered lines around her cool blue eyes hinted at her age. She had one of those bony, strong faces that retained its firmness and shape for a long time.

"Francis," she said. She put out her hand, and he took it in his own.

"Philippa," he answered, squeezing her hand. "I do mean it. It's wonderful to see a face from home, and especially yours."

"That's kind," she answered.

"Have you come from my lord brother? Do you wish to see the Prince?"

"No," she said. She gave him a level look. "I carry a letter from Margareth to His Highness, but it's meaningless. It's a cover." At his lifted eyebrows, she nodded. "It's you I've come to see, Francis. And William must know nothing about it."

PHILIPPA had spent many months in Arlton years before. Prince Nicolas had not yet taken his father's throne at the time, but it was clear, even then, that he was a man inclined to indolence.

Still, his corpulence surprised her when Francis escorted her into the salon where the Prince sat with two secretaries and an older man.

Philippa inclined her head, and the Prince laughed. "Never curtsy, you horsemistresses!"

"No, Your Highness," Philippa said. "It is not our custom."

"I know." He chuckled. "None of this lot here will curtsy, either."

"No offense is intended, my lord."

Nicolas waved a hand. "None taken, Mistress. Tell me, what brings you here? Word from Duke William, perhaps?"

"No, Prince Nicolas." Philippa took a step closer, and drew an ivory envelope from her pocket. "My headmistress, Margareth Morgan, greets you, and asks for advice on a small detail regarding the flight you have here at the Palace."

Some polite conversation followed, remembrances of Margareth's days spent with Nicolas's father, when she was still Margareth Highflyer, and Nicolas was a boy. Nicolas asked after William and expressed his regrets over the death of Duke Frederick. He barely glanced at Margareth's letter before he passed it to a secretary. "Answer that," he ordered. "Use your best judgment." The secretary bowed and departed, and Philippa and Francis were soon able to take their leave as well.

They strolled past the stables and paddocks and out into the rolling parks of the Palace grounds. A well-kept path wound between shrubs and groves, descending to a clear stream that burbled happily away toward the eastern sea. "Autumn comes so late here in Arlton," Philippa mused, trailing her hand through the drooping, still-leafy branches of a vine maple. "The leaves have all fallen in Osham, and the nights are drawing in."

Francis smiled. "It is a gentler climate," he said. "But I miss the air of Oc. It seems—cleaner, somehow. Sharper."

Philippa cast a glance at him from beneath the brim of her riding cap, thinking how appealing the Fleckham features were on this younger brother, when they were so hard on William. The Duke's black eyes were cold and full of danger. Perhaps it was simply because she knew Francis so well, but in him, those same eyes spoke to her of his sympathetic nature, his intelligence and sensitivity. He was a little shorter, a little more slender than his brother. Even his hair seemed softer, framing his face with ice-blond wisps.

She wondered how he managed, here in the Princely City, where politics ruled and every word had two meanings.

"Francis," she said abruptly. "I presume upon our old acquaintance."

"Feel free," he said. "We've been friends since we were young."

She inclined her head, accepting the assurance. "Your brother's accession has been fraught with problems."

Francis raised one pale eyebrow and waited for her to go on. They reached a carved stone bench, and he gestured for Philippa to sit. She did, but stood again almost immediately, feeling restless. She pulled her gloves from her belt and creased them between her fingers.

"Duke William removed our Master Breeder and replaced him with a young man with no experience. Eduard Crisp accused him of violating the bloodlines, but the Council refused to prosecute the charge."

"Then that must not be why you've come."

Philippa lifted her face to meet his eyes. "No," she said shortly. "At least, not that alone. There's been a raid, Francis. On a tiny northern fishing village."

"Aeskland?" he asked, frowning. "But the barbarians have been quiet for years."

"They killed several villagers—including one very dear to us at the Academy, our stable-girl. They stole two children. We have all heard the terrible tales of how such kidnapped children are treated, Francis, but William—with the support of the majority of the Council—refuses to do anything."

Francis dropped his chin, thinking. "It surprises me."

"His attention is engaged elsewhere," Philippa said. "And that is why I think the two events are connected."

"The Master Breeder?" Francis said. "Then this is about the winged horses."

Philippa breathed a sigh of relief at Francis's quick grasp of the situation. "It is indeed, Francis," she said. "It's about the winged horses. And about treason."

He looked around them then and put a hand under her arm. "Come," he said. "I doubt anyone is nearby, but let's be certain. We can walk farther, and you can tell me all of it."

FIVE

FRANCIS left Philippa at the stables after hearing her out and walked alone toward his rooms in the Palace. The bustle had begun, as it did every afternoon, cooks and servants and delivery people hurrying this way and that. No evening passed at the Palace without some sort of official entertainment, visitors from Marin or Crossmount or Oc, or simply a reception for one of the nobles of Isamar. Francis didn't know who it might be this evening, but he knew he would be expected at dinner, to speak of import tariffs or the need for stronger diplomatic ties with Klee or with setting export prices. Everyone present would have an opinion on every issue. Such debates were the part of his duties he hated most. He didn't mind being a sort of glorified accountant for the Prince—accounts had to be kept, after all, and might as well be kept properly—but the posing and pretensions of diplomats irritated him.

Tonight, in particular, he doubted he was capable of pretending interest in such matters. His mind teemed with the images of nightmare, barbarians descending on a peaceful village, their painted warboats carving the cold green sea of the Strait, old men slaughtered in the streets, mothers wailing for dead children, two innocent ones carried off. The thought that his brother

would allow such a thing to pass without retribution made his
jaw ache with fury.

"Philippa," he had said finally, after she recited the whole
story, "I don't understand my brother. William was never altru-
istic, but this is Oc! These are our citizens!"

"I'm sorry to speak ill of your brother. It's his obsession
with the winged horses."

"My father was obsessed with them, too," Francis said. "But
he put his people's interests first."

"He did," Philippa agreed. "I think 'obsession' is the wrong
word for the way Duke Frederick felt about the bloodlines. I
know you and William sometimes felt he cared more for the
horses than he did for you—"

At this Francis put up a hand. "Those were childish feelings,
Philippa. It troubled William far more than it did me."

"I know." She had nodded then, and let her eyes stray to the
west, where the mountains rose like pale ghosts beyond the
foothills. He watched her profile, appreciating its ascetic strength.
She was not a beautiful woman, and she was ten years older than
he, but he had always admired her. He would have been happy to
have Philippa Islington as his sister.

"It's different for William," she said finally, then bit her lip
in uncharacteristic hesitation. He waited, wondering what mystery might unfold.

Philippa dropped her eyes to her hands, where she had folded
her gloves into a nearly flat square of black leather. "Francis,
William has altered his body."

"Sorry?" Francis thought he must have misheard her.

She looked up. "I believe he is taking some potion, some
medicament. His—" She made a gesture over her own meager
bosom. "He swells, here. Like a woman."

"But that can't be!"

"No, it can't. Not without interference."

"Why would my brother do such a thing? Is he mad?"

"Perhaps he is. But this is how much he wants to fly a
winged horse."

"But men can't fly—" Francis heard his voice rise, and he
swallowed, trying to wrap his mind around this offense.

"No," Philippa said flatly. "Men can't. But William, it seems,
will stop at nothing to change the fact."

Quietly, there by the flowing water, Philippa had told Francis of William's illegal breeding attempts, of his removal of the Master Breeder from his post, of his interest in a crossbred winter colt foaled in the cow barn of an Uplands farm. And now, at the end of the day, Francis was left to wonder what William hoped to gain. He had always known his brother to put his own interests before those of others—any others, including parents and siblings. He also knew how fiercely William had resented his father's obsession with the winged horses, and with the girls and women who flew them. Francis could guess that if William intended to fly a winged horse, he expected to profit from it. He could also guess where that profit was meant to be found, and it was a truth he did not want to accept. Philippa had come to ask for his help, and as yet, he had no idea how to provide it.

As he had expected, the dining room with its silk draperies and banks of candles was full of elaborately dressed emissaries and lordlings with their ladies. Prince Nicolas was already present, a glass of champagne in his hand, his cheeks red and perspiring, laughing. Francis slipped into the room unnoticed, and stood beside an arched doorway, eyeing the crowd.

"My lord Francis," a voice murmured, with the unmistakable accent of the east.

Francis turned to the side, and found the ambassador from Klee standing at his elbow. He bowed. "Baron Rys," he said. "No champagne for you?"

The Baron, a short, slender man with graying hair and finely cut features, shook his head. "There are weighty matters to discuss tonight," he said. "I prefer a clear head."

"Ah." Francis sighed and turned his eyes back to the crowded room. "It never ends."

"No." Rys's lips curved. "And I hear you, too, have matters to deal with."

Francis gave a short, humorless laugh. "My lord," he said. "Your ears must be the sharpest in all of Klee."

"News has ways of reaching me, it's true," the Baron said. "You had a distinguished visitor today."

"She's an old friend," Francis said. "Almost a sister to me."

Rys gave him a slantwise look. "Of course," he said smoothly. "And a friend of the new Duke as well, I believe?"

Francis shook his head, chuckling. "Baron Rys, I suspect

there is little I can tell you of Horsemistress Winter's relationship with my brother that you don't already know."

"Hmm. Well, one does hear things . . . about arguments on the floor of Oc's Council of Lords, for example."

Francis pursed his lips. "Spies, my lord?"

"Not at all." Rys gave a cool smile. "Business associates. But I understand your wariness. Peace between our lands is tenuous, is it not?" Rys made a gesture to invite Francis out of the over-heated dining room. Francis glanced around to be certain his prince did not need him at the moment, then followed the Klee Baron out into the cooler air of an anteroom. They sank into comfortable chairs, and Rys leaned forward.

"I've heard," he began, "that Oc suffered an attack on its northern coast by a band of barbarians."

"My brother calls it a skirmish," Francis said. "A minor raid."

Rys straightened, and shrugged expressively. "Minor, perhaps. Not to the dead. Or to the families of the kidnapped children."

Francis nodded, and clenched his jaw.

"Further," Rys said, "I'm told that Duke William refuses to spend money retrieving these small citizens."

Francis looked away, but anger burned in his cheeks.

"Yes, I see this shames you," the Baron said evenly. "I'm not surprised, Lord Francis. Your reputation is an honorable one."

"You flatter me."

"Not at all. I'm a diplomat. I know character when I see it."

"I am powerless in this matter," Francis said. "The Council has ruled with my brother."

"Ah. But I have a proposition that may help you."

Francis leaned back in his chair. In the dining room the clatter of china and glass had begun. "Tell me your proposition, my lord," he said. "Although I can promise nothing. I am—as are you, I believe—only a younger son."

"I am exactly that," Rys said. He sat back, too, and steepled his fingers. Francis eyed him, seeing the gleam of intelligence in his eye, the easy confidence that made him, although a small man, seem an imposing presence. "My older brother inherited the title of viscount, which carries with it lands and the position," Rys went on. "But we have an amicable relationship, and in the normal way of things, I enjoy diplomatic work. This situation, however, provides me with an opportunity to satisfy a secret ambition."

Francis waited. Rys gave him a small smile, and said, "I have a daughter—well, to be honest, I have three daughters, but this one is my particular pride. She's bright, and she's fiercely independent. She's not pretty, though I care nothing about that. I want her to have a life of her own, not to be married off like some expensive doll, to do a husband's wishes and abandon her own abilities."

"And what does she want, Rys?"

Rys said, with evident pride, "She yearns to fly a winged horse."

Francis's mouth opened, but for a long moment he could say nothing. The idea was revolutionary, but it had merit. Even Francis, who disdained politics, could see how such an alliance—the bonding of a Klee daughter to one of the winged horses—could help to stabilize relations between Klee and Isamar. "My lord," he said slowly. "What would you offer the Duchy of Oc to secure such an honor?"

"I," Baron Rys said, "will fund a war party, and lead it. To rescue the children."

PHILIPPA planned an early departure for the long flight back to Osham. One of the resident horsemistresses of the Palace arranged an early breakfast for her, and went to order Winter Sunset saddled. Philippa drank a cup of strong coffee and ate a dish of coddled eggs the cook had waiting. The cook also had prepared a packet of sandwiches, which Philippa accepted gratefully. She would rest Sunny halfway, then press on. With luck and good weather, she was hopeful of having dinner in the Hall tonight.

She walked across the courtyard to the stables, buttoning her coat over her habit, pulling on her warmest gloves. Frost rimed the grass in the paddocks, and her nose tingled with the early morning chill. Flying would be easier for Sunny, in the cold air, but Philippa knew she would have cold toes and icy fingers for the first hour, until the sun was well up into the sky.

Sunny was ready and waiting when she reached the flight

paddock. She took the reins from the stable-girl and removed Sunny's wingclips, slipping them into the pocket of her tabard. She was preparing to mount when she heard her name called. She turned and was startled to see Lord Francis sprinting across the courtyard. He stopped at the paddock fence, out of breath.

"Philippa! I hadn't thought you would be away so early," he panted.

"Why, Francis," she said. "I didn't expect to see you again this morning. I know there was a dinner last night, and you must have been late to bed."

He shrugged his slender shoulders and gave her a wry smile. "There's a dinner every night here," he said. "I excused myself early."

"It's kind of you to come to say goodbye," she said.

He leaned against the fence, catching his breath. "I did want to wish you a good flight, of course. But there's something else." He looked over his shoulder, and across to the stables, and gestured her toward him. She dropped Sunny's reins and crossed to the fence.

"I had not thought there would be anything I could do to help," Francis said quietly. "But now it seems there might be something."

Philippa put one gloved hand on the top rail. "What is it?"

"Do you know Baron Rys, of Klee?"

"No. We have not met."

"He's a clever man, and I believe an honest one," Francis said. "As much as any diplomat can afford to be honest, that is. He has offered to fund a war party to rescue the children from the Aesks."

Philippa drew a swift breath. "Francis—to do such a thing, the Baron must be asking a high price."

"Yes," Francis said. "But it may be one we can afford."

"Tell me."

"His youngest daughter—Amelia, her name is—longs to fly a winged horse."

Philippa dropped her hand from the fence, and folded her arms. "This is his price. That we bond his daughter—a daughter of Klee—to one of Kalla's creatures."

Francis nodded. "It's a good trade, Philippa. It's politically expedient, and it gives us a chance, at least, to recover the children."

"But we know nothing about this girl."

Francis smiled. "I think you often know little about the girls who bond to the winged horses, Philippa. You accept the recommendations of their parents and their tutors. Rys assures me his daughter is strong and intelligent. And independent," he added.

"Independent," Philippa repeated. "That may be a parent's euphemism for 'ill behaved.' "

Francis shrugged again. "It may be. Can you trust a father's word?"

Philippa snorted. "Sometimes not," she said. "But you're right. We've done it before."

Francis sobered. "Philippa, I think you must decide this, here and now. There's no time to waste, and Amelia Rys is already eighteen."

Philippa nodded. Francis was right. With every day that passed, hopes dimmed for the safety of the two children from Onmarin. And for a girl to be bonded, eighteen was none too young. She bent her head, thinking hard. "I gather you trust Baron Rys's judgment."

"I believe I can. I like him, even admire him. Of course, parents and their children . . ."

"He and his daughter must both understand that she will be bound to Oc for the length of her horse's life."

"He tells me they do."

"Well. Kalla's heels, this is odd, but I believe I can persuade Margareth," Philippa said. "It is your lord brother who may object."

"And the new Master Breeder."

Philippa shook her head. "Jinson is in over his head in almost everything relating to the bloodlines. He will say what William tells him to say and no more."

"Ah." Francis ran a hand over his fine hair. "Will the Council Lords support us?"

"Some of them," she answered. "Certainly Lord Beeth will. He knows I came to beg your help. And there are several who stood with him in the Rotunda, demanding action."

Francis gave a small nod. "I shall tell Baron Rys, then, to send for his daughter. The Prince will give me leave to be away for a time, if I ask him carefully. I had better send word to my brother myself."

"I think you must," Philippa said. "I wish you joy with it."

Francis laughed, a sound without mirth. "Thank you."

Philippa inclined her head. "I thank you, Francis, and the people of Onmarin will be grateful. Come to see us when you arrive."

"Look for me in three days."

A few minutes later, Philippa turned Sunny's head for the gallop down the flight paddock. As the mare's wings drove them up and away from the Palace, Philippa glanced back over her shoulder. Francis still stood beside the paddock fence, a slender figure in a long dark coat, shading his eyes to watch her flight. She lifted one hand in farewell, and he raised his arm in return.

As she settled into her saddle, Philippa thrust away, for the moment, her worries over the missing children, the coming conflict with the Duke, the dissent among the Council Lords. There was nothing more she could do today but enjoy the freedom of flight. She put one hand on Sunny's withers, feeling the heat of her muscles, the wondrous strength of her body.

William was wrong to toy with the bloodlines, wrong to endanger these amazing creatures. She would not give in to his meddling. She would fight him every step of the way.

SIX

LARK and Hester and the rest of the second-level girls were in
the dry paddock behind the stables when they saw Philippa
Winter and Winter Sunset winging toward the Academy through
the dusk. Hester tipped her head back to watch them and lost
her place.

Their instructor, Suzanne Star, had been drilling them in un-
mounted Points. On foot, the girls moved in the figures they
would later translate into flight, practicing the formations over
and over until they became second nature. "Hester," the horsemistress said sharply, "you will not learn the pattern if you
don't pay attention. Remember, it is not only you who could be
at risk. Whoever flies close to you depends upon your accu-
racy."

Hester said, "Yes, Mistress Star. I'm sorry." She stepped
back into place. Lark tried to keep track of where she was supposed to be, but her eyes strayed to the sky, too, watching the
sorrel mare's descent. Both girls hoped that Mistress Winter
had gone in search of help.

Hester had heard through her mamá that the Council Lords
had declined to act in the matter of the attack on the northern
village. The death toll, they said, was small, only six, and the
kidnapped children were probably dead already. No one seemed

to care that one of those slaughtered by the Aesk was a stable-girl from the Academy. Thinking of poor Rosellen's savage death dismissed in such a heartless way made Lark's eyes blur, and she stumbled out of the pattern.

Mistress Star clicked her tongue. "Larkyn, not you, too. Kalla's teeth, you girls must concentrate! Now, again. Anabel, you're first on the left. Everyone, mark your own position and that of the girls on either side—remember to make wing room—and now, right for a count of five—watch your leader! Descend, and left for a count of five. Half Reverse, and . . ."

It seemed to Lark to go on forever. Hester, on a Grand Reverse, grimaced at her. Lark closed her eyes briefly. Neither of them had been able to concentrate on their studies since the tragedy. Only flying distracted them, however briefly, from grief and worry and awful memories.

When Mistress Star released them at last to go and blanket their horses for the night, Winter Sunset was already in her stall. The new stable-girl, Erna, was filling her water bucket and shredding a flake of hay into her bin. Hester and Lark paused in the sawdust-strewn aisle and waited for the other girls to walk past.

"Erna," Hester said, when the others had gone. "Where is Mistress Winter?"

Erna gave the two girls a disinterested glance. "Gone to the Hall, 's far 's I know," she said offhandedly. "Prob'ly wants her dinner. Just left me with her mare to see to."

Hester rolled her eyes at Lark as they turned away. When they rounded the corner into their own wing of the stables, she whispered, "That one won't last long. What a sourpuss!"

"Aye. She is that. Rosellen would never—" Lark's throat closed.

Hester put a hand on her shoulder. "Give it time," she said softly. "We'll get over it."

"A thousand days to grieve, we say in the Uplands," Lark said. "And we've only been through a few so far." She sighed. "I only hope Mistress Winter—" A crash of hooves on wood interrupted her, followed by a girl's shout. She gasped, "Oh, Zito's ears! That's Tup!" She started to run. Hester was close on her heels.

They rounded the corner into the aisle where Tup and Golden Morning had their stalls, and both skidded to a stop in the sawdust.

Tup's hindquarters were turned toward the gate of his stall. Just as they got there, he kicked out, his hooves banging hard on the gate. The latch creaked so Lark thought it might break. Molly, the little brown goat, cowered in one corner of the stall.

Petra Sweet, pale and furious, stood with her back against the opposite wall, shouting, "Quiet, Seraph! Quiet!"

And beyond Petra, quirt in hand and face like a thundercloud, stood William of Oc.

"What's going on?" Lark demanded. At the sound of her voice, Tup whirled, and pressed his rump against the back wall. His head was high, his ears laid back, and sweat dripped down his sides, striping his folded wings. Lark hurried to let herself into the stall and cross to him.

With one hand on Tup's hot neck, she glared at the Duke and Petra. "What did you do to him?" she demanded.

"Nothing!" Petra shrilled. "What's the matter with your crybaby that a person can't walk past—"

"He's always been bad-tempered," the Duke said lightly. He stepped forward, and Lark felt Tup tense.

"Hush," she murmured to the horse. She pressed her body against his shoulder. "Hush, now, Tup, it's all right."

"It is *not* all right!" Petra declared.

Lark said, through a tight jaw, "What were you doing?" She meant to speak to the Duke, but Petra intervened.

"The Duke was only strolling through the stables." Petra shook a finger at Lark. "As is his right, and no other horse behaved in such a way. Seraph is out of control, if you ask me!"

"Good job I didn't ask you, then," Lark snapped.

Duke William's lip curled. "But it's true," he said. He turned the quirt in his hands. "Your little stallion has a terrible temper."

Lark thrust her chin out. "He does not," she said. "What he has is a good memory."

The Duke scowled. "You would be wise, brat, to mind your own memory. Remember to whom you're speaking."

A retort sprang to Lark's lips, but she thought of her brothers, and of the threat to Deeping Farm, and she bit it back.

"Yes," William said, with a cold smile. "I see you understand." He slapped the quirt into his palm. "You may have passed your first Ribbon Day, Miss Hamley, though we hardly expected it—"

Petra smirked at that, and Lark's heart began to pound with fury.

"But you have other tests still facing you," the Duke said. "And with an unruly stallion." He took a single step closer. Tup trembled against Lark's shoulder, and she felt him tense. She gripped a handful of his mane and willed him to be still.

"One failure," William murmured. His eyes were like black ice. "Just one, Miss Hamley, and he's gone."

"It won't happen," she managed to say through tight lips.

"I do hope not," William said in the silky voice that chilled anyone who recognized it. "What a shame that would be." He slapped the quirt into his palm one more time, and Tup flinched. William's smile grew, seeing it. "Good luck to you." He tucked the quirt under his arm, wheeled about, and strode away down the aisle.

Petra stood with her hands on her hips, glaring at Lark. "How dare you speak to His Grace that way? Your behavior was inexcusable! I believe the Headmistress should—"

"Oh, give over, Sweet," Hester snapped. "There are things you don't understand."

"What does that mean?" Petra asked, spinning about to face Hester. "Why do you always act like you know more than anyone else? Just because your father is one of the Lords of the Council—"

Lark said in a low tone, "Let it go, Hester. It doesn't matter what she thinks."

Petra cried, "I'm telling you, Larkyn Black, I'm going to speak to the Head about this!"

And Hester said firmly, "Do that, Petra. Enjoy yourself."

Petra made an exasperated sound and stalked out of the stables. Beside Lark, Tup relaxed his muscles and lowered his head. She stroked his cheek. Molly trotted across the stall to press against her knees.

"Is Seraph all right?" Hester put her elbows on the gate, leaning into the stall.

Tup's ears flicked forward at her voice, at ease now. "Aye," Lark said. "But I worry about what he'll do."

"Seraph, or the Duke?" Hester asked.

Lark said bitterly, "Both." She crossed the stall to take Tup's blanket from its shelf, and shook it out. "The Duke hates me," she said. "Because I stopped him getting what he wanted. And Tup hates the Duke because he beat him."

"You, at least," Hester said, straightening, "will be protected by the Council. Mamá assures me the Council will draw the line at allowing the Duke to interfere with one of the girls of the Academy."

Lark buckled Tup's blanket around him and checked to see that his water bucket was full. "But our farm," she said, as she gave the brown goat one last pat, and opened the half-gate to step through. "The Duke has the power to take it right away from the Hamleys, after we've held it for more than three hundred years."

"Try not to worry, Black. Mamá and Papá will do their best."

"I know. I'm grateful."

"Now, come help me with Goldie," Hester said. "We'll be late."

"Aye," Lark said.

She filled Golden Morning's water bucket while Hester blanketed her. As they turned to leave the stables, the oc-hound, Bramble, came pacing toward them.

Hester stroked her silky head. "Where have you been, Bramble?"

Lark patted the dog, too, and said, "She's been watching the Duke."

"How do you know that?"

"'Tis what she does. Ever since he stole Tup from the stables." She knelt in the sawdust, and murmured, "You're a lovely fine dog, Bramble. Watch over my Tup, now will you?"

Bramble's plumy tail waved gently, and she turned toward Tup's stall. As Lark stood, Bramble settled herself just outside the stall gate.

"That's amazing, Black," Hester said. "How do you do that?"

"Do what?"

"Talk to animals that way. You do it with Bramble, with Pig, with Molly. And they always seem to understand!"

Lark gave a small laugh. "I don't think Pig always understood!"

"Well—he's a difficult pony," Hester admitted. "But still."

Lark considered this as they crossed the courtyard. The lights of the Hall were on, and the aromas of supper reached them through the chill air. Despite her sadness, Lark was hungry. "I think," she said to Hester, as they climbed the steps, "that it's because I grew up with animals. No mother, no father—my brothers were wonderful to me, but they were always working. I had the goats, the cows, the chickens." They reached the tall doors, and Hester opened one. "And I had Char, for a time," Lark added sadly.

"Oh, Black," Hester said. "You've had a hard time of it."

Lark managed a smile up at her tall friend. "We grieve for a thousand days. 'Tis better now," she said.

Hester smiled back. "Yes, I think so."

But Lark couldn't help the thought, as they found their seats, that it would never get better for Rosellen. She doubted she would ever cease mourning her friend. Or Char, her magical little mare, or the mother she had never known. The world seemed full of grief. If only something could be done for the bereft parents of Onmarin!

Lark looked up at the high table, where the instructors sat. The Headmistress's seat was empty, and so, she saw, was Philippa Winter's. As Lark gazed at their empty chairs, the icon that hung around her neck, the little carved image of the horse goddess, grew warm against her skin. She touched it with her fingers and wondered what Kalla was trying to tell her.

SEVEN

THE day after Philippa's return from Arlton, a horsemistress arrived with a message for the Academy.

It was a cool afternoon, the shadows already beginning to slant across the Academy grounds. Philippa was in the flight paddock with her students when she saw the dun Ocmarin approaching from the south. She knew the horse, Sky Mouse, and knew the courier who flew him. She excused herself from her class and hurried to the return paddock, calling for Erna.

By the time the stable-girl plodded out, the courier was already leaping down from her horse, tapping his shoulder with her quirt, touching her cap to Philippa. As Sky Mouse folded his wings, Philippa said, "It's always good to see you, Catherine, but I suspect your errand is urgent."

"It is." Catherine Sky gave her reins to Erna.

Erna turned away, yanking on the reins, and Sky Mouse tossed his head in complaint.

Philippa said sternly, "Erna! Don't pull a horse's head that way."

Erna flashed her a sullen look. "Yes, Horsemistress."

"Mouse has flown a long way. He needs a walk and a rubdown. When he's cool—and not till then—give him water, and a feed of oats and flake of hay. Do you understand me?"

The girl nodded and set off toward the stables with the horse at her heels. As the two horsemistresses crossed the courtyard, Philippa said, "Erna hasn't been here long, and she makes mistakes. I'll send one of the girls out to check on Mouse."

"Thank you."

Philippa said bitterly, "We miss Rosellen even more when Erna gives us trouble."

"Was Rosellen the one killed in Onmarin?"

Philippa nodded. "I still can hardly believe it. It was an awful thing. Brutal."

"Lord Francis told me," Catherine said.

"You've come from him, I gather?"

"Yes." Catherine touched the leather pouch at her belt. "I have a letter for Duke William from Prince Nicolas. But my message for you and Margareth is from Lord Francis. Private."

"Come," Philippa said, opening the tall door to the Hall. "You can tell us together."

Both horsemistresses pulled off their caps and gloves as they crossed the foyer of the Hall. Philippa saw how Catherine scanned the familiar paintings, how she breathed in the old, comforting scents of polish and wax and leather. Before she knocked on Margareth's door, she said, "It's good to be back, isn't it?"

Catherine breathed a sigh of pleasure. "It feels more like home than my own."

Margareth was at her desk when they entered her office. She looked up, and smiled, but she didn't rise. She had grown thinner in the past weeks. Philippa wished she could believe it was only her worry over the current troubles, but she feared it was worse than that. Over the past two years, the Headmistress had grown increasingly weak, tiring easily, and she had a poor appetite. It was time and past time for her to retire, Philippa thought, but for her own sake, she dreaded that day.

"Catherine Sky," Margareth said. "What a pleasure to see you, my dear."

Catherine inclined her head to Margareth. If she, too, noticed that Margareth did not look well, she hid her feelings about it. "Headmistress," she said, "I was glad to know that my errand would bring me here."

"Catherine has a message for us from Francis," Philippa said. Margareth indicated the chairs across from her desk, and they seated themselves. Catherine glanced at the door to be certain it was closed before she said, "Lord Francis has arranged a war party to go in search of the children."

"Ah," Margareth said. "The agreement with Klee."

Catherine nodded. "Depending, of course, on whether you will accept Amelia Rys as a bondmate to one of the winged horses."

"Philippa explained this to me," Margareth said. "And she has persuaded me to endorse the plan. But the Duke may not, and the Master Breeder is his puppet."

"Yes, Lord Francis understands that." Catherine touched the messenger pouch at her belt. "I carry a letter for the Duke. But Lord Francis wants Philippa to deliver it."

"Philippa? But she and the Duke—" Margareth sat back in her chair, shaking her head. "I don't understand."

Philippa closed her eyes briefly, feeling the weight of responsibility. "I do, Margareth," she said heavily. "Francis knows I can put pressure on his brother."

Catherine untied the pouch and held it out to Philippa. "Lord Francis said he knew you would understand."

Philippa crossed to her and accepted the pouch. "I could wish I did not," she said. "But this must be done. Not only for the kidnapped children, but for the honor of Oc."

Margareth, with difficulty, came to her feet. "Be cautious, Philippa."

Philippa said, "It is far too late for that, Margareth. William has set himself against me. And our conflict has old roots." She tied the pouch to her own belt and nodded to Catherine and to Margareth. "He will be angry with me, no doubt. But there is no going back now. And what can he do, really? I'm a horsemistress of Oc. I have my own rights."

A few unseasonable snowflakes drifted around Philippa as she and Sunny came to ground in the park of the Ducal Palace. Sunny blew and danced as she trotted up the ride toward the stables. A few morsels of glittering white caught on her red mane and quickly vanished.

Philippa stroked her neck. "You like the cold weather, don't you, my girl?"

The mare came to a stop, tossing her head. Jolinda, the old stable-girl who had been in the Ducal stables since Frederick's day, came across the frosty grass to meet them. She smiled, a hundred wrinkles creasing her face. "Acting like a filly, isn't she, Mistress?"

"She is, Jolinda." Philippa swung one leg over the cantle and jumped to the ground. She winced a little, feeling the jolt in her knees. "I guess neither one of us is a filly anymore, though," she said wryly. "Nineteen years in the saddle this season."

Jolinda took Sunny's reins and clucked to her. Over her shoulder she said, "Thirty in the stables for me, Mistress Winter. Sorry to tell you, the knees is what feels it first."

Philippa laughed. "Thanks for the encouragement!"

Jolinda grinned and led Sunny off in the direction of the stables. Philippa watched them go, then turned to her left to cross the circular courtyard to the Palace steps.

Everything about the Palace grounds was painfully familiar. The window of Frederick's old apartment was just above the entryway, and the room where she herself had lived, so long ago, was to her right, around the corner and through the garden. She remembered the flush of excitement she had felt when she first arrived here to take up her duties in the Duke's service. She and Sunny had both been young then, nervous and proud at the same time. They had served well, Philippa thought, served both the Duke and the Duchy.

She climbed the steps, stripping off her gloves as she went. Tension gripped the back of her neck. In some strange way, she thought, she still served Frederick, though he had been gone more than a year. She knew what his dreams and ambitions had been, all for Oc, and for the winged horses. By tradition, she owed loyalty to William, because he was now the Duke. She had been taught that principle since childhood, and her training at the Academy had reinforced it. But, she reflected, she was incapable of blind loyalty.

"Kalla's teeth," she muttered under her breath. "If the Duke doesn't serve the Duchy, who will?"

There was no answer, of course. The heavy doors before her opened, and Parkson, William's steward, was bowing to her. She took off her cap as she followed him inside, and moments later, found herself in a comfortable study, warm with heat from a sturdy fire. She tucked her cap into her belt and paced back and forth before the study's wide window, pleating her gloves between her fingers.

William did not keep her waiting long. He stood just inside the room, one hand on a lean hip, the fingers of the other tucked into the pocket of his elaborate vest. Keeping his distance, Philippa thought. As if that would make a difference.

"I have a letter for you from Arlton," she said without preamble.

William's expression didn't change or his eyelids flicker. He said icily, "Why, Philippa. When did you become a courier for the Prince?"

"I have not done so," Philippa said. "This message is from your brother. The courier brought it to the Academy, at Lord Francis' express wish." She untied the messenger pouch from her belt and crossed the room, holding it out.

William did not move his feet, but Philippa could have sworn he leaned back, away from her. He stretched out his long arm and took the pouch. She eyed him a moment, one brow raised, then went to the hearth to stand near the warmth of the flames.

William started to undo the leather thongs, but stopped with the ties dangling from his fingers. His narrowed eyes lifted to Philippa's face. "Why you, Philippa? Surely Francis understands there is no love lost between us."

"I have not read the letter," she said. "Perhaps when you do, you will understand."

"I can guess."

"Yes," she said with deliberation. "I suppose you can."

William pulled the letter from its carrier. He moved to a velvet sofa and smoothed the pages on the small table beside it. Philippa watched as he read it, then read it again. There was a long silence as he rerolled the letter and tucked it inside his vest. He stood and walked to the fireplace to stand opposite her, staring into the flames.

She waited. After perhaps a minute, he drew a slow breath and lifted his head. His eyes glittered. Like a snake's, she thought. Like one of the Old Ones.

"I dislike having my private affairs discussed," he said at last. His tone was tight, his face like stone. "Especially because you have used them to manipulate me."

"I told Francis you have shirked your responsibility."

"You mean to those yokels of Onmarin?" he spat at her. "Don't be ridiculous, Philippa! I have greater things to worry about than that."

"You are the Duke," Philippa said. "Your duty to your people should come first."

His face flooded with dark color. "How dare you presume to tell me my duty?"

Philippa folded her arms and tapped her fingers irritably on her elbows. "Your father would be appalled to know that you care nothing for your citizens, however low their station."

"I care for Oc," he snapped. "Everything I do is for the Duchy."

"Indeed?" She unfolded her arms and raised one hand, the palm out as if to touch his breast. "Does that include changing your body, William?" Her omission of the title was deliberate, and she saw by the flicker of his eyelids that he knew it. "Are you violating the bloodlines for the people's sake, or because you wish to shatter the traditions of the winged horses? I hardly think that's the act of an altruist."

"Why not expose me, then? You have friends in the Council, I believe."

Philippa dropped her hand. "I'm concerned about our Duchy, of course. What will become of Oc if the rest of Isamar learns of your depravity?"

He sucked in a breath. She saw that his hand went to his belt, but it came away empty. The quirt, the one Larkyn was convinced was magicked, was not there.

Philippa stepped back, and she, too, drew a deep breath. "Your Grace," she said, in as moderate a tone as she could manage in the tense atmosphere. "It's not too late. Give up this madness, let your body return to its natural state. Restore the Master Breeder." His silence encouraged her, and she said swiftly, "You could make peace with your sister as well."

He threw up his head and fixed her with a furious gaze. "You go too far," he said, his voice so tight it was barely audible.

"What has passed between Pamella and me is none of your business."

"It is my business, I'm sorry to say," she said heavily. "In the ordinary way of things, I wouldn't care. But of course you fear what she can tell us, and that gives me power over you." His mouth twisted, and she shrugged. "I wouldn't care about that, either, if it were not for your interference with the winged horses."

He folded his arms, outlining the slight but unmistakable swell of his bosom beneath the extravagant vest. The sight made Philippa feel faintly queasy. It seemed to her that his lips were fuller, his jaw narrower, than when she had last seen him. He made an odd picture, as if painted by someone of perverse talent.

He said stiffly, "I will allow my brother to accept the offer of Baron Rys. And I will inform Jinson—Master Jinson, that is—that the Baron's daughter is to be bonded to a winged foal. However," he added, "you are forbidden to mention these other matters ever again."

"Or what, William?" Philippa said wearily. "There's nothing you can do to me."

"Oh," he said, "but there is." He leaned forward a little, his thin lips curving. "There is that farm in the Uplands—Deeping Farm, I believe. The little Hamley girl is from there."

The familiar pain began to radiate up Philippa's neck. She grimaced and rubbed at it.

He gave a hollow chuckle. "Yes, I see that you understand. A single word from me, and the Hamleys lose Deeping Farm."

"The Hamleys are caring for your sister," Philippa said. "And for her child. Does that mean nothing to you?"

"Ah, Philippa, I've shocked you. Did you think, because they took Pamella in, that they would be spared?"

"Of course I did," Philippa said.

He gave an elegant shrug. "Then you were wrong. These are the things that give a leader power, and I will use them if I must."

Philippa pulled her cap from her belt and smoothed it over her head. She moved toward the door and opened it, then stopped, the latch still in her hand. She looked at him over her shoulder. "Your father would be ashamed."

"My father was a weakling."

"He was a man of honor," Philippa said.

"Why? Because he wouldn't lift a finger without the approval of that lot of old men on the Council?"

"I warn you, William. I will not see Duke Frederick's legacy destroyed."

"And I," William said, "will see every bitch of a horsemistress curtsy to me before I am done."

EIGHT

THE girls of the Academy were atwitter about the forthcoming visit of the Duke's younger brother, but Lark felt nervy and anxious.

"What are you worried about, Black?" Hester asked her quietly. All three flights were gathered in the Hall, awaiting the arrival of Duke William's younger brother. An elaborate reception had been arranged, and the girls, hungry as always, hovered near the tables, awaiting the signal that meant they could start on the tiny sandwiches, buttery biscuits, and iced cakes laid out in readiness. Lark and Hester stood before the windows in the foyer, watching the courtyard for Lord Francis's entourage. Unseasonable snow had begun to fall in small, dry flakes that made swirling patterns on the cobblestones.

"I just have a bad feeling." Lark twisted the icon of Kalla that hung around her neck. It felt hot all the time. It made her skin burn, and she had taken to wearing it outside her tabard. She wished she knew a witchwoman she could trust, here in Osham, who could explain it to her.

"Well," Hester said darkly. "I can't tell you not to have a bad feeling. These are dark times, as Mamá says. The Council is divided, the Duke is negligent, and the Prince is lazy."

She broke off when they caught sight of two riders, coming

at a posting trot from the road. They wore the Prince's crown and lily on their fluttering cloaks, and behind them came a well-sprung carriage, drawn by two draught horses. The royal insignia was gilded onto its doors, and embroidered on the heavy jackets of the footmen who clung to its rear posts. Two more liveried riders followed the carriage, but it was the pair behind them that caught Lark's attention.

There was no mistaking the white-blond hair of the Fleckhams. On this member of the Duke's family, it was softer than on William. Its strands lifted in the breeze like spider silk.

"Lord Francis," Hester murmured.

"I thought it must be," Lark said. She cupped her hands around her eyes to see better through the glass. Lord Francis Fleckham was a bit shorter than his brother the Duke, and younger. He had the same lean figure, and dressed in the black and silver colors of the Duchy. As he pulled up his horse before the Hall, threw one lean leg over the cantle and dismounted, she saw that he had the same narrow features as his brother, too. Lark's arms prickled with unease. He brushed snow from his sleeves as he waited for the other rider, a shorter, darker man, to dismount and join him. His companion preceded him up the steps. Lark shrank back into the window, a familiar chill stealing through her chest and stomach.

"Lord Francis is bookish, according to Papá," Hester said. "More interested in libraries than in government."

Bookish or not, to Lark he looked like another William, another threat to Tup and to her family. The doors were thrown open, and the two men, with two of the liveried riders behind them, came into the foyer on a gust of cold wind and a dusting of snow that melted swiftly on the tiles. Lark stayed behind Hester, but she watched with held breath, hugging her elbows.

Headmistress Morgan stood in the very center of the entryway, supporting herself with one hand on the newel post at the bottom of the stairs. She looked elegant in her black riding habit, her white hair smoothed into the rider's knot. Her back was very straight. She waited for the men to come to her, and bow, before she inclined her head to them. The girls in the Hall and in the foyer fell instantly silent, listening.

"Mistress Morgan," Lord Francis said. "How good to see you again."

"Welcome home, Lord Francis."

"I've looked forward to it." He gestured to the man beside him. "May I present Baron Rys, of Klee? My lord, this is the Headmistress of the Academy of the Air, Margareth Morgan."

The Baron bowed again, and murmured greetings. Mistress Morgan answered him, then turned to Mistress Winter, who stepped forward from the corridor behind the staircase. Introductions were repeated, and the group moved into the Hall. Lark and Hester followed at a little distance. By the time they came into the crowded Hall, most of the other girls had filled their plates and were chattering among themselves. The dignitaries had taken seats at the high table, and two maids were bringing them cups of tea and platters of food.

Hester said, "Hurry, Lark! All the cakes will be gone."

Lark followed her, but her eyes strayed again and again to Francis Fleckham. She was hungry, too. But she wished she could flee to the stables.

FRANCIS followed Philippa and the Baron on a cursory circuit of the dining hall. The young flyers inclined their heads as they passed. He and Rys greeted the horsemistresses waiting at the head table and drank obligatory cups of tea. Francis had always liked visiting the Academy. The fresh faces of the students, the weathered and experienced faces of the instructors, refreshed him. It was a beautiful old place, elegant and utilitarian at the same time. He liked the scent of horseflesh that permeated everything, and he liked the sense that these women and girls were doing work that mattered. There was, as a rule, less talk and more action here than in any other place his duties took him.

As they walked out through the doors of the Hall, Francis felt someone's gaze on him, and he looked around.

One girl had left her companions and stood watching him. She was small, and she wore her black hair differently from the others, cropped very short so that it curled over her forehead and behind her ears. Her eyes were violet, and they fixed on him with an intensity that made his skin prickle. He nodded to her, and she bent her head solemnly, as if the moment were important to her. Francis hurried on after Philippa and the Baron, frowning. He would have to ask Philippa who the girl was.

There was no time at the moment. Philippa showed them into the Headmistress's office, and Margareth waved them all to seats. She sat behind her desk, resting her head against the back of her carved chair. She had aged greatly since Francis had last seen her.

Baron Rys said, "We've gone ahead with arrangements. My ship will arrive on your northern coast within the next two days, if all goes well. The winter tides are beginning, and there can be ice in the Strait."

"We're grateful for your help," Philippa said.

The Baron nodded. "It's a mutually beneficial arrangement." He brought a miniature from an inner breast pocket and opened its chased-silver lid. "My daughter, Amelia."

Philippa leaned forward to take the miniature, then stood to cross to Margareth's desk and lay it on the polished wood. Francis moved behind her. He had not yet seen the picture.

A thin girl with brown hair looked out of the little silver frame. She looked very like her father, with a narrow chin and small, sharp nose. There was something direct in her gaze, even in the painted miniature. She was not smiling.

Baron Rys said, with a deprecating gesture, "I know she's not beautiful."

"She resembles you," Philippa said.

"She's bright, and she's brave. I think you'll be glad to have her."

"You understand," Margareth said, "that she will become a citizen of Oc upon her bonding. The winged horses live thirty years or more, and she will be ours for all that time."

Rys's voice was steady. "I assure you, Headmistress, that I considered that."

"You must care a great deal," Margareth said, her eyes still on the miniature, "to risk your soldiers on our behalf, and hers."

"I do, of course. I care for Amelia, and I care about the fisher-folk who live and work near the glacier. The Klee have long experience with Aeskland." His voice hardened. "We share our northern border with them, and we know how brutal they are. It may already be too late for these children."

"Let us hope it is not," Margareth said. "And we appreciate your haste."

Philippa asked, "How will you find them? I understand they're nomadic, these tribes."

He said tonelessly, "In the ordinary way of things, Mistress Winter, we would petition Oc for one of your Foundation flyers to help us find them."

"Yes." Philippa folded her arms. "But in this case . . ."

"In this case," Francis said, "we can hardly ask my brother for such a service."

"Then what—" Margareth began.

Philippa interrupted her. "I will go," she said flatly.

Margareth hesitated, her faded eyes on Philippa's face. "Are you certain, my dear?" she asked quietly.

"Of course, Margareth." Philippa gave a firm nod. "I must."

Francis drew breath to protest, but then released it. The set of Philippa's jaw, the resigned sigh of Margareth Morgan, confirmed there was no other choice. Fresh anger at William burned in Francis's chest. Philippa Winter had performed extraordinary service at the battle for the South Tower. It was unfair that she and her mare should be put at risk again, at a time when they were meant to be pursuing peaceful activities.

A long moment of heavy silence passed, in which Esmond Rys shifted his weight. He pursed his lips but said nothing. Francis admired his patience. He was, wisely, giving everyone time to reflect and accept the necessity of this decision.

Margareth said at last, "Baron Rys, I trust you will not allow Philippa to be in more danger than necessary."

Rys bowed to her from his chair. "That, at least, I can promise you, Mistress Morgan."

Philippa snorted. "I am no novice flyer," she said in her sharpest tone. "Worry about me and Sunny if you like, but trust us to know what we're about."

"Of course, Philippa," Margareth said. Her tone was as mild as Philippa's was harsh. "But remember," she went on, one pale finger raised. "Winter comes much earlier in the north. The winds and snow will be unpredictable."

"You may count upon me," Philippa said, "to take every care. But I promised Rosellen's mother."

"When will you leave?"

Rys stood, his slight figure full of purpose. "A week has already passed," he said. "There is no time to lose. We will meet my ship at the dock of Onmarin, ready to set sail."

Margareth got to her feet, a little grunt of effort escaping her lips. Philippa stepped toward her, hand outstretched, but Margareth shook her head, forestalling her help. "My lord Rys," she said. "We are already committed to bonding your daughter Amelia. Don't take unnecessary chances for yourself, either. Do what you can, and no more."

Rys bowed again. "I am not a man given to wild gestures. I have my family to think of, and my men to consider. But these children—" His thin features darkened, and his mouth turned down. "I have three children of my own. I love each one differently, but deeply. These poor children of Onmarin must be saved if they still live. Life as an Aesk slave is not to be borne."

Francis felt a turning in his heart. Esmond Rys's calm courage stirred his blood. What Oc might have become had such a man succeeded to the Dukedom! William, alas, suffered no lack of courage, but his spirit was turned inward, feeding upon envy and resentment and shallow ambition. He would never lead Oc as Rys might have done, nor would Rys in all likelihood have the opportunity to lead a duchy of his own.

Francis stood and bowed to Rys. "It will be a privilege to serve with you, my lord."

Rys gave him a grim smile. "Let's hope so, Francis. We have a great task ahead of us."

Francis did not miss the glance that passed between Margareth and Philippa. It, too, was grim, and determined. Again his heart turned. He would be proud to be part of such an alliance, a brave man and two brave women. He hoped his own courage would not fail in the test ahead.

LARK rose before dawn the next morning, propelled by unease at knowing that a Fleckham slept beneath the roofs of the Residence. The other girls still slept, lulled by the unusual feast of cakes and biscuits the evening before. Lark pulled on her riding habit and tugged her cap down over her short curls. She carried her boots in her hand. She sat on the bottom of the stairs from the sleeping porch to pull them on and let herself out as quietly as she could through the heavy door.

She was relieved to find Tup waiting for her in his stall, ears flicked forward. He had sensed her early rising, and now was eager for whatever exercise or adventure awaited. She unbuckled his blanket and slipped a bridle over his head. Surely, while everyone else at the Academy was still abed, a little private practice in the air would go unnoticed. Dutifully, Lark lifted the flying saddle from its peg. She put the saddle blanket on Tup, smoothing his coat beneath it so it would be comfortable, then put the saddle on him, too. He twisted his neck back, nipping at her coat to protest.

"Hush, my Tup," she murmured. "We have to learn to fly with it. You and I both!"

He sidestepped and whimpered, making her task difficult. Molly bleated once at this activity, and when the saddle was secure, Lark bent to nuzzle her warm neck. The little goat's winter coat was coming on quickly, a long undercoat of fibers like strong silk, much prized in the Uplands. It smelled like home to Lark. "Just wait for us, Molly mine," she said. "We won't be long. Back before breakfast is laid in the Hall!"

She whispered to Tup to be quiet and led him out through the back of the stables and around to the flight paddock. The sky had brightened to a pale blue, with wisps of rippled, grayish cloud drifting gently before the steady breeze from the mountains. They could be off and back before anyone noticed.

The snowfall had stopped during the night, leaving the grass crisp with crystals but not slippery. Everything was perfect. Lark braced herself for the standing mount, then leaped into the saddle, her belly touching first, her leg swinging easily over the cantle. The standing mount, at least, she had mastered. It had been easier for her than for most of the girls, because though her legs were short, her weight was slight, and her muscles were strong from spending the years of her childhood heaving and stacking and carrying around Deeping Farm.

She lifted the rein and leaned forward. "Let's go, Tup," she called. "Hup!"

Tup was now two and a half years old, sturdy and strong although still small. When he began his gallop down the paddock, she could feel the bunch and stretch of his muscles beneath her hands and wished for the hundredth time she could fly without the saddle. When she flew bareback, she felt every muscle flex beneath her thighs, felt every tilt and flex of his wings. When there was no leather and steel to impede them, they executed Reverses sharper and swifter than any other pair in their class.

But today, with the saddle, Lark confined their practice to the drills Mistress Star would no doubt put to them later this same day.

She laid a rein against Tup's glossy black neck and pressed her left knee into his shoulder. Obediently, he performed a Half Reverse. She held him at Quarters for four wingbeats, then urged him into a Full Reverse, something he performed deftly, quickly. She had learned to snug her thighs hard beneath the thigh rolls to keep from slipping. Without the saddle, there was no need. Her body knew what his was going to do before he began the movement. There was never a question of slipping. They were as one body at those moments.

But the Academy was not satisfied with that. Mistress Star insisted that the two of them learn the Airs and Graces with a flying saddle. Lark understood they worried about her safety. She had no words to convince them that she and Tup would work better unhindered by tack. She knew in her bones that she could fly Arrows without a saddle, but it was that Air in particular that troubled her instructor. That, of course, and the balletic Graces, which would be the seal of her second-level test. All she could do to earn her second-level Ribbon was to master the saddle as she had everything else. When she did, all doubts about her future would fade.

The sun had risen above the mountains, and the icy branches of the treetops glistened in the light. It was time to return to the Academy. Lark spoke to Tup with her hands and her feet, and though he tossed his head, loath to give up their brief taste of freedom in the air, he tilted obediently to the left to circle the grounds, beginning his descent. He flew past the gambrel roofs of the stables and on toward the end of the flight paddock, where the stand of spruce trees guarded the hedgerow beyond. Lark closed her eyes, just for a moment, to feel the chill wind on her cheeks. Tup's wings stilled, and he began his glide.

She opened her eyes, looking ahead. Just outside the paddock, between the stables and the pole fence, stood a slender figure in a black cloak. His hair was almost as pale as the snow that clung to the roof and the post-caps. Lark's heart missed a beat, and she cried, "No, Tup!"

Willingly, even eagerly, Tup gave a strong downward beat of his wings, and they began to ascend again. Beyond the man,

Lark saw Erna come out of the stables, leading a winged horse. In the hall, lights were burning through the dim winter morning, and a door opened in the Residence. She would be late for breakfast, perhaps miss it altogether. She would be scolded for going out without telling anyone, for being aloft by herself.

Which Fleckham was watching her from the end of the paddock? Duke William, or Lord Francis? It didn't matter. They both terrified her.

Tup soared higher, turning away from the Academy. They flew past the grove, past the hedgerow, past the turning of the lane into the road. And Lark, in the grip of an irresistible impulse, turned her bondmate toward the Uplands. Home.

Against the skin of her breast, the little icon of Kalla grew cool, its smooth wood as comforting as a mother's hand.

NINE

PHILIPPA was at breakfast in the Hall when Matron came in, threaded her way through the students, and approached the high table. She stepped up on the dais, walking behind the other instructors. When she reached Philippa's chair, she bent, and murmured, "Mistress Winter. Lord Islington is here to see you."

Philippa stiffened, and Margareth, next to her, lifted her eyebrows. "Is it Meredith?"

Philippa laid down her napkin. "It must be. There is no other Lord Islington as yet." She pushed back her chair and stood up. "Thank you, Matron. Is he in the foyer?"

"I put his lordship in the Headmistress's office," Matron said. "I didn't feel he would wish to come into the dining hall." She directed this statement to Margareth, who nodded. "I ordered coffee for him and asked him if he had breakfasted. He said he had." She turned and bustled away. Philippa followed.

In Margareth's office, she found her brother standing before the tall window behind the desk. He had opened the heavy drapes and stood looking out into the cold gray morning. When the door clicked behind Philippa, he turned.

"Philippa. It's been a very long time since we've seen you at Islington House."

"Good morning, Meredith." Philippa walked with deliberate steps toward the desk and stood facing her brother across its mahogany expanse. She laid her fingertips on the leather-bound genealogy that lay on it, mimicking Margareth's habitual gesture. "I do apologize for not coming for Erdlin. I was otherwise occupied."

"Yes, Jessica told me you had sent a note."

"And how is Jessica?" Philippa asked. She hated small talk, but she needed a moment to assess Meredith's mood, to try to guess why he was here. He wanted something, naturally. There was not the slightest chance he had come merely from filial affection. None had ever existed between them.

Meredith's cool blue eyes told her nothing. The features which on herself looked bony and plain were striking on Meredith. He had always been a handsome man, but now, approaching middle age, the slight silvering of his red hair had added a distinguished air. He carried himself with confidence, even arrogance. He had high hopes for the advancement of the Islingtons, for more power and more profit from their ventures. Her refusal to be his liaison with Duke Frederick, when she was still flying for the Ducal Palace, had infuriated him.

"Jessica is well," Meredith said. "And our daughters thrive."

"I am glad to hear it."

"You're making a great mistake, Philippa."

Philippa said dryly, "Why, Meredith, because I'm glad your family is well?"

"Don't be a fool," he said. He left the window and came to lean on the high back of Margareth's chair. "Your mistake is in taking Lord Francis's part against that of the Duke."

"Oh, by Kalla's heels, Meredith! Surely that's not why you're here?"

"That is exactly why I'm here," her brother answered. "This is our chance to mend the relationship of Islington House and Fleckham House. I won't stand by and see you destroy it."

"It's you playing the fool, Meredith." Philippa drew her gloves from her belt and slapped them into one palm. "You can't have been paying attention! Duke William's tenure is likely to be a short one. Where will you be if he's deposed?"

"Deposed?" Meredith gave an incredulous laugh. "Where

do you come up with such ideas? His Grace settled the issue of Onmarin in the Council. What gives you and Francis the right to gainsay him?"

"William didn't settle the issue." Anger roughened Philippa's voice. "He ignored it."

"He is the Duke, and it falls to him to make these decisions."

"Or not make them. And how, pray tell, do you think there is anything I could do that would improve relations with William?"

"Duke William, Philippa. Show him the respect he's due."

"When he earns it, I will."

Meredith drew himself up very straight and looked down his nose at her. She recognized the posture. She had the same habit.

"Philippa," he said, "I want you to refuse Lord Francis's plan. Decline the Klee girl, and turn your back on this ridiculous scheme."

Philippa laid her palm flat on the book of the bloodlines, feeling its bulk and substance beneath her hand. She narrowed her eyes at her brother. "You," she said bitingly, "cannot give me orders. I am a *horsemistress*, Meredith."

"You are an Islington, and I am the head of our house. You owe me loyalty."

Now Philippa did laugh, though there was little mirth in it. "Loyalty," she said sourly. "You mean, such as the loyalty you always showed to me when I was a girl?"

Meredith's lips pulled down. "I was young, Philippa."

"I was sixteen. And you laughed at me, you and William. You have daughters now, Meredith. Would you like them to have that experience?"

His eyes flickered away from her. He turned back to the window, and his posture softened a little. "I'm sorry about that," he said. "It was cruel."

"Ours was always a cruel family," Philippa said. "I suppose you should not bear all the blame. And it did work out for me, after all. Duke Frederick not only bonded me to Sunny, but he became the affectionate father our own never was."

A silence stretched between them. Philippa closed her eyes for a moment, tasting the comforting scents of leather and wax and lamp oil. There was also, of course, the omnipresent smell of horses in this room, as in every room at the Academy. She should explain to Meredith how much she loved this life, how little she regretted that other life that might have been.

She opened her eyes, and opened her mouth to tell him, but he forestalled her, turning abruptly to face her. "None of that matters now, Philippa. What matters is the future. And William can help or hinder our fortunes."

"Duke William," Philippa said slyly.

Meredith's eyes narrowed. "Don't take part in this, Philippa. It's madness."

"Madness." Philippa lowered her voice. "Meredith, listen. In all truth, I fear for William's sanity. You and I have known him since childhood, and he is much changed recently."

"That's a treasonous remark," Meredith said.

"Some would say abandoning two young citizens to the barbarians is treason."

"That's not a decision for us to make. I don't want you involved, Philippa. I order you."

"Order me? I'm a horsemistress of Oc, Meredith. I take orders from no man."

"Except the Duke."

She shrugged. "Even the Duke. He has to answer to the Council Lords, and that is by no means a foregone conclusion in this instance. The Academy—and Francis, I should point out—have supporters in the Council."

"Damn you, Philippa! I swear—"

"Swear away, Meredith. It will do you no good."

FRANCIS and Rys were to leave a day before Philippa. As she would be flying, her journey would be swifter than theirs. Lord and Lady Beeth had offered a carriage for the two men and their servants. Francis had directed his man not even to unpack, other than what was needed immediately, and so there was nothing for him to do but wait for the Beeth carriage. He was standing in the foyer of the Academy Hall, gazing at the paintings of the winged horses that hung on its walls. One, in particular, interested him. It was a lean, muscular brown horse, painted with its wings extended over a snowy landscape, no tack or rider to obscure its sleek lines, the depth of its chest, the neat cut of its hooves.

"He was one of the founders of the Ocmarin line."

Francis turned his head at the sound of Philippa's voice. She had come to stand beside him, her riding boots making almost no sound on the tiled floor. "He's beautiful," he said.

"They say he was. And he threw nothing but winged foals," she told him.

"What was his name?"

"Seraph," she said. "One of our girls—Larkyn Hamley— flies a colt named for him. Her horse is named Black Seraph, in honor of his forebear. Black Seraph is a good bit smaller than his ancestor, though, I think."

"Larkyn? That's an unusual name, is it not?"

Philippa's lips pursed. "She is an unusual girl," she said in a dry tone. "With an unusual history. And, Francis . . ."

"What is it, Philippa? It's not like you to hesitate."

"I don't know how much your brother has told you of the events of the past year."

Francis turned away from the painting and faced Philippa. Her features were drawn with fatigue and tension. He supposed his own were no better. He hated to admit it, even to himself, but he was afraid of what was coming in Aeskland. He cleared his throat. "William and I have not corresponded on anything but official business," he said. "Nor have we spoken privately since my father died."

"Have you heard from your sister?"

"No. My father's old steward tells me she's in seclusion, residing with a family in an outlying district."

"The family is called Hamley," Philippa said bluntly.

"Hamley? The same name as your student?"

"The very family," Philippa answered. "The Hamleys of Deeping Farm, the Uplands."

"How did such a coincidence come about?"

"It's a long story, Francis, but coincidence has no part of it. There is still a mystery to be solved, but your sister is unable to speak."

Francis frowned. "She could have written to me, surely. If she needed help . . ."

"I do not wish to interfere in your family's affairs," Philippa said. She glanced around, and Francis followed her gaze. The foyer was empty. Margareth was in her office, and the instructors and students were in the paddocks.

Francis put a hand under Philippa's elbow and led her to one of the long benches opposite the windows. "Tell me, Philippa," he said. "I never doubt you have only our best interests at heart."

Her mouth twisted. "Well, yours at least."

"Tell me."

Philippa had been right. It was a long story, of intrigue, of an illegitimate child, of deceit and sacrifice. Francis dropped his head, listening, trying to imagine his pretty, prideful sister banished to an Uplands village, cared for through a traumatic pregnancy by a village witchwoman, residing in the end in a sympathetic farmer's house.

"Brye Hamley," Philippa finished at last, "is a man of honor, the sort of man Oc can be most proud of. William now has two reasons to hate him and to threaten to confiscate the lands the Hamleys have held for centuries."

"Two reasons."

"I fear so." Philippa had pulled her gloves from her belt, and was creasing them in her fingers. "William is obsessed with Black Seraph, Larkyn's winged horse. He was furious when he found she had bonded with the foal, and he tried once to take him from her. But he fears what Pamella might tell the Hamleys should she begin to speak again."

"Who is the father of her child?" Francis asked. His heart weighed heavy in his breast. He knew how such a thing must have wounded his father, and he understood also that his mother would never allow Pamella to return to Osham with a bastard brat at her knee. Poor Pamella! It seemed her life was ruined, in more ways than one.

"Do you know, Francis," Philippa said slowly, "that is something she will not reveal. The secret seems to weigh upon her more than any other."

"She can write, surely?"

"Yes," Philippa answered. "But all she has written is the name of her son, so that we would know what to call him. Brandon."

"Brandon," Francis mused. "We had an uncle by that name, and a great-great-grandfather. Pamella remembered."

"He looks just like you and William," Philippa said. "A true Fleckham." Her eyes softened, and Francis wondered what it must be like for her, and for all the horsemistresses. If their horses lived out their full span, the women were too old to have children by the time they lost their bondmates. He had no children himself, but he had both time and freedom to have a family. The bonded flyers had no choice in the matter.

"I wish I could see Pamella while I'm here."

"You can, Francis. When we return from Aeskland, you can go to the Uplands. The Hamleys will welcome you. You'll like them."

Francis cast her a surreptitious glance. Something changed in her voice when she spoke the Hamley name, and that softness stayed in her eyes. It was unlike Philippa to be sentimental. Perhaps it was the child Brandon that caused her to have such feelings. Or perhaps it was affection for the girl, her student.

"Well, now." Philippa stood up abruptly and brushed her hands together as if to rid herself of unnecessary emotions. "You have preparations to make, no doubt. Have you breakfasted? Do you need anything?"

He was about to explain the way he had spent the morning when one of the students burst through a door on the floor above the foyer and came hurrying down the wide staircase. Philippa looked up, and said, "Hester? Whatever is the matter?"

Francis recognized the tall girl as the daughter of the Beeths. She reached the bottom of the stair and whirled to face Philippa, one hand on the newel post. "Mistress Winter," she panted. "Have you seen Black? She missed breakfast, and now she's missed our Points drill. Mistress Star is furious, and I'm worried. I've looked in the library, in the classroom, on the sleeping porch. I can't find her anywhere!"

PHILIPPA pressed the palms of her hands against her eyes. Curse the girl! Were there not enough problems without Larkyn taking it into her head that she must fly away, without telling anyone, without any warning or message?

It had taken only moments for Francis to explain that he had seen someone circling the return paddock when he went for an early walk that morning. It must have been Larkyn.

Philippa's stomach roiled with tension. Margareth's patience was already sorely tested by Larkyn's various escapades, and Suzanne Star would have every right to censure the child for missing her drill. If she didn't return quickly, with appropriate apologies, she would be back to practicing her drills on the wingless pony and repeating her first-year studies.

"How long ago did this happen, Francis?" Philippa asked.

"No one else was about yet," he said. "Except the stable-girl. I was surprised to see someone flying so early, and I stood at the end of the paddock to watch her."

Hester said, "I'll go after her, Mistress Winter."

"Go where, Hester?" rapped Philippa. "You have no idea where she is. And I am not going to send one fool of a girl after another!"

Hester subsided, her face reddening. Philippa regretted her sharpness, but the pressure of the upcoming mission and the utter lack of time to resolve the current crisis were simply too much. "I'll go, Hester," she said. "I'll go immediately, and see if I can guess where she's got to. You see to Lord Francis's needs, will you?"

"Yes, Mistress Winter. And I'll tell Erna to saddle Winter Sunset for you."

Philippa nodded. "Thank you. I'm going to go change into my winter habit. It will be cold aloft."

"I hope Black wore hers," Hester said, as she turned to leave.

"Indeed," Philippa said. Her neck began to ache. "And I hope the snow doesn't return."

TEN

PHILIPPA turned Sunny to face down the flight paddock. In the early morning hours, the sky had been a clear, cold blue, but clouds had rolled in from the mountains, obscuring the low hills to the west, erasing the glitter of the thin fall of snow from the night before. Her heart sank.

"We'd better hurry, Sunny," she said. "And not to get too far from home."

Sunny tossed her head and blew plumes of frost. When Philippa loosened her rein, she broke into a brisk canter as if she understood the urgency. She sped to the hand gallop and launched herself well before the end of the paddock. The grass was crisp and a little slippery beneath her hooves, but she ascended sharply, her great scarlet wings driving them upward as surely as Philippa might have climbed stairs.

Flying was good in cold weather, the horses' wings more efficient. Even in rainy weather, the winged horses could fly long distances, no matter how sodden their manes and tails became, how wet and miserable their riders. But snow was another issue altogether.

Winter birds—the goldfinches and siskins—flew easily through drifts of snow, though Philippa believed they preferred to huddle in the inner branches of the spruce and pine that protected them in the worst weather. She and Sunny had watched from the warm security of the stables more than once, envious of the birds in this one thing. Perhaps, Philippa thought, if Sunny's wings were feathered rather than membranous, she, too, could fly through falling snow.

Philippa and Sunny had been caught in a sudden snowstorm once, flying to Crossmount for Duke Frederick. That duchy lay south and west of Oc, beyond the mountains, and the season had been early spring. An unseasonable storm blew into the pass without warning, and Philippa had watched with alarm as the expanse of membrane between the ribs of Sunny's wings filled with snow. Her wings, warm with exertion, melted the snowflakes almost immediately, but as the storm intensified, more snow fell on the chill wetness to create a sort of white mud.

As Sunny's wings chilled under the weight of the snow, the rhythm of her wingbeats faltered. She struggled, her effort evident in the ripple of the muscles across her chest and down her ribs. Philippa shivered with cold and fear as she did her best to guide Sunny down through the storm. She could only hope there would be a place to come to ground.

They had made a precipitous descent through fluttering snowflakes and emerged from the clouds to find themselves above a grassy meadow just where the pass opened into the plains of Crossmount. The grass was barely misted with white, the snow already melting on the spring-warmed ground. Skeptic though she was, once Sunny had safely touched down, Philippa thanked the horse goddess with all her soul. She rubbed Sunny's wings dry and walked her until they were both warm again. Her hands trembled for an hour afterward, and she promised herself she would never again have such an experience.

But now Larkyn was aloft somewhere, with a snowstorm coming, and no experience of bad weather.

Philippa turned Sunny to the west. The air was ominously still. Philippa peered ahead, but as the storm swept eastward, visibility was growing worse by the moment. She twisted in her saddle to look back toward Osham, wondering if Larkyn and Seraph might have turned that way. If so, Philippa had no idea where to look for her. Indeed, searching for one pair of flyers who had left the Academy hours ago was an impossible challenge. They could be anywhere.

Philippa freed one hand to pull her collar higher against the chill. If there wasn't a student missing, she would never be aloft in this weather. But they were out there, somewhere, possibly lost, possibly needing help.

She lifted her eyes once again to the bank of clouds shrouding the western horizon.

She blinked, and blinked again, wary of wishful thinking. But no, it was true! She could see them, silhouetted against the silver clouds, Seraph's black wings stretched wide, beating steadily, Larkyn a mere speck in the sky.

Relief made Philippa's heart skip a beat. Praise Kalla, she thought, praise whatever icon or fetish it was that Larkyn put her trust in. They were coming back.

She let Sunny fly on, and in moments they were close enough for her to see Larkyn's face, her cheeks rosy with cold. She signaled to her with her quirt as she circled around and above Seraph, so that she and Sunny could escort the young flyers safely home.

The clouds rolled behind them, surging and curling against the sky. In moments, they were circling the roofs of the Academy. Black Seraph's wings rippled with exuberant energy, and his tail flickered up and out. Pride, Philippa thought. He was proud to be flying with Sunny, to be high in the cold air with his bondmate, to be making an elegant and smooth descent toward the return paddock. Larkyn kept her eyes straight ahead, her back self-consciously straight, her hands in the perfect low position.

Philippa's lips twitched. She would have to mete out some suitable punishment, but her relief was greater than her irritation, and there was the gratification of seeing Larkyn in a proper flying saddle. Kalla's teeth, the child was difficult! And Kalla had bonded her to a difficult horse in the bargain, a horse with an independent spirit and an attitude that would suit a flyer twice his size.

She watched with a critical eye as Larkyn guided Black Seraph over the grove and down into the paddock, as she loosened the reins and balanced for the landing. Seraph reached with his forefeet, neck nicely extended, hind hooves curled and ready to touch the frosty grass. It seemed Larkyn did everything correctly, and yet, at the moment of coming to ground, she slipped in the seat of her saddle, grabbed at the pommel, seemed to stiffen in her stirrups. Seraph's hooves made an irregular pattern as he began his gallop, but he soon recovered, cantering smoothly up the paddock. He slowed to the trot, and whirled at the far end, head high, ears pricked toward Sunny.

Philippa and Sunny came up the paddock at a posting trot, and when they reached the younger flyers, Philippa saw that Larkyn's chin was up, her eyes blazing defiance. Before Philippa could speak a word, Larkyn cried, "I was afraid to come to ground! The Duke was in the return paddock!"

"It was Lord Francis," Philippa said wearily. "And you have missed your Points drill, to say nothing of worrying us all."

"I came back the moment I smelled snow in the air."

"You smelled it," Philippa said flatly.

"Of course. I know how a snowstorm smells when it's building." The girl's color surged and faded, and she dropped her eyes to her pommel. "Mistress Winter, the Duke wants Tup, you know that. There was no one about, and I didn't know what he might do."

"He can't take Black Seraph from you, Larkyn."

"He has that magicked quirt—"

"Nonsense. There's no such thing," Philippa snapped. "Now dismount, and stable your horse. I will meet you in the Head-mistress's office."

The girl swung her leg over her pommel to leap to the ground. Philippa dismounted more slowly and followed her through the gate toward the stables. As she watched Larkyn's slight figure and the elegant lift of Black Seraph's tail as he pranced away, she felt a pang of compunction. It was true that she did not believe in simples, in magics and spells. But William's quirt did have strange properties. She had felt them herself, though she had spent months trying to convince herself it was her imagination. She had decided, in the end, it was William's own strength that made the little whip seem to have a power of its own.

She shut the gate of Sunny's stall with a decisive click. Such speculation was meaningless. No doubt they all suffered from heightened nerves at the moment, and were ready to believe anything. Nonetheless, while she was away with Francis and the Baron, she would set someone to keep watch over Black Seraph.

And over Larkyn. She sensed, deep in her bones, that William's fragile sanity was a real threat, with the aid of magic or not, to Larkyn Hamley.

THE next day Lark, shivering in the cold, stood with Hester to watch Mistress Winter's departure for the Angles. Chores awaited her in the stables, her penalty for missing her Points drill the day before, but she let them wait.

Mistress Winter's riding habit was invisible beneath a heavy fur coat, one that Lark had never seen before. Her narrow face was set above the thick woolen scarf wound around her neck.

"Take a blink at those gloves," Lark whispered to Hester. "'Tis a wonder she can hold the reins!"

"She has a long, cold flight ahead of her," Hester murmured back.

"She will stay low, won't she? Where it's warmer?"

"She'll have to. But the winds are in her favor." Hester put her head back to scan the sky. "And at least it's stopped snowing."

The flight paddock was buried by an inch of pristine, perfect white, unmarked yet by hooves or boots. Mistress Winter tested it with her foot before leaping up into her flying saddle, gathering Sunny's reins in the thick, clumsy-looking gloves.

Lark heard a footstep behind her, and turned. Headmistress Morgan had come across the courtyard and stood with one hand on the rail fence. "Take care, Philippa," she called, her voice quavering slightly. "Remember."

Lark turned back to watch Mistress Winter's face as she answered, but there was no hint of feeling in her set expression. "I will," she said. She lifted her quirt in a half salute. "I will be back the moment I can, Margareth."

Lark found herself gripping Hester's elbow as Winter Sunset spun about on her hindquarters and began her canter down the flight paddock. Her hooves kicked up sparkling puffs of powder as she ran, and when she launched, her fetlocks glittered white. But her wings were clean and dry, and she rose steadily above the grove, skimming the hedgerow and the lane, a steady arrow of red against the high gray clouds.

"What will she do if it begins to snow, Hester?"

"That depends how heavy the snow is," Hester told her. "If it's too strong, she'll have to come to ground and wait it out." She patted Lark's hand. "Try not to worry, Black. We have our own work to do."

"Aye," Lark said. "I know." But as she turned toward the stables, to assist the dour Erna with the mucking out, her stomach churned with tension, and threatened to return the breakfast she had so hurriedly eaten an hour before.

Working with Erna made her miss her old friend Rosellen even more. As she wielded the pitchfork, scattered fresh sawdust, and swept the tack room, she thought of Rosellen's wide, gappy smile, the way her freckles spread across her round cheeks. She remembered, as she watched Erna splashing water negligently into the stall buckets, how much Rosellen had loved the winged horses, what devotion she had given to them. It made her doubt Kalla's purpose, that now the Academy should have this sullen incompetent while Rosellen had met such a bitter end.

The early darkness was closing in around the Academy by the time she finished all the chores set for her by Mistress Morgan to expiate her faults of yesterday. She still had studies to make up after dinner. Her bed was hours away yet.

She walked toward the Dormitory to put on a clean tabard before supper. As she went, she cast an uneasy glance skyward. Where would Mistress Winter be now? The snow had returned, sparse, dry flakes that swirled in the darkness. Would it be snowing in Onmarin, too? Lark tried to picture Winter Sunset soaring in over the beaches as she and Hester had done. It seemed a very long time ago now, and yet the memory of those ghastly boats, the snarling wardogs, the screams from the village, was as fresh as yesterday. Lark shivered and hurried on across the courtyard.

Everyone at dinner seemed to share Lark's mood. The horsemistresses whispered together at the high table, and Mistress Morgan hardly spoke at all. Even the students were subdued. The moment Mistress Morgan rose, Lark bade Hester and Anabel good night, and dashed up the stairs to the library, her assignment book under her arm.

A lamp had been left on in the small library, but the fire had almost gone out, leaving the room uncomfortably chilly. Lark stirred the embers with the poker and added two small logs. As she waited for them to blaze up, she stood beside the window, rubbing her arms for warmth.

The snow had thickened, making ghostly shapes of the stables across the courtyard, of the solid bulk of the Dormitory. Just so would the buildings look at Deeping Farm, the farmhouse, the barn, the chicken coop shrouded by drifting flakes. The blackstone fence around the kitchen garden would wear a white mantle along its top, and the empty fields would stretch clean and unbroken in every direction. With a pang, Lark thought of her brothers in the great old kitchen, the close stove blazing, a teakettle whistling, the table set for a winter supper. Cheese and soup, perhaps, and a loaf Nick would have brought from Willakeep. Crooks for dessert, and cups of black tea. Peony was a good cook, and she had Pamella to help her now. Lark hoped they had remembered to lay extra straw for the hens and to be certain the goats were snug in their night pen. She could see, in her imagination, Edmar dandling little Brandon, teasing him to laughter. The little boy had transformed silent Edmar into an avuncular jokester.

Tears of homesickness stung Lark's eyes. Behind her, the fire began to crackle, and the room to warm, but still she stood by the window, her cheek against the heavy curtain, her eyes gazing unseeing into the blank whiteness drifting past the window.

A blur of darkness passed before the lighted squares of the Dormitory windows. Lark sniffed, and rubbed her eyes. She looked again.

The blur resolved into a dark figure, with swirling coatskirts and a wide-brimmed hat. As she watched, the figure's head lifted, and seemed to stare at the library window.

Lark sucked in a breath. Too late, she pulled the curtain forward to hide herself. She must be outlined perfectly by the lamplight, by the rising flicker of the fire. She stared in horror as he lifted his arm and pointed something at her, something small and thin and dark against the falling snow.

The icon of Kalla against Lark's breast began to burn, and she gripped it in her hand. Her enemy was here. He must have known when Mistress Winter left to meet Lord Francis and Baron Rys, and he had wasted no time.

There was no doubt in Lark's mind. Duke William was watching her.

She whirled, dropping her assignment book in her haste. She dashed out of the library and down the stairs, racing across the courtyard to the stables, heedless of the slippery snow on the cobblestones, of the cold on her neck and hands. Bramble, the ochound, bounded to meet her, and followed close on her heels as she hurried into the warmth of the stables.

Not till she reached Tup's stall did she think that William might have followed her. She opened the gate and went in, Bramble with her. She glanced behind her to see that the door of the stables remained closed, that there was no sound of boots on the sawdust. Molly and Tup crowded against her. Bramble whirled, facing the gate, her hackles up, her ears laid back. Tup whickered a question and nosed Lark's shoulder.

"I don't know," she whispered to him, circling his neck with her arm. "I don't know if he would try to take you again, or if it's me he wants. But we have to stay together!"

ELEVEN

FRANCIS was glad to see Philippa and Winter Sunset circling above the tumbled huts of Onmarin. He had watched for her all day, and darkness was already creeping across the bay. She gave him and Rys a brief greeting and went straight to the village to meet with the bereft mothers and visit the graves of the dead.

The village prefect had turned over his modest house to Francis and Rys, and one of the village women had come to cook for them. The hour had grown very late when Philippa joined them at last, bringing the scent of horse with her and a slight tang of fish. She sat at the table, where they were finishing a simple meal of chowder and some sort of sour black bread.

Philippa pulled off her hat and her gloves and laid them on the table. "It's too cold to leave Sunny outside," she said. "I've had to stable her in the hut next door."

Rys pushed the bread platter toward her. "What did the family have to say about that?"

"They're afraid of her," Philippa said. "They gathered their things and vanished the moment the prefect told them what we needed. Sunny's none too easy in that fish-smelling house, either. I'll have to sleep there with her."

"We hope to make an early start," Rys said. "Before the snow comes back."

"You know, then, that snow is a problem for me."

He nodded. "All we need is for you to find them," he said. His voice held an edge, and his lips set. All vestiges of the urbane diplomat Francis had known in Arlton had vanished. "My captains have fought the Aesks before. We have thirty-five men, and a half dozen matchlock guns. The challenge is to get a clear shot for our marksmen." He waved one slender hand. "Archers are more accurate, but the barbarians' spears are no defense against bullets. Just the sounds of the matchlocks terrify them, though I doubt we've actually hit one of their people. We have to ascertain if the children are alive—"

At Philippa's wince, he made an apologetic sound. "I know, Mistress Winter. But these are the facts of the case. And, in fact, we must tread carefully. The Aesks are not above slaughtering hostages in order to deter us."

"I understand," she said.

"Then Philippa can return to Onmarin once we've found them," Francis said. He was gratified to hear that his own voice was steady. Rys had even suggested that he need not accompany the war party, but Francis knew he could never live with the idea that he was not brave enough, or strong enough, to face the barbarians. He knew well enough that most of Oc—and especially his brother—considered him soft and bookish. He did not relish the idea of the conflict ahead, but he could not imagine standing by while others did what needed doing.

"It would be best if she did," Rys said.

Philippa inclined her head. "We never risk the winged horses unless we must," she said. "If you believe in any gods, pray the weather holds."

Rys smiled. "Do you, Horsemistress? Do you believe in the gods?"

Philippa's answering smile was wry. "I'm afraid not, my lord."

Before they retired, an old woman appeared at the door of the house, wrapped in a shawl, her gray hair falling in tired strands around a careworn face.

"Mistress Brown," Philippa said, when she saw her. She stood up and crossed to the door, holding out her hand to the woman, escorting her to the table, and urging her into a chair. Francis watched, bemused, as Philippa pressed tea on the woman, asked her if she was hungry, if she was warm enough.

Apparently satisfied that their visitor was comfortable, Philippa turned to Francis and Rys. "This," she said gravely, "is Evalee Brown. Our stable-girl, Rosellen, was her daughter. Lissie, whom we hope to rescue, is her youngest."

Francis opened his mouth, but he could think of nothing to say. "I—I am so sorry for your loss," he finally stammered. "Oc—Oc grieves with you."

The look she turned on him, bitter and wise, told her she knew that Oc had done nothing to help her. Shame burned in his heart, and he dropped his gaze.

Rys seemed more confident. "We will do everything we can to bring your daughter home," he said, leaning forward. "You have my solemn promise, Mistress Brown."

The bereaved mother said softly, "I came only to thank you, me lords. For trying."

Rys said, "We will do more than try."

She nodded, but Francis saw that there was no hope in her dull eyes.

She didn't stay long. Philippa rose to see her to the door, but Francis shook his head. He got up himself and went out the door with Evalee Brown. "I will escort you home, Mistress," he said gently.

She sighed. "Safe enough here in Onmarin, me lord. That is, until—until it happened."

Francis put his hand under the old woman's arm. Her elbow felt light as pigeon bones beneath his fingers. He walked with her through the cramped and crooked streets until she stopped before a tumbledown hut.

"Mistress Brown," he said impulsively. "I want to apologize for my brother. For the Duke."

She gave a shrug that was almost imperceptible in the darkness. "Fisher-folk are of no account in the White City, I suppose."

"I pledge to you that will not be the case," Francis said formally. As he said the words, he felt purpose form in his breast, a need to make them true. "Every citizen of Oc matters."

She squinted up at him. "I'll be holding you all in my prayers," she said.

He bowed. "I thank you for that," he said gravely. "It may make all the difference."

* * *

EARLY the next morning, Francis stood on the dock of On-marin. The drying racks lay in ruins, smashed by the barbar-ians, and bloodstains still marked the boards beneath his feet. He looked out to the bay, where Rys's ship bobbed at anchor. A cold salt wind riffled his hair, and he pulled his cloak closer around him. For the first time in a week, he had slept soundly. Meeting the villagers of Onmarin, seeing the ruined huts and freshly dug graves, had strengthened his determination.

It seemed that Rys, too, felt called to their purpose. Francis had reconciled himself to the thought that the Baron had made a political decision in trading this enterprise for his daughter's fu-ture. But now, as Francis watched him give orders, confer with his captains, plan their foray against the Aesks, he believed Rys was as committed as he himself was. Whatever happened, what-ever fate awaited all of them, there was nothing else they could have done.

And now, in the cold light of morning, with the glacier gleam-ing dully from across the sea, it was time.

The weather was steady. The clouds were high and flat above the icy water of the Strait. The glacier was a smear of dull white in the distance. The Klee ship, a narrow-prowed craft built for speed and maneuverability, was turned toward the distant shore, aimed like an arrow at their goal. The Klee soldiers, in blue wool uniforms, stood in orderly ranks on its deck, awaiting their captains, who were even now rowing out from the beach in a flat-bottomed dinghy.

"Ready, Francis?" Rys said.

"Yes." Francis pulled on his gloves. "Philippa, good luck."

"Thank you," she said quietly. The ground beyond the dock was slick with moisture, and Francis noted that she did not use the standing mount she was known for, but stood on a wooden block to fit her foot into her stirrup. Mounted in the flying sad-dle, she saluted him with her quirt and turned Winter Sunset to-ward the dunes. She would launch from there, where the ground was dry. The mare's folded wings began to open as she trotted away. Her tail arched, and fluttering in the wind, a proud plume of red against the gray sand.

Francis and Rys boarded the second dinghy and set out for

the ship. As they climbed the rope ladder, Francis glanced over his shoulder just in time to see Philippa and Winter Sunset launch. He paused, one foot still on the ladder, to watch their ascent. What must it be like to shake off the bonds of earth as the two did now, to rise into the air with the freedom of a great bird, to look down from aloft on those who were tied forever to the land? It was perhaps no wonder that his brother William, always intense in whatever took his interest, had become obsessed with the winged horses.

But now was not the time to worry over William. Francis climbed aboard the ship and joined Rys in the bow as they turned their faces toward Aeskland and the mission at hand.

TWELVE

"YOUR Grace," said Slater, bowing in his awkward way, his greatcoat flapping around him.

"Ye gods, Slater," William said snappishly, "can't you find a better coat? You look like a giant crow."

Slater grinned, showing his yellow teeth. "Aye, me lord, if you like." He held out a grimy palm.

William gave a short, humorless bark of laughter. "I've paid you enough," he said.

"Could have had my company last night, me lord," Slater said, retracting his hand and stuffing it into one of the capacious pockets of the offending coat.

"What are you talking about?" William said offhandedly. He was in the midst of dressing, buttoning his embroidered vest over a full-sleeved white shirt. He had that damned Council to attend today, when he would rather have had a lie-in.

"No need to go out alone," Slater said, his eyelids drooping suggestively. "'Twas past midnight when you returned."

"I don't need a nursemaid," William said.

"Protection, then, mayhap?"

"No." William shrugged into his coat and tugged at the vest. It was getting harder to disguise his changing body. He let his hand linger on his chest, beneath the lapel of his jacket. The swelling there had doubled with the doubling of his dose. It had never been his intention, nor his desire, but it would be worth it, he told himself. It would all be worth it.

He turned to the mirror and surveyed himself. If he kept his jacket pulled close, no one would be able to tell. He eyed his smooth jaw and touched one eyebrow with a long, slender finger. His eyebrows, like his hair, were pale as snow. Not like Larkyn Hamley. She was raven-dark, like the wings of her little stallion.

The thought of her made him tremble with renewed fury. The bloody brat stood in that window staring down at him, bold as brass. She thought he couldn't touch her now, he supposed. Thought she and her horse—the horse that should have been his—she thought they were safe from him now. He would like to have Slater procure *her*, just once. Give him an hour alone with her, and he'd wipe that insolent look off her pretty face.

He could have gotten to her last night, if it weren't for that damned dog. Maybe, he thought now, as he smoothed his hair into its queue, and took his quirt from its hook, maybe he could have Slater take care of that bloody oc-hound. One slash of a good sharp knife . . . waste of a dog, he supposed. But it would be one less obstacle between him and the brat.

He smiled to himself as he went down the stairs and out to where his brown gelding was saddled and waiting. There could be no better way to pay Philippa Winter back for her insolence than to get his hands on the Hamley brat, do her a little serious damage. If he took care of Larkyn Hamley, and thereby stalled Philippa's interfering in his affairs, he wouldn't have to worry anymore about what Pamella might say.

The thought filled him with frantic energy. He snatched the reins from his stable-boy and swung himself up into the saddle, wrenching his gelding's head around and applying his spurs. The gelding grunted and burst into a teeth-jarring gallop. William yanked him again to settle him down, then felt a moment's remorse. It wasn't the horse's fault that the rest of the world caused him such irritation. He reined the gelding back, giving Slater a chance to catch up with him on his ugly pony.

They set out for the Council Rotunda at a trot, Slater bouncing from side to side in his saddle. William passed the time imagining Pamella and Philippa, both weeping, Larkyn Hamley's small body bruised and broken. A thrill surged through him, a spasm of delight that was purely physical. Oh, yes, he told himself. Oh, yes. Now that would satisfy.

THIRTEEN

FROM high above the Strait, Philippa could see the approach of winter from the north. It was as if giant boots stamped southward from the glaciers, leaving great snowy footprints. Beneath Sunny's wings, the Klee ship arrowed toward Aeskland, its narrow black silhouette slicing the green water. Sunny's wings beat effortlessly in the cold air as they left the ship behind, and the biting wind held steady. Philippa pulled the collar of her riding jacket higher. She let Sunny choose her own direction, while she kept an eye on the shore ahead, knowing that when they reached it, the winds would change.

The Strait was not wide, and before the morning was half-over, the flyers were making their first high circle inland. The wind shifted as they left the water, but Sunny adjusted to it without difficulty. Philippa kept her thighs pressed tight under the knee rolls of her saddle, shifting as Sunny tilted with the updrafts, and scanned the ground below.

It hardly seemed possible that the topography of one shore could differ so much from the other. The north coast of Oc was sandy, lined by dunes and long grasses, with abundant inlets and bays for the fisher-folk to use. Aeskland's coastline was rocky and rough. Between the glacier's edge and the coastline stretched a vast, treeless plateau, covered now with snow.

Philippa understood that the nature of a people was shaped by its environment. From the indolence of Isamarians to the toughness of the Uplanders, she had seen how hardship or ease affected character. Those they called barbarians were the product of a barbaric land. She could find nothing in the country beneath her that offered warmth or comfort.

She knew little about the Aesks except for the tales of their savage wardogs, of their barbed arrows and double-tipped spears, the viciousness with which they treated their slaves. Some said they killed horses when they could get them, ate the meat, and used their skins. Philippa scanned the horizon, looking for the smoke of cookfires, the outlines of tents against the snow. Soon, perhaps, Klee and Isamar would know what was fable and what was truth about Aeskland.

Rys had said that though Klee had often been at war with Aeskland in the past decade, the Klee never followed them into their own lands. Klee's lands abutted the Aesk territories, and their battles had been skirmishes, raids and counterraids, the barbarians biting at Klee's borders like dogs nipping at a deer's flanks. Not since Klee and Isamar had been one kingdom had any of the civilized lands invaded the north country. Aeskland had nothing they wanted.

Philippa let Sunny make a lower circle. A bit of midday sun broke through the cloud cover and glimmered on the sails of the Klee ship as it hove to off the coast. Ice crystals flashed from the snowfield below. Philippa squinted against the brightness, but she could see nothing. She and Sunny made another circuit, still lower, then banked back toward the ship, dipping over the cliffs and down to the shore. They flew along the strand, looking for a place to come to ground.

At the end of a long finger of water that thrust inland through the rocks, Philippa spied a more or less level space, just upslope from the beach, running between stands of the dwarf trees. Snow covered everything now, of course, so she had no way to tell how trustworthy the ground might be. But Sunny had been aloft for many hours, and it was time to rest her. Philippa lifted her rein and shifted her weight. Obediently, Sunny tilted her wings and began her descent.

Philippa loosened the reins. Sunny knew how to choose her landing spot, and on uncertain ground it was best to let a winged horse follow her instinct. Sunny stretched out her neck, her ears flicking forward, and reached with her forefeet. Philippa kept her hands low, her weight a little back, her thighs flexed against the leathers of her stirrups.

Sunny's forefeet touched, and her back hooves reached, but she kept her extended wings tensed. Philippa felt her caution at landing on the snow, at not knowing what might be beneath it. Her left front hoof slipped, and she might have stumbled, but her wings flexed, catching the air, steadying her. Her canter was tentative, wings still fluttering. She bowed her neck, seeking balance. Philippa swayed with her and stood in her stirrups as Sunny slowed to a trot.

When she stopped, panting, Philippa leaned forward over her lathered neck. She smoothed her ruffled mane, and murmured, "Sunny, I am barely worthy of you." Sunny tossed her head and flicked her ears, making Philippa laugh. "All right, my girl," she said, swinging her leg over the cantle. "I know what that means. And I'm as hungry as you are."

She turned to see that the two dinghies from the ship were moving in toward the shore. A man in the front of each bent over the bow, testing the depth of the water with a pole as the boats sought a safe path to the rock-strewn beach. By the time Philippa had cooled Sunny, removed her tack, and rubbed her down, the boats had grounded, and the soldiers were pulling them up onto the shore. Some of the Klee soldiers went straight to work putting up tents, economical affairs constructed with poles and sheets of jute canvas, arranged in circular fashion. Others set to with buckets to tote water from the stream that ran through the rocks to the beach, carving a sandy path to the sea.

Sunny pushed at the feed bag. "In a little while, my girl," Philippa said, picking up her halter lead. "It's a bit too soon after your flight. But we could get you some water." She led her down the slope of the beach, both of them picking their way through sharp rocks and piles of cold seaweed.

Francis joined her at the stream's edge, while Sunny dipped her muzzle into the water. "You didn't see anything, I gather?" he asked.

"Snow and more snow," Philippa said. "And rocks. How do the Aesks eke a living from this place?"

Francis lifted his head to gaze up at the plateau beyond the cliff. The wind ruffled his pale hair. "Even the fisher-folk of On-marin must seem rich to them," he said thoughtfully.

"I was thinking just that," Philippa said. She tugged at Sunny's lead. "Enough, Sunny. Give your belly a chance. You can have more soon."

Francis, from a careful distance, asked, "Can I do anything to help you?"

"I'll need Sunny's blanket from my things. I believe my lord Rys's men were to bring them ashore."

Obligingly, Francis went back to the swiftly growing camp-site and sorted through the piles of baggage. When he returned with the horse blanket folded over his arm, he said, "They're setting up a separate shelter for you."

"And for Sunny?"

Francis smiled. "I think that's up to you. It looks big enough for three horses."

"Good." Philippa looked up into the sky. Great patches of blue separated the clouds now, opened by a rising wind. "It's going to clear," she said. "It will be damnably cold tonight."

"Rys says it's too late to start the search today."

"He's right. Sunny needs to rest now," Philippa said. "We'll go aloft first thing tomorrow. The plateau is huge, and they could be anywhere. This could take time."

Francis made a slight sound that might have been a groan or might have been a laugh. Philippa, with one hand on Sunny's neck, looked at him curiously. "What is it, Francis?"

He shrugged, and avoided her eyes. "I was—I was afraid, actually. But now that we're here, now that it's close—I find I can hardly wait to begin. I feel a bit silly, like a young boy eager to prove his courage."

"There's nothing silly about that," Philippa said. "You were right to be afraid, and it's natural to be impatient to get it over with."

"I lack your experience, Philippa."

"Lucky you," she said.

A rumor had reached the Academy, and the girls whispered it to each other in the Hall and in the Dormitory. Lark heard it first from Anabel, who came to bend over Tup's stall gate. "It's

Geraldine," Anabel murmured, her eyes wide with excitement. "It's Geraldine's baby!"

Lark had been brushing tangles from Molly's winter coat. She straightened, the stiff-bristled brush in her hands. "Geraldine's baby? It must be six months old by now, or more."

Geraldine had been, for a time, Geraldine Prince, bonded to a winged horse, with a bright future before her. Her pregnancy, which no winged horse could tolerate, had put an untimely end to her career and meant the death of her bondmate. Lark would never forget the death of New Prince, and her part in it. And she would never, as long as she lived, understand how Geraldine could have allowed such a thing to happen.

Anabel waved one hand. "I don't know how old it is—he is, I mean—but Geraldine's father has brought suit in the Council."

"Suit? About what?"

"About the baby's *father*, Black!" Anabel said. "Everyone's talking about it!"

Lark crossed the stall with Molly at her heels. Tup whimpered and pressed close behind them. "Anabel," Lark said, "what is everyone talking about? I don't understand."

Anabel opened the gate for her, and Lark went through. She shut it, then leaned against it, gazing at Tup's shining coat, his wide, bright eyes. She remembered how the light had gone out of New Prince's eyes, how his breath had rattled as he died. It made her shudder anew at the horror of it.

"What's the matter?" Anabel asked.

"I was thinking about New Prince."

"Don't think about that now," Anabel said. She tugged at Lark's hand. "Come on, let's hurry and change. We'll be late for supper, and I'm ravenous."

Lark turned with her, and they started down the aisle. Anabel said, "You still don't see, do you? Geraldine's father has accused someone of fathering her child!"

"Can you do that?" Lark asked. "At home, in Willakeep . . . everyone just knows. I mean, the girl will say, and usually the baby looks like someone we all recognize."

"That's just it!" Anabel said triumphantly.

"What is?"

At that moment, Hester came dashing around the corner

from the tack room, and fell into step with them as they started across the courtyard. "Have you heard?" she demanded.

"You mean, about Geraldine and the Duke?" Anabel said. She drew breath to say something else, but Lark put a hand on her arm and held her back. Hester stopped, too.

"The *Duke*?" Lark said, her voice tight in her throat. "They're accusing Duke William?"

Anabel's pale complexion colored with excitement. "That's what I've been trying to tell you! Geraldine's little boy looks *exactly* like Duke William!"

Hester nodded. "Papá just came from the Council of Lords. It's true, Geraldine's family is bringing a paternity suit against the Duke."

"And the little boy . . ." Lark began. Her voice trailed off as the realization struck her.

"Yes!" Anabel exclaimed. "He has the same light hair, the same black eyes . . . he looks just like all the Fleckhams."

Lark felt as if she couldn't breathe. The image of little Brandon rose in her mind, his hair pale as ice, his midnight-dark eyes sparkling with laughter as Edmar teased him. Brandon, too, looked just like William. He looked just like his mother Pamella, as well . . . Pamella, the Duke's own sister.

Hester's thoughts had traveled the same path, she could see. Her eyes met Lark's, widening with shock. "Oh," she said. "Oh, no, Black, that can't be."

Anabel said, "What? What are you two talking about? Why can't it be?"

Hester drew a breath, then shook her head. "Never mind, Anabel. It's nothing."

"But what—do you know something you're not telling me? What is it?"

Lark bit her lip and turned away from Anabel's burning curiosity. She and Hester had promised Lady Beeth not to speak of what had happened in the Uplands months ago. Lady Beeth, and Lark's brother Brye as well, had convinced them that their silence was in the best interests of everyone, Pamella, Brandon, Oc itself—and Deeping Farm.

But the idea that Geraldine's baby might be William's troubled Lark deeply. So often, she knew, bulls and billies and stallions threw offspring that resembled them. It was one of the ways farm-folk kept track of which sires were most potent. What if—would it be possible that poor Pamella's little one, little Brandon—

No, she told herself. It was too disgusting an idea even for Duke William.

It would explain, though, why Pamella steadfastly refused to return to Osham, or to see anyone in her family. And it might explain why she could not speak. Such an experience . . . Lark couldn't imagine it.

And maybe it wasn't true.

She glanced across at Hester as they took their places at the long table, and saw that Hester, too, had been thinking dark thoughts. Hester gave her a slow, deliberate shake of the head. Lark nodded in return. There was nothing they could do and no point in speculating. But when the chores of the day were finished at last, she lay in her cot staring out at the brilliant winter stars. For a long time sleep eluded her as she thought of poor Pamella—Lady Pamella—and what might have befallen her. The last image in her mind, before her eyelids finally closed, was of Duke William's hard, pale face and the cold braided leather of his magicked quirt.

FOURTEEN

PHILIPPA slept poorly in the shelter. Its sheets of canvas protected her and Sunny from the worst of the cold, but the packed sand beneath her blankets and furs was unforgiving to the points of her hips and shoulders, and the pillow, made of a folded blanket, scratched at her cheek and neck. She rose when the first gray light stole in through the spaces between the panels and the poles that supported them, rubbing her neck and grimacing. There had been a time when she slept easily on hard ground, but her body was not so flexible as it had been at twenty-four.

Sunny seemed to have fared better. She dropped her head willingly to receive her bridle, and her steps were light as Philippa led her outside and down to the stream to drink. The watchmen, arrayed around the campsite, nodded silent greetings. Philippa nodded back. As Sunny drank, she scanned the sky.

It looked to be a perfect day for flying. The weather held clear and cold. She would be glad of her woolen vest and thick stockings, but Sunny would find the frigid air invigorating. To the north, the glaciers shone like sheets of dull silver. To the south, the green waters of the Strait flickered and gleamed. It was into the east that they would turn today, toward the black beaches and the scrubby forests that stretched beyond the great plateau.

Francis and Rys emerged from one of the tents as Philippa was seeing to Sunny's feed. She turned, leaving Sunny to it, and went to meet the men. A table had been set up in the open, and as she approached, one of the soldiers put a platter of steaming meat and sliced bread on it, with a stack of battered metal plates and flatware. Another had a huge camp pot of coffee and poured out mugs of it. Philippa sat at one end, with Francis and Rys opposite, and they made quick, silent work of their breakfast. Moments later, Philippa was saddling Sunny, checking her gear, and preparing to launch.

Francis stood well to one side, sensitive to Sunny's aversion, but close enough that he could speak quietly. "Philippa," he said. "I've been thinking."

Philippa ran her hands over Sunny's breastband and rested her palm on the pommel of her flying saddle. Everything was in order. She glanced at Francis from beneath the brim of her riding cap. "About what, Francis?"

He hesitated, his slender features tightening. "It's about risk. About priorities."

"Yes?" She was ready to mount, and she felt a slight impatience. Francis had always been deliberate, but now, both she and Sunny were ready to fly.

His voice dropped. "Philippa, I completely support this effort, as you know . . . I care about it . . . but—"

She lifted her chin and pointed at the circle of jute tents. "A little late for second thoughts, I think."

He managed a small, tense smile. "I'm not having second thoughts. But I want you to remember—that is, I am my father's son, after all."

That made her chuckle. "Out with it, Francis! A snowstorm could reach us while you decide how to say whatever it is."

His smile grew, too, but his dark gaze was bleak. "It's this, Philippa: I cannot, as a member of the Duke's household, equate the value of a winged horse and her rider with that of two fisherfolk children, however unfair that may seem. I must—" He cleared his throat, and looked at his boots. "I must order you, I'm afraid. To put yourself first."

A strange warmth spread through Philippa, and she very

much feared her cheeks had gone pink. She turned to Sunny, and leaped up into the saddle. She allowed herself a moment of satisfaction; she might have difficulty sleeping on the ground, but she could still perform a perfect standing mount. Keeping her face averted, she said, "Have no fear, Francis. It would not be myself, but Sunny I would always put first." She wished her voice did not sound so hard, but she didn't trust it not to tremble. Francis's concern reminded her of Frederick's devotion, and she had not thought such a commitment would come again from a Fleckham.

He answered with mild irony. "Of course, Philippa. But Sunny can't be protected unless you are."

She took a steadying breath, and met his gaze. "Exactly so. Thank you, Francis."

He bowed. She inclined her head and lifted her hand to Baron Rys, standing just outside his tent. Sunny spun on her hindquarters and set off at an eager canter. When she launched, the thrust of her hindquarters thrilled Philippa as it always did with its strength. She leaned forward, urging Sunny up and over the cliff. The beach dropped away below them until she could no longer make out the upturned faces of the men watching. Philippa lifted the rein and laid it against the left side of Sunny's neck, shifting her weight into her right stirrup, and the mare banked to the east to begin their search anew.

FRANCIS stood on the beach to watch Philippa and Sunny leave, and he was in the same place when they returned hours later. It had been a long, idle day for him. Rys had sent a few men to climb up the cliff and scout the seaward edge of the great plateau, but there was little else to be done until Philippa found the tribe.

"They keep a great distance from each other," Rys had said when they were still in Osham. "If one tribe trespasses on another's hunting territory, they fight. We can expect that the tribe we find will be the one responsible for the attack on Onmarin." He had been honing his smallsword with a whetstone, handling the weapon with the ease of long practice.

Francis had always been forbidden to use matchlocks because of the danger of their exploding in the face of the shooter, but he did have a smallsword. He had, in his youth, had some training with it. He spent the empty day waiting for Philippa's return in sharpening and cleaning the blade, trying to remember how his fighting-master had told him to use it.

Rys came to stand beside him at about midday and gave him an easy smile. "You have not been in battle before, I expect."

Blushing, Francis sheathed the blade, shaking his head.

"Natural to be nervous."

That made Francis laugh. "You'll find me ridiculous, Rys," he said diffidently, "but in fact, I'm not so much nervous as impatient."

"Ah." Rys touched his shoulder lightly. "I remember the feeling." He pointed to his men, lounging around the warmth of the fire pit in the center of the circle of tents. They kept the fire blazing hot, feeding it with driftwood. A thin, clear smoke rose from it to dissipate quickly in the cold air. "If you fight enough wars, Francis, you acquire the attitude of these men. You save your energy, postpone thinking about it. You learn to let tomorrow take care of tomorrow."

Francis turned to face seaward, where the shore of Oc was a distant smudge beyond the icy gray water. "It is another of the burdens of being born into a Duke's family, I'm afraid. Our experiences are rather closely controlled." He shrugged. "I wasn't allowed any real danger, not even true sword practice. I'm expected to keep myself intact. If something were to happen to my elder brother, I'm meant to step into the title."

"I would be surprised if that were an ambition of yours."

"And so you should be, Rys!" Francis's laugh sounded thin in his own ears. "The last thing I have ever wanted was to sit on that throne."

Rys sobered after a moment, and Francis saw that his gaze, too, strayed to the southern horizon. Klee, of course, was a great distance from where they stood, but Francis thought he understood the Baron's thoughts. "You feel differently about your own inheritance, I think," he said softly.

"Indeed I do," Rys said, just as quietly, but with an edge to his voice. "It's not that I want to be the Viscount . . . I don't . . . but I cannot bear the idea of spending my life fawning at various courts, with no authority to actually do anything."

"We are at least in agreement about that," Francis said.

Rys pointed to his soldiers around the snapping fire. "In any case, Lord Francis," he said, "you can trust my men to take care of the fighting." He grinned and slapped Francis's shoulder. "I don't want His Grace of Oc blaming me for damage to his brother!"

Francis laughed, too, but he felt a pang of something like premonition in his gut. He drew a sharp breath, trying to banish it, and turned back to watching the sky for Philippa. At length he saw her, a tiny figure on the eastern horizon, growing steadily as she flew into the west.

The winged horses were often compared to birds in song and story, but Francis thought their magnificence outshone any bird. And their partnership with the horsemistresses set them apart from all other beasts, making them the most remarkable and the most mysterious creatures in all of creation.

Philippa and Sunny were close now. Winter Sunset spread her broad, scarlet wings, and the last of the setting sun shone through them like lamplight through parchment. She soared down past the cliff, and settled swiftly onto the narrow beach. She cantered toward the camp, wings outspread, fluttering in the breeze. She trotted to a stop, blowing clouds of mist from her flared nostrils. Sweat lathered the jointure of her wings, and Philippa said sharply, when they were near enough, "Francis! Could you fetch me Sunny's blanket? She's overheated."

Francis, hiding his smile at being ordered about like a stableman, obeyed, and stood watching as Philippa stripped the saddle from Winter Sunset, rubbed her dry, bade her fold her wings, then buckled the blanket around her. "I must walk her till she's cool," she said over her shoulder. "We flew a bit too far, but I saw something."

"We'll wait," Rys said. He gestured to the fire. "Join us as soon as you can, and we'll have a hot drink for you."

Francis followed Rys to the fire and stood with the others as Philippa and Sunny paced back and forth on the beach. They made desultory conversation, and Francis feigned casualness as the mulled wine began to steam on the fire and Philippa filled Sunny's water bucket near her shelter, but his gut was tight with impatience. He had time, as Philippa shook grain into a feed bag, to scoff at himself for his bloody thoughts. He was the bookish one, the gentle one, after all, and here he was, eager as a boy to get into his first real battle.

At last, Philippa patted Sunny and started up the beach toward the fire. She pulled off her cap and gloves, and folded them into her belt. By the time she reached the circle, one of the soldiers had poured out a mug of the hot wine for her, handing it to her with a bow. She gave him a nod of thanks and came to stand beside Francis.

"You saw something," Rys said.

"I did." Philippa sipped from the mug, and held her free hand out to the fire. Her cheeks and nose were reddened, and strands of gray and red hair were slipping from her rider's knot. "I saw smoke, and what looked like buildings, just inland from the sea." She indicated the eastern horizon with her chin. "It's at least three days' walk, I expect. They must have crossed the plateau and dropped down on the eastern side. There's a valley there. I kept a prudent distance, but there must be some way to climb down from the plateau. Perhaps this is their winter camp. It has some shelter, trees for a windbreak. There's a bay quite close. You can reach them by water and climb up from the shore."

"They didn't see you, then?" Rys asked.

Philippa set down her mug. "I don't think so," she said. Francis saw how the lines fanned around her eyes, the toll the chapping of the wind took on her face. He took her mug from her and refilled it himself from the kettle. She tucked the loose strands of hair back into her rider's knot. "There are several buildings, low, rather long. A sort of compound."

"Then you couldn't see if the children were there," Francis mused, then felt foolish. "Oh, sorry. Of course you couldn't see."

Philippa gave him one of her restrained smiles. "I did try," she said. "But I didn't want them to see us. If Rys and his men—and you," she amended, "if you retain the element of surprise, you'll have a better chance."

"Very good," Rys said. Francis glanced at him and saw that he had brought a sheet of thick paper and a charcoal stick. He began to sketch what they already knew of the coastline. "Can you show me, Mistress Winter?" he said, handing the charcoal to Philippa.

"I think so." Setting down her mug, she took the charcoal and spread the paper across her lap. She began to draw with a sure hand, with Rys watching over her shoulder. She drew several inlets as landmarks and showed a few stands of the scrubby trees. "Here," she said, reaching a point to the east. "You'll see a great black rock formation thrusting up from the sea. Sea stacks, I think they call them in the Angles. Beyond it is the bay. Sunny and I will guide you. There are many such rocks, and I can't think how you could tell this one from the others."

Rys was nodding and chewing on his lower lip. He called one of his captains to him, and together they pored over Philippa's map. A moment later, they excused themselves and went to confer with the other men.

Philippa sighed then and rubbed her eyes with her fingers. They must be burning, Francis thought, after so many hours of peering down on the snowfields. "You're tired, Philippa," he said. "You must eat something, then rest. I wish you didn't have to fly tomorrow."

"One more day," she said. She dropped her hands, and her eyes met his. "I can make it one more day," she repeated. "But tonight I feel every one of my years."

"Well done, though, Philippa," Francis said warmly. "Oc will remember this."

"Don't speak too soon, Francis," she answered. "We don't have them yet."

FIFTEEN

WHENEVER she was not required in the classrooms or the library or the Hall, Lark haunted the stables. When she was forced to go to the Dormitory, to sleep, she left Bramble in Tup's stall, though Erna frowned at her. She tried to explain to the stable-girl that she was worried about Tup, but the girl was so slow Lark ended up simply commanding her to leave be. Erna looked at her dully, and said, "Yes, Miss," in a way that made Lark feel a bit guilty. But it was necessary. As it was, even with Bramble sleeping in the stall with Molly and Tup, she herself could hardly sleep at night for worrying about what Duke William might do.

Every evening she and Hester watched the skies, hoping for the return of Mistress Winter and Winter Sunset, wishing for good news of the kidnapped children, praying the weather would hold. Once Lark looked across the courtyard from the Dormitory and saw Mistress Morgan standing in the window of her office, also gazing at the northern horizon. Lark almost started across the cobblestones to go to her, to share her vigil, but then she remembered who and what she was, and she turned to the stables instead. She glanced back before going in, and saw Mistress Morgan still standing there, one hand on the sash.

And in the middle of this time of waiting, the Klee girl arrived at the Academy.

The Honorable Amelia Rys was narrow of body and face, with brown eyes and unremarkable brown hair. She wore a vivid blue tabard girdled in gold, with a full and elegantly draped skirt. Her hair was caught back in a jeweled net, and her boots, when she stepped down from her carriage, were small and high-heeled. Two footmen hurried to unload several trunks and a tapestry valise. A maidservant trailed Mistress Rys as she swept up the stairs to the Hall, the footmen following.

Hester and Lark and the other second-levels came out of the dry paddock, where they had spent the morning drilling with Mistress Star. They goggled at the entourage invading the Hall. Mistress Morgan appeared in the doorway and stood waiting, her hands linked before her.

Lark whispered, "Just have a blink at all that fuss!" as the Klee girl, with the practiced grace of a courtier, dropped a curtsy to Mistress Morgan.

Everyone in the courtyard could hear Mistress Morgan's firm admonishment. "That will be your last curtsy, my dear. Ever."

Amelia Rys rose and stared at the Headmistress. There was a frozen, awkward moment, when the footmen's mouths fell open and the maidservant put her hand to her throat. At length, the Baron's daughter nodded. "Have I erred, Mistress?" she said in a matter-of-fact tone. "I do apologize. I hope you will soon instruct me as to the proper comportment."

Mistress Morgan inclined her head, held out a hand to indicate that the girl should follow her inside, then turned with a flip of her riding skirt's hem and went into the Hall. The maidservant started to follow, but Matron appeared, and pointed, wordlessly, to the Dormitory. The doors closed behind the Headmistress and the new student, and the Klee servants, laden with baggage, trooped back down the stairs and across the courtyard toward the Dormitory. The carriage, with its driver and four magnificent gray draught horses, stayed where it was.

The second-level girls dashed across the courtyard to circle the big grays, admiring them. The driver gazed down at them in amazed silence as they exclaimed over various distinctions of the horses.

"Look at those fetlocks!" Anabel exclaimed. "Why, you could fit two of my Chance's onto those big bones!"

"And so tall!" Grace breathed. "Their withers are higher than my head."

Lark smiled up at the driver. "They're well matched, aren't they?" she said. "And so beautifully groomed. Tails like silk, I would say."

The driver lifted his cap. "Thank you, Miss. I would ask you young ladies not to startle them."

Hester said indignantly, "Don't be ridiculous! We would never startle horses."

She was right, of course. The girls circled the animals, and spoke to them in soft voices, but made no sudden moves. In moments, the big horses were bending their necks, sniffing at the girls' faces, their ears flicking comfortably back and forth.

"May we bring them a treat?" Beatrice asked, and dashed off toward the kitchen without waiting for permission. When she came back, she carried a pocketful of carrots and slightly withered apples, and when the driver, laughing now, nodded his permission, the four enormous carriage horses were soon munching, tossing their heads, standing hipshot and comfortable in the cold sunshine.

"Larkyn!"

Lark looked up from scratching behind one of the horses' ears to see Mistress Morgan beckoning to her from the doorway of the Hall. Lark glanced at Hester, who shrugged and grinned, and Anabel, whose forehead creased with worry. Lark shook her head at her. "Don't worry, Anabel," she said hastily, as she spun about to run up the steps. "I haven't done anything wrong in days!"

When she reached Mistress Morgan, she saw that the Baron's daughter stood in the shadows of the foyer. The Headmistress stepped back to allow Lark to pass inside, saying, "Larkyn Black, this is Amelia Rys, our new student."

"Aye," Lark said cheerfully. "So we guessed. Welcome to the Academy, Amelia."

She saw the girl's thin eyebrows rise, and her narrow lips pursed a little, but she inclined her head. "How do you do, Miss."

"Oh, you can call me Black," Lark said with a smile. "Everyone does."

The thin eyebrows rose farther, and the purse of the lips

remained. "Indeed," the Klee girl said. Her tone was neither cold nor warm. It was, Lark thought, perfectly noncommittal.

Lark glanced at Mistress Morgan for guidance, and thought she saw the dance of humor in her eyes. "Like yourself, Larkyn," the Headmistress said, "Amelia comes to the Academy alone. Her beginning is as unusual as yours, in its own way. You had a foal born out of season, and Amelia comes with no bondmate yet. It will be difficult for her, I think, to feel a part of the Academy. Under the circumstances, I thought you would make the perfect sponsor for her."

Lark inclined her head. "Aye." She grinned at Amelia, a little wickedly. "Would you like a blink at the stables?" The Headmistress's lips twitched, but the Klee girl only fixed Lark with her brown gaze.

"A blink?" she said. "You must translate for me, Miss—that is, Black. This is not a term I'm familiar with."

Lark laughed. "Never should you be! I'm a farm girl from the Uplands, as my own sponsor will remind you at every opportunity, and I speak our dialect. Come, with the Headmistress's leave, I'll give you a tour."

She put a hand under Amelia's slender arm, finding it hard and muscled beneath her fingers. The girl tolerated her touch for a moment, and then, subtly, lifted her arm away.

Lark bit her lip, trying not to be offended. She led the way out of the Hall, trusting the girl would follow. Mistress Morgan's bemused gaze warmed her back as she and the new student went out the double doors and down the steps.

"A loner, my mamá would say." Hester had finished Goldie's grooming, and she came to hang over the gate of Tup's stall, watching Lark finish her chores. She kept her voice low, though Amelia Rys was not in the stables. She was in the Hall, receiving instruction from the Headmistress herself. Her trunks and valise had been arranged in the Dormitory, the maidservant unpacking everything, arranging things in drawers, badgering Matron for storage space.

"Wait till she finds out her maid has to go." This was Anabel, who draped her long, slender form next to Hester's, and idly held out her thin white fingers for Molly to nibble at.

"Did you come with maids, both of you?" Lark wondered. "No one in the Uplands has such, except perhaps the horse-mistress in Dickering Park."

"We didn't," Hester said. "But Petra did!"

Lark and Anabel both giggled. "Maybe Petra should have been her sponsor," Anabel said. "They might have a lot in common."

"Oh, I don't think so. Amelia doesn't seem like a snob to me. She's just—aloof." Lark put the currycomb on its shelf and gave Tup one more pat. She hated to leave him, but she gave a low whistle, and Bramble came at a trot, obligingly going into the stall when Lark opened the gate.

"Why do you put Bramble in Seraph's stall?" Anabel asked.

Lark avoided Hester's eyes. "Oh, he just likes her," she said weakly. "And Bramble doesn't mind."

Hester said briskly, "Come on, you lot. Suppertime at last!" The three of them hurried out and across the courtyard to the Hall, joining the other girls streaming in out of the cold.

Lark cast a look up at the sky as they went, and a little shiver of unease went through her. The stars were invisible tonight, hidden by high, thin clouds. "Smells like snow," she said, half to herself.

Hester laughed. "Black! How can you smell snow?"

"I just can," Lark said. "When you live in the hills, you learn it."

Hester put an arm around her shoulders. "Mistress Winter knows what she's about," she said. "You have to trust her."

"I know," Lark said. "But I wish—I just wish she would come back. The weather could turn at any time."

They were caught up in the tide of girls, swept along to their places at the long tables. Mistress Morgan brought Amelia in after everyone was seated, and the girls at Lark and Hester's table had to move while a place was set. Amelia Rys stood watching this proceeding without reaction, her eyes running up and down the table as if assessing every girl. Lark had the impression she would remember every face and know exactly where they were sitting.

Lark put a hand on the back of the empty chair and smiled. "Do you sit here, lass," she said. "And I will introduce you."

Amelia Rys's eyebrows quirked at the "lass," but she took

the chair, and sat. Lark had just begun to name the girls on either side when a hush fell over the dining room. Lark stopped speaking and followed the turned heads to the doors. Her mouth dried, and her heart sped when she saw who had interrupted the Academy's supper.

Duke William, tall and lean in his black coat and narrow trousers, silver buckles, and embroidered vest, strode in from the foyer. His quirt was tucked under his arm. Lark folded her arms tightly, aware that Amelia gave her an inquiring glance.

The Headmistress, at the high table, rose. "Your Grace," she said, with a stiff inclination of her head.

The Duke did not acknowledge her greeting. He stepped up onto the dais with a lithe movement and turned to survey the room. "Where is the Baron's daughter?" he asked. His voice carried in the quiet room, high and clear.

A cool smile curved Mistress Morgan's lips. "We have several barons' daughters at the Academy," she said smoothly. "I believe Your Grace knows that."

Duke William took his quirt in his hand and lightly slapped his thigh. "You know whom I mean, Headmistress," he said lightly. "Rys's daughter. The Klee girl." His eyes raked the room. "Whose bonding has been bought and paid for."

A collective indrawn breath seemed almost to dim the light in the room. Lark, shocked at the insult, let her eyes slip sideways to Amelia Rys's thin face. To her surprise, a light of something like defiance, or perhaps recognition, shone in Amelia's eyes. With a slight clearing of her throat, the Klee girl rose in her place.

Lark almost put out a hand to stop her from curtsying to the Duke, but it seemed Amelia Rys had already learned that lesson. In a clear voice, she said, "Your Grace of Oc. I am here." She inclined her head, and she didn't smile. "Amelia, youngest daughter of Baron Esmond Rys."

The Duke stepped down from the dais and came to stand near their table. The room was silent, the servers holding back with their steaming platters, the girls and the horsemistresses frozen in their places. Lark shrank down in her chair, wishing Amelia had not sat next to her. William's black eyes glittered in the light from the wall sconces. "You look like him," he said to Amelia.

"So I am told," she said evenly. Lark could hardly breathe, but still she felt a rush of admiration. Would that she had such composure in the presence of the Duke! But then, Amelia did not know all that she knew about William of Oc.

William slapped his thigh once again with his quirt, and Lark flinched. His eyes passed over her, and his mouth tightened. "We would warn you against keeping the wrong company," he said lightly.

"I assure Your Grace," Amelia said, "that I need no such warning, though I thank you for your concern."

William frowned. "We shall see." He tucked the quirt back under his arm, flicked a glance over Lark, and looked back at Amelia. "We will discuss your future with the Baron when—indeed, we should say *if*—he returns from Aeskland." He turned around and stalked out of the dining room without looking back. A long moment of silence stretched around the room, until a burst of nervous conversation broke it.

Amelia, slowly, resumed her seat. Lark leaned closer to her. "I'm sure your father will come back safely," she said. "He was trying to frighten you."

Amelia's cool brown gaze met hers. "I know," she said. She picked up her salad fork as a server set a tiny plate of chilled bloodbeets before her. She speared one, delicately, then held it on her fork as she looked back at Lark. "He's angry at being forced to allow me to bond with a winged horse." She put the bloodbeet in her mouth and chewed it thoughtfully. When she had swallowed, she added, "My father is a clever man. He's thinking of the future. My being here strengthens Oc's ties to Klee, and the Council of Lords likes that."

"And you?" Lark dared to ask. She started on her own salad, watching this unusual girl from beneath her eyelids. "Are you glad to be here?"

Amelia laid down her fork and turned to face Lark directly, her face as composed as ever. She said, "I have wanted nothing else since I was a child."

Lark couldn't answer. She herself, as a girl in the Uplands, could never have dreamed of such a possibility.

As the meal went forward, the soup course and the fish course and the meat course, her eyes strayed again and again to the doorway where Duke William had gone out. She was hungry, as always, but a knot of anxiety tightened in her stomach, and she longed for the meal to be over.

The moment the servers cleared away the ice, Lark jumped up from the table and started toward the door. Before she reached it, the Headmistress's voice stopped her. "Larkyn! Will you please show Amelia to the Dormitory, and her bed?"

Lark stopped where she was and turned around slowly. Mistress Morgan had almost reached her. Lark was alarmed to see how weak and pale the Headmistress looked, how her hand shook. When had she started using a walking stick? Lark hadn't noticed before.

Amelia Rys joined them, and stood, brows slightly raised, waiting for Lark's response.

"Oh—oh, aye, of course, Mistress Morgan," Lark stammered. She couldn't help glancing longingly at the doorway. She could just see the lamplight in the stables beyond the foyer windows.

Amelia's eyebrows rose farther. She followed Lark's gaze, then said easily, "Thank you, Larkyn. But perhaps first we could go to the stables? I would so like to see your horse."

Lark cast her a glance full of gratitude. She bade the Headmistress good evening and walked as swiftly as she dared across the courtyard and into the stables. Amelia stayed close beside her, asking no questions, but her own steps were as quick as Lark's.

A wave of relief swept over Lark as she reached Tup's stall. Though the light was dim, she could see that he was there, safe and sound. Molly and he were huddled against one wall, and Bramble stood, glaring into the darkness. Lark let herself into the stall. She put out a hand to touch Bramble as she passed and found that the oc-hound's hackles were up, her neck stiff. She didn't move when Lark stroked her, but stared fixedly out into the aisle.

Molly and Tup were both trembling. Tup's ears drooped, one to either side, in that oddly confused way he had when William had been near.

"Kalla's tail," she hissed. "What was he doing here?"

"What is it?" Amelia asked, from outside the stall.

Lark whirled. She had forgotten Amelia was there. "It's him," she said in a tight undertone. "The Duke. He's been here with Tup."

SIXTEEN

PHILIPPA let Sunny choose her own pace, circling back once in a while when the ships fell too far behind them. The glare of sun on snow of the day before had given way to a gray layer of cloud that cast shifting shadows on the dull sea below her. She felt as if she had been flying over snow, ice, and water for weeks instead of only days. Her joints ached from sleeping on the ground, and her face felt stiff and dry from exposure. Sunny, too, seemed tired, her launch a little labored, her wingbeats steady, but hardly the effortless strokes they had been when they left the Academy.

"One more day, Sunny," Philippa murmured to her, beneath the whine of the wind aloft. "Just one more day, and we can go home." Teaching her third-level girls would feel like a holiday, she thought, after these difficult days. Sleeping in her own bed, with her own quilt and pillow, would be bliss. And she had no doubt Sunny yearned for her straw-filled stall, the heated stables, and the occasional treat of hot mash Herbert cooked up in the cold weather.

They skirted the ragged coastline, keeping an eye on the Baron's ships. Philippa also kept an eye on the lowering clouds, tasting the bite of snow in the air, frowning at the darkness of the northern horizon. She found that the landmark she had chosen was not so easy to identify again. There were dozens of such sea stacks, monoliths rising from the water, worn smooth by the splashing of the waves. They flew inland a half dozen times, searching for the right place, finding only empty snow-covered ground. They followed narrow inlets, estuaries, one or two broader bays than the one she remembered, without success. She began to doubt her memory and worry that she had somehow missed the spot.

They had been aloft for a long time when she saw the landmark at last. Its crenellated shape looked familiar, but in the cloud-filtered light, it was hard to be certain. The bay beyond it was oval, with a narrow, curving beach of black sand giving way to steep walls of rock on either side. She breathed a sigh of relief when she saw smoke rising from beyond the bay. She and Sunny would take a quick flight inland, to make sure this was the right spot, then they would turn for home at last. They would rest in Onmarin for a night, and tomorrow, they would be at the Academy, warm, well fed, surrounded by the soothing sounds of feminine voices.

She reined Sunny to her left. She would fly just far enough to confirm this was the Aesk camp, then she could circle back, staying low in hopes she and Sunny would look like one of the large seabirds swooping and circling over the shore.

As Sunny banked, Philippa glanced to the north. Alarm thrilled through her body.

The northern horizon had disappeared in a bank of gray, and the threatened snowstorm had begun in earnest over the great plateau. Now that she had moved far enough to the east, she could see that the storm was sweeping down from the glaciers in a rolling march.

She leaned forward as the mare veered around the black sea stack. "Better hurry, my girl," she called. Sunny responded with stronger wingbeats. Philippa shaded her eyes with her hand and peered ahead.

Now that she was so close, she saw that the Aesk compound was farther inland than she had thought. She dropped low over the tumbled boulders that marked a break in the cliff. They were black, too, like the sand, and dull in the gray light. She flew over a rock-strewn rise, and the shallow valley opened before them. To the west, the plateau rose, with its wall of forbidding gray stone. To the east, a forest of the stunted trees stretched raggedly across the horizon. And there, at last, Philippa saw the buildings she had spotted the day before.

There were eight of them, long, low structures arranged around a central fire pit. Two smaller buildings, little more than huts, stood at each end of the compound. She was close enough now to see the Aesks themselves, a dozen or more squat, thick figures moving between the longhouses, and more of them out among the trees. She reined Sunny sharply back, hoping to get back over the bay without being seen.

She was a moment too late. Just as Sunny banked, tilting her wings to turn in that precarious spot between land and sea, someone saw them.

There was a figure on the little strip of beach, one she hadn't seen against the dark sand. An arrow sliced the cold air toward them. Philippa cried out, and Sunny responded.

Their discipline served them well. They had drilled this a thousand times, and the maneuver was automatic. Philippa shifted her weight, and Sunny's wings tilted, her body shaking with effort. First, Arrows, descending precipitously in a path no attacker could predict. Then a Grand Reverse, a full turn, a change of altitude. Another arrow followed the first, and Sunny swerved again, driving higher, her wings shivering as she flew up and out of the archer's range. A dog's savage baying rose from the ground, echoing against the cliffs. No oc-hound was capable of such a noise. Philippa trembled at the sound.

Just as Sunny completed her second Grand Reverse, the snow reached them. It came on a fist of wind that slammed over the edge of the plateau and drove into Philippa's face with shocking force. Sunny's wings faltered, and Philippa felt the spasm that rippled through her body.

In a moment, the mare steadied, finding the lift of the wind, balancing on the conflicting currents of air rushing in from the sea. Philippa reined her to the west, back toward the convoy, to give them the prearranged signal. She waved the scarlet flag she had tied to her pommel for the purpose and saw the answering wave from Francis. It was at this moment that she and Sunny were to bank to the south, to fly across the Strait to Onmarin, and their well-deserved rest.

But they were too late. Thick flakes fell fast and hard, swirling around Sunny's head, settling on her wings, melting quickly with the heat of her blood, making a pool where more snow caught and stayed.

There was nothing for it but to turn back to the land, to find a place to return to ground as swiftly as they could. The cliffs loomed ahead of them, ghostly and grim. The plateau offered the best surface if Sunny could ascend high enough.

Philippa felt her wing muscles laboring beneath her calves. Her own thighs clenched with sympathetic effort, and she felt Sunny's heat rising through the saddle. Snow caught on her eyelashes and her lips. She saw the mix of water and snow on Sunny's wings, and fear made her heart thud in her ears.

They had only moments to climb high enough so that Sunny could land. Under normal circumstances, the height of the cliff would be no challenge at all, but the snow and the wind beat them back. Philippa had to remind herself to breathe, to stay loose. If she tightened her hands or stiffened her spine, Sunny would have to work even harder.

Sunny's wings shuddered, and drove again. And again. They rose, it seemed, by inches. The snow was coming so fast now that they were almost blind. Philippa didn't bother looking backward for the ships. She would never see them through the storm. She peered ahead, and she could see little there either, except for the looming grayness of the rock, the whirling snowflakes around them.

And then the gray was gone. Ahead was only white snow falling sideways past Sunny's straining neck, her now-flailing wings.

But she had done it! They were above the cliff, and the plateau stretched before them, flat, slippery with snow, its pitfalls hidden. There would be rocks and holes, snags that could trip Sunny as she came to ground. But Sunny had to land. The membranes of her wings glistened with water, and snow gathered between the ribs, white and deadly.

Philippa did not look down at the treacherous surface. It was up to Sunny, and there was nothing she could do to help. Her fate was matched to her bondmate's.

Sunny's wings stilled, and her forefeet reached. Her neck stretched forward, ears laid back against the falling snow, hindquarters gathered beneath her.

"Just do your best," Philippa called to her. She settled deep into the saddle, her weight a little back, her heels down. She gripped Sunny's barrel with her calves, tucked her chin, and loosened the rein.

She felt the touch of Sunny's hooves on the snow, the slide as her hind feet came down and found no purchase. Sunny lifted from the ground again, perhaps half a rod, and Philippa felt the single strong beat of her wings as she rose, then settled a second time. Her hooves skidded to one side, and Philippa compensated, leaning into the skid, staying with it until Sunny found her balance on the slippery surface, tipped her wings to catch the air, and slowed her speed.

Sunny's wings fluttered above the snow as she cantered, then trotted roughly, and came to a stumbling halt, her head down, her wings drooping, her sides heaving.

Philippa leaped from the saddle and began brushing the snow and water from Sunny's wings with her gloved hands. She pulled off her coat and used the woolen lining to dry the membranes before she touched Sunny's shoulder. As Sunny folded her wings, Philippa leaned her head against her bondmate's hot neck, shivering with dread over what might have happened. "Bravely done," she murmured, into Sunny's mane, hugging her tight. "Bravely done, my girl."

She didn't hear them coming. She didn't know they were there until Sunny suddenly threw up her head and backed away from the hated scent. Philippa whirled to see what had frightened her, and found the dull point of a long, ugly knife pointed directly at her throat.

She gave an involuntary cry. The deep, fierce bark of a large dog made Sunny squeal in answer, and back again, hastily, ripping the rein from Philippa's hand. Philippa backed, too, trying to stay near her.

The barbarians had sneaked up on them, their footsteps silent in the snow. There were six of them, dark-skinned, short, bearded men, swathed in thick furs and wearing greasy leather helmets. One was hauling on the lead of an enormous black wardog that snarled without ceasing, its mouth dripping froth. Others brandished double-pointed spears. They tried to form a circle around Philippa and Sunny, but Sunny squealed, rearing, scrambling away from them. The men shrank from her stamping hooves, but the moment she was far enough away, they closed their circle around Philippa. They looked hideous to her, squat, fearsome creatures with flat faces and narrow, cruel eyes.

The man with the knife said something in a guttural language. He withdrew the knife from beneath Philippa's chin to gesture with it, then pointed it at her breastbone. The wardog whined as his handler jerked at him.

Philippa, her belly tight with the tension of being separated from Sunny, glared down into the windburned face of the man with the knife. "You'll regret this," she snapped.

No understanding showed in his eyes. He shouted something at her, puffing his chest and making wild circles with the knifepoint. One of his gestures caught the exposed skin of her neck with the blade. She felt a hot trickle of blood run down beneath her tabard, and Sunny squealed again, prancing frantically around the circle of men, trying to get back to Philippa.

Philippa touched her neck, then swore over the blood on her gloved hand. The man with the knife gurgled more words in his ugly language. The wardog, who wore a spiked collar, snapped at his handler, pulling on his lead until he choked. The barbarians muttered among themselves and looked nervously over their shoulders at the winged horse stamping behind them. Only the leader stood his ground, his narrow eyes glittering in his dark face. He spoke again, and pointed to the east, but he kept the knife at Philippa's throat.

Philippa set her jaw. "I suppose I have no choice at the moment."

The man gave some command that made two spearmen circle back behind Sunny. Two others leveled their spears at Philippa's back, and as the leader started off through the drifting snow, they prodded her with their double points to make her follow. The man with the wardog flanked the rest of the party. Philippa could see he had his hands full controlling the dog, and she cast Sunny an anxious look. Her wings fluttered open, closed again, flexed. "Sunny, keep them closed! Close your wings!"

Sunny slid on the snow, and whinnied nervously, but her wings folded again over the stirrups of the flying saddle.

The Aesk leader shouted something at Philippa. Philippa lifted one shoulder. "Shout at me all you want. I don't understand a word of it." She slogged forward, following his footsteps in the fresh snow. "But have no fear," she added. "Baron Rys speaks a language you will understand."

FRANCIS stood in the prow of Rys's ship and scanned the sky anxiously. He could no longer see Philippa and Winter Sunset. The storm had blown in from the north with stunning swiftness, a wall of white tumbling across the plateau. He had seen her wave the red flag, as arranged, but only moments later she had disappeared.

"She must have landed," Rys said quietly at Francis's shoulder.

"She can't fly in snow this heavy," Francis answered. "The horse's wings collect it . . ." He felt as if he couldn't catch his breath. "But where could she have gone? She was over the bay when we saw her last, when the—" He broke off, clenching his jaw to stop himself from babbling.

"What do you want to do, Francis?" Rys kept his eyes ahead, on the black rock rising from the sea, the sea stack that marked their goal.

"I want to complete our mission, Rys. And hope we find Philippa safe on the beach."

"With her horse," Rys added.

Francis said grimly, "If her mare isn't safe, Philippa won't be either."

The ship heeled about, and slipped, rocking and splashing, past the rock guarding the bay. The snow that was so treacherous for Philippa was a boon for the Klee soldiers. The white sails of the ship were indistinguishable among the snow flurries. Even from the deck, as Francis looked up, he couldn't see the tops of the masts or the folds of the sails as they were struck. They were heavy with snow as the sailors furled them, but they managed to get them down, swearing, calling to each other. They lowered a dinghy, just big enough for Rys, Francis, and eight soldiers. The soldiers rowed with a will, sweating with effort. Francis, sitting still, was thoroughly chilled by the time the dinghy drew up to the black sand beach.

It was an eerie place. The snow muffled every sound, even the captains' orders and the clanking of the oars in their locks. The snow fell silently on the water and dusted the black boulders that guarded the landward side of the beach. Francis loosened his smallsword in its scabbard and prepared to follow Rys and his captains off the ship.

He remembered reading accounts of the raid on the South Tower, descriptions of bravery and sacrifice and blood. He had been young then, barely in his teens, and he had thrilled to the battle tale, felt both glad and sorry that he hadn't been present. Facing the reality now, he felt no thrill. He felt only determination. There was neither fear nor joy, only a compelling sense of duty. His only anxiety was for Philippa and Winter Sunset.

The stones of the beach were slick with snow, and the storm showed no signs of abating. Rys sent a half dozen of his soldiers ahead, and he and Francis followed, coats buttoned up to their throats and hats pulled low over their eyes. The soldiers were impressively efficient. They hardly spoke at all. Six of them carried the matchlocks strapped to their backs, swords and knives at the ready in their hands. The rest came behind Rys and Francis, while three sailors stood guard. To a man, their faces were impassive. Surely, Francis thought, their stoic expressions hid some emotion, but he could not have guessed what it might be.

They climbed up through the litter of big rocks and crouched behind them to look inland. To their left, in the west, a dizzying cliff rose, obscured by falling snow. To their right was a line of scrubby trees, bent and twisted as if the wind from the sea had beaten them into submission. Directly ahead was a valley, just deep enough to be out of the worst of the wind.

There were eight structures built in the flattest part of the valley. Six were longhouses with thatched roofs, laid out around a central fire pit. At each end of the compound were smallish huts. Smoke rose from holes in the thatched roofs to vanish in the falling snow. Francis peered past the shoulder of one of the captains to make out the shapes of a few thickset figures, faces and bodies hidden by heavy furs. One had a great dog beside him, at least half as tall as he was.

With them, Francis saw with sinking heart, was Philippa. And coming behind her, reins trailing, slender legs struggling through the snow, was Winter Sunset, with two more barbarians at her back. Snow clung to her mane and tail and dusted her flying saddle. Her ears flicked anxiously forward and back, forward and back. Through the snow, Francis heard her whinny, and knew she was pleading to be reunited with Philippa.

Rys threw up his hand. In silence, his men withdrew, keeping low behind the jumble of boulders, and retreated toward the beach. There was nothing Francis could do but go with them.

SEVENTEEN

PHILIPPA heard the name of the leader of the Aesks, the one who had scratched her with his knife, as Urg, or perhaps Hurg. He led the way down a steep crevice, where Philippa stumbled over rocks and ice, barely keeping her feet. She had lost her coat on the plateau, and she saw that one of the barbarians had it over his shoulders. She was shivering and wet by the time they descended into the valley, and miserable at not being able to respond to Sunny's anxious calls.

The longhouses of the compound were made of sod, braced on footings of stone, thatched with some kind of grass or straw. The fire pit was enormous, circled with more stone, a great spit across it. The longhouses looked old, with their sharply slanted roofs and crooked doorways. Two huts on either end of the compound seemed to be empty, their thatched roofs crumbling, but smoke rose from holes in the roofs of the other buildings, mingling with the falling snow. Everything smelled of smoke and salt and fish, and the whole place had an air of hardship and meanness. They must have lived in these sod dwellings, oppressed by harsh weather and scant resources, for centuries, all the while Oc built its beautiful cities and cultivated its rich fields.

The snow kept coming in thick wet flakes. Philippa eyed the Aesk who had her coat, but he showed no sign of being willing to give it back. People came out of the longhouses to stare. They stood on the rough stone steps or peered around corners. The women wore long cloth dresses with greasy furs thrown over them. Dirty children peeked from behind their mothers' skirts. Old men, one or two of them maimed, hobbled forward on crutches or in one case, on hands and knees, pointing at the winged horse and exclaiming in their harsh tongue.

Philippa kept her eyes forward, and willed Sunny to follow quietly. She was exhausted, sweaty and chilled at the same time, and she knew Sunny must be the same.

The spears worried her. Sunny's wings were her most vulnerable part, and Philippa feared she might open them, flutter them in her anxiety to be close to her bondmate.

The procession wound past the fire pit and on past the last of the longhouses, stopping before one of the empty huts. It had no door, but a leather flap, stained and cracked, hanging over its opening. Hurg gestured at the men behind Sunny and shouted some command.

They babbled something back at him and waved their spears at Sunny's hindquarters.

Philippa cried, "No! Don't touch her, I beg you!" and tried to push past the guards.

One of them held his spear sideways, barring her path. As she thrust at it with her hands, he laughed.

She forgot the cold, and her fear, in a rush of fury. "That's a *winged horse*, you cretin!" she shouted at the man. She lifted her fist and shook it in his face. His mouth opened in amazement, and he stared at her as if no woman had ever done such a thing to him.

Before he could collect himself, Philippa heard more laughter, first from Hurg, a great guffaw, and then from some of the other Aesks. The dark face of her tormentor grew even darker. He snarled something and shoved at her with the horizontal spear, the shaft catching her hard at the waist. She stumbled backward, lost her footing, and sprawled her length in the snow.

The wardog erupted in fury at this, barking and snarling. For one long, awful moment, Philippa thought his handler might lose control of him, that he would be on her, those terrible teeth ripping her flesh. More dogs, from somewhere Philippa couldn't see, began to howl and bark in response. She heard the thump and slide of Sunny's hooves beating a frantic rhythm on the frozen ground, trying to get to Philippa while at the same time staying away from the hated scent of men.

Philippa struggled to her knees, then to her feet. Hurg was watching Winter Sunset, his laughter gone. He stood with his hands on his hips. The dog settled a bit, though it still growled a steady monotone. The howling, which seemed to come from behind one of the longhouses, subsided.

Philippa spoke to Hurg, in as level a voice as she could manage. "You have to stay back," she said. She pointed to Sunny, and then to the men, and made a gesture with both palms apart, trying to explain. "Keep a distance."

The Aesk chieftain's skin was like old leather. His lips were so dark they were almost purple. He squinted at her, brows drawn together as if in hard thought. Philippa felt a little spurt of relief that perhaps he had understood her. He gave commands, and the men between her and Sunny stepped aside. Sunny, with an eager whicker, trotted to Philippa, splashing through the thin snow cover, and pressed as close to her as she could. Philippa seized her rein with one hand, and circled the mare's neck with the other. Sunny's body was blessedly warm against her cold one. She raised her face to Hurg then and waited for what would happen next.

He pointed to the hut and said something. A woman hurried forward to lift the leather panel and held it aside. She turned to face Philippa, to gesture to her to go in, and Philippa saw with a pang that one side of her face was ruined by a horrible scar, a burn perhaps, or a wound that had never healed. She averted her eyes, involuntarily, and hurried to lead Winter Sunset into the dark, noisome hut.

She stood just inside the door, assessing it. There was no fire pit in this one, and no chimney hole in the thatched roof. It was cramped, with a dirt floor. Parts of the thatch were drooping, as if the whole roof could fall apart at any moment. There was no water for Sunny, no bed for Philippa, no amenities at all.

She turned to Sunny, thinking that she should get her flying saddle off, rub her down, even if she had to use her own tabard. Then perhaps she could persuade someone—

Her thought was broken off when the scarred woman seized her arm and pulled her toward the door.

Philippa cried out, trying to get her arm free, and the woman produced an ugly knife from beneath her furs. She brandished it in Philippa's face, all the while holding her arm with a grip like iron.

"What do you want?" Philippa exclaimed.

The woman only pulled on her arm again, waving the knife threateningly near Philippa's cheek. She outweighed Philippa by half, and her fingers were thick and hard. Philippa knew her arm would be bruised, and she didn't want that rusty knife to touch her. She let the woman draw her a step toward the door, then another. She cast one look back at Sunny, but before she could even speak to her, one of the warriors had grabbed her other arm, and between the two Aesks, Philippa found herself hauled bodily back out into the falling snow.

She cried frantically, "No! No! I need to be with Sunny!" But neither of them faltered.

She twisted her head to look over her shoulder and saw Hurg, the leader, approaching the doorway to Sunny's hut. She screamed some imprecation, she hardly knew what, but she had no power. Her two captors dragged her the length of the compound and thrust her in through the door of a hut no larger than the one that now held Sunny, and the Aesk woman pulled the leather flap over it and tied it down from the outside.

Philippa stood helplessly in the windowless sod hut, staring at the leather panel, the door to her prison that had shut her off from the fresh air, freedom, and Winter Sunset.

FRANCIS had been in favor of rushing into the Aesk compound, but Rys demurred. "They're capable of anything," he said. We need to have a plan first."

Francis sagged back against the rock he was leaning on. Unspent nervous energy made his head ache, and the smallsword at his belt seemed to have grown heavy.

The Klee captains had been conferring, and one of them came up now to murmur something in Rys's ear. As they talked, Francis lifted his face and let the drifting snowflakes cool his burning cheeks. He had hoped it would all be over by now. That they might have rescued the children, if they lived, and that he would have proved himself. William would never let him forget this if they failed, especially if a winged horse were harmed.

"Francis," Rys said.

Francis turned to see Rys and the captain standing beside him. Self-consciously, he brushed the snow from his face and adjusted the smallsword at his belt. Rys's grim expression gave Francis no comfort. "Yes," he said.

"My captains feel we should return to the ship and get out of the bay before the Aesks spot us."

"Is there no other choice?" Francis asked. He looked back toward the narrow, boulder-strewn passage that led to the encampment. He yearned to dash in among the Aesks, blade swinging, shouting his fury. He could see it in his mind, the Klee soldiers appearing like dark demons out of the snow, matchlocks blazing, the barbarians fleeing in disarray before them.

The captain spoke with deference, but with authority, too. "No, my lord," he said firmly. "I've fought the Aesks before, and I've seen what they can do to hostages. The risk to the winged horse is too great."

"And to her rider," Rys said.

"Yes, of course," the captain said. "I think we must hope the horsemistress can find a way to escape on her own."

"How is she going to do that?"

"I don't know, Francis," Rys said. "Not yet, in any case. We will withdraw and try to devise a scheme."

Francis's heart rebelled at the delay, and at leaving Philippa and Sunny in Aesk hands, but he could think of no argument. His own burning desire to try his courage would hardly serve. He bowed his head and gave in though it grieved him.

As quickly and silently as they had come to shore, the soldiers and the two noblemen made their way back to the ship under cover of swiftly falling darkness. Francis climbed aboard, his fingers and his feet chilled to the bone, but even then he didn't go below, where dinner was being laid out in Rys's cabin. He stood in the prow of the ship and stared inland. The snow had stopped though the clouds remained. The high plateau and the twisted coastal vegetation gleamed with fresh snowfall. A sharp breeze snapped the edges of the furled sails, and the empty masts groaned. The ship had pulled back behind the sea stack so that the Aesks could not see it.

Francis hoped Philippa would have something to eat tonight. What about Winter Sunset? How long could she manage without the grain and hay she was accustomed to?

"My lord," came a voice behind him. Francis turned to see Rys standing in a lighted doorway. "Come and eat," the Baron said. "You will be no good to them if you're exhausted. Or frozen," he added.

"I know," Francis said heavily. He turned away from the vista of land and dark sea and joined Rys in the doorway. "It's just so damned hard to do nothing."

"That's war, Francis," Rys answered. He stood back to let Francis precede him down the short stair. "War is long stretches of idleness interrupted by episodes of rather shocking violence. I know no other way to conduct it."

PHILIPPA paced her prison, back and forth, back and forth. She shuddered with cold and fatigue and worry, and every sound from outside made her body quiver with anxiety for Sunny. Daylight faded with staggering swiftness, and she had neither light nor fire to brighten the dank hut. It smelled of dirt and fish and animal droppings. At one end was a stack of empty barrels she supposed had held foodstuffs of some kind, but which now offered only the tang of long-gone roots and dried fish and other substances she couldn't identify. The hut had never, she felt certain, been intended for human habitation.

More than once she pulled at the edge of the leather door panel, trying to see what was happening. Every time, a guard brandished a spear at her. One of the wardogs lay at his feet, and each time she put her eye to the opening, the dog leaped up, bristling and growling. She could see just enough to know that a fire had been set in the fire pit. Flames leaped into the darkness, sparks fading into the sky. The snow had stopped, but it seemed the sky was still cloudy. No starlight penetrated that Philippa could see, and soon she could see almost nothing inside her hut.

She tried to examine the walls with her fingers, to find any weakness, any hole. She was rewarded with splinters and handfuls of crumbling mud, but no door or window or other opening. There was certainly nothing like a chamber pot, which she would need soon. She thrust that concern aside, and continued her examination, wiping her dirty hands on her skirt.

It seemed to her that the rear wall, behind the barrels, slanted inward, possibly on the verge of collapse. She might be able to break that down. She didn't dare try it now, though. She couldn't leave Sunny in their hands. She would—and she faced the thought without flinching—rather die.

The Aesks, it seemed, gathered for a communal meal around the central fire pit. She heard the babble of conversation grow and could detect the smell of cooking. She heard voices as people walked past her jail, and the wardog snapped and growled as if it hated everything and everyone.

When Philippa had begun to think she would be left utterly alone all night long, the flap over the door was pulled back, and the scarred woman reappeared. She tied back the flap, allowing some of the light from the fire pit to penetrate the darkness of the hut.

She had a broad, low forehead over a thick nose and eyes so small it seemed inconceivable she had full use of her vision. Her mouth pulled hard to one side, and as she came closer, Philippa saw that the scar that so distorted her face had a thick center of corded flesh, as if she had been slashed with a knife, the edges of the wound inexpertly sewn together. It must have been unbearably painful, Philippa thought, with a rush of pity.

The woman stepped through the door and held the panel aside for someone else.

Behind her, carrying a wooden bowl and spoon, her head hanging so low Philippa hardly recognized her, was a young girl with sandy hair and a pale, freckled face.

"Lissie!" Philippa exclaimed.

The child did not so much as lift her eyes at the sound of her name.

EIGHTEEN

"YOU'RE supposed to do your own chores, Goat-girl." Petra leaned back against the gate of her horse's stall, propping herself on her elbows, her riding boots crossed at the ankle. Sweet Reason put his nose over the gate, nodding above her shoulder at Lark, until Petra hissed at him, and he stepped back. Petra fixed Lark with a stony gaze. "The Head wouldn't be pleased with you giving your jobs to a baron's daughter."

Lark had been trundling a wheelbarrow down the aisle, full of soiled straw to be put into the refuse heap. Amelia Rys carried a shovel in one hand and a pitchfork in the other. Her tabard and skirt were littered with bits of hay and other dirt. She stopped midstride and looked at Petra for a long moment, until the older girl began to redden.

"Naturally I felt it was proper to offer to help my sponsor with her work, since I have little else to do until my foal arrives," Amelia said in her uninflected voice. Lark, who had been about to protest Petra's accusation, put down the handles of the wheelbarrow. She would not want to miss this exchange. The past day had given her reason to believe Amelia Rys could deal with anyone or anything that came her way.

Petra's forced accent intensified. "I hardly think you should be shoveling muck from that little crossbred's stall, Miss Rys. You'll have enough of that to do for your own foal."

"I wonder," Amelia said, almost casually, "why you concern yourself with the way I spend my time? I've observed how busy all you third-level flyers are."

Petra's blush darkened, and she dropped her elbows from the gate and attempted a casual shrug. "You will do as you please, of course," she said, with a dismissive wave of her hand. "It's unfortunate there was no more suitable person assigned as your sponsor."

Lark laughed at that. "As you were suitable for me, Sweet? Calling me names and predicting my failure every other day?"

Petra's lip curled. "It's hardly an accident that the Duke himself is keeping an eye on you, Black. I merely share his concerns."

Lark drew an outraged breath, but Amelia spoke. "How nice for you," she said in that modulated voice, "to be in His Grace's confidence."

Petra's eyes narrowed, and one hand strayed uneasily to her throat. Lark guessed she was not certain whether Amelia had insulted her or not. "Well," she said, after a pause, "if you insist on doing Black's work for her, you'd better get on with it."

"Yes," Amelia said. "Do excuse us."

She nodded to Petra and turned away. Lark, biting her lip to suppress a giggle, picked up the handles of the wheelbarrow again and trundled it down the aisle.

Once the muck had been dumped in the refuse heap and mixed with the rest of the compost, she and Amelia stowed the tools in the tack room and walked back to Tup's stall. The first emotion Lark had seen on Amelia's face had been when she had introduced the Klee girl to Tup. Amelia's eyes softened, and her lips parted as she watched Tup drop his nose into Lark's hand, as he rustled his gleaming wings, as Lark fed him, brushed him, polished his hooves. Her voice softened, too, when she spoke to him.

They went into the stall now, and Amelia stood back, allowing Lark to touch Tup first. Lark smiled over her shoulder. "He likes you, Amelia. You can stroke him if you like."

Amelia's smile brought something like beauty to her narrow

face. She stepped forward, without fear but without hurrying and laid her palm on Tup's gleaming neck. "You beautiful creature," she said softly. "I've never seen anything more beautiful than you are." His ears flicked in her direction, and he blew air through his nostrils.

Lark chuckled. "Tup's a one for compliments."

Amelia drew her hand down Tup's muscled neck, over the jointure of his wings, up to ruffle his silky mane. "It's a miracle," she said, her voice a little throaty.

"Kalla's miracle," Lark said as she poured grain into Tup's feed bucket.

"That, of course," Amelia said quietly. "But I meant, it's a miracle that I'm here. That one of these glorious horses will one day bond to me."

"It was for me, too," Lark said.

Amelia turned to look at her, her face settling again into its still lines. "Was it?"

"Oh, aye," Lark assured her. She opened the stall gate and held it for Amelia. "'Twas never meant to be that I should bond with a winged horse. 'Tis why the Duke hates me so."

"Does he hate you?" Amelia asked.

"He does." Lark called to Bramble and let her into the stall.

Amelia watched this ritual, her eyebrows rising. "Do you always leave an oc-hound in his stall? The other winged horses don't have one."

"Well, they don't have them anymore. They did, when they were foals. Oc-hounds keep the foals company when they're small."

"But Seraph has that sweet little goat."

"Aye." Lark shrugged. "I just feel better if Bramble's there, too."

Amelia seemed to accept this without comment. Lark led the way out of the stables and across the courtyard. "My bonding was a mistake, in Duke William's view."

"But not in yours," Amelia said.

Lark ran her fingers through her short curls, dislodging bits of straw and no small amount of horsehair. "Tup's coming to me was no accident. I believe the horse goddess sent his dam, the sweetest little mare you could ever hope to know, to us at Deeping Farm. We didn't know she was with foal, but we cared for her when she was almost dead from hunger. Tup was Kalla's gift to me. That's why I wear this." She lifted the icon of Kalla on its thong and held it out for Amelia to see. As they turned into the Dormitory to change for dinner, she said, "I had never even seen a winged horse before he came. And once he was foaled, I slept in the barn for the better part of two weeks!"

Amelia Rys said, "Of course. I would have done precisely the same."

IN the morning, Lark and Hester escorted Amelia to the Headmistress's office. Hester's mamá wanted to meet the daughter of Baron Rys of Klee. Hester and Amelia had not yet spoken together. They kept a careful distance apart, and their expressions were neither friendly nor unfriendly. Lark watched this with bemusement. Surely, the two had much in common, growing up as they had. Lark would not believe Hester capable of envy, but her friend seemed wary around Amelia, as if loath to reveal anything of herself.

The girls found the Headmistress standing on the steps of the Hall, shading her eyes as she peered to the north. A thin snowfall had come during the night, frosting the paddocks and the hedgerows faintly with white. The air was cold enough to make lungs ache.

Lark said absently, "The bite of winter has sharp teeth."

Amelia turned her cool glance her way. "Is that another Uplands saying?"

Lark nodded, and said distractedly, "Oh, aye." Like Mistress Morgan, she searched the horizon, longing to see a winged horse appear above the towers of the White City on its return flight. There was no sign of Winter Sunset.

Mistress Morgan turned when she heard the girls' footsteps and made some greeting, but Lark saw the worry in her eyes, and the quiver of anxiety she had felt herself ever since Mistress Winter set out for Onmarin and Aeskland intensified. The icon at her breast seemed to burn through her tabard, and she scanned the grounds of the Academy, fearful of seeing Duke William's brown gelding. She breathed a little easier when she saw Lady Beeth's carriage turn into the drive.

Hester kissed her mother, then she and Lark left Amelia to

go into the Hall with Lady Beeth and Mistress Morgan. They crossed the courtyard to the stables, where Mistress Star was expecting them. Lark asked quietly, "Do you not like Amelia, Hester?"

Hester didn't meet her eyes. "It's not a question of liking. It's a question of trust."

"You don't trust her?"

"Oc has plenty of reason not to trust Klee. And Amelia Rys is Klee."

"But—Baron Rys is trying to save Lissie and Peter!"

They had reached Goldie's stall, and Hester stopped. "Black, the Baron is a politician, and Amelia is a politician's daughter."

Lark grinned. "So are you, Morning."

Hester laughed, and shrugged. "Yes," she said. "That's why I'm withholding judgment."

"Lord Francis trusts the Baron."

"Lord Francis is no politician. And I'm afraid he's rather naive."

"Don't you think the Baron is sincere about finding the children, then? About bonding his daughter to a winged horse?"

"I think it is expedient for him."

Lark shook her head. "You should have seen Amelia yesterday with Tup. She—she came alive, for the first time since she's come here. I believe she, at least, is sincere."

"Perhaps." Hester opened the gate to Golden Morning's stall and went in. She lifted a halter from its hook, then turned with the halter in her hands. "Ask me about the Ryses again, Black, when Mistress Winter is back safely."

Hester turned to her horse, leaving Lark staring at her back. Something cold clutched at her heart. Hester, she saw, was as worried as she was.

She shivered and turned to hurry down the aisle to Tup's stall.

THERE was still no sign of Mistress Winter by evening. Amelia Rys spent most of the day in the Headmistress's office. The early darkness of winter enfolded the Academy grounds before suppertime, and the girls blanketed their horses and laid down extra straw for their feet. Hester finished with Goldie, and begged Lark to hurry.

Lark promised she would. She stepped outside the stables to call for Bramble just as cold white stars were beginning to prick the night sky.

The sound of her calling brought Herbert out of the tack room. "What are you needing the oc-hound for, Miss?" he asked brusquely. "Surely your little black is past needing her for company."

Lark bit her lip. She liked Herbert, and she knew he was missing Rosellen as much as she was. But she was fearful of expressing her fears about Duke William, despite what had happened the year before. The very walls, it seemed, listened for a stray word. "I—" she began, and then faltered. Bramble saved her by bounding up, thrusting her sleek head beneath Lark's hand, her plume of tail waving.

Herbert's wizened face creased in gloomy lines. "Your little stallion doesn't need protection now," he said. "I mean, anyone who tries to come in these stables again—that is, I wouldn't let it happen, Miss Hamley."

"It was never your fault, Herbert!" Lark said hastily. "And I know you—I mean—Oh, Herbert, I just sleep better, knowing Bramble is with Tup."

Herbert considered this for a moment, one finger rubbing the side of his nose. At last he sighed, and said, "Well, I suppose it doesn't matter, Miss. She's not needed elsewhere until the spring foaling."

Lark gave him a grateful smile and led Bramble back inside. She leaned on the stall gate a moment, watching the beasts settle themselves for the night. Tup stood hipshot, nose tucked, eyes gazing peacefully at nothing. Molly curled at his feet, nestled deep into the straw. Bramble lay down, too, but she faced the aisle, her head on her paws, her eyes alert.

"Lovely smart dog you are, Bramble," Lark murmured. "I'll see you all in the morning." She hurried off to change. As she crossed the courtyard, her eyes strayed again to the northern horizon, but there was nothing to see.

Halfway through dinner, the icon around Lark's neck started

to burn. She shifted it, startled by its heat, and glanced around. Hester was busy talking to her mamá, who had stayed for dinner, and Amelia was gazing around the room as if memorizing faces.

Lark forced herself to pick up her fork and take a sliver of steamed trout. What did this mean? What was Kalla trying to tell her? She wanted to get up, leave the table, but she had no good excuse. She wasn't ill, and her chores were done. She chafed and fidgeted, waiting through what seemed interminable courses. She barely tasted the braised rabbit or the tiny cup of pudding she was served, though she ate everything, out of habit. The moment the Headmistress rose, she made her escape and dashed across the courtyard to the stables.

She met Herbert just coming out, his eyes wide, his step hurried. "Herbert! What is it? What's happened?"

He stopped, muttering, "Don't know just what to do! Gate open, beast gone—"

"Beast gone!" Lark seized Herbert's arm, feeling the trembling muscles beneath his shirtsleeve. "What beast? What gate?"

His eyes focused on her face, all at once, as if he had only just realized she was there. "Black Seraph's gate! And it's Bramble . . . I can't find her nowhere!"

He tore his arm free and hurried across the courtyard toward the Hall. Lark left him to it, and dashed inside the stable, her heart pounding. She raced to Tup's stall and almost collapsed with relief at seeing that he and Molly were still inside. Herbert had closed the stall gate again, evidently, but Lark could see that the sawdust of the aisle had been disturbed. There was a large furrow down the middle, as if something had been dragged along it.

With a cry, she followed the track, around the corner, past Goldie's stall, and Sweet Reason's, on to the rear entrance that led to the dry paddock. There the track continued, marked in the snow now, and it broadened and roughened as if there had been a struggle.

"Oh, Bramble!" Lark cried aloud. "Bramble, where are you?" A stab of guilt rent her breast, and she seized the icon of the horse goddess in her hand. "Kalla, please, watch over Bramble! This is all my fault!"

NINETEEN

THE Aesk woman grunted something at Lissie. Her language sounded tortured to Philippa, as if it must hurt to pronounce it. Vowels were hard to distinguish, and consonants seem to come as much from the teeth as the tongue. Both Lissie and the scarred woman were dirty-faced, wearing the long cloth dresses and draped in ancient furs. Lissie carried a wooden bowl and spoon, and the scarred woman had an armload of ragged blankets.

"Lissie," Philippa said. "Do you understand what this woman is saying?"

The girl from Onmarin kept her eyes down but came forward with the bowl and held it out to Philippa. The Aesk woman said something else. Lissie, still with her eyes on her boots, held the bowl a little higher, until Philippa took it from her. It smelled of fish and some odd spice, but at least it was warm. Philippa was surprised to find that, despite her anxiety for Sunny, she was hungry. And she would need strength for whatever was to come.

"Thank you," she said, nodding to the woman.

The woman peered at her from those nearly invisible eyes, then pointed to herself. She said, "Jonka," or something like it.

"Jonka?" Philippa ventured. She won a nod, and a little burst of words from Jonka. When Philippa shook her head, under-standing none of it, Jonka gave Lissie a clout on the back of her head and snapped something at her.

"Don't!" Philippa said, taking a step forward. "There's no need to—"

Jonka seized Lissie's hair and pulled on it until Philippa stopped where she was. She grunted something, and Lissie drew a shuddering breath. She spoke at last, almost inaudibly. "Jonka says don't move."

"Move?" Philippa said, frowning. "Not move, Lissie?"

One thin shoulder rose beneath her swath of furs. "I think so, Missus."

"How much can you understand, Lissie?"

The shrug again.

There was a pause, during which Lissie seemed to droop even more, her too-thin body sagging under the heavy fur coat someone had hung over her shoulders. She turned halfway, so that she faced neither Philippa nor Jonka, and spoke a couple of words in the Aesk language.

Jonka lifted one thick finger and pointed at the bowl Philippa held, then made a scooping motion with her hand toward her own mouth.

Philipa took a spoonful of the fishy soup, repressing a grimace at its raw saltiness. She took another as she looked Lissie over.

The child was freckled, as Rosellen had been, but she was bone-thin, and she wore bruises on both cheeks. Her eyes were shadowed, and flicked anxiously from left to right. She looked as if any sudden movement might send her flying from the tent.

"Lissie," Philippa said. "I'm glad to find you well."

The girl's eyes dropped again.

"And Peter?" Philippa asked gently. "Is Peter—is he here?"

Jonka interrupted with a spurt of words, and Lissie whis-pered, "She says, 'hurry.' "

Philippa took another spoonful of soup and swallowed. "Lissie, my mare needs water. Grain or grass if there is any, but she needs her tack removed, a rubdown, but above all, water."

Lissie's eyes lifted to hers and away again.

"You can't say that? Even part of it?"

The girl turned her body in that odd way again, halfway

toward Jonka, half-away from Philippa. One pale hand appeared from the furs, fingers opening as she tried to translate.

Jonka grinned up at Philippa, a hideous expression showing as many missing teeth as whole ones. She said something, and Philippa turned hopefully back to Lissie.

Lissie would not lift her eyes this time.

Not knowing what else to do, Philippa finished the last of the soup. She held the bowl out, and Lissie took it. "At least tell me about Peter, Lissie."

Lissie dropped her head to one side, as if that could stop Jonka hearing her as she whispered, "Peter's always in trouble. Them barbarians hit children, and they hit Peter a lot."

Jonka growled something, and Lissie immediately turned about and carried the bowl and spoon out of the tent. Jonka started to follow her.

"Jonka!" Philippa pleaded. "Please—my horse needs water." She tried to mime the drinking of water, and pointed to the opposite end of the compound, where she had been tricked into leaving Sunny. "Water!" she said, cupping her hands, pretending to sip from them.

The woman mimicked her gesture, then opened her hands, spilling the pretend water uselessly on the dirt floor, and barked with laughter. She dropped the armload of blankets she was carrying right where she was standing. She pointed at the far end of the hut, where the barrels were stacked. She pretended to squat as if to relieve herself, then pointed at Philippa. Philippa stared at her, shocked and offended, and the Aesk woman laughed again.

She was still chuckling as she went out of the hut. She dropped the flap over the door and tied it, leaving Philippa alone in the dark. The wardog outside snarled as Jonka walked away.

THE oily fish soup roiled in Philippa's stomach as she waited for the compound to grow quiet. As the cold deepened, her shivering became unbearable, and she knew that Sunny, too, would be cold. She plucked one of the blankets from Jonka's pile and pulled it around her shoulders. It reeked of fish and smoke and age, but it helped to shut out the chill a bit. She huddled near the door, listening to sounds diminish as people went to their beds. Even the wardogs quieted. The wind snapped through the thatch of the hut, but after what seemed an eternity of cold and dark, there was no other sound.

Philippa was forced to use one corner of the hut, just as Jonka had so crudely suggested, since there was no chamber pot. This indignity fired her with angry energy.

She rose, pulling the stinking blanket tightly around her shoulders, and peered with one eye through a narrow space between the leather and the wood frame of the door. The guard was still standing outside her hut, or it might have been a new guard, she couldn't tell. In their leather helmets and thick fur vests, they looked alike to her. He leaned on his spear, his eyes half-closed. The wardog drowsed at his feet, eyes closed, its head resting on a pair of the most enormous paws Philippa had ever seen.

This wardog, at least, she knew was different. It was black, like the first, but with white spots on its chest and head. When Philippa put one finger in the opening of the door flap, widening it just a bit, the dog's eyes opened and fixed upon her. She froze, hardly daring to breathe. The dog lifted its head, but it made no sound. Its eyes gleamed, and after a moment it thumped its long tail, once, and put its head back on its paws.

Philippa released the leather panel and drew back. As quietly as she possibly could, she went to the back of the hut and began to pick at the slanting wall with her hands.

EVERYONE on the Klee ship retired immediately after dinner. Francis tried to do the same, but could not even bring himself to take off his clothes. He waited until he thought most of the Klee soldiers were asleep, and then he went silently up the stair to the deck. He nodded to the night watchman stationed above the Baron's quarters, and walked to the prow to gaze out over the water. Around him the ship was dark, curtains drawn, all external lamps extinguished.

The last of the clouds had cleared. There was no moon. Sky and water were evenly black, stars steady above, dancing in reflection on the choppy waves. The land glowed white with its blanket of snow, only the rocky shore left bare. Francis remembered something he had read years before, in his school days, lines by some poet of the Angles:

> *Erd rules over the frozen land,*
> *crushing all beneath his hand.*
> *Of human want or human need*
> *the fist of winter takes no heed.*

Francis wished, at this moment, that he believed in the cold-hearted god of the north, so he could beg him for guidance. But he was no peasant, to take comfort in superstition. He felt utterly alone at this moment.

He thought he could just make out the glimmer of firelight from the Aesk compound. He leaned forward into the dark, trying to see better. The ship had backed out of the bay and dropped anchor behind the sea stack that marked it, but should the Aesk climb up to the plateau for any reason, they would spot it. They could fortify their position, set up their spearmen and archers. Worse, they could use Philippa and Winter Sunset to force the Klee fighters to withdraw.

Francis spun about, thinking to wake Rys, to try again to prod him to action, but the night watchman's stolid face dissuaded him. They would not listen, not now. Several ideas had been bandied about at dinner, but none had been settled upon.

Francis paced along the starboard deck. The dinghy bobbed below him upon the water, tugging at its thick rope tether. He bent over the polished railing, trying to see if the oars were shipped. The boat was small. Perhaps, he thought, a single man could handle it.

"Not a good idea, Francis," came a dry voice.

Francis whirled and found that Rys had come out of his quarters. He, too, was still dressed, and he had a pipe between his teeth. A silvery plume of smoke drifted before his face.

Francis managed a light laugh. "Are you reading my mind, Rys?"

"I know it's hard," the Baron said. He joined Francis at the railing and stared down at the dark water. He drew on his pipe, making the bowl glow in the darkness. "Waiting."

"I wouldn't mind it," Francis said, "if I could believe some action was imminent."

Rys's eyes narrowed against the pipe smoke. "Conflict between us will not help."

"Coming all this way without trying won't help, either."

Rys regarded him for a long moment. Francis met Rys's gaze directly and let his silence speak for him.

In the end, the Baron smiled, the cool, controlled smile Francis remembered from the Palace. "You're right, of course, my lord," Rys said easily. "And I promise you, we will try."

"When?"

"We're watching for an opportunity."

Francis pressed his lips together and turned his eyes back toward the water. This was pointless, he thought. This sparring between Rys and himself could not help Philippa or the missing children. At last he said, "I'm willing to go in on my own."

"Then I will list you among the half dozen other volunteers I already have."

Francis said, startled, "You do?"

"Of course I do, Lord Francis. These are brave men."

Abashed, Francis turned to face Rys and bowed slightly. "I apologize. I just—it's all very strange to me. And Philippa is more valuable to us than I can tell you."

Rys nodded. "I can see that for myself, Francis. Now, come. Rest. It may well be that our chance will come tomorrow."

Francis agreed and followed Rys back across the deck. He went down the stair to his cabin, stripped off his clothes, and rolled himself into the narrow cot that served as a shipboard bed. He closed his eyes, but sleep was still a long time coming. When he woke, it was to snow falling again, thick, swirling flakes that obscured the land and seemed to silence even the rush of the sea.

He stood in his cramped quarters, looking out at the white weather. Philippa could not fly in these conditions. They would have to wait another day, leave Philippa in barbarian hands even longer.

He was shocked to realize, as he tried to pull on his clothes, that the ship was moving. He hurried back to the porthole. The ship was moving away from the shore, rather than toward the bay.

With an exclamation, his shirt still unbuttoned and flapping about him, he charged out of his quarters and up onto the deck.

TWENTY

WILLIAM glared at Jinson, who stood beside the stall gate, his head hanging.

"Why the devil did you bring her here?" William roared. "Why didn't you just dispatch her out there in the woods?"

In the stall behind Jinson, the oc-hound whimpered. William glanced over the gate, where the dog lay limp and exhausted in the straw. "You half strangled her anyway, you damned fool," he snapped. "Why not finish it?"

Jinson's shoulders appeared to contract, as if he were shrinking. "M'lord," he whispered. "I couldn't do it. Such a great dog, she is."

"Erd's teeth," William grated. "I should have left you in the stables where you belonged, you misbegotten fool! What do I care about her? She's vicious."

"Oh, no, m'lord," Jinson said, lifting his head a little. He glanced at William's face, then shifted his gaze hastily, down to his chest, then away to the blank wall behind him. "Oh, no," he repeated, weakly. "Not a bit vicious. She—she—"

"Stop whining, man," William said. He felt his temper fray like a broken rope, and it gave him a murderous energy. He shoved Jinson aside, and the smaller man stumbled. "Give me your knife. I'll do it now if you haven't the nerve."

Jinson fumbled at his belt and drew a short blade from a leather sheath. William snatched at it, catching the side of his forefinger on the blade and bringing a drop of blood to his skin. He cursed, and sucked at the finger.

The oc-hound bitch struggled to her feet, and she stood glaring at him, her hackles up, her silvery fur marked with dirt and straw. She growled and lifted her lip to show her teeth.

The sound gave William a thrill of pleasure. "Growl at me, will you?" he murmured. "We'll see about that."

He shot the bolt of the gate and threw it back. Jinson groaned, "M'lord—just consider—"

William shot him a furious glance. "You damned coward! Either be quiet, or get out of my sight!"

Jinson fell back a step. The oc-hound's growl grew, a loud sound that echoed through the stables, causing the horses to whicker uneasily and stamp their feet. William, brandishing the knife, stepped into the stall.

The dog barked, once, and leaped past him, aiming for the open gate.

William swore, and slashed at her with the knife.

He felt the blade catch in the long coat, dig into flesh, grate against bone. She yelped, and fell her full body length in the sawdust of the aisle. He raised the knife high above his head to slash at her again.

And Jinson—Jinson, choosing this odd moment to show some backbone—seized his arm and jerked at it.

A heartbeat later the dog was up and running, silent now, disappearing out of the stable and into the night like a gray ghost.

William spun about and pointed the bloody knife straight at his Master Breeder. "How dare you?" he roared.

For once, the man stood his ground, though he trembled so William thought he might fall right over. "I—I'm sorry, m'lord, I—I don't know what came over me."

"Give me one reason I shouldn't run you through with your own knife, man!"

Jinson took a step back, and his face went white as a sheet. "You've killed her, anyway, m'lord, for sure. Look at the blood." He pointed to the sawdust.

William looked down. A thick stream of blood stained the

clean sawdust, trailed down the aisle and out into the darkness beyond. Slowly, he lowered the knife. He fixed Jinson with a hard gaze as he reversed the knife, and held it out, hilt first. "Never again," he grated. "Never, ever, interfere with me again. I promise you, I will put an end to you with no more qualms than I felt over that oc-hound bitch."

"Yes, m'lord," Jinson quavered. He kept a wary eye on the blade as it approached him, and seized the hilt with shaking fingers. The dog's blood was already turning dark on the steel.

"Go after her," William ordered. "Find her body and bury it. I don't want any complaints from those damned horsemistresses."

"Yes, m'lord." Jinson bowed, looking like a badly strung puppet as he jerked his body upright and staggered away.

William wiped his fingers on his trouser leg and tugged down his vest. He felt a sense of satisfaction, of satiety. It was almost, he thought, as good as having a girl.

But not quite.

He spun about, and strode out of the stable and toward the Palace. He would call for Slater. The night was yet young.

TWENTY-ONE

PHILIPPA was nearly collapsing from exhaustion by the time she had worked three sod bricks from the back wall of her jail. Her back ached, her skin itched, and her flying gloves were in tatters, but she thought she could just wriggle through the opening. She gazed at it with tired eyes. It took her a moment to understand that she could actually see it for the first time.

With a shock, she realized that morning had caught her at her clandestine task. She had scraped and pulled at the ancient blocks of turf right through the night. The snow had returned, falling in impenetrable sheets. Even if she could get Winter Sunset free, even if she were willing to abandon Lissie and Peter, she could not fly.

With a strangled cry of pure frustration, she crouched on the dirt floor, and pounded it with one fist. A whole night! Poor Sunny must have worn her tack, gone without water or food, for the whole night!

It took Philippa several moments to collect herself. She stood, gathering the dirty blanket around her, and tried to think what to do.

The sounds of voices outside the hut forced her to action. Hurriedly, she restacked the empty barrels to hide the opening she had made. She used the corner of the hut again, wrinkling her nose at the smell already beginning to build there, and went to huddle beside the door, to pretend to have been asleep, to await her chance.

Jonka came not long after, tying back the leather panel, leering at Philippa as if she knew just how miserable her night must have been. Behind her, Lissie trailed, head down, feet scuffing in the new snow. A rabble of children hung about behind the guard, trying to peer past him at the curiosity of a strange woman. The guard snapped at them and cuffed the nearest one, making Philippa clench her teeth. She had yet to find anything about these people to excite her sympathy.

Even Jonka's ghastly scar could not move her this morning. Jonka pushed Lissie forward, and Philippa saw that the girl held another bowl. The contents looked about the same as those of the night before. "Lissie," Philippa said, trying to speak mildly. "Have you seen my mare? My winged horse? Is anyone taking care of her?"

The girl flicked a wary glance at Jonka, and held the bowl out as she had done before.

"Lissie, please," Philippa repeated. She took the bowl from the girl but only held it in her hands. "I can't eat until I know Sunny is all right."

The girl's eyes came up to hers, and her lips trembled, but didn't part. Philippa sighed, and took up the spoon. "All right," she said. "If I eat this, will you tell me?" She took a spoonful and swallowed. It was cold and oily, and threatened to come right back again. She put the spoon back in the bowl and tried to give it back to Lissie.

Jonka snarled something, and swatted Lissie's shoulder. The girl stammered, "Jonka says, 'eat.' "

Philippa gritted her teeth for a long moment, watching the scarred woman through narrowed eyes. Finally, she took the bowl in both hands, pretended to sip as Jonka had pretended to sip water the night before. Then, slowly deliberately, she spilled all of its contents onto the dirt floor.

Lissie burst into tears, and Jonka's response, as always, was to draw out her ugly knife and point it at Philippa.

Philippa snapped, "Go ahead, wretch! Let's see if you have the nerve!"

For one awful moment, as Jonka pulled back her hand as if to strike, Philippa feared she might learn just how much courage the Aesk woman had. But a deep voice sounded from outside the hut, accompanied by the barking of one of the wardogs, and Hurg appeared in the open doorway.

The chieftain took in the situation, snarled one short word, and backhanded the hapless Jonka directly across the face. She fell to one side, dropping her knife, clutching her nose. It began to bleed immediately, trickling down her ruined cheek and lip. Lissie seized her opportunity and ran from the tent, hands over her head as if expecting to be Hurg's next victim.

Philippa glared at Hurg, her hands on her hips. She was now as filthy as he was, but so filled with fury she didn't care. "What do you want from me?" she demanded, knowing he couldn't understand her words, but utterly out of patience. Pain shot through the back of her neck, a pain born of tension. She wanted to push past Hurg, to run down through the compound to Sunny. For a breathless moment, she was tempted to try.

But her guard was still there, standing in the snow like a pillar, his spear in his hand. The spotted wardog stood beside him, ears up, tail straight out. And Hurg, who obviously had no hesitation in striking one of his own citizens, was no doubt as likely to stick his knife in her as stand out of her way.

He said something over his shoulder and gave a tug on a rope that was in his hand. Philippa had not noticed the rope.

The small creature who hobbled forward was swathed in ancient furs, like everyone else in this place, his light hair and freckles barely emerging above them. His hands were tied, and the rope was wrapped several times around his shoulders for good measure, but unlike Lissie, a rebellious spark glowed in his blue eyes.

"Peter!" Philippa breathed. "You must be Peter!"

The boy reached Hurg's side, relieving the pressure on the rope. He looked up at Philippa. An enormous bruise spread across one of his cheekbones, and when he grinned at her, she saw that one of his teeth was gone. "Aye," he said, with something very like cheer. "I'm Peter. And I'm that glad to see you, Missus! I'm awful tired of the smell of fish and barbarian!"

The length of this speech evidently offended Hurg, who yanked on the rope, making Peter stumble.

Philippa's anger flared hotter. "Why does he tie you, Peter? Lissie's not tied."

Peter, now pulled tight against Hurg's massive thigh, grinned again. "'Cause I keep running away," he said matter-of-factly. "I'll do it again, too, first chance."

Philippa nodded. "We'll do that together, Peter," she said evenly, keeping an eye on Hurg. "Just as soon as we can."

Hurg looked back at her, suspicion clouding his rough-skinned brow. He slapped Peter's shoulder, but lightly, and said something.

Peter pushed away from him a little, and this time Hurg didn't tighten the rope. "Hurg says," Peter began, "that you should help him."

"You can understand him?"

"Sort of." Behind Peter, Jonka struggled to her feet, keeping a wary eye on Hurg. Her knife lay where she had dropped it, and Philippa could feel her yearning toward it, her only defense. Philippa supposed that for a woman like Jonka, disfigured and unwanted, she had only her own strength to defend her. An unwelcome spurt of sympathy flickered in her breast.

Hurg spoke again, at length, and Peter stuttered a few words in answer, then turned to Philippa. "Come out," he said. "He wants you to come out."

"Have you seen my mare, Peter?" Philippa said, as she took a step forward.

He shook his head. "No, Missus." He looked fearful for the first time since he had come into the hut. "But Hurg wants you to come help him. He wants to fly."

A second time Philippa was herded through the compound, making her think, oddly, of Larkyn Hamley herding her goats. This time Peter walked beside her, Hurg having loosened his rope enough so that the boy could go ahead of him. Behind her, Hurg and the guard came, the guard with his spear at the ready, the spotted wardog padding beside him.

When they had passed the dog on their way out of the hut, the beast had risen and gazed at Philippa, mouth open, long red tongue lolling. Peter looked at it curiously. "Dog likes you, Missus," he said. "Why's that? Them dogs hates everybody."

Philippa glanced back at the spotted wardog. "It could be like the oc-hounds," she said. "The dogs that foster winged foals. They have a special bond with flyers."

Hurg had noticed, too, and he prodded the big dog with his spear. It obliged him by snapping at his hand, lunging forward, making the guard yank on his spiked collar.

"They're so cruel," Philippa said in an undertone to Peter.

"Mean as they are ugly," he answered.

Philippa looked ahead, to the hut at the end of the compound, hoping to see Sunny at last, and to think of some way to deal with a barbarian who thought he could fly a winged horse.

FRANCIS knocked on Rys's door. "Enter," the Baron said, and he went in, closing the door behind him with a decisive bang.

"Francis," Rys said, rising from the table where he had spread a wide sheet of parchment.

"Esmond. I want an explanation." Francis stood just inside the door, his hands on his hips. "You made a promise to me. And to Philippa."

"Did you think I had forgotten it?" Rys said mildly.

"This ship is going in the wrong direction."

"You sound angry, my lord."

"I am." Francis took a deep, quivering breath. "I'm angry at the Aesks, I'm angry at my brother . . . and now—" He laughed a little, bitterly, with a touch of self-deprecation. "Now I feel anger toward you and your captains, because while we cruise here in comfort, Philippa Winter is held prisoner."

Esmond Rys came around the table to Francis. He put a hand under his arm and led him to the table, gesturing to the parchment. "I'll call my captains," he said. "They will show you what we spent most of the night working on. We've agreed it's time to move, but it's dangerous for Philippa. We've seen what the Aesks can do to their prisoners when they're cornered."

Francis breathed again and buried his fists in his pockets to hide the whiteness of his knuckles. "How long, Esmond?"

"Just till dark." Rys beckoned to him, and bent over the parchment, pointing with one manicured finger at a sketch of the bay, the Aesk compound, the plateau and the valley. "We have a plan, but it is by no means perfect. We are sailing away from the Aesk encampment, you're right, but only for a short distance. We want to take no chance of being seen, to lose our advantage of surprise. We will turn back soon enough. But you must prepare yourself. Our venture has become much more complicated than we had hoped."

Francis nodded, staring at the map, his teeth clenched so hard his jaw hurt. He promised himself that if he made it back from this, William would pay.

TWENTY-TWO

THE sun rose over the Academy in a perfect blue sky, glittering on the distant spires of the White City, dissolving the remnants of the early snowfall. The pause in winter's march meant that flights could drill in the air again. Mistress Star's second-level students launched from the flight paddock, the horses exuberant in the cold, the girls wrapped in their winter flying coats and thickest gloves.

Lark followed Hester in the formation, Tup's wings sweeping chilly air over her thighs, the cold saddle leather warming gradually as they banked above the stables' gambrel roofs and turned to the west, where open farmland stretched in patterns of beige and rust to the foothills. Lark tried to feel Tup's muscles through the stiff leather of her stirrups, to sense his movement through the iron and wood of the saddle tree. Everything about the day was brilliant, the distant mountains gleaming with snow, the coats of the winged horses glistening in the sunshine, but her heart felt dark as night.

Mistress Star had refused to excuse her to join Herbert in his search for Bramble.

"It's pointless, Larkyn," she had said. "Herbert has no idea where the dog might be. Don't miss your drill."

Lark knew it would do no good to state her suspicions. Only

Hester understood, but Hester agreed with Mistress Star. "Wait for Mistress Winter, Black," she had said. "There's nothing you can do by yourself."

As the flyers moved into a Half Reverse, Lark glanced to the north and east, where the tall facade of the Ducal Palace gleamed against the brown landscape. Someone there knew what had happened to Bramble, she had no doubt. Duke William. Her enemy.

But no one would believe her. She had not dared even to tell Herbert what she suspected.

Mistress Star signaled with her quirt, and the flyers executed their turn, most of them smoothly, although Anabel, as she often did, had trouble maintaining her altitude. Lark and Tup, even though the flying saddle bothered them both, had no difficulty with it.

She and Tup made their turn and swept away from the formation for a dozen wingbeats, then wheeled back, holding at Quarters while they watched Anabel and Chance repeat the maneuver, once, then again. When Mistress Star gave the return signal, Lark urged Tup back to the formation, to fall in behind Hester and Goldie for Open Columns, flying two by two in a looping circle that led them west, then north. They flew low, just skimming the tops of the spruces and the bare branches of oak and cottonwood.

Lark lifted her face, letting the cold sunshine gild her cheeks. Tup's gleaming black wings, like ribbons of ebony silk, beat joyously against the dense winter air, and his mane rippled in the wind. Lark wished she could banish her anxiety and give herself up to the pleasure of the flight, of being far above the land and its troubles.

But she kept seeing the marks in the snow, the disturbance in the sawdust where Bramble must have struggled, must have scrabbled with her feet, trying to get away . . .

A spasm of grief made her throat ache. She dropped her chin, trying to swallow it away, and it was then that she saw it.

Her eyes, practiced at spotting a missing goat or a lost calf, caught the splash of silvery gray against the sparse green of a hedgerow. She leaned forward to look more closely, and Tup, misunderstanding, began to bank out of the formation. Lark started to correct him, but even as she lifted the rein she saw the silver-gray form, just a huddle of fur at first, move a little. The icon of Kalla blazed against her chest, and she urged Tup lower to circle back the way they had come. She felt Hester's questioning eyes on her, and knew that Mistress Star would scold her for breaking formation, but she thought she knew what was resting there against the hedgerow, and the heat of her icon confirmed her suspicion.

The hedgerow ran along an empty field where a crop had been plowed under, ready for planting in the spring. It was a long, narrow space, and Lark knew the dirt would be full of clods and stiff with cold, but Tup could manage those. She hoped there were no worse obstacles. She flew to the end of it, so that she could turn Tup back, into the wind. It was always easier to land, or to launch, into the wind. Tup stretched his neck eagerly.

She had almost forgotten about the stiff saddle, but when Tup's forefeet reached for the ground, she remembered. She had to do everything consciously, instead of instinctively. She settled deep in the saddle, tried to stay centered, to feel Tup's balance. If she made a mistake now, if anything went wrong, she would be cleaning stables for weeks!

But she didn't fall, and Tup came to ground smoothly, forefeet reaching, hindquarters gathering, and Lark, though she jounced a little at the landing, stayed securely in her seat. Tup cantered, then trotted directly to the mound of silver-gray. He, too, had seen it, Lark realized. He stopped beside the hedgerow and gave his wings a shake, then lowered his nose to sniff. Lark threw her right leg over the pommel and jumped down. They had found the missing oc-hound.

Her heart leaped to her throat at the blood on Bramble's fur. She knelt in the dirt beside the dog, murmuring her name. There was no response.

Steeling herself, Lark put her hands under Bramble's neck, searching with her fingers for the beat of Bramble's heart.

It was there! Bramble's throat pulsed lightly. Her breathing was shallow, almost imperceptible. "Oh, Bramble," Lark whispered. "Poor Bramble!" She quickly unbuttoned her flying coat and wrapped it around the dog. She found the wound with her fingers, a deep slash that had cut through the oc-hound's long coat and into the flesh of her neck. The bleeding had stopped, but the edges of the wound still seeped stickily. Lark searched in her pockets for a handkerchief, for anything she could bind the cut with. Finding nothing, she ripped a section from the hem of her divided skirt. She would have to mend it later, but she couldn't worry about that now.

Just as she finished tying the piece of black cloth around Bramble's neck, the dog stirred. Her eyes opened, rolling to one side, showing the whites. She whimpered when she saw Lark, and tried to lick her hand.

"Nay, Bramble," Lark said. Her voice broke. "Lie still, Bramble. Don't move."

Bramble gave a great sigh, and she lay still. Lark kept one hand on her belly, the other on her narrow head. Tup dropped his nose down over Lark's shoulder, giving his little whimper. The sound was not much different from the dog's.

"I know, Tup," Lark said sadly. "She's hurt. And I don't know what to do now. I need to get her home, but it's such a long walk."

Tup blew air through his nostrils, and rustled his wings.

"No, we can't fly with her," Lark said. "She's much too heavy, and the balance would be wrong." She lifted her head, and looked past the hedgerow and plowed field to the formation of winged horses, now far in the distance. "Mistress Star will be furious with me," she said. "She must think I simply abandoned the flight, and now they're on their way back to the Academy without us!"

Bramble moaned, and Lark patted her flank gingerly. "Nay, we won't leave you, Bramble. We would never leave you. The flight doesn't matter."

Long moments passed, and Bramble's breath, now that the bleeding had been staunched and she was warmer, seemed a bit deeper. Lark had seen hurt animals before, and she knew the cut on Bramble's neck had cost her a lot of blood. She was afraid to try to carry the dog, lest the injury to begin to bleed again. She looked behind her, where the plowed pasture stretched to a small farmhouse, nestled beneath the bare branches of an ancient oak tree. "What we need, Tup," she said, half to herself, "is a farmer. Or a farmwife. Someone who can help us."

Tup lifted his head, following her gaze as if he understood her meaning. His wings flexed, and he whickered softly.

"Do you see someone?" Lark asked. "They couldn't have seen us, or surely they would have come out . . ."

Tup lowered his muzzle and blew his breath on her cheek. She reached up to pat his neck, but before her hand touched him, he backed away from her, and went cantering down the field, wingtips fluttering, empty stirrups flying, the irons banging on his ribs. "Tup!" Lark cried. What was he doing? Surely he would not fly off and abandon her!

Tup, head high, wings half-extended, galloped straight to the farmhouse. He whinnied, and spun in a circle, then stopped, head up, ears pricked forward. When no one appeared right away, he made a larger circle, cantering, his neck arched and his tail flying. He whinnied again, and again, the commanding bell of a young stallion, and pounded his front feet on the cold ground. Lark watched him, marveling. She touched the icon of Kalla at her neck, and was startled to find that the heat which had bothered her for days had cooled.

At last a window blind lifted, and a moment later, the door of the farmhouse opened just a crack.

Tup neighed, and whirled on his hindquarters. He dashed a few steps back down the pasture and then stopped, turning back to stare at whoever was in that doorway. When the figure didn't move, he repeated his invitation, running a few steps, turning, waiting. Lark held Bramble in her lap, caressing the silky head and watching Tup, while the cold began to pierce her tabard and her torn skirt.

Three times Tup repeated his invitation before the figure in the farmhouse door stepped outside. It moved slowly, and Lark now saw that whoever it was used a walking stick. Tup whinnied one more time, and dashed back down the pasture, skidding to a stop near Lark and Bramble, tossing his head triumphantly.

"Well done, Tup!" Lark said. "Well done! Now someone will come and take a blink at poor Bramble, and maybe loan us a cart to bring her home."

It took some time for the woman, as it turned out to be, to walk up the long pasture from the farmhouse. She was elderly, with wispy white hair and sunken cheeks, and she peered at Lark through thick glasses much in need of cleaning.

"Good day to you, Mistress," Lark said. "I thank you for coming out."

"What is it?" the woman quavered. "What is it there? A dog?"

"Aye," Lark said. "An oc-hound. From the Academy of the Air. She's been hurt."

The old woman said, "When I saw yon winged horse dancing in my front yard, I thought you must be from the Academy. But a dog . . . I didn't see the dog. I thought you was the one hurt, Miss."

"I'm not," Lark said. "But we need help—a cart, or something, to take Bramble back to the Academy."

The farmwife nodded, leaning on her stick. "Oh, aye, Miss, that's all right, then. We farm this portion for the Palace, you see. My husband went there to ask someone to come."

Lark pressed her hand to her heart, which felt as if it had stopped beating. "Not—oh, not the Palace!"

The woman tipped her head to one side, frowning. "Not the Palace? Why not?"

Lark dropped her eyes to Bramble's limp form, and bit her lip. She dared not say anything more.

It was a long, cold wait there in the empty field. The farmwife, who wore a full-length goat-hair coat, seemed not to notice Lark's shivering as the morning wore on to noon. Bramble lay still, panting slightly, her eyes closed. She needed water, Lark knew, and she needed to be truly warm, not lying on the half-frozen ground. Tup stamped his feet restlessly, but he stayed close. Lark cast him a grateful look. The farmwife seemed unimpressed by a winged horse in her pasture, but then Lark supposed the Academy flights drilled above her house often. Perhaps she had grown used to them.

Just when Lark thought her jaw would burst from trying to clench her chattering teeth, a cart drawn by a pony pulled in at the far end of the field, circled around the stone fence that divided it from the lane, and bumped over the plowed furrows toward them. Lark tucked her coat around Bramble again and stood slowly, stretching her cramped knees, rubbing her icy hands up and down the sleeves of her tabard. Her pulse beat in her ears, and the icon of Kalla grew warm against her chest again, the only thing about her that wasn't cold.

The cart rattled to a stop beside them, the pony tossing his head and blowing clouds of fog. The farmer climbed out, stiffly and slowly, and joined his wife. The driver of the cart jumped down, and Tup snorted and backed away.

Lark knew this man. The icon began to burn, and she plucked it away from her tabard with her fingers.

It was the Duke's Master Breeder who had come to fetch Bramble. It was Jinson. He looked down at the oc-hound huddled on the cold dirt, and his face was as pale as mountain snow. When he raised his eyes to Lark's, she caught her breath at the look in them.

"Is she dead?" he asked.

Lark hesitated. She had no doubt he had known before he arrived that it was Bramble in the farmer's field. "She's half-dead," Lark finally said. "She needs help."

The look on his face made her stomach turn. It was the face of a tormented man, a man with no choices left. He sidled closer, as if reluctant. "I'll take her," he said.

Lark gripped the icon of Kalla in her cold fingers, and prayed.

The old farmwife exclaimed, "Who's that, then?" and pointed back to the lane beyond the stone fence.

Lark and Jinson both looked up, and Lark's heart leaped with joy.

It was the Beeth carriage, with its footmen and two swift draught horses, coming down the lane toward the farmhouse, pulling up beside the entrance to the pasture. The door with its painted crest flew open, and Hester—Hester, tall, rangy, and strong—jumped out, and dashed toward them over the rough ground.

"Oh!" Lark breathed. "Oh, Kalla's heels, was there ever a more beautiful sight!"

WITH the help of Lady Beeth's footmen, they bore Bramble tenderly home, still wrapped in Lark's coat, laid on the cushions in the warmth of the carriage. Tup followed, his lead attached to a hitch ring on one side of the carriage, the footmen well to the opposite side so as not to upset him. Lark put his wingclips on before they set out, and spoke to him sternly about staying close to the draught horses, and to her. He tossed his head and snorted, as if to tell her he didn't need any such warning.

When everything was in order and they were on their way, having bid farewell to the farmer and his wife, and to a pale and anxious Jinson, Lark said, "Hester. He tried to kill her." Her voice dropped to a whisper. "Duke William tried to kill Bramble."

"You don't know that, Black." Hester spoke in an even tone, but her eyes were dark with worry, too. "You couldn't prove it."

"I couldn't prove it, but I know it just the same. That's why Jinson—" Lark's voice broke. She bent to put her cheek on Bramble's silky head, and the oc-hound sighed. " 'Tis because of me. He blames me for—for everything! For Tup, and for Pamella, and for passing my Airs when he wanted so much for me to fail."

Hester didn't speak for a long moment. She leaned forward to stroke Bramble, then settled back against the cushioned seat, frowning at the passing scenery. "Papá and two of the other Council Lords have had a meeting. Mamá arranged it. They believe the Duke to be unfit to rule."

"Then who?" Lark said.

"Lord Francis," Hester said with some regret. "Poor Lord Francis who prefers libraries to palaces. We like him, everyone does, but he has never wanted his brother's position. He is too gentle to be Duke."

"What will the Council of Lords do about Duke William?" Lark asked cautiously.

Hester turned away from watching the bare winter fields spin by. "Nothing," she said. "Nothing at all. It requires a unanimous decision, and most of the Council, Mamá says, reveres the rule of succession. It would take something truly awful—and more than just rumor—for them to depose the Duke."

"So the paternity suit . . ."

"Has come to nothing. Everyone believes the girl is telling the truth, but the court found she could not prove it."

"Which leaves only Pamella."

Hester nodded, her face grim. "And she will never speak of it, I suspect."

"I wish Mistress Winter were here," Lark said, a little plaintively. She was tired of worrying, tired of watching over her shoulder day and night.

"So do we all," Hester said. "So do we all."

TWENTY-THREE

PETER was sent ahead to pull back the leather panel covering the hut, and Philippa hurried past him, ducking under the sagging doorframe into the dark, noisome space. Sunny stood at one side, her head hanging, her wings drooping. She still wore her flying saddle. Her flanks were frighteningly gaunt, and there was no sign of water anywhere.

"Sunny," Philippa murmured. She hurried to her, saying over her shoulder, "Peter, water! Sunny needs water, and right away!"

Sunny's head came up at the sound of her voice, and the horse stumbled forward a couple of steps. She whickered, but it was a dry, weak sort of sound.

"Damn them," Philippa said, but she said it softly, even as she held Sunny's head close in her arms. "Damn them! Oh, Sunny, Kalla's teeth, what have they done?"

Sunny pressed close against her, snorting faintly, breathing in her scent. Philippa stroked her a moment, and then stepped to her side to undo the breast strap and cinches, to slide the flying saddle off, and the saddle blanket after that. She bit her lip at the cold, wet coat beneath it. It must have been a misery all night. She turned the saddle blanket, and began to scrub at Sunny's back with it, cursing steadily and fervently under her breath.

Peter came back and stood staring openmouthed at her.

Sunny smelled the water in the bowl he held and stepped forward to plunge her muzzle into it. Peter held the bowl as she drank, his thin arms shaking.

Philippa looked past him to where Hurg, feet planted wide as if to claim the place for his own, stood in the doorway, framed by the snowy background beyond. She gestured with her chin at him. "Even if she would let you fly, you'd fall and kill yourself," she said.

He stared back at her, his eyes flat and stubborn. She knew he didn't understand her words, but she suspected the meaning was clear enough.

Peter said, "Missus. He wants you to tie him on."

Philippa snorted. "Tie him on? He'll never get near her. Does he know that?"

"I tried to explain," Peter said. "But I don't know enough words. And now he thinks, because your horse lets me near . . ."

"You're only a boy," Philippa said. "Two more years, and she wouldn't have anything to do with you."

"I know that, Missus, he don't. He don't know nothing about winged horses."

Sunny finished the water and lipped around the bowl, searching for more. "Later, Sunny," Philippa said, patting her. "Not too much yet." She was relieved to see Sunny pick up her wings and fold them, rib to rib. Her eyes looked a bit brighter, and her breathing sounded better already.

"Will she be all right, then?" Peter asked.

Philippa nodded, keeping a protective arm around the mare's neck. "She's all right for the moment," she said. "But we have to get away from here, Peter."

"Can she fly with us? Both of us?"

"No." Philippa cast a glance at Hurg, who had taken a step closer. "No," she repeated. "Together we would be too heavy."

"There's no place to go, anyway," Peter said sadly. "I've tried it lots of times. They always find me. The last time Hurg knocked me in the head, and I lost my tooth."

Philippa touched his shoulder, wishing she could comfort him. Sunny, with a snort of fear, laid her ears flat and began to back up.

Philippa spun about.

Hurg was coming toward them, his rolling gait making him look like some sort of bearded drunkard. He had the rope he had used on Peter in his hands, coiled, but with one end free. He had made a loop in it, and was holding it out, ready to put it over Sunny's head.

The Aesk chieftain had such an aura of sweat and fish and ancient furs about him that Philippa wondered it didn't choke him. Sunny's nostrils flared, showing red. She had little room to move, and when her hindquarters struck the sod wall, her hocks bent as if she would try to back right through it.

"No!" Philippa shouted at Hurg. "She won't tolerate it!"

But Hurg, his narrow eyes gleaming with avarice, pressed forward. He even began to swing the rope, as if to throw it. Philippa tried to step in his path, but he batted her away with the coiled rope. She dragged at his heavy arm with both hands, and he swung a fist at her. She fell back just enough that the blow missed, but she lost her footing in the dirt. By the time she regained her balance, Hurg was within rope's throw distance of Sunny. The mare whinnied in fear, and reared, her front hooves clawing the air a hand's breadth from the barbarian's face.

Hurg hesitated for the first time. A winged horse on its hind legs, hooves flailing, teeth bared, was a daunting sight. He even took a half step backward, but then, with a muttered exclamation, lunged forward again. Perhaps he had meant to surprise the horse, to get the rope around her neck before she could evade it.

Winter Sunset exploded. Her wings opened, though Philippa cried out to her to keep them closed, and they beat uselessly in the cramped space. Her forefeet came down, barely missing Hurg's face, and she reared again, striking her head on the thatched roof so that pieces of it fell in dusty clods over her back, over Hurg's head, over Philippa. Hurg roared something, and one of his guards, the whites of his eyes showing, ran into the hut and froze, openmouthed, transfixed by the sight of a winged horse in fury.

Philippa said, "Peter! She might kill him if he doesn't—" But it was too late. Sunny whirled, and fired at Hurg with both hind feet, so fast the movement was impossible to see. She caught him directly in the chest.

Hurg's body sailed across the hut, slamming against the wall, slumping to the dirt floor. The guard shrieked, and ran.

But Sunny wasn't finished. She had been pushed too far, and until Philippa could get her away from the smell of men, she wouldn't be calm. She bucked, and squealed, and her wings flapped against the walls, against the floor, against Philippa as she tried to get close. She kicked at random, so that even Philippa had to fall back.

"Peter! I have to get her outside!"

And Peter, shouting something in the Aesk language, managed to clear the guards from the door, to get Jonka out of the way. Leaving Hurg where he was, stunned and still, Philippa seized Sunny's rein, and pulled, calling her name.

At last, with Aesks shouting and running around them, Philippa and Sunny were out in the clean air, where Sunny stood, sides heaving, breathing the cold scent of snow, cleansing her nostrils of Hurg's scent. Philippa finally succeeded in persuading her to fold her wings. Warriors, keeping their distance but with spears at the ready, circled them. Jonka, having retrieved her knife, stood to one side with the weapon in her fist, a look of satisfaction on her ruined face. Peter stayed by Philippa's side, the two of them with their backs to the winged horse, facing the enemy all around them.

Hurg, looking dazed, staggered out of the hut. He lurched over to Jonka and seized her knife from her hand. He turned, with the knife held out before him, and loudly proclaimed something.

Peter said, "Nay! Nay!" His freckles stood out on his ashen face.

Philippa said, "What is it, Peter? What's happening?"

Peter said, in a tone of pure horror, "Missus! Zito's ears, Missus. He says if he can't fly her, he might as well eat her!"

SNOW fell intermittently all day, covering the meanness of the compound with clean, glittering white. Not until evening did the snow stop. A hard wind blew in from the sea, and the clouds lifted, showing cold white stars and a frozen landscape. Philippa and Peter shivered together in the hut, where they had been forced to go by Hurg and the guards. Through the crack in the door, they saw that a great fire had been started in the fire pit.

"I can't believe he would do this," Philippa said, over and over, in an agony of fear for her mare. "It's an abomination."

"All I know is," Peter said once, "there's been no meat in this place since we came. Only fish, fish, and more fish."

Many times, Philippa pulled back the leather panel to beg to see Jonka, or Lissie, or Hurg. Each time the guard leveled his spear at her, flat face unreadable. Only the wardog seemed to respond, so that the last time she had gone out, the beast wagged its tail when it saw her. This won it a vicious yank on the collar, but it still watched Philippa with something like intelligence.

My only ally, she thought. A dog.

Sunny had been circling the shallow valley all through the afternoon, whinnying, calling to her bondmate. Philippa had screamed at her, when the Aesks dragged her and Peter away, to run, and Sunny had, her wings rippling beside her, her red mane and tail flecked with snow. One or two of the warriors, to Philippa's horror, had thrown spears at her, but their weapons were clumsy, with their double points, and their range was short. Still, Sunny would not go far, not with Philippa still in the compound. She galloped around the rim of the valley, neighing frantically, and the wardogs responded with barks and howls. By the time the bonfire was raging, Philippa was dry-mouthed and shaking with fear.

"They can't catch her," Peter said.

"But she won't leave," Philippa told him. Her voice cracked, and she struggled to maintain her composure. If Sunny would stay far enough away, until the darkness fell, until the Aesks gave up and went to sleep . . . Exhaustion blurred her mind, confused her thoughts. She had to concentrate, to focus on what to do next.

When Hurg appeared at the door, the bonfire was raging into the night sky behind him. He snapped something at Philippa, pointing with a thick finger, and Peter translated. "He wants you to come out," he said.

Sudden alarm sent a sharp pain up Philippa's neck. "Why?"

Peter stammered some Aesk word, and Hurg laughed. He gestured, and when Philippa did not move at once, he came toward her, gripping her arm with a hairy hand, and dragged her forward. He leered at Peter, and said one short word.

Peter gasped, and paled. "What is it, Peter?" Philippa cried. The Aesk's fingers were like iron. She struggled to keep her feet as he hauled her through the door. "What did he say?" she begged. "What?"

Peter followed on uncertain feet. "Bait," he whimpered. "He said, 'bait.'"

A great shudder ran through Philippa. Peter was right, of course. There was only one way Hurg could get Sunny to come into the compound, and that was to use her, Philippa, as a lure. Her thoughts swirled desperately, but she couldn't think what to do about it.

She would have to sacrifice herself first. There was nothing else.

The fire blazed in the center of the compound. The snow-fields around the longhouses glistened with reflected flame, and the stars faded before its brilliance. The Aesks were gathered, avid gazes fixed on their chieftain dragging the foreigner along by her arm. The guard in front of the hut came after, his spear leveled at her back.

Philippa, with the last of her strength, set her feet, and ripped her arm from Hurg's grasp. She turned to face the guard, and his spear, and she screamed, wordlessly, but with intent, and threw herself toward him. Let him stab her, let him put an end to her, and Sunny would never come into the compound, never let herself be taken. What would happen to her after that, Philippa could not bear to think about, but she would not, could not, allow Hurg and these primitives to commit this abomination.

The guard's lip lifted from his teeth in a gleeful snarl, as if he were one of the wardogs, and he lifted his spear.

Philippa shouted again, gathering her courage, and ran at him.

But the spotted wardog, with a roar, leaped on the guard from behind. Its great teeth closed on his arm, and its claws tore at his back. Blood spurted from somewhere and spattered the snow with scarlet drops. The guard shrieked in shock and pain.

Tumult broke out, shouts and yells, the howling of wardogs, the screams of the guard. From beyond the compound, Sunny whinnied. The spotted wardog growled and snarled, and Hurg leaped forward to try to pull it off his man.

Philippa, her strength gone, collapsed. She was barely aware of young Peter dragging her away from the fray, all the way through the compound and back into the hut where she had spent the night. She slumped on the cold dirt floor, and Peter knelt beside her, calling to her, "Missus! Missus! Are you all right? Did he hurt you?"

At that moment, an explosion rocked through the compound from the eastern side. There was a breathless moment of silence, filled only by the reverberation of the blast, then another explosion filled the night.

Philippa roused, staring up at Peter with unbelieving eyes. Another crash of sound came from the west of the compound, and a child began to scream.

Philippa's mind cleared, all at once, as the night wind had cleared the sky, and she understood exactly what Rys must be doing. "They're here! They've come! Peter, we have to get out of this place!"

It took only moments to topple the empty barrels at the back of the hut, but it took a few more to pull out the bricks of sod Philippa had loosened the night before. They climbed through, and saw that the compound behind them was full of smoke, people running this way and that, confused by the explosions of the matchlock guns. Philippa could see that the Klee were coming from two flanks, but the shock and the shattering noise must have made it seem to the Aesks that there were hundreds of attackers.

She gave it no more thought. Winter Sunset was all that mattered to her now, and Sunny, too, would be terrified by these explosions. She had to find her. With the very last of her strength, Philippa seized Peter's hand and began to run.

THE deadly efficiency of Rys's soldiers stunned Francis. The matchlocks were unwieldy and awkward, but the practiced way the men fired them, then reloaded, waiting till the flanking force had fired theirs, then firing again, was something he would never forget. The Aesks ran like frightened ants from one side of their compound to the other. The enormous fire blazing in the center of the longhouses made the scene even more threatening, more chaotic. Beyond the circle of lurid light and black smoke, Francis could see nothing. Within that circle, he saw men and women, and what he feared were children, go sprawling. Had he not been so angry at Philippa's imprisonment, such carnage might have turned his stomach. No doubt, one day, the memory would do just that, but for now he could not help exulting in the Klee soldiers' overwhelming advantage.

Rys had told him to stay back, out of the line of fire. The initial barrage would go on for a time, until the enemy was thoroughly bewildered and disheartened, and then the soldiers would go down into the compound, and take control with their smallswords and daggers. Francis paced behind the line, torn between bloodthirsty satisfaction at seeing the Aesks punished and fear for Philippa. He scanned the longhouses, and the space between them, wondering where she was, hoping she was safe. He walked a little away from the smoke and flame, and it was then that he saw the horse.

It was Winter Sunset, it had to be! She was too far away for him to see her wings, but Francis knew there were no horses, or indeed any large animals, in this northern land. She was galloping wildly, this way and that, on the rim of the valley, her head high, her tail arched. But what was she doing, out there in the snow, by herself? Where was Philippa?

Fear clutched Francis's heart. The Klee soldiers were intent upon their goal. Rys, who had taken the opposite flank, strode purposefully behind his men, calling orders. There was no one to look for Philippa or the children. No one but Francis himself.

"Zito's ass," he swore, drawing his smallsword. "I did not come this far to watch from the battlements like some fainting girl."

None of the Klee fighters took any notice as he strode away from the firing line and down the slope toward the compound. He circled to the north, to stay out of range of the matchlocks. He moved more slowly as he came near the longhouses, where he could hear the moans of the wounded. He saw spears hurled aimlessly into the darkness by frantic men shouting in fury at an enemy they could not see. He heard the raging of dogs, deep-throated barks and desperate howls. And then, ahead of him, he saw Philippa and a small boy, just emerging from the broken wall of one of the sod huts, racing away from the battle through the unbroken snow. Francis dropped down the slope to run along the rear of the longhouses, to intercept them.

On the far side of the valley, Winter Sunset sensed her mistress's flight and came galloping down the slope, mane and tail and loose reins flying, whinnying to her bondmate.

One of the Aesk warriors appeared suddenly from between the longhouses, his thick figure outlined against the firelight. He was no more than an arm's length from Francis, but his attention was fixed on the winged horse. He lifted his arm, and took aim with his spear.

Francis took no time to consider. A winged horse of Oc was being threatened. He spun on his toes, his body remembering those long-ago drills, and he ran the man through with his smallsword.

When he pulled the weapon free, there was a noise he would remember all his days, the sound of blood and ruptured flesh and the gurgling of a dying man. Francis felt the rising of his gorge, but he fought it. He left the warrior where he was and sprinted after Philippa.

THE relief Philippa felt, when Winter Sunset skidded to a halt before her, wings shivering, foam on her chest and on her lips, almost sent her to her knees. She seized Sunny's dangling rein, pulled her mare's head down to her chest, and held it there for one long moment, while Sunny and she both struggled to regain their breath.

In the valley, smoke from the bonfire and from the guns obscured the battle, but could not deaden the sounds. Peter stood staring at the billowing gray clouds, his eyes wide, his mouth open. "Oh, Missus," he breathed. "What about Lissie?"

TWENTY-FOUR

"WE didn't think we dared wait another day," Rys said to Philippa.

They sat on the beach in the cold morning, Philippa wrapped in a blanket, Sunny nearby. Philippa cast Rys a weary look. "Sunny couldn't have waited another day, my lord, so you were right." She shuddered, remembering. "It's hard to comprehend such evil," she said. "And I'm having difficulty believing I'm free of it—that it's over, and Sunny unhurt."

"It's a great relief to me, as well."

"But how did you—I looked around at those men, and those dogs, and I couldn't see how you were going to pull it off."

"Classic flanking maneuver. And of course, we had the matchlocks. They aren't very accurate, but they make a terrifying noise and a lot of smoke. Confusion, and surprise . . . there was risk to you, of course. You broke free at the perfect moment."

The Baron nodded to his cook, who came around the campfire to pour more of his excellent coffee into Philippa's cup. Before she drank it, she looked over her shoulder to where Sunny stood, now warmly blanketed and brushed, with a bucket of fresh water before her. In an hour or two, when Philippa could be sure Sunny had had enough to drink, she could give her some of the grain Rys had ordered brought from the ship. She would rest her all day, and tomorrow, they could fly home. Tomorrow, Sunny would be strong enough, and the sky bade fair to be clear and cold.

Philippa turned her gaze up beyond the beach. Smoke still roiled from the Aesk compound. Rys's soldiers were "mopping up," the Baron had told her. The firing of the matchlocks had ceased when the soldiers poured down into the compound. They were archers, Philippa knew, and swordsmen, and their attack was lethal. There had been screams among the Aesks throughout the night, wails and shouting. Now, a weighted silence filled the little valley.

As Francis had led her and Sunny, with Peter close by, in a circle far from the battle, down to the safety of the beach, Philippa had seen the bodies already piled up at one end of the compound, and had averted her eyes. It was hard to feel sympathy for the Aesks, after what they had done to Rosellen, and what they had threatened to do to Sunny, but she had no stomach for killing. The thatched roofs had burned with alacrity, and she could only hope that the people—especially the children, whose screaming haunted her—had gotten out of the longhouses before the flaming thatches collapsed.

And Lissie was still there, somewhere.

The peace and order here on the beach was shocking, by contrast, in its civility. There had been a substantial breakfast, prepared over an open fire. Rys's cook had produced scrambled eggs, some kind of pan bread, rich with soda and butter, and thick rashers of bacon. Young Peter ate until Philippa feared he would burst, grinning at everyone, showing his missing tooth, giving voluble thanks that there was no fish being served. She herself, despite her worry over the still-missing Lissie, ate heartily after two days of nothing but greasy fish soup. When the cook tried to persuade her to eat more bread, she protested. "I must fly tomorrow," she said with a little laugh. "You will make me as fat as that gull over there, if you persist."

He bowed and took her plate and linen napkin. The sun was fully up now, and the black sand and boulders glittered. Philippa even had a chair to sit in. It was more of a stool, really, canvas and wood, but it was set up before a well-laid table with a sheet of framed canvas as a windbreak. It was hard to believe that only a short distance away a battle was being concluded. People had died, could still be dying, but the cook appeared unperturbed by the circumstance.

Baron Rys, on the other hand, looked somber, sitting a little apart, head bent to speak with one of his captains. Francis paced the black sand and stared up at the smoke swirling into the sunshine with a hard expression Philippa had never thought to see on his gentle features. She left Peter devouring the last of the pan bread and went to join him.

He looked up at her approach. "Winter Sunset will be all right, I think," he said.

"She's fine," Philippa said. "Tomorrow she'll be able to fly."

"And you?"

"I'm well enough, none the worse for the last two days. Though I am in desperate need of a bath," she added, with a little laugh.

He didn't smile. "I was frantic for you," he said. "This should never have happened. We should have gone after them the moment they attacked the village."

"You've done all you could, Francis."

He shook his head. "Not yet. There's still a child missing."

A breeze from the sea gusted around them. Philippa wrapped her arms around herself, feeling the chill through her tabard. Francis frowned. "Where's your coat?"

"Some barbarian has it," Philippa said. "It's probably burned to ash by now."

Francis shrugged out of his own cloak, a finely made piece of black wool with a worked-silver clasp at the throat. "Here, Philippa. Please."

She accepted it. As he wrapped it around her shoulders, enveloping her in a circle of warmth, all the sweeter after the reeking blankets of the Aesks, he said, "You have blood on your neck, Philippa. Are you hurt?"

"It was only a scratch."

He didn't answer. A muscle jumped at the corner of his mouth, and his eyes strayed again to the smoke above the beach. He put his hand on the hilt of his smallsword. "I'm going back there," he said in an undertone.

Philippa said hastily, "No—Francis, no. Let Rys's soldiers do what needs to be done."

"I can't. My whole life has been one of privilege. We are effete, we lords of Oc."

"Francis, you've never been effete."

"I've never done anything real," he said, shaking his head. "And I'll never again be content to think of myself that way."

"Francis, don't talk nonsense! You arranged all of this! None of it would have been possible without your diplomacy—that young boy would still be a captive, and the Aesks—"

"They still have one of my citizens."

Philippa was so struck by his phrasing that for a moment she could think of nothing to say. What a fine duke he could make, however reluctant! He could restore integrity to Oc, leadership to the Palace. When he strode away from her, his boots sinking deep into the fine black sand, she watched his tall, lean figure with a regretful admiration.

She turned about, half-expecting Baron Rys to dissuade him. But she found Esmond Rys gazing after Francis, nodding slightly. Approvingly.

FRANCIS paused in his climb through the scattered black boulders to look back at the camp on the beach. He was so relieved by seeing Philippa seated there, the winged horse blanketed, tethered, and safe, that his blood seemed to run warmer in his veins, his breath move easier in his lungs. Why did William not feel these things? How could it be that William did not feel the compulsion he, Francis, felt, at knowing one of Oc's citizens was still held captive?

It may be that the girl Lissie was past saving, but he could not go back across the Strait until he knew. He, it seemed, was the only Fleckham left to answer to his people.

He drew a deep breath, spun about, and marched up toward the compound.

Francis saw, as he approached the smoldering longhouses, that the row of bodies had lengthened. Some corpses lay in quite staggering pools of blood, and one of them, at least, had died at his hand. There were children among the dead, and Francis supposed such tragedies had been unavoidable. He tried to remember the deaths that had sparked this mission, the dead fishermen and the stable-girl Rosellen, but the stillness of the corpses sickened him.

His only consolation was that none of them wore Klee uniforms. Or a flyer's habit.

The fighting seemed to be at an end. He paced through the center of the compound, smoke billowing about his ankles. Someone, huddled in the ruins of one of the longhouses, was sobbing endlessly. Francis turned. An Aesk woman squatted in the ashes with something in her arms, something small. Francis looked away, not wanting to know for whom she grieved.

Rys's men had herded the survivors of the battle to the far end of the compound, where a couple of buildings still stood, more or less intact. One was a sort of hut, with the same walls of sod and thatched roof as the longhouses. The other was a covered pen, and here he found several enormous dogs that whined and cowered against the far wall, as far as their tethers would reach. A center pole still held them fast. If the fire had reached this enclosure, these dogs, great creatures with huge teeth and restrained by the heavy spiked collars, would have died where they were. As it was, Francis could see that the fire and noise and smoke terrified them. He supposed they could smell the blood on the air. He could smell it himself.

One of the soldiers turned at his approach and pointed to a sagging hut next to the dogs' pen. "That's where they kept the horsemistress," he said shortly.

Francis stared at it, aghast. It was little more than a cave, dark and stinking and cold. He turned back to the soldier. "Are these all the people left? Surely there were more."

The soldier nodded toward the Aesks huddling together, with Klee soldiers surrounding them. Francis looked at them more closely, and frowned. "They're all women and children."

A captain heard his question and threaded his way through his men to stand beside Francis. "The men fled," he said. "Those that weren't killed in the initial incursion."

Francis eyed the clutch of people, thinking he had never seen such misery. They were short, square people. The women wore cloth dresses beneath layers of animal skins that were matted and greasy-looking. Their hair looked no better than the furs. "They left them," he said. "Ran off and abandoned their families."

The captain shrugged. "Barbarians."

"Barbarians, perhaps," Francis mused, "but they are people."

The captain fixed him with a level gaze. "They kill children, my lord."

"Yes. I do remember." Francis approached the group of Aesks, noting that none shrank away from him. Several of the women gave him fierce looks as they pushed their children behind them. One or two boys, on the verge of manhood, thrust their chests out and did their best to look brave, though their dirty faces were haggard with fear and shock. Francis circled them, trying not to let his own dismay show. He had no heart for this. He was sure he would have made a terrible soldier.

"Don't get too close, my lord," the captain said at his shoulder.

Francis looked back in surprise. He hadn't known the man was following him. "Surely there's no danger now," Francis said.

"There is always danger," the captain answered.

"I need to find the girl from Onmarin," Francis said.

"You may need to look among the dead," the captain said. "This lot all look alike to me."

Francis's belly clenched at the thought of telling the grieving mother that she had lost another daughter. He glanced back at the far end of the compound, where the dead lay cold and still, then he surveyed the disheveled survivors. He would look here first. He had to try.

They looked back at him as he walked around them, their eyes slitted and wary. A child whimpered in the little group, and was quickly shushed. Some of them sat on the hard ground, others knelt or stood. All faced outward, reminding Francis of a hunt he had once been on, when a herd of deer gathered in a protective circle. And there was, he thought uncharitably, something animal about these people. They were dirty, and they smelled bad, but it was more than that. The veneer of society had never touched these creatures, never softened their edges, disguised their drives, or cushioned them from the basic necessities of survival. These people lived as close to the land as it was possible to do, and the land that was theirs had not been kind to them.

Suppose, Francis thought, with jarring irrelevance, suppose we were to help them, rather than hunt them? Suppose we employed our ships to send them goods, grain or cloth or tools—

He stopped, and gestured to two women standing shoulder

to shoulder in front of him. One was a crone, grizzled and tiny. The other was younger, but hideously scarred, one half of her face ruined, the other flat-featured and stoic. "Stand aside," he ordered, his confused emotions making his voice harsh. "Who is that behind you?"

The women stared at him, and for a moment, he thought they would not move. He put his hand on the hilt of his smallsword and pulled it from its scabbard. The soldier behind him moved closer.

Slowly, the old woman moved, a half step to her left. The scarred one didn't budge, except to put one hand inside her furs.

There was no mistaking the girl from Onmarin, now that Francis could see her. Though she was shockingly dirty, her pale hair and pinched features set her apart from the Aesks. She knelt on the ground, held there by the scarred woman, who kept one grimy hand clamped on the back of her thin neck. As the old woman moved aside, Lissie's eyes lifted to Francis's face. Tears streaked her pitifully bruised cheeks, and she began to sob.

"Lissie?" he asked, stepping forward. "Lissie of Onmarin?"

She put out her hand. Giddy with relief at having found her, he bent to help her stand. The Klee captain said, "Have a care, my lord."

Lissie's eyes rolled to her right, stretching wide with alarm.

Francis didn't see the scarred woman's knife, but he felt it. It was not pain, not exactly. It seemed to burn, and yet to freeze at the same time, as if were a blade of ice. It cut through his wool shirt, sliced his skin, and drove in through his flesh until it struck bone.

Distantly, he heard the captain's shout, but he could not turn, impaled as he was. He still faced the girl from Onmarin, the thin, shaking child. The last color drained from her face as she opened her mouth to scream. He tried to lift his own weapon, to defend her, and himself, but his arm was nerveless. He managed only to pull it out of its scabbard, and then he dropped it.

The Klee captain seized him from behind with both hands, and the girl from Onmarin, suddenly shrieking, leaped to her feet, and reached with both hands for Francis's smallsword.

The world blurred before Francis's eyes, and a wave of cold swept his body. He hoped, rather faintly, that he was not dying.

He watched, with wonderment and a sort of detachment, as the slip of a girl, the child of Oc, seized the hilt of his smallsword and thrust the blade at the Aesk woman who had stabbed him.

Francis felt as if he were falling head over heels into a gulf of darkness. He flailed with his hands, trying to grasp at something to stop himself, but he found nothing. He couldn't tell up from down, left from right. He couldn't breathe, and the darkness was rising to his waist, to his chest, to his neck. When it closed over his head, all sound faded from his ears, and he sighed, giving in. How foolish he had been, when success had been within his grasp! William would be triumphant. He had failed after all.

TWENTY-FIVE

HERBERT took one look at the nasty cut on Bramble's neck, and said, "Needs stitches."

"Aye," Lark said. "I know it does. Can you do it? I'll help you."

Hester had left them to go and explain to Mistress Morgan what had happened, to try to excuse Lark for leaving her flight. There would certainly be consequences for her infraction, but Lark couldn't think about that now.

They laid the oc-hound on a pallet of blankets in the tack room, and Herbert brought a needle and a spool of fine silk thread. Lark knelt beside Bramble and took the dog's head into her lap. She murmured encouragement to her while Herbert cut the long hair away from the wound, and threaded careful stitches through the torn edges of her neck. Bramble whimpered at each piercing of the needle, and Lark felt each pain as if it were her own. "I know, lass, I know," she said, through a tight throat. "A little bit longer. It will only hurt a moment."

The oc-hound flinched, but she didn't try to pull away. She licked Lark's hand when it was all over, bringing tears to Lark's eyes.

"Saved her life, you did," Herbert said as he spread a fresh, dry bandage over the wound. "She might have bled to death, out there in that field." He pinned the bandage together and sat back on his heels.

"Hester helped," Lark said. "Or we might still have lost her."

He lifted his eyebrows, and glanced over his shoulder to be certain they were alone. The Beeth carriage had departed, and the horsemistresses and girls were at supper in the Hall. There was only Erna to worry about, and she had gone into the kitchens for her own meal. "The Beeths' footman told me the Master Breeder showed up," Herbert said quietly. "After the farmer went to the Palace for help."

Lark stroked Bramble's shoulder. "Aye, Herbert," she said. Now that she believed Bramble would survive, she trembled with the knowledge of how close they had come to losing the oc-hound. She lifted her eyes to meet the old stable-man's. "I don't think Jinson wanted to kill her," she said. "But the Duke would have made him do it."

Herbert's jaw set hard. "Don't understand it," he said bitterly. "When I think of the foals this dog has fostered . . ."

"Aye." Lark smoothed the blanket beneath Bramble and held a cup of water so she could lap a bit. " 'Twas a cruel thing they did."

"Don't understand why," Herbert muttered. "What's to gain?"

Lark caught her lip between her teeth and didn't answer. It didn't seem fair to drag Herbert into her troubles with the Duke. "The important thing is," she said after a moment, "they won't try it again. They wouldn't dare."

"I'll watch over her, I promise you that."

"Aye, Herbert. I know."

"None of them other girls would do what you did tonight," he said. There was a gruffness in his voice, and Lark looked up to find that his eyes had reddened.

"I'm a country girl," she said softly. "The beasts love me, and I them."

"I know, Larkyn," he said. He cleared his throat abruptly. "You're a good girl, you are."

She smiled at him and touched his hand. "Thank you, Herbert." As he got stiffly to his feet, she said, "Herbert—do you have a Tarn?"

He gave her a startled look. "A Tarn?"

"Or some other fetish." Lark's cheeks warmed, and she

shrugged a little. "I know we're not supposed to believe in small-magics, but—"

He put a finger on the side of his nose, frowning. "I think—seems to me there might have been something Rosellen favored."

"Do you still have it?"

"Give me a minute." He turned and went up the stairs to the room Rosellen had used before Erna. In minutes he was back, a worn and faded object in his hand. He handed it to Lark.

"Don't know what it's called. But Rosellen was a great one for charms and simples."

Lark caressed it between her fingers. It seemed to her that a touch of sea air still clung to it, and though it was almost shapeless, little more than a bundle of soft yarn and some sort of dried grass, it must surely retain some of the power Rosellen had believed it to have.

She twirled the little fetish above Bramble's wound, as she had once twirled her own Tarn over a teapot or a pot of soup, then she tucked it close to the dog's head in a fold of blanket. Bramble's eyes fluttered closed, and she gave a deep sigh.

"There," Lark whispered, stroking the oc-hound's flank. "There you are, lass. Rosellen's little charm will watch over you."

When she emerged from the stables, she shivered in the hard cold. Automatically, she let her eyes stray to the northern horizon, hoping to see Mistress Winter and Winter Sunset winging toward them, though it was so late. She saw nothing except sharp white stars in a black night sky, not even a sliver of moon. She paused, hugging herself against the chill, and took the icon of Kalla into her fingers to whisper a prayer for their safe return.

Across the courtyard the lights of the Hall still glowed in the Headmistress's office and in the dining hall. The Domicile was brightly lit, its reading room awaiting the horsemistresses. The Dormitory entryway shone with lamplight, vivid in the darkness. With the icon still in her hand, Lark felt a quiver of anxiety, but she couldn't think why. She saw no tall, dark figure with ice-blond hair lurking between the buildings or creeping across the courtyard. Bramble was safe inside the stables, with Herbert keeping watch. Tup was in his stall, with Molly beside him. Still, something was wrong. She didn't know what, nor did she even know why she knew.

She walked on trembling feet across the cobblestones toward the Hall, trying to convince herself that it was her imagination, that it was exhaustion after the stressful day, and her fear for Bramble, but she couldn't drive away the feeling that something had happened, some further disaster.

"Zito's ears," she muttered, an epithet that had not come to her lips since she left the Uplands. "Will no one tell me what is happening?"

LARK tossed and turned on her cot until the pale dawn washed the stars from the sky. Only then did she fall into a fitful sleep, with dreams and alarms disturbing her often. When Matron roused the girls on the sleeping porch, Lark felt exhausted and dry in that way she had felt during lambing season, when sleep came in short bursts, and was always interrupted. She struggled into her clothes, grateful that she had no need to spend time on her rider's knot as the other girls did. She ran a comb through her short curls, splashed water on her face, cleaned her teeth, and was ready.

Despite her anxiety, she was ravenous. As she sat down to breakfast between Hester and Amelia, it occurred to her that she had not eaten since breakfast the day before. She ate everything she was given and took every scrap of buttered toast from the tray when the others were done.

Amelia only looked at her in that unreadable way she had, but Hester laughed. "Black, you've eaten enough to make Goldie full!"

"I know," she said. "Are you going to eat those apple slices?"

Hester chuckled, and passed her plate so that Lark could have the last of her fruit. "Poor Black Seraph," she said, as she brought it back to her place, empty now of every scrap. "I hope he feels strong this morning, now that you've eaten enough for two! We're supposed to be drilling Grand Reverses."

Lark groaned, and Amelia raised her eyebrows. "Are they difficult?" she asked.

"No," Hester said, leaning forward to see Amelia past Lark. "Except Black would rather fly them bareback."

Lark was about to answer, but Matron interrupted her, bustling up behind her to tap her shoulder. "Larkyn," she hissed. "The Headmistress wants you, quick!"

Lark pushed her chair back, trembling with renewed anxiety. "Has something happened, Matron?" she asked.

Hester stood, too. "What is it, Black? What's wrong?"

Lark shook her head. "I don't know," she said.

"Maybe," Hester said with a wry grin, "it's about your punishment for yesterday."

"No doubt," Lark sighed.

Matron, already at the door, turned and gestured to Lark to hurry. Lark said hastily, "Hester, explain to Mistress Star for me, will you? I'll be there as soon as I can." She hurried after Matron, leaving Hester shaking her head.

As she trotted after Matron to the Hall, Lark thought Hester probably was right. Mistress Morgan had no doubt thought of some task she could do to show her penitence, something hard so that she would not repeat her offense. But why now? Why not wait until after her flight? Her stomach roiled with the big breakfast she had eaten so quickly.

Matron opened Mistress Morgan's door and stood back. Lark, trying to moisten her dry lips with her tongue, walked past her on trembling legs.

When she saw the tall, burly man in the Headmistress's office, his broomstraw hat in his hand, standing with his feet apart in his old, well-polished farm boots, for a moment she couldn't speak. She stared at him, caught in an undertow between fear at what might have brought him here and joy at seeing him for the first time in months.

He gave her a nod. "Lark," he said, in his familiar rumbling voice.

"Oh! Oh, Brye!" And she threw herself into her eldest brother's arms.

"WON'T Pamella come to speak for us?" Lark said anxiously. "After all you've done?"

Brye shook his head, heavily, sadly. "The poor lass is so terrified of her brother," he said. "Edmar got it out of her, somehow."

"Is she speaking, then?"

"Nay, not to me. But Edmar, when he comes home from the quarry, spends most of his time with her and the little boy, and he learns things. You can see for yourself, in any case, that whenever the Duke's name is mentioned she turns that white, it would frighten you."

"But to lose Deeping Farm . . ." Lark shuddered, hardly able to take it in.

"Now, Larkyn," said Mistress Morgan. "You must not give up hope. The Council of Lords has to vote on such a confiscation."

"And what's the charge?" Lark demanded. " 'Tis the Duke who has committed crimes!"

"Hush, child," the Headmistress said. "Even here, his spies may be listening."

Lark put her fingers to her lips. Brye reached out one big hand and laid it gently on her shoulder. She had forgotten how hard his hands were. Indeed, his whole big body was rigid with muscle. The Hamleys often marveled that Lark should be so different from her brothers. Silent Edmar and handsome Nick were both muscled and tall, though not so tall as Brye. They had teased Lark as a child, calling her bobbin, and button, and mouse.

"Mistress Morgan has the right of it," Brye said heavily. "I will speak before the Council, as is my right since the Duke wants to take our farm. But I had thought that Mistress Winter—if she would—could support me. If it doesn't cause trouble for her."

They had explained Philippa's absence to him and their hope that she would return any moment. "Mistress Winter won't care about trouble," Lark said stoutly. "But Brye, Duke William must have learned that Pamella can't speak. We always thought he was afraid of what she would say, and that would keep Deeping Farm safe from him."

"We had a stranger with the bloodbeets crew," Brye said. His shoulders sagged at the admission. "Should have known better. Should have suspected . . . but he seemed all right."

"You think he was a spy," Lark said.

"Aye, I fear so." Brye turned his broad-brimmed hat in his hands. "The summons came soon as he left Willakeep."

"How did you get here?" Lark asked. "I didn't see the ox-cart."

"I took the mail coach," he said. "Nick needed the cart. And I don't know how long all this might take."

"What is the charge against you, Master Hamley?" Mistress Morgan asked.

"Treason," he said bluntly. "For harboring a winged horse of the bloodlines."

•

WILLIAM laid his quirt across Jinson's neck, enjoying the blanching of the man's color as the power of the cold leather closed his throat. "Give me a reason," he purred, "why I should not kill you the way I told you to kill that dog."

"M' lord," Jinson choked, "I'm sorry. I told you, I thought she was dying, I didn't think she could last much longer . . ."

"You thought?" William said. He pressed the quirt harder, seeing Jinson's flesh crease, hearing his breath rasp. "You should have made sure."

"I know, m'lord, it's just that . . . she's such a nice dog, and the flyers . . ."

"Don't talk to me about the flyers, I don't care about that! I gave you your position, and you owe me fealty."

"I do," Jinson croaked. "And I—I've proved it, my lord." He didn't try to push the quirt away, but lay where he was, trying to breathe. His eyes pled with William, and his pitiful look turned William's stomach.

William sighed and lifted the quirt. He couldn't, after all, kill everyone who irritated him. "What does that mean, Jinson, you've proved it? Speak plainly, man."

Jinson took a ragged breath, and sat up, keeping a cautious eye on the quirt. "M'lord," he said. "Come to the stables. At Fleckham House. I've something to show you."

William stood back and let Jinson get up from the floor, where he had shoved him in his spasm of fury. He supposed he should give the stable-man—that is, his Master Breeder—a bit of latitude. It went with the job, no doubt, a love for animals, a soft heart for beasts in pain. A lopsided smile twisted his lips. He could leave the soft heart to Jinson; fortunately, he himself suffered no such affliction. He would be the one to see that things got done, that changes were made. Such a revolution required a strength of will no one else possessed. Certainly his father had not had it.

They went alone to Fleckham House, William riding his tall brown gelding, Jinson his own rather chicken-necked piebald mare. The day was clear, the air dry and cold. Clouds hung low over the western hills, but the spire and towers of the White City caught the pale sunshine.

It was not far from the Palace to Fleckham House, but Jinson's mare had nothing like the speed of William's horse. Her trot looked, to William, like riding in a cart over boulders. Jinson jigged and bounced until William wondered his teeth didn't rattle. "You need a better horse, man," he said with a laugh.

"Aye, m'lord," Jinson said, his voice uneven. "But I prefer a carriage."

William shook his head. He would have to find a better Master Breeder soon. Jinson was an embarrassment.

Except for a housekeeper and two gardeners, Fleckham House had been left empty when William and Lady Constance moved into the Ducal Palace. Though there was no family left to live in it, William had declined several offers to purchase the estate, having his own reasons for keeping it. He glanced up at the house now, its curtainless windows blank, its doors locked, its stone entryway littered by fallen leaves. The house of his boyhood looked abandoned. Lonely.

His lip curled at his own romantic thought. Careful, he admonished himself. You'll be as soft as Francis if you don't keep a firm hand.

Jinson urged his mare through the grove of beech trees that masked the small stable from the main house. He dismounted and looped her reins over the hitching post. He loosened her cinches before he turned toward the stable.

William only leaped down from his own gelding and dropped the reins where they were. It was not his job to see to the horse's comfort. He had more pressing concerns.

It was warmer inside the stable. William shrugged out of his long black cloak and tossed it over the nearest gate. He followed Jinson down the aisle to the farthest stall.

Jinson reached the stall, opened the half-gate, and stood back. His thin features twisted into a sort of conflicted pride, and William eyed him briefly, thinking the man must decide, once and for all, whom he would serve. Then he turned to look into the stall, and what he saw there drove all other thoughts from his mind.

The smells of soil and foaling still permeated the box stall, but these things, for once, made no impression on William's senses. The world dropped away, and he brought his entire focus to the foal in the stall. It was a tiny, trembling, big-eared creature staggering beside its dam on long, thin legs. The mare was white, and wingless. The foal was gray, like the one that had died the year before, but lighter, with ghostly dapples over the back and hindquarters. The mane and tail were the silvery color of winter moonlight, so pale they glowed in the dimness of the stall.

But what made William's breath catch in his throat, made a thrill run through his nerves and tingle in his fingers, were the delicate silver wings, fragile, shining things, clamped to the foal's sides.

"Colt or filly?" he breathed.

"Filly, m'lord," Jinson said.

Filly. This could be the foundress of his new bloodline, the one he had spent most of his adult life striving for.

She showed her Noble sire's breeding in the line of her back, the depth of her chest. The Foundation strain, from the wingless horses William had experimented with, showed in the shape of her hoof, the flatness of her croup, her color. But her head was finely made, with the wide eyes and delicate muzzle of an Ocmarin, which her dam was. She was perfect, this little silver filly. She could spawn a whole line of perfectly crossbred horses. Winged horses.

Horses who would, William was determined, fly with men.

Cautiously, he stepped into the stall, smoothing his embroidered vest as he went.

From the aisle, Jinson said, "M'lord, please, if this one doesn't take to you either—please, sir, there's the Rys girl at the Academy. She'd be glad of a winter foal. It might take to her, even if we wait until tomorrow, and we wouldn't need to tell 'em when she was foaled."

William ignored him. His attention was all for the filly. *His* filly. "She's bigger than I expected," he murmured.

"She'll be strong," Jinson said.

"Such a pretty color," William said, surprising himself. He was not normally given to girlish notions.

But she *was* pretty, her coat shining in the gloom as if sprinkled with diamond dust. "A silver horse, a winged horse," he murmured. "A little diamond of a horse who will carry the Duke of Oc into the sky."

Jinson made a small sound in his throat, and now William did look up. He fixed him with a hard gaze. "If you can't be quiet, leave," he said.

"It's just—m'lord—" Jinson turned his hat in his hands, and shuffled his feet, the picture of misery. "I wouldn't want you to—I mean, the last one—you—"

"It died. Say it."

"M'lord, a winged horse! If it won't bond to you . . ."

"If it won't bond to me, it's worthless."

"Please," Jinson begged. "I'll do whatever you say, if you just—"

"You're a weakling, Jinson," William said conversationally. "And I'm not." He turned his eyes back on the little filly, who had buried her nose beneath her dam and begun to suckle. "Get out now, man. Leave me alone with my foal."

TWENTY-SIX

IT was hard for Lark to concentrate on her duties when she knew Brye had gone off to stand alone in the Council of Lords, that great marble Rotunda that sat like an Erdlin cake in the center of the White City. Mistress Morgan had sent a note to Lord Beeth, in hopes of securing a sympathetic ear in the Council, but Lark knew all too well how the highborn Lords would sneer at the Uplands farmer in his thick boots and worn winter coat. Trying to keep her nerves in check, she brushed Tup till he gleamed, and cleaned his stall until she could have eaten her own supper on its floor.

Tup caught her mood and pranced in his stall, whimpering. When she remonstrated, he kicked at the back wall as he had done when he was younger, when he had almost destroyed his stall. He needed exercise, but their flight had been necessarily short this morning. The lowering sky was gray and threatening, and the air was perilously cold for horses and girls alike.

The hand of the year had begun to open, as they said in the Uplands, bleaching the land of color, drying the grass, turning the hills white with frost. The first snowfall had melted, but more was coming, perhaps even today. Lark worried about Brye, and Deeping Farm, but she worried about Mistress Winter, too. By the middle of the day, her nerves and Tup's were

frayed to threads. Lark went to the tack room, where Bramble
still lay on her pallet of blankets, and spent a few minutes
changing her bandage, persuading her to drink a bit of warmed
water. She was there when she heard hoofbeats in the courtyard, and she ran to the window to look out.

A battered and weathered hackney coach, with much-
mended wheels, circled the courtyard to come to a rattling stop
before the Hall. Two plain horses, one gray, the other brown,
champed at their bits and switched their tails against the traces
as the driver reined them in. The families of the Academy girls
all had their own carriages, with matched pairs, and Lark had
not seen a rented coach since she had been here. She leaned farther into the window casement, trying to see who might have
come in such an odd conveyance.

When she saw Winter Sunset behind the coach, blanketed
and wingclipped, on a long halter lead, her heart missed a beat.

"Kalla's teeth!" Lark breathed. "Something's happened to
Mistress Winter!" She whirled away from the window and dashed
headlong down the stairs.

She reached the courtyard at the same moment that the carriage door opened. Relief made her giddy as she saw the horsemistress climb down, looking lean and weary, but blessedly
standing on her own two feet. Mistress Winter glanced at Winter Sunset, then leaned back into the carriage as Lark raced
across the cobblestones. She skidded to a stop, crying, "Oh,
Mistress Winter! We've been so—"

Philippa Winter turned about, suddenly, her finger to her lips.
Lark stopped and stared past her into the interior of the coach.

Baron Rys was there, with two men Lark didn't recognize,
both in the blue wool uniforms of the Klee. With careful movements, they were lifting someone, someone wrapped in blankets. The Baron himself pillowed the person's head as Mistress
Winter guided them out of the coach and down to the cobblestones. Lark, on tiptoe, saw only the white-blond hair of the
Fleckhams above the blankets.

Lark spun about to run up the stairs of the Hall to tell Mistress Morgan. The faces of the Baron, of Mistress Winter, and
of the Klee soldiers, and the limpness of the blanketed form,
made it clear that something grave had happened, and that it
had happened to Lord Francis.

The first snow began to fall in tiny flakes that clung to the coats of the soldiers as they laid Lord Francis on a litter of poles and canvas. They started up the steps, maneuvering with care. Philippa Winter and Baron Rys followed, their breath pluming in the frigid air. Mistress Morgan had come down, and she held the doors open for them to pass through.

Mistress Winter's nose and chin looked sharp as knife blades, and her cheeks were hollow. She stood to one side as the men carried the litter into the Hall, her hands knotted together before her. As she turned to follow them, she paused in the doorway, and looked up into the swirling snow. "Larkyn," she said hoarsely. "Winter Sunset . . . if you could . . ."

"Oh, aye, Mistress!" Larkyn said, relieved at having something to do. "I'll see to her, I promise! I'll rub her down and get her some warm water and grain."

As she ran down the stairs to take Winter Sunset's lead, she wondered if that gleam in Philippa Winter's eyes had been the shine of tears. But surely not, she told herself, as she led the winged horse across the courtyard to the stables. Mistress Winter was always strong, always clear in her purpose. She would never shed tears.

Lark spent an hour with Winter Sunset. She removed her blanket, rubbed her vigorously with a clean towel, then brushed her. It took a long time to get the rough spots out of her sorrel coat, to comb the tangles out of her mane and tail. She brought her a bucket of warmed water, and when the mare had drunk her fill, Lark put a measure of grain in her feed bin. She went to the tack room to find a clean blanket, carrying the soiled one over her arm. Erna came in just as she was dropping the dirty blanket into the wash pile.

"What's this, then?" she asked in her sullen way. "More work for me?"

Lark was too relieved at Mistress Winter's safe return to snap at the stable-girl. "Winter Sunset's blanket was filthy," she said mildly. "She needed a clean one."

She could see Erna looking for some way to object to that and finding none. She left the girl staring at the wash pile as if it would hie itself into the tub on its own if she glared at it long enough. At another time, Lark might have let Erna know in some detail just how many loads of wash she herself had scrubbed in a tin tub on Deeping Farm, but at this moment, she wanted only to assure herself that Winter Sunset was as clean and warm and comfortable as she could make her. She stroked Bramble on her way out of the tack room, and the oc-hound thumped her tail without opening her eyes.

Tup had calmed, no doubt because Lark herself was so much calmer. He was happily drowsing in one corner of his stall, Molly the goat snuggled up against him. Sunny was munching grain. Lark buckled the fresh blanket around her and dashed across the courtyard through steady snowfall to see what else she might do to help.

She found that Lord Francis had been installed in the tiny guest room on the second floor of the Hall, opposite the reading room. The two blue-uniformed Klee soldiers guarded the half-open door to the apartment. The door to the reading room stood wide open, and Amelia Rys was there with her father.

The afternoon was wearing on to dusk, and the falling snow blotted out what little light was left. Even as Amelia stood to invite Lark into the reading room, one of the maids came along with a taper, lighting the lamps and the wall sconces. The fire crackled nicely in the reading room, but Baron Rys looked cold and tired.

"Black," Amelia said. Her manner reflected nothing of the drama of the day. "Do come and meet my father. Father, this is my sponsor. Larkyn Hamley, now called Black."

Baron Rys bowed, and Lark inclined her head.

"Father says," Amelia told her, "that the children of Onmarin have been restored to their parents."

"Oh," Lark said weakly. "Oh, my lord, that is wonderful news. Rosellen—my friend—she would be so grateful."

"They've had a bad time of it," he said. His voice was hard, and his eyes looked as weary as Mistress Winter's. "But the Aesks have paid the price for their suffering."

"And Lord Francis?" Lark dared to ask. "Will he live?"

"That, I'm afraid," Baron Rys answered her, "is something we don't know yet."

PHILIPPA left Francis to Matron's care. Margareth had dispatched Herbert to the Palace for the Duke's own physician, and there was nothing further to be done until he arrived. Matron, diffidently, suggested the witchwoman who lived just beyond the Academy, but Philippa and Margareth both disdained the suggestion. Francis was comfortable for the moment, at least, though he occasionally moaned and protested something about having failed.

Philippa heard Rys whisper to Francis, bending close to his ear. "You did not fail, my friend," he said. "Both children are safe." But Francis evidently was past comprehension.

Philippa knew she had no need to check on Winter Sunset. No one could take better care of her mare than the Uplands farm girl. With a weariness beyond belief, Philippa went down the staircase and into the dining room. She would eat, and bathe, then sleep, and try to erase from her memory the images of dead bodies on a bloodstained field of snow.

Conversation in the dining room was subdued, and when the students and the horsemistresses saw Philippa, it died away completely. She walked to the high table, feeling every pair of eyes on her back, and took a seat. Kathryn Dancer signaled for someone to bring her a plate, and she nodded her gratitude.

"Are you all right, Philippa?" Kathryn asked her.

"Cold, dirty, and hungry," Philippa said. "But otherwise well."

"We hear," Suzanne Star said softly, "that Lord Francis lies dying upstairs."

Philippa had just picked up her soup spoon, but she laid it down again, staring at the fragrant, pale broth in her bowl. Everything sparkled in the lamplight, the crystal, the silver, the white tablecloths. She looked up at her colleagues, and at the young women seated at the long tables. Their clean faces and hands, their neat hair, their immaculate riding habits, reproached her. "Kalla's teeth," she gritted, "I hope he's not dying."

"A barbarian stabbed him?" someone said.

Philippa fingered her spoon and didn't answer for a long moment. When she found a way to put her thoughts into words, she found that her voice was more gentle than usual. "Yes," she said. "I suppose you could say that. But I don't know that I will ever think of the Aesks as barbarians again, though they live a barbaric life. They have—" She swept the elegant dining room with her glance, the old, graceful wall sconces, the carved oak chairs, the sideboards laden with savory dishes. "They have nothing," she finished. "Nothing but snow and rocks and fish to sustain them."

"But they attack innocent folk," Suzanne protested. "And take hostages!"

"I know." Philippa took a spoonful of soup, and closed her eyes at the perfection of its delicate taste. "I know they do. And they have been punished for it." She took another spoonful as her colleagues watched her. One or two were shaking their heads doubtfully. Philippa put down the spoon again and folded her arms. "It's easy for you, sitting here with a good meal and a warm room and clean clothes. But I wonder, if we had to live as they do, if we might not behave in ways we now think barbaric."

"Ridiculous!" someone said, and several women agreed. "Never!"

"You know nothing about it, any of you," Philippa began. She felt the heat of her temper, and she preferred it to the fear and sorrow she had suffered in the last days.

"Hush." It wasn't clear who Kathryn was speaking to, but as she pressed a fresh yeast roll on Philippa, she said, "Philippa is exhausted. Let's talk about it another time."

Philippa cast her a grateful glance. She took the roll and dropped her eyes to her soup bowl. Another time, yes, but not soon. It would be a long time before she knew how to think of the Aesks and what had happened to Lissie, and Peter, and herself.

And Francis. At the thought of Francis, his ghastly wound, the blood and the pain and the worry, her throat closed.

Kathryn touched her arm. "Eat, Philippa. You're all bones."

Philippa nodded. She did her best to swallow away the tightness and resumed her meal.

LARK left the dining room with the other girls, and crossed the courtyard to the stables. She spoke to Tup as she passed, but went on to Winter Sunset's stall. Mistress Winter had gone straight to her apartment, looking as if she could sleep for a week. Lark murmured to her as she walked by, "Leave your mare to me, Mistress," and received a nod of thanks.

She found Winter Sunset content, sleepily munching the last of her grain. There was water still in her bucket. Lark brought a pitchfork and cleaned the stall a bit so she would have perfectly fresh straw to rest on if she decided to lie down. "Tired, aren't you, girl?" Lark said. "Lovely brave, you were. Such an adventure."

She patted Sunny's smooth neck and left her drowsing in a corner. She had just reached Tup's stall when she heard Petra Sweet's nasal voice. "Truly, Miss Rys," she was saying. "I do think it shows bad judgment to make the goat-girl your sponsor."

"Goat-girl?" Amelia asked. "Do you mean Lark?"

Petra sighed. "Oh, yes, Lark. With her crybaby horse and that perfectly *filthy* little goat."

"Filthy?" Amelia said in a colorless tone.

Lark was on the point of marching around the corner to confront Petra, but she stopped with one hand on the stall gate. Molly came and gazed up at her, her little beard trembling in anticipation of a treat. Tup turned his head toward Petra's voice, ears pricked, listening.

Petra dropped her voice confidingly. "You know, she's only an Uplands farm girl. Hardly the thing for the Academy. And her colt—he's not really of the bloodlines. Anyone can see he's crossbred."

There was a pause. Lark caught her lip between her teeth, not knowing whether to dash out and demand Petra apologize or wait to hear what Amelia Rys would say.

At last, Amelia spoke, with a clarity to her tone that reminded Lark of the Baron. "One so often finds crossbreeding energizes the line, doesn't one?" Petra seemed to have no answer for that, and Amelia went on, "Horses, dogs, even *people*." Lark heard the slight emphasis on the final word. "As my lord father so often says, every family needs fresh blood now and then."

"W-well," Petra stammered. "I suppose . . . of course, Baron Rys . . . I mean to say, there are standards . . ."

Amelia laughed, lightly, noncommittally. "Oh, standards," she said. "When I left Klee, standards for ladies meant skirts a rod wide and hair teased up to the ceiling. I'm so glad not to be subject to other people's standards."

There was a rustle of feet in sawdust, and Lark, her cheeks burning, hurried into Tup's stall, closing the gate behind her. She busied herself with a hoof pick, searching for a nonexistent stone so as not to be caught eavesdropping. She waited what she thought was a safe interval, then straightened. Molly stood inside the gate, looking up at Amelia Rys.

Amelia put both elbows on the gate. "Do you know, Black," she said. "I do believe that is the cleanest little goat I have ever seen."

PHILIPPA woke early the next morning to a world so dark at first she thought it must still have been night. She went to her window, wrapping her quilt around her against the cold, and sat in her armchair, where she could look out into the peaceful courtyard of the Academy. Never in her life had she been so glad to be home.

The floor was cold, and she tucked her bare feet up under her to keep them warm. She let her head fall back against the cushion and gazed out at the wintry scene. Intermittent snowflakes dashed themselves against the glass, and the clouds were so low it seemed if she leaned out of her window she could touch them. The paddocks were still under their pristine covering of snow. Nothing moved in the courtyard or the stables, not even an oc-hound.

It suddenly occurred to Philippa that Bramble had not come to greet her the day before. She frowned and sat up again, the last of her drowsiness gone. Perhaps, before breakfast, she would just run across to the stables, check on Sunny, make sure that Bramble was there.

She dropped her quilt where it was, and hurried to dress. She wore her thick wool stockings, as if she were going to fly, and a warm vest beneath her tabard. She wound her hair hastily into the rider's knot.

When she was dressed, she tiptoed downstairs. The other horsemistresses were still in their apartments. The lamps were not yet lighted, and the Residence was cold and quiet at this early hour. She heard Matron just beginning to move about in the small kitchen beneath the stairs.

She could have gone in and asked for a cup of tea, but she decided to wait. The question of Bramble troubled her. She pulled on her riding coat as she went out into the snow, not bothering with her cap, and strode across the icy cobblestones to the stables.

The smell of horses and hay and leather greeted her on a gust of warm air as she went in. She didn't see Bramble, but she slowed her steps, savoring the sensations. "Kalla's heels, it's good to be here," she said aloud as she strolled down the aisles, nodding to the beautiful creatures in the stalls, sorrels, grays, bays, and duns, all groomed and blanketed, their precious wings carefully wingclipped against undue harm. Their ears flicked toward her as she passed, and their eyes glowed with recognition. Larkyn's Black Seraph made his little whimpering cry as she came near, and Philippa paused at his stall.

He crossed to her, and pressed his muzzle into her hand. "You little rascal," she said fondly. "You're the most vocal horse I've ever met." She caressed his satiny cheek with the backs of her fingers.

A step behind her made her turn so quickly she almost lost her balance.

"He is a noisy one, isn't he?"

Philippa felt her cheeks burn with an unaccustomed flush. "Why," she exclaimed. "Master Hamley! You are the very last person I expected to see here!"

He kept a careful distance from the stall, so as not to upset Black Seraph, but he bowed, and she remembered how oddly elegant a picture he made, though he was such a big man. "My sister must be that glad to see you back, Mistress."

Philippa ran her hands over her hair and wished she had taken more pains with it, or at least rubbed a little cream into her skin. She gave a rather embarrassed laugh. "I'm glad to be back, myself, Master Hamley. But do tell me what brings you to the Academy—and why you're in the stables so early!"

"Having a blink at Lark's little black, there," he said. "And wanted to see Lark once again before I go back to Deeping Farm."

"Did you come all this way to see her?"

"Nay, Mistress. Trouble with His Grace, I'm afraid." Brye Hamley glanced about him, but no one else had come in yet. "I came here yestermorn. Hoping to find you, as it happens."

Philippa found this so unlikely she could think of no answer.

He nodded, as if in understanding. "Thought perhaps you could speak for me, in the Council Rotunda."

"Oh, Brye," she said, abandoning formality in their shared trouble. "William didn't try to confiscate Deeping Farm after all!"

"He did." Brye folded his arms and leaned against a support post. He appeared to be perfectly at ease in the stables. But then, he was a farmer. He would be at ease here.

He went on, keeping an eye out for anyone who might overhear. "Had a spy in our bloodbeets crew. The Duke knows now, I fear, that Pamella doesn't speak. Not long after that man left Willakeep, got the summons from our prefect."

"And the charge was interfering with the bloodlines."

"Aye. Mistress Morgan asked Lord Beeth to stand up for me among the Lords, and he was kindly ready to do so. But Duke William didn't show. The charge is postponed."

"The Duke wasn't there? Does anyone know why?"

"Nay." In typical Uplands fashion, he apparently felt this needed no elaboration. He straightened and put his hat on his head. It was a winter hat, boiled wool, with a neatly turned brim. His eyes looked deep and dark in its shadow. "Best I be going, Mistress. The mail coach is to stop for me out at the road."

"Do you not care to breakfast first?"

He paused, and then shook his head. "Nay. Just a blink at Lark."

"I hear the girls coming out now. We can go and find her."

As they turn to go out of the stables, Philippa remembered what had drawn her here so early in the first place. "A moment, please, Brye," she said. Said glanced around, looking for Bramble. She called her name, and heard a little yip of response from the tack room.

By the time she had opened the door, and found the oc-hound on her bed of blankets, Herbert had joined her. Brye Hamley seemed to take in the situation at once, and strode across the tack room to kneel beside the dog.

Herbert said, "Someone cut her, and bad enough it was."

Philippa crouched beside the dog's head. "Bramble! Who would do this to you?"

She whined a little, and thumped her tail. Philippa stroked

her, and her fingers encountered something soft beneath her neck. "What's this?"

Herbert cleared his throat. "Well, Mistress . . . I stitched up her wound, with Larkyn's help. And then Larkyn thought—well, she wanted a fetish, and Rosellen had left this one. I thought it couldn't hurt."

Byre Hamley was carefully lifting the bandage from Bramble's neck, smoothing long silky hairs away from the wound to examine the stitching. Under his careful ministrations, she laid her head down again, and sighed. "Good job you made of this, sir," Brye said.

Herbert nodded. "Aye. Bad business."

" 'Twill heal fast. The stitches can come out soon."

"Aye. I thought the same."

Philippa said, belatedly, "This is Larkyn's brother, Herbert. Brye Hamley, of the Uplands."

The two men nodded at each other, then Brye smoothed the bandage back over Bramble's wound, and tied it deftly around her neck. He let his fingers linger on it, just for a moment, looking down at the dog. When he looked up, the anger in his face was so intense Philippa almost gasped.

"If I knew who did this—" he began, then stopped. His jaw worked, and he stood up in a sudden, fluid motion. "I don't hold with hurting animals," he said, his eyes on Bramble.

"Aye," Herbert said. "But we can't prove nothing."

Brye's eyes, not violet like Larkyn's, but the dark blue of a winter sky, met Philippa's. "Dark days for Oc," was all he said.

She could only shake her head. He was right, of course. And she would never want that look of fury turned her way. But as they walked together out of the stables, it was the tenderness in his big hands she remembered, the precision with which he had touched Bramble's wound, replaced her bandage. Not for the first time, she thought how fortunate Larkyn was, though motherless and fatherless, to have been brought up by such a man.

Philippa caught sight of Larkyn coming out of the Dormitory, and called to her. She stood back as the brother and sister said their farewells. She watched Brye Hamley stride out of the courtyard and down the lane a moment later. His heavy boots stirred the snow as he walked, and his shoulders soon bore a frosting of snowflakes.

"So strange, Mistress Winter, isn't it?"

Philippa looked down to see that Larkyn had come to stand beside her. The girl waved one last time to her brother, and he touched the brim of his hat. "What's strange, Larkyn?"

"That the Duke made Brye come all this way, then didn't appear in the Council."

"Ah. That." Philippa turned to go to the Hall, suddenly as hungry as the girls always were. "Yes. Well, let's just be grateful. Put it out of your mind for now, Larkyn. You have work to do."

She tried to follow her own advice, but it was hard. She kept wishing she had been present in the Rotunda, to see how this Uplands farmer fared. She had an idea that Brye Hamley would be just as poised, just as sure of himself, among the Lords of the Council as he was kneeling on a dusty floor beside an injured oc-hound.

TWENTY-SEVEN

WILLIAM felt as if his whole world had become one of the smell of horses, the crunch of straw, the taste of sawdust. He stayed in the filly's stall day and night, watching her suckle, seeing her begin to strengthen. Her slender legs steadied, and her coat of puppy fur thickened. He summoned Jinson when the stall needed mucking out, but otherwise no one came near the foal except her dam and himself.

The dam, being wingless, accepted William's presence. The foal, however, was wary. He saw her nostrils widen when he approached her, heard the intake of her breath as she sniffed at him. He kept a careful distance. He didn't want a disaster like the last one.

He sent Jinson to fetch Slater, and when he arrived, he ordered, "Slater! Get to the apothecary. Tell him to make it stronger."

Behind Slater, Jinson frowned, but Slater only grinned, showing his snaggleteeth, and said, "Aye, me lord. Back in two hours, then."

"M'lord," Jinson said, when Slater had gone out into the snow. "D'you think that's wise?"

"It's not a question of wisdom," William said. "It's a question of courage."

"But, m'lord, you—the changes—"

"Poor Jinson. You just don't understand, do you? I've had a bellyful of those horsemistresses and their monopoly. Men like you will praise my name one day."

"Your Grace, the risk—"

William made an exasperated noise. "That's enough, Jinson. When I want your views, I'll ask for them. Now get me some food, and a bottle, port, or brandy. Both."

Jinson did as he was ordered, but to William's irritation, he was not done making suggestions. He stood in the aisle outside the stall, a covered plate in his hands, a bottle under each arm. "M'lord," he said, with evident diffidence, "the foal should have a dog with her, an oc-hound. Then you can—"

"Not yet," William said. He took the plate and set the bottles in the straw. "Now go. I won't need you for a while."

"But, Your Grace, if she has a dog for a companion, you don't have to—"

"Damn you, Jinson! Don't you see how important this is? Do you want another dead foal?"

Jinson's look of misery at this made William want to throw one of the bottles at his head. "Oh, Zito's ass, Jinson, leave. Let me do what needs doing."

"Aye, m'lord," Jinson said. He walked away, shoulders slumping, feet dragging with reluctance.

William turned back to his filly, admiring the way the filtered light coming through the small, high window shone on the ghostly dapples across her back. He pried the cork out of the bottle of port and sat down, his back against the wall, his legs stretched across the pallet of blankets that had served as his bed for the past two nights. He took a long draught of rich red wine, then sighed, a deep sigh of satisfaction.

The filly lifted her head at the sound and cocked her ears toward him. *Toward* him, he noted, with a thrill of pleasure. Not away, not laid back. Toward him. Even better, she took one cautious step in his direction.

He sat very still. When she didn't move away, he said, softly, "You're exquisite, my little friend. You're like a perfectly cut diamond, aren't you? Every facet catching the light, every detail glorious." Her ears flickered, and he chuckled again. "Not that I would hesitate to put you down, little friend. But I confess, I would be sorry to lose something as beautiful as you are."

When she took yet another step toward him, he held his breath. She was everything he had dreamed, the realization of every ambition. She was, of course, merely a means to an end, but . . . the liquid glory of those eyes, the delicate cut of her muzzle, the silver glow of her mane and tail . . . He would have been less than human had he not felt moved by such a creature.

And she was his. His filly. His little diamond.

She took another step closer, and William almost wept with joy.

TWENTY-EIGHT

HESTER and Lark stood in the shadow of the stable door watching Amelia Rys bid her father farewell. The snow had persisted in the week since Baron Rys and Mistress Winter had brought the injured Lord Francis to the Academy. There had been no flying, and little exercise, and every girl and horse at the Academy was restless.

"I don't trust her," Hester told Lark.

"I like her, Hester."

"It's not that I dislike her. But the Klee are known to be devious, have always been so."

"Have they?"

"So Mamá says. She and Papá asked me to keep an eye on her, and as you're her sponsor, they wanted me to speak to you as well."

Lark frowned. "She's been kind to me," she said. "I don't want to spy on her."

"Not spy. Just watch." Lark glanced up at Hester's plain profile and saw that her features were set, making her look older than her nineteen years. Making her look, indeed, very like her mamá.

"Hester," Lark said softly, "shouldn't we give her the benefit of the doubt? That she simply wants to fly, as we do?"

"We shall see," Hester said, turning away from the view of the courtyard. "But there are political forces at work, and horse-mistresses should always be aware of them."

Lark remained where she was, watching Amelia and her father embrace. The Baron climbed into the waiting carriage, and Amelia stood, the light snowfall dusting her brown hair and her black tabard. No emotion showed on her narrow features, nor on the Baron's as he leaned out of the carriage to wave a final goodbye. They didn't look deceitful to Lark, but they did look . . . purposeful was the word that came to mind. Like Brye when he was negotiating for a bloodbeet crew, or haggling over the price of broomstraw.

From within the stables came a banging of hooves on wood. Lark spun about. "Oh, Kalla's heels, Tup!" she muttered, and hurried down the aisle to stop him before he broke something.

It was a relief to everyone when the snow stopped. The clouds lightened, allowing a thin sunshine to pierce the gray. It was still not safe to send up the flights, but the girls were allowed to ride in the yearlings' paddock, their horses wingclipped and warmly blanketed. They made something of a festival out of it, the third-years and the second-years all cantering about the paddock, down to the bare-limbed grove, back to the gate. Larkyn was there, with Black Seraph prancing, his tail arching, his mane rippling. Hester and Golden Morning trotted beside them, Hester as graceful in the saddle as she was awkward on the ground. Amelia Rys, Philippa noted, was perched on the fence near th dry paddock watching everything with that measured look always wore. Someday, perhaps they would know what sh thinking. For now, she was as closemouthed as any diplomat, her father's daughter through and through.

Philippa stood outside the pole fence, savoring young girls and bright-coated horses against th white snow and black tree branches. Bramble, gic, pressed against her side, and Philippa str silky head with her palm.

The story of Bramble's injury was o weighing on her mind. Larkyn, as He had happened, had pressed her lips her "snappy tongue," Philippa supposed. When she asked her later, Larkyn shook her head, and said that no one would believe her, so she would say nothing. There was something troubling about the whole thing, more troubling than simply an injured oc-hound, but Philippa couldn't think it through. Francis still lay in semiconsciousness, and concern for his recovery blurred her thoughts.

The guest room was too small to keep Francis in comfort for long, and the Hall was too noisy, with horsemistresses and students coming and going all day long. Margareth and Philippa spoke at length about the problem, until Philippa remembered that Fleckham House was now empty, since William and the Lady Constance had removed to the Ducal Palace.

They decided to send word to the Duke, explaining that his brother had been wounded and asking if Francis could be installed at Fleckham House while he recovered. They waited a day for an answer from the Palace, then two days, but none had come. Philippa worried over this, teasing it in her mind, trying to fathom what William's silence meant. He had opposed the whole mission, of course, but surely even William would not hold that against his brother, now grievously injured in an honorable cause. It seemed to Philippa more likely that if William was still angry he would send a curt letter of refusal.

The third day she asked Margareth to send a letter, marked, as her own had been, for the Duke's eyes alone. Again there had ... according to all reports, the Duke had not been ... e city for several days. It was gener- ... broad with some secret purpose.

... ecovered her strength quickly, and ... the agony over Francis, and the ... nerves.

... horses galloping in the sunshine, ... could stay clear. Tomorrow, she ... nd make the arrangements her- ... eckham. He had a right to the

... ite and vivid blue, crisp fields ... sky. It gave the Academy a festive look, and indeed, the Erdlin holiday was coming soon, when the girls and the horsemistresses would go off to their homes for the holiday. Philippa had not heard from Meredith. She squinted up into the snowy hills, and thought that, even though she had defied her brother, the summons to Islington House would no doubt come in due course. She supposed she should make a brief visit, but the idea of spending the whole ten days with her family filled her with ennui.

Today, in any case, she would fly. It had been too long, and both she and Sunny were restive, eager for some kind of activity.

Margareth had asked her to take Larkyn aloft with her. "She's being punished again," she said dryly. "Let us call it a drill with a senior instructor, meant to polish her skills with the flying saddle."

Philippa snorted. "Margareth. Larkyn is hardly going to think a flight to Fleckham House with me and Sunny is punishment."

Margareth smiled, wrinkles wreathing her faded blue eyes. She smoothed her white rider's knot and laid her left hand on the embossed genealogy on her desk. "I was forced to discipline her," she said, "because she deserted her flight. But by doing so, she saved an oc-hound, and I have been careful not to let her penance be onerous. We must have rules and standards, of course, but every girl in her flight understood what happened. Hester Beeth came running in from the return paddock as if her tail was on fire, demanding I allow her to fetch her mamá's carriage to save Bramble's life."

"Do you have any idea what happened to the poor dog, Margareth?"

Margareth's smile faded, and she stood, bracing herself on her hands. "I can only speculate," she said in a confidential tone. "But I have never, in all my life, been so worried about the future of Oc. The next time you see the Duke, Philippa, have a care. He is more dangerous now, I fear, than ever before. And less predictable."

"I know, Margareth. But I won't see him today. He hasn't lived at Fleckham House since his succession, and in any case, they say he's gone abroad." She had bid Margareth farewell, climbed the stairs one more time to check on Francis, then, pulling on her cap and gloves as she went, she walked to the flight paddock.

Erna brought Sunny out, prancing and blowing, energized by the sparkling day. "Sunny," Philippa chided, as her mare side-stepped and tossed her head. "You're behaving like a two-year-old."

Larkyn and Black Seraph appeared, the little black stallion whickering at Sunny, strutting as he came into the flight paddock, arching his tail. Philippa hid a smile as the two of them crossed to her. Larkyn's step was so light she almost bounced. Her cheeks were pink with anticipation of a flight, and her short curls shone like black glass in the sunlight. She certainly did not look like someone doing penance for yet another infraction of the Academy rules.

Larkyn knelt beside Bramble and ran careful fingers over the oc-hound's neck. "Almost healed, this is, Mistress," she said. "She'll always bear the scar, but her fur will hide it. I think she'll feel like her old self in a few days."

"I'm glad," Philippa said. She stroked Bramble once more. "I'm fond of her."

"Aye, she's a fine lass, she is." Larkyn stood. "Off with you now, Bramble," she said, with a flicker of her fingers. "Stay warm today."

Philippa's throat tightened as she watched the oc-hound rise stiffly to her feet. Bramble paced slowly back toward the gate and stood beside it, waiting for Erna. Before she was hurt, she would have leaped over it without hesitation. Philippa set her jaw, wishing she knew who had attacked the dog, and why. Anger made her voice sharp as she addressed Larkyn. "Now," she said, "let's see how you and Seraph are doing with the flying saddle."

In truth, she was glad to have a chance to monitor the pair's progress herself. Suzanne Star was an excellent instructor, but Larkyn and Black Seraph had been struggling to catch up with their class since their very first day at the Academy. She and Sunny hung back to watch their launch.

Seraph's gait was lovely to watch, his small, fine hooves precise in their rhythm, even on the snowy ground of the flight paddock. He sped to the hand gallop, then leaped into the air as easily as a bird might do. Larkyn's thighs snugged tightly beneath the knee rolls of the flying saddle, and her hands were light on the reins, her spine straight, her chin tucked. As Seraph banked to the left, to hover at Quarters and wait for Sunny, Philippa watched from the corner of her eye. Larkyn did nothing wrong. She did everything as she had been taught, everything in the classical way, as all the flyers of the Academy were trained.

But Philippa remembered seeing the two of them, Larkyn and Seraph, racing through the trees at the end of this very paddock, looking as if they were one creature, one heart, one mind, one body—with no saddle between them. They had no such union now, though there was nothing specific she could have said troubled her. Sometimes Philippa lay awake at night, and wondered how to teach Larkyn to sense her bondmate's movements as easily with the saddle as she did without it. Surely, she thought, the strap Larkyn had created to get them through their first Ribbon Day, those first Airs and Graces, would never be adequate for Arrows, or for any of the complicated Graces required of advanced flyers. Larkyn must learn to use the saddle. She would have to master it through sheer will if her instinct could not do it for her. Philippa could see no other way.

She and Sunny rose above the grove and banked around to join Larkyn and Seraph. Philippa signaled with her quirt that Larkyn and Seraph should fly ahead, and she and Sunny came behind, a little above, so she could watch. Larkyn flashed her a grin of sheer pleasure. And though Philippa signaled to her, and made the two young flyers execute a Half Reverse, then a brief Points pattern, when she and Sunny surged past them to lead the way over the White City, she indulged herself in a brief smile at the girl. No one knew what awaited any flyers, and perhaps less so with this pair than any other. Larkyn should be joyous when she could.

They circled the copper dome of the Tower of the Seasons, and soared high above the Rotunda of the Council of Lords, its rooftop astream with the colorful pennants of the noble families. The wings of the horses, the red and the black, were no less colorful, vivid and shining against the white spires of Osham. The sea shone emerald green in the distance.

Philippa felt, as she so often did in the air, that the troubles and worries of the ground lost their import. With reluctance, she laid her rein against Sunny's neck and turned her toward the Ducal Palace and beyond, to the familiar grounds of Fleckham House.

LARK took every care to show Mistress Winter that she had learned her lessons. She remembered to keep her heels down, to sit deep in the saddle, to tuck her chin. She would never, she thought, prefer flying in the saddle to flying bareback, but she would do what she needed to do. Though there were still months to go till Ribbon Day, she wanted no one to doubt that she would pass every test.

Still, she knew how much nimbler she and Tup were without the burden of leather and wood and steel. Though they followed obediently behind Winter Sunset as she flew her sedate pattern around the Tower of the Seasons, and above the Council Rotunda, Lark knew they could have darted close enough to see inside the windows of the tower, could have dipped low enough over the Rotunda to snatch a pennant from its staff. The thought made her laugh, and Tup flicked an ear in her direction. She touched his neck with her gloved fingers and felt the surge of energy in his muscles. He stretched his neck farther, and his wings beat faster, until she had to rein him in a bit so as not to overtake Winter Sunset.

"No, no, Tup," she called, above the wind. "We have to follow. Our day will come!" To her relief, he obeyed her, but she felt simmering rebellion in every beat of his wings.

The grounds of Fleckham House came up all too soon. Tup followed Sunny in, and Lark only jounced a little on the landing. Tup cantered beautifully, collected and graceful, and they reached the end of the park just a few strides behind Sunny. Mistress Winter dismounted, and Lark slid quickly down from her saddle.

"There's no one in the stables," Mistress Winter said. "We'll have to take them in ourselves."

"I'll do it, Mistress Winter," Lark said. "Why don't you go on to the house?"

Mistress Winter nodded, her eyes already on the big house. Its windows were shuttered, and its gravel courtyard lay covered with snow. The steps and porch were also blanketed in unbroken snow, as if no one had used the front entrance in some time. "Thank you, Larkyn," she said. "That will save time."

Moments later, the horsemistress was gone, striding around the side of the house to the service entrance. Lark led Sunny and Tup into the stables.

The stables, too, had an abandoned air. They felt cold, and there was no straw in the stalls. Blankets and towels and saddles waited on racks in the tack room, all coated with a layer of dust. She put the horses in adjoining stalls, and told Tup to wait while she took Sunny's saddle off and rubbed her down. When Tup was done, too, she went in search of water.

She found buckets and a tap in back of the stables, and pumped water for each of the horses. It would have been better, on this cold day, if she could have warmed it, but there was no wood for the close stove. She carried the buckets to the stalls, then went back to the tack room.

She took two blankets from a stack and shook them out, sneezing at the cloud of dust that rose from them. Everything had the look of having lain untouched for months, as if no one had been in these stables or this tack room for a very long time. She hung the blankets over her arm and started back to the horses. She was almost out the door when she noticed the clean, new-looking bin set in one corner. There was a grain measure hanging on a hook next to it. Neither bin nor measure bore any trace of dust.

Curious, she turned aside and lifted the lid of the bin with her free hand. It was full to the brim with fresh oats.

"Handy," she murmured. She went to blanket the horses, thinking she might as well feed them each a half measure while they waited. It was not until that was done, and she was scooping oats with the measure, that she realized that the icon inside her tabard had grown warm as toast. Busy as she was, she hadn't noticed it at first.

Alarm shot through her, and she straightened, dropping the measure into the bin. She pulled the icon outside of her tabard before it should burn her skin, and looked around, her breath coming faster. Something was wrong.

She fairly ran back down the aisle to check on the winged horses, but they were standing peacefully in their stalls. Even Tup, for once, was still. Lark went outside to look across the courtyard toward the house. Mistress Winter had apparently gone around to the service entrance. Lark saw a light in the kitchen, where Mistress Winter was probably having tea with the housekeeper. There was no other sign of life, neither in the grounds nor in the upper floors.

Slowly, cautiously, Lark moved around the back of the stables and looked down at the copse of beeches. She knew what was past those bare trees. There was a small, secret stable there. Lark had seen it, one terrible day. She did not, truly, want to see it again. But the icon burned against her breast, and she had to know why.

TWENTY-NINE

THE branches of the beech trees were bare and gray in the winter sun. The roof of the stable showed just beyond the leafless grove. The meadow that sloped up on the far side to the wood at the top of the hill was the very one through which Lark and Tup had run for their lives. It seemed a lifetime ago.

A slender, clear stream of smoke rose from beyond the grove to dissipate in the cold air. The stable beyond the beech grove, unlike the one where Sunny and Tup waited, was being heated.

Lark puzzled over this. Everyone at the Academy knew that when the Duke had removed to the Palace, he had taken all of his horses with him, along with his stable-men. There had been some resentment that Duke Frederick's favorite stable-girl, old Jolinda, had been sent away from the Palace in favor of the new staff.

Lark took a step forward, then another. It would take too long to go around by the road, but she could climb down the snowy bank behind the main stables, slip through the beech copse, have a look out the other side. She glanced back over her shoulder, but there was no sign of Mistress Winter. She could go down to the copse, see who was using the stable, and be back before Mistress Winter was finished with her arrangements. She buttoned her riding coat to the neck, and started out.

The bank was steeper than it looked. Her riding boots were soft, with no traction. After only two steps, she lost her footing, and half slid down the sharp incline toward the grove. Her riding gloves filled with snow as she braced herself on her hands. At the bottom she took them off, shaking out the snow so they wouldn't be ruined, and tucked them into her belt. She brushed snow and bits of dry bracken from the back of her habit as she walked through the trees. She stood behind the thickest one she could find, peering at the stable.

She remembered it well, a simple rectangular place, without the gambrel roofs of the Academy stables, and with only one paddock and a long, fenced pasture. A little drive, with a hitching post and a mounting block, separated the beech grove from the stable. The nearest door, closed now against the cold, led directly into the tack room. Both halves of the door leading into the back paddock were also closed, and the gates of the paddock and the pasture beyond it were latched. She saw no horses. Had it not been for that smoke, the clear gray smoke of well-dried wood burning, she would have believed the place deserted.

She stayed where she was, watching for any sign of movement. She saw none, and almost gave it up, even turning around to climb the bank again. But when she turned away, the icon of Kalla burned hotter against her tabard, driving her back to gaze across the little drive. Something was there, in that stable. Something she was supposed to see.

At the opposite end from the tack room was a glazed window. There would be a box stall there, perhaps even the very one where Tup had been held. The window was a problem, though, set half a rod's height from the ground. Even on tiptoe, she wouldn't be able to see in.

She waited another moment, watching and wondering. She tried to persuade herself that the warmth of her icon might be her imagination, or the heat of her body, created when she stumbled and slid down the bank, but she failed.

She took one last look over her shoulder to assure herself there was no one about, then dashed across the drive. The mounting block scraped on snow and rock as she half dragged, half pushed it to the wall. It wasn't heavy, but she took a sliver in her thumb and lamented having taken her gloves off. She sucked at the sliver as she climbed up on the mounting block, steadying herself with her other hand on the sill, and peered into the dimness within.

The bright sunshine made the glass opaque, and only her own reflection looked back at her. Lark gave up on the sliver and cupped both her hands to the glass.

There was a horse there, wingless, gray, munching hay from a bin.

She pressed her nose to the glass, trying to get a better look.

The stall looked as if it were well provided, straw on the floor, water bucket in its place. Lark moved her hands to get a better perspective, and looked again.

She drew a quick, delighted breath. There was a winter foal in the stall, a tiny thing, its fluff of mane and tail silvery white in the gloom. Lark smiled to herself as the little one nosed beneath its dam and started to suckle.

Her smile faded a moment later as the foal moved into a slender shaft of light from her window. "Oh," she whispered. "Wings!"

Her heart began to pound with the import of her discovery. She leaped down from the mounting block, and spun about, to hasten to find Mistress Winter.

She cried out when she found her way blocked.

Duke William wore a long black coat, littered with bits of straw. His narrow trousers were dirty, too, and his boots were scuffed. His pale hair hung untidily around his shoulders. She barely had time to register all of this before his hand shot out, and he gripped her arm with iron fingers. "Aha, brat," he hissed. "I have you now!" In his other hand he held the magicked quirt, and as she tried to pull away, he struck her with it, a painful blow directly at her face, raking her cheekbone so hard that her vision blurred.

The sudden violence shocked her. She struggled against him, and when she couldn't get her arm free, she kicked at him, catching his shin with her riding boot. It was a feeble effort, but he swore, and struck at her again with the quirt. She threw up her left hand to protect her face, and briefly caught the cold, hard leather. She couldn't hold it. The touch of the leather was worse than the pain of her arm, twisted in his grasp. She felt her skin break and a hot trickle of blood start down her arm.

William started to laugh, a low, exultant sound that sent icy tremors of fear through her belly. He pulled her half off her feet as he dragged her toward the tack-room door. He shoved the door open with his foot and threw her inside as easily as if she were a sack of grain.

She fell headlong on the hard wood floor, and twisted around to face him. Her cheek stung, and she knew she would be bruised by morning—if she lived till the morning.

"So, brat," Duke William said lightly. He tapped the quirt into his right palm and smiled crookedly down at her. "What a nice surprise. We're going to have some fun."

PHILIPPA bade the housekeeper of Fleckham House farewell and promised that someone would come with Lord Francis to see to his nursing care.

"Aye, Mistress," the housekeeper said. "His Grace left us shorthanded here, right enough." She was a thin woman with a tight expression and a tendency to speak sharply. Philippa thought she had best send two nurses, one for the night and one for the day, lest Francis be dependent upon this cold woman. She was efficient, but she was hardly sympathetic. "I don't suppose you know how long he'll be here?"

"Of course not," Philippa said with asperity. "I take it, Paulina, that you don't look forward to the extra work."

The woman had the grace to flush. "I only meant . . . I was thinking of getting in extra supplies—food and linens and the like."

"Yes," Philippa said. "You should do that. And you would do well to remember whose home this is."

"Aye, Mistress," Paulina said, her voice a little softer. "I do remember. And I'm very sorry his lordship was injured. A terrible business, that."

Philippa stood up. "It was in a good cause, but we're worried about him."

"You rescued the babes, though, they say."

Philippa took her cap and gloves from her belt. No one was saying much about the state of the Onmarin children. On the voyage home, young Peter had told his story over and over, with drama and much colorful detail. By the time they docked in

Onmarin, he had made a dozen friends among the Klee and earned Baron Rys's admiration.

"The boy will be fine, I think," she said. At Paulina's look of interest, she shook her head. "I don't know what to say about the girl."

"Did they savage the lass, then?"

"I don't know," Philippa said. "But she's a little thing, and she was frightened half to death. She was a sort of slave to this awful woman, and she took a great deal of abuse."

"What happened to that woman, then?"

Philippa paused, looking around at the housekeeper's spotless kitchen, every counter and pot and glass gleaming. She was reluctant to speak of how Lissie, in a fit of repressed fury, had stabbed the scarred Jonka to death. It sounded like a triumph, a sort of justified vengeance, but she feared it would be the final, perhaps even the lethal, blow to Lissie's soul. She settled for saying merely, "The woman died in the attack."

Paulina nodded, apparently satisfied with this rude justice. Philippa pulled on her riding coat. "I will see you tomorrow, then I'll be visiting his lordship often."

"Well. You'll always be welcome, of course, but we're not really set up for visitors."

Philippa did not bother to answer this. She let herself out the kitchen door without farewell, more preoccupied with thoughts of Lissie than of this cranky servant.

Lissie had not spoken a word on the voyage home. She had neither eaten nor slept, but sat staring into the cold waves until the ship docked in Onmarin. Her mother had taken one look at her pale, stricken daughter, and swept her up in her arms, carried her through the streets of the village as if she were still a baby.

Philippa nourished a hope that a mother's care could rekindle the flame of life in the girl, but she had her doubts.

She secured her cap on her head and began to pull on her gloves as she started across the courtyard. Beneath the snow, the gravel crunched under her boots. Everything looked orderly and pristine under its layer of snow, and her heart lifted a bit. She had been able to address one problem, at least, and there was still reason to hope for Francis.

She was halfway to the stables when a shrill neigh shattered the peace of the morning. Hooves battered on wood with a sound that scraped her nerves. She quickened her step. "Larkyn?" she called.

There was another whinny, and more banging. This time Philippa was certain she heard wood splinter, and hinges shriek. "Kalla's heels!" she swore. "Seraph!"

She heard Sunny's answering neigh, loud and demanding, calling to her for help. She dashed into the stables and down the aisle, rounding the corner just in time to see Seraph blast the gate to his stall with his hind feet, again, and then again.

"Seraph! No!" Philippa shouted. He threw up his head to glare at her, the whites of his eyes showing, his muzzle flecked with foam.

Where was Larkyn? Philippa didn't think she could calm Seraph without her.

He bashed at the wood one last time, and this time it broke into four jagged pieces. By Kalla's good grace, Philippa saw, he was wearing his wingclips. Though he charged through the broken gate, head shaking from side to side, snorting and sweating, his wings were safely folded beneath a blanket. But the door to the courtyard stood open, and Seraph spied it. Before she could think what to do, or how to stop him, he was off.

He raced through the door, and plowed through the snow and gravel to the center of the courtyard, where he whirled on his hindquarters, sniffing the air. Philippa ran after him, calling his name, but when she came close, he reared, and slashed the air with his hooves, driving her back. He wheeled once more, his tail grazing the snow, then, with the scream of a young stallion in hot fury, he pounded away from Fleckham House, his tail high and his ears laid back.

Philippa stood helplessly in the courtyard, watching him go. She would never catch him. Seraph was looking for Larkyn.

LARK lay where she had fallen, where she had been pushed, and William held his magicked quirt across her chest, stealing her breath and her voice. When he twisted her small breast with his hard fingers, she could only whimper her pain and her fear.

"Louder, little bitch," he hissed at her. "I want to hear you howl." He drew out the word on a long breath, giving her nipple a vicious pinch, pressing into her thighs with his knees so that she couldn't move. Somewhere behind her, the mare snorted uneasily, and her hooves clattered as she paced in her stall.

Lark struggled to breathe. Black stars danced before her eyes and coalesced into dark clouds. She had to get that quirt away from her, far enough from her lungs that they could function again. She gagged, but no air came into her throat. Her heart pounded in her ears. She thrust her hands against his shoulders, but he was too tall and too heavy.

"Make some noise, brat!" She heard his words, his mouth so close to her that she could smell his odd, incongruous scent, but she could make no sound. "I said," he shouted, "noise!" And he pulled the quirt away so that he could cut at her legs with it.

It hurt, even through her riding skirt, a slashing pain across her shin and knee, but she hardly noticed. The quirt was gone from her chest, and she drew a desperately needed breath.

"Scream, you little bitch!" he panted. His arm lifted and fell again, and the quirt cut her like a knife.

The mare whinnied alarm. Lark sucked more air through her gritted teeth. William was not sane. His madness had a power of its own, a force that was hardly human. He wanted to savage her. He wanted to hurt her, to hear her cry out.

And then what? If the stories were true, he could beat her to death. Or, worse, he could rape her, ruin her if he made her pregnant . . .

All these thoughts raced through her mind in a flash, reminding her of Geraldine Prince, of her suspicions about Pamella . . . but there was no time to ponder them.

She caught another deep breath and used the strength it gave her to shove, with every bit of muscle in her small body, at William's chest.

Something soft met her fingers, gave way under her palms.

He knew, and he straightened, seizing both her wrists in one long hand, and twisting until she thought the bones would break. "Don't—you—*ever*!" he grated. He gave her wrists another wrench, then lifted the quirt above his head.

She rolled her face to one side, just in time. The little whip caught her skull just above her ear, and her stomach lurched. "Scream!" he shouted. He leaned over her, his knees rolling off her thighs as he shifted, his hand vicious on her wrists. "Scream, brat, or I swear I'll break your country neck!"

And Lark, in pain and real terror, screamed, and screamed a second time as he struck her again. Though her hands were captured, with his weight off her legs, she kicked with all her might. She had practiced a thousand standing mounts, and she had labored in her family's fields since she was a child. She was small, but she was strong, and she managed to throw her body to one side, ripping her arms free of his grip. He grabbed at her, getting a fistful of her cropped hair. It was too short, and he couldn't hold it. Her scalp stung, and she knew he must have strands of her hair in his fingers, but she was free.

In a flash, she was up and running, down the aisle. The bar was thrown across the divided door at the back of the stables. He was coming behind her, and there was nowhere to go. She saw the gate to the box stall, unlatched it with one practiced motion, and threw herself in to land on her knees in the straw.

The mare whinnied, and backed to the wall, flattening her ears. The foal froze, head up, ears forward, eyes wide.

Just as William reached the gate, Lark jumped to her feet. The window was too high, and had no latch in any case. There was a pallet of blankets in one corner, which was no help to her. There was nowhere to go. She murmured a plea to the mare for calm, then scurried behind the winged foal, putting the little creature between her and the aisle. It tried to back closer to its mother, stopping when its hindquarters touched Lark. She put one hand on its croup, and whispered, "Hold still, little one. Oh, please hold still . . ."

William stopped when he saw her behind the foal. His face was scarlet, and sweat darkened his pale hair. He panted, the lust for her pain still on him. "Come out," he commanded.

She shook her head, and said, "Nay," as stoutly as she was able. She wasn't sure if he would strike the foal to get to her. She would have to step forward if he did. She couldn't let him hurt a winged foal, but he didn't know that.

William held his quirt in one fist, indecision plain on his face, and in the angle of his body. For the first time since she had met him, he wore no embroidered vest. Her eyes strayed to his chest. It was obvious now, that swelling, that strangeness:

After a long moment, he lowered the quirt, letting his arm hang by his side. His color began to fade, and his breathing to slow as he regained control. "You're bleeding, brat," he said.

Lark lifted her chin. "Aye."

"I've told you before to stay out of my business."

"'Tis you bashing about in mine, my lord."

He raised one pale brow. "My, my. Spunky, aren't we?"

"'Tis only the truth," she said. "Threatening to take Deeping Farm, stealing my horse." The trickle of blood ran across her eyebrow, down to her eyelid, and she dashed at it with a finger. William's lip curled at this.

"That's what you like, isn't it?" Lark said. She held out her shaking finger to show him. "Blood, and hurting."

"I love it," he murmured. "I truly love it." He turned the quirt in his fingers. "I could kill you now, and that would be even better."

"Mistress Winter knows I'm here."

His eyes narrowed. "Then I'd better hurry," he said, and he took a step toward her. Lark thought the foal under her hand would flee at that, dash behind its mother, but it didn't move.

Surely the Duke was too close for a winged horse to tolerate. Surely her last hope was about to vanish, and this madman would have what he wanted. She shrank back against the mare's warmth, and a crooked smile curved the Duke's lips.

"She's only a wingless horse," he said lightly. "What does she care if a flyer dies?"

"But the foal—" she began, without much real hope.

"This is *my* foal, brat." He took another step. "My filly. Bonded."

"It can't be!" she wailed. She looked frantically about for a way to escape. The Duke blocked the gate, her only way out. The mare behind her, though she could feel her nervousness, would be no help, and the foal . . .

The foal took a tottering step closer to William, extending her nose. Lark stared, mouth open in wonderment.

The foal took another step, and put her nose in the Duke's hand, and stood perfectly still while—

He *stroked* her.

Lark put a hand to her throat. A winged horse—it wasn't possible. It shouldn't be possible. But it was happening, right before her.

William fondled the filly, smiling, caressing one delicate wing, before he moved her out of his way with the gentlest of touches and reached for Lark.

THIRTY

PHILIPPA raced back inside the stables, grabbing Sunny's bridle from the hook where Lark had hung it. Sunny whickered and stamped as she opened the gate, and a tense moment passed before Philippa could settle her enough to fit the bridle over her head. She didn't waste a thought for her flying saddle, but leaped up on Sunny's back, snugging her legs over the blanket, and pressing her thighs down over her folded wings. "Go, Sunny," she cried. "We have to catch Seraph!" At the last second, as Sunny trotted down the aisle, Philippa reached to snatch Seraph's bridle off its hook. She laid it across Sunny's withers, reined her toward the road Seraph had charged down, and gave her her head.

Sunny, sensing the urgency of their purpose, surged into a gallop. Seraph's footprints were still visible in the thin layer of snow, but the bright sun had begun to make the road slushy and slippery. They reached the end of the estate lane in moments, but in the main road, the last of the snow had melted. The trail disappeared, but Sunny seemed to have no doubts. She changed leads neatly, as if the surface were good turf instead of slick gravel, and turned left.

They followed the road for only a few strides before a narrow drive led down toward a stand of bare trees. A fresh alarm gripped

Philippa as the memory came flooding back to her, the little hidden stable, the crisis that had started here. There was still snow in the drive, shaded as it was, and she saw hoofprints. She turned Sunny, and they raced toward the beech copse. Philippa did not urge more speed on her mare, knowing Sunny was running as fast as she dared on the uncertain ground. Philippa gripped the mare's barrel with her thighs. She didn't dare fall now, but it had been a long time since she had ridden without a saddle.

The drive led around the grove, and Philippa could hear Seraph before she saw him. When they cleared the trees, she saw the little stallion dashing back and forth, whinnying frantically. There could be no doubt that Lark was there.

Sunny skidded to a rough stop, and Philippa swung her leg over her back, half-falling to the ground. She raced toward the tack-room door and threw it open. She heard the voices. Larkyn was there, and so was William.

She ran toward them. She didn't realize at first that Seraph was at her heels.

FROM outside, Lark heard her bondmate's shrill whinnying, his frantic feet pounding back and forth, but she couldn't call out to him. William had one hand clamped over her mouth, and with the other he lifted her off her feet, pressing her back to him as he maneuvered his way out of the stall, careful of the filly. When he had kicked the gate shut, he threw Lark against the opposite wall and put both his hands around her neck. His hands squeezed until she thought her eyes would fall out of her head.

"William! No!" It was Mistress Winter's voice, sharp with desperation.

And then there was Tup. Mistress Winter fell to one side as he charged past her, his lips pulled back, his ears flat. He reached for the Duke's shoulder, and his teeth closed on it. He shook him, like an oc-hound might shake a rat, and William howled with shock and pain, a thin, high cry. The mare in the stall gave a nervous whinny, and the colt dashed back and forth in the stall, whickering anxiously.

William released Lark, all at once, and the moment he did, Tup loosened his bite. The Duke whirled, lifting his quirt to strike.

Tup snorted, and backed away, his hindquarters deeply flexed, his tail brushing the sawdust of the aisle.

Philippa had recovered her balance, and she strode past Tup, hands on hips, glaring at William. "What is the meaning of this?" she demanded.

Lark sagged against the wall, her hands to her throat. "He tried to kill me!"

The Duke snapped, "Don't be ridiculous, brat. Why would I do that?"

She stared up at him. "He did!" she said faintly. "Tup knew it, that's why he—"

Mistress Winter said, "William, have you lost your mind?"

"That will be Duke William, to you, Horsemistress," he said. He spoke as easily as if they were sitting down together over tea, as if he had not just had murder in his heart. He dropped his hand, and Lark saw that blood from Tup's bite seeped through his white shirt near his collarbone.

"You dishonor your title," Mistress Winter said. "Abusing a child this way."

The Duke adopted a negligent pose, leaning against the wall of the box stall, switching at his thigh with the quirt. "I have abused no one," he said.

"Larkyn is bleeding," Mistress Winter pointed out. "And I saw you with your hands around her neck."

"She's not hurt. Not that I have the slightest need to explain to *you*, Philippa, but I have simply stopped an impetuous brat from interfering with my horses."

"Your horses?" She stepped forward, and looked past the Duke into the box stall. Lark pressed her hands to her trembling lips, and watched as Mistress Winter took a long look at the silvery foal. It trotted back and forth, ears flicking in its anxiety, its little plume of white tail swishing. She eyed the mare, who huddled fearfully against the far wall, and then she turned to look at the Duke's dirty coat and trousers, his soiled boots. "William," she said deliberately. "What have you done?"

He ran a hand through his tumbled hair and pushed it behind one ear. "You can see perfectly well what I've done, Philippa. I've bred a beautiful winged filly, from a wingless dam and a wingless stallion."

"It's treason."

He straightened, and his voice grew silky. "It's a triumph."

"What do you hope to gain from it? What's the point?"

Lark stepped up behind Mistress Winter, but she kept a wary distance from the Duke. "Mistress," she whispered fearfully. "I saw him touch her. And she didn't—she—"

Mistress Winter glanced down at her, then looked back at William, her face set in sharp lines. "What is this about?"

His cold smile made Lark's belly quake anew. Involuntarily, her hand strayed to her throat, still throbbing from the pressure of his hard fingers. He said, "It's a new bloodline, Philippa. A glorious step forward in the history of the winged horses."

Mistress Winter shook her head slightly, frowning. Lark took a deep breath, steadying herself. She said, in a swift undertone, "He bonded with her, Mistress. He's changed his body so he could bond with a winged horse."

The Duke's eyes flashed something frightening, but Lark forced herself to hold her ground. He couldn't hurt her with Mistress Winter here. Or Tup.

Tup, too, stood his ground, now that he was out of reach of that quirt. His head was high, his legs stiff, his tail arched above his croup. His nostrils flared red, and Lark cast him a look of pride and gratitude. He would have killed for her, she felt sure.

"Your grandfathers would turn in their graves if they knew, William," Philippa said.

"Then," he said with a forced laugh, "I hope their coffins are spacious."

"I will bring this before the Council."

"Don't waste your time." He tucked his quirt under his arm, and brushed bits of straw from his coat. "I'm not the only one who thinks men should be able to fly winged horses."

Mistress Winter gave her famous snort. "You underestimate me, William, and not for the first time." She turned her back on him and put a hand under Lark's arm. "Come, Larkyn. Collect your stallion, and let's go home."

Lark, trembling with the aftermath of too much emotion, stumbled toward Tup, glad to have his neck to lean on as she preceded Mistress Winter out of the stable. She hurt all over, her legs, her head, her cheek. Her knees felt weak.

Winter Sunset came to meet them, blowing nervously. Lark

patted her, then threw her arms around Tup's neck. She whispered, "Oh, lovely Tup! Lovely brave, you are!" He dropped his head and nuzzled her shoulder.

Mistress Winter stopped in the tack-room doorway, and spoke once more to the Duke. "I suppose this is why you haven't answered our letters, William. Certainly you look as if you've been living in the stable."

"Why did you write?"

"To tell you that your brother has been injured."

There was a little moment of silence, then the Duke growled, "What? How?"

"Rescuing two Onmarin children from the Aesks," Mistress Winter said. Her voice, Lark thought, was as hard and cold as the Duke's quirt. "A job you should have done, William."

"I was otherwise occupied," he said, but his voice seemed to falter slightly.

"Indeed."

"Philippa—is Francis going to survive?"

"I don't know. This is why we came here. There's not adequate room for him at the Academy, and it's not restful. We thought Fleckham House was empty. I suppose we will have to find some other place now."

"Not at all. Of course he should come here to recuperate. In fact, I'll order it. And I'll visit him."

"I'm sure," Mistress Winter said in a dry tone, "that he'll find that restorative."

PHILIPPA and Larkyn went back to the stables of Fleckham House to retrieve their saddles and replace the borrowed blankets in the tack room. Philippa saw how Larkyn winced when she jumped down from Seraph's back and that her face was already beginning to bruise. When she put her fingers on the girl's cheek, Larkyn's indrawn breath led her to lift the dark curls aside and see the great welt beneath her hair.

"What other hurts do you have, child?" she asked, anger constricting her throat.

Larkyn lifted one side of her divided skirt to show the scarlet stripes where William had struck her. As she leaned forward, Philippa saw the contusions on her slender neck. There were more on her wrists. Philippa had to fight a startling urge to draw the girl into her arms and hold her there, but she knew better. Flyers must learn to deal with adversity, and softness would not help them. "The Council Lords should see these," she said grimly.

"And then Duke William would take Deeping Farm for certain," the girl said. She lifted Seraph's saddle to his back and began to do up the breast strap and the cinches.

"That's a possibility, I fear." Philippa finished tacking Sunny and turned to face Larkyn again. The girl was pale beneath her bruises, but her chin was lifted, her eyes bright with courage. "Margareth and I would stand up for you in the Council, of course. But there are some Council Lords who will back the Duke no matter what, simply because he is the Duke."

Larkyn didn't answer, but she revealed how much pain she felt by leading Seraph to a mounting block. When she was in the saddle, her knees tucked beneath the thigh rolls, she reined Seraph around and gazed out over the melting snowfields. "I doubt the lords will care much about a girl from the Uplands," she said. "Flyer or no."

"I won't lie to you, Larkyn. The breeding violation will be considered at least as serious as the Duke's attacking you, I'm afraid."

Larkyn shrugged. "Not to my family."

"Of course not." Philippa mounted, suppressing a groan of her own. Seraph, when he had charged at the Duke, had banged one of his hooves on her shin, and she knew it must be black-and-blue and swollen by now. She had no intention of letting Larkyn know of it. Enough had happened to weigh on the child, and there was one more warning that had to be made. "Larkyn, I fear for the Duke's safety if your brothers should hear of this attack."

Larkyn's eyes turned to her. Their violet color was so dark it was almost black, and the cruel stripe across her cheek was vivid scarlet against her white skin. "Mistress Winter," she said softly. "We mustn't tell them. There would be such trouble."

Philippa gave an approving nod. "You're a wise girl, Larkyn. And you will one day be a wise horsemistress. We flyers will stick together in this, then, as we do in everything. Come, let's get home, and we'll talk with Margareth."

They launched from the park and circled to the east and south. Philippa and Sunny led, but Philippa kept a worried eye on Larkyn and Seraph. The pair looked steady to her, and Larkyn, despite her injuries, sat straight in her saddle, leaning as Seraph banked, secure as they picked up speed. By the time they had reached Osham, Philippa felt confident in the young flyers.

She looked ahead to the slate roof of the Academy Hall glistening under a thin sheen of snow and ice. Shadows already stretched toward the east, the early evening of winter fast approaching. Philippa spared a look to the west, to the hills of the Uplands, and beyond to the Marins, their peaks mantled in white, framed by the bright pale blue of a winter sky. It was a time Philippa usually looked forward to, when the weather enfolded the Academy in its cold embrace, and the Hall and the Residence and the stables were warm havens where horses, ochounds, and women settled in to wait out the season. She wondered if there would be any peace this winter. Conflict seemed to be building on every side, trapping her in a web of tension.

She and Larkyn flew back over the roofs of the White City, made a long, gradual descent to the Academy, and came to ground in the return paddock. Philippa watched Larkyn and Seraph's landing, the little stallion's ebony hooves flashing against the snow, the girl's slight body flexing and balancing just as it should.

They cantered, then trotted up the paddock to the stables. Erna came out, but Philippa waved her off. "I'll rub her down myself," she said. "But Larkyn—perhaps you would like Erna to take Seraph?"

She was not surprised when Larkyn shook her head. "Nay, Mistress. He'll worry if I don't do it."

Erna, incurious and stolid, went back into the tack room, where a merry fire crackled in the close stove.

Philippa and Larkyn went into the stables, side by side, their horses walking quietly behind them. "I'll ask Matron to arrange a hot bath for you, Larkyn," Philippa said, as they reached Seraph's stall. "Do you need a potion? Are you in pain?"

Larkyn shook her head. "Nothing's broken, Mistress. But a hot bath will help." She let Seraph into his stall. "The other girls will talk if they see these marks," she said. She pointed to her bruised face. "Especially my sponsor."

Philippa tutted. "I'll speak to Petra, Larkyn. You're a second-level flyer now, and have no need of a sponsor. And as to the talk—there's no way around that."

"I don't want them to think I fell."

"You can't control what they think, I'm afraid." Philippa bent her head, thinking. "If you speak of what really happened, you'll be open to all sorts of accusations and slanders. The Duke will deny everything. He'll say you made up the story to prevent him from confiscating Deeping Farm—and it will be his word against yours."

"Aye." Larkyn nodded and followed Seraph into his stall. "I'll just say nothing, then," she said. "And pretend I don't hear them whispering."

"It's hard on you, Larkyn, but I think it's best." Sunny whickered, eager for her stall, and nudged Philippa with her nose. Still she hesitated. "Are you—you're quite certain you're all right, Larkyn? He didn't—" She couldn't bring herself to say it.

"'Tis not pricking he wants, Mistress," Larkyn said. "He pressed me against that wall with his own body. If rape had been on his mind, I would have known."

Philippa nodded and turned to lead Sunny to her own stall. Larkyn was wise beyond her years, perhaps beyond her experience. She could very well rise above her country manners, her Uplands accent, and her lack of breeding to become one of the great horsemistresses of Oc.

If they could protect her from the mad Duke.

THIRTY-ONE

PHILIPPA and Margareth dispatched one of the third-level girls the very next morning with a missive for Lord and Lady Beeth, requesting their protection. Lady Beeth responded by sending one of her footmen, a tall, silent man who brought a letter of explanation. He was introduced to Herbert, and shown where he could stand night guard outside the stables of the Academy. The girls looked at him curiously as Philippa showed him about. She informed them he had come to assist Herbert, and they frowned, knowing Herbert had never needed assistance before. Only Larkyn and Hester looked relieved. The girls had proved already they could be trusted to keep silent, and Larkyn would sleep better knowing there was someone keeping night watch.

After much discussion of the risks, Margareth sent a formal complaint to the Council, alleging a breeding violation by Duke William. She and Philippa both understood that if the decision did not go their way, there could be trouble. They couldn't see how else to deal with the situation. With Francis ill, and the Master Breeder in William's control, the Council Lords were all they had to rely upon.

The confirmation of their suit was to come by post, which

meant two days of waiting, Philippa pacing, Margareth mostly sitting in her big chair, wrapped in a heavy shawl.

"You're ill, Margareth," Philippa said, on the first day. "You should be in your bed."

"No, no," the Headmistress said faintly. "I just feel cold. Don't you think it's cold?"

Philippa walked to the window to hide her frown. A lively fire crackled in the hearth, and Margareth's office was so warm that she herself had been on the point of opening the window to the crisp air. She stood gazing out, glad her students had already returned from their commissions. Clouds had rolled down from the mountains in the night to shroud the countryside in cottony gray folds. She could see neither the hills to the west nor the spires of Osham to the east. She folded her arms, and tapped her elbows peevishly with her fingertips. She couldn't shake the memory of Larkyn with William's hands at her throat, of Tup crashing past her to sink his teeth into William's shoulder. And the winged filly's wide, innocent eyes haunted her.

"She's so beautiful, Margareth," Philippa said for the tenth time. "Pale gray, the faintest dapples across her back and croup, and her mane and tail are like silver. Her wings will be gray, too, I think, and her legs are long for her body. I'd think she were a Noble if it weren't for her color. She should have been Amelia's, but of course it's too late for that now. What will become of the poor little thing?"

"I don't know," Margareth repeated. "It will depend on the Council."

"It's too late," Philippa said again, feeling cross and restive. "She'll die if we take her from him, but I fear she'll die if we don't . . ."

Across the courtyard, she saw the stable door open, and Herbert came out, carrying a bucket and a spade. Bramble paced at his heels, slowly, but her tail up and waving. Philippa put one hand on the cold sash, and watched the oc-hound as she followed the stable-man around to the dry paddock. "At least Bramble is recovering," she said, half to herself.

"Thanks to Larkyn," Margareth said. Philippa glanced at her, and saw that the Headmistress had leaned her head against the high back of her chair and closed her eyes.

"Margareth. Go to bed. How will you be strong enough to appear before the Council?"

After a moment, Margareth opened her eyes, but they were red and unfocused. "I suppose you're right," she said weakly. "Call Matron for me, will you?"

Matron took charge of Margareth, helping her down the stairs and across to the Residence, up the stairs into her apartment. She installed her in her bed with a blazing fire and a heated brick between her sheets. Philippa oversaw all of this before she went down to the kitchens to see that everything was in order for the midday meal. Then, feeling itchy and out of sorts, she wandered across the courtyard to the stables.

Bramble came to meet her, and Philippa crouched to hug her, to stroke her, and to take a look for herself at the wound on her neck. Whoever had administered it had been serious, she thought. It had been a deep cut, intended to kill. But why?

When she stood up, she found Amelia Rys standing in the doorway, watching her.

"Hello, Amelia," Philippa said.

"Hello, Mistress Winter." The girl stood aside to let her pass.

"I hope you're finding enough to occupy you?"

"Oh, yes," the girl said, in that noncommittal voice. "I've been studying the genealogies, and helping in the stalls where I can. Where I am allowed, I should say."

Philippa had started to turn away, but this stopped her. She lifted one eyebrow. "Is there a problem here?"

Amelia shrugged. "The other girls neither like me nor trust me," she said. "But I'm not surprised by it. It's an uneasy alliance between our two principalities. We have a long history."

Philippa said lightly, "We do, indeed. I am part of that history, as it happens."

"The battle of the South Tower," Amelia said. Her eyes flicked away, just briefly, and for the barest moment she looked like the eighteen-year-old girl she was. When she brought her gaze back to Philippa, though, her face had resumed the expression of a seasoned diplomat. Philippa wondered if she had had any childhood at all.

"How did you know about that, Amelia?"

"My father told me," the girl said. "He felt the more I knew, the better I would fare."

"It was not your father's government who raided the South Tower. I know that." Philippa pleated her gloves between her fingers. It was her turn to look away, out into the snow-filled clouds that hung low over the Academy. "Alana Rose died that day, and her beautiful Ocmarin, Summer Rose. It was the worst day of my life. Two precious creatures dead, and nothing gained. Our prince would never have ceded Klee the port of the South Tower."

"And you resent us still." The statement was made without emotion, without inflection.

Philippa sighed. "Amelia. You were an infant."

"But I am Klee."

Philippa met the girl's level brown gaze, and nodded. "Yes. But if we don't put the past behind us and look forward, we are no better than those barbarians I so recently met." She pointed behind her, down the aisle of the stables. "Would you help me with Sunny's stall? I've been away so much, it's rather a mess."

"Of course," Amelia said. "I could have taken care of it while you were gone, if I'd known."

"I would never have thought to ask you. In the days when Rosellen was our stable-girl, it wouldn't have been necessary. Erna is—"

"Less than satisfactory, yes," Amelia Rys said, and turned to walk by Philippa's side. "I can see that. I hope that next time you'll remember to ask me, Horsemistress."

"I will, Amelia. That is, until you have your own horse and stall to care for."

Amelia looked up at her, and her narrow face brightened. "I can hardly wait," she said, with a little throb of urgency in her voice. "It's all I think about."

Philippa felt a rare smile curve her lips. "Indeed," she said softly. "I was the same."

THE storm began during supper. The horsemistresses and students came out of the Hall into a world of snow, big dry flakes filling the sky, softening the cobblestones of the courtyard, muffling every sound. Philippa glanced to her left, where she could just the see the corner of the dry paddock, and saw that Lady Beeth's man was there, with a lantern and a hooded coat to protect him. It would be a long, cold night. She must tell Herbert to see to it the man had something warm to drink.

The lane leading to the road was already filled with snow, the paddocks disappearing behind shifting curtains of white. The girls, laughing, turned their faces up to catch fat flakes on their lips and eyelashes as they trooped across the courtyard. Philippa had blanketed Sunny, and she turned toward the Domicile, looking forward to an early night.

As she crept between the sheets and pulled her quilt up to her chin, she blessed Lady Beeth. It was a simple thing, sending her man to stand watch, but it was a great comfort. A shame, she thought, that more of the nobility did not possess the practicality of Hester's mamá. Lady Beeth could be counted on to take action where action was needed, not to dither about asking permission or seeking approval for every small thing.

She rolled to her side to watch the drifts of snowflakes dance past her window. It was wonderful to feel snug and safe, Sunny in her stall and she in her own bed, in her rightful place. She fell asleep at once.

Snow was still falling and the sky gray with early morning light when the urgent knocking woke her.

Philippa struggled out of a heavy sleep, with a momentary sense of displacement. The knock came again, and Matron's voice called, "Mistress Winter! Mistress Winter!"

Philippa put her feet on the floor, and almost gasped at the cold. She didn't bother hunting for her slippers but went to the door, pulling her hair back from her face and rubbing her eyes. She opened the door, and found Matron standing outside, tears streaming down her face.

She stared at her. "Matron! Kalla's heels, what's the matter?"

She should have known, of course. She should have suspected, and she should have visited Margareth before she went to her own bed. For days afterward, she would try to remember what she had said to her old friend, what her last words had been, if she had shown her affection in any gesture or word. But it was too late now. It was not as if she could have saved her, postponed the inevitable in any way. It was only that—if she had had some idea—she might have said goodbye.

She threw a dressing gown on, found her slippers, and hurried after Matron to Margareth's apartment. Margareth lay as Matron had found her, curled on her side. Her hair spread across her pillow like a fan, almost as white as the pillowcase. Her eyes were half-open, gazing peacefully on the next world.

Philippa knelt beside the bed and touched Margareth's cheek, finding it icy cold beneath her fingertips. She gently, tenderly, closed the papery eyelids. She gathered the strands of her hair and wound them into a long braid. Margareth would not want to be seen with her hair disordered.

Matron, still weeping, came to the other side of the bed, and together they turned Margareth to lie on her back, and folded her pale hands on her bosom. The blue tracery of her veins still showed in delicate lines like those of a spider's web. They smoothed the quilt over her and folded it back to her waist.

Philippa laid a hand on Margareth's arm, then straightened, and stood back. "There's nothing more to do for now," she said. "Until the deaner can come."

Matron burst into fresh tears. "Oh, Mistress Winter! I had no idea she was so ill! I should have stayed with her . . ."

"Nonsense, Matron," Philippa said, but her tone was gentle. "Margareth was old, and tired. And now she flies with Highflyer again. She would not want us to grieve."

But later, in her own apartment, she sat down in her chair beside the window, put her face in her hands, and wept for a very long time, not for Margareth, but for herself.

PHILIPPA prevailed upon Suzanne Star to make the announcement. The excuse she gave was that she knew her own manner of speaking was brusque, when gentleness was needed. Suzanne gave her a close look, and Philippa thought she probably had not fooled her. The truth was that she did not trust herself. The tears she had shed lingered in her throat and behind her eyes, and her eyelids were swollen. It would do neither the girls nor herself any good for her to break down at the high table.

Philippa listened, her head bowed, as Suzanne told the assembly of Margareth's passing, bracing herself against the gasps and cries of shock. She wished she had Suzanne's gift for being direct without sounding harsh. She tried to focus on her words, but she kept seeing Margareth's thin hands, once so strong and capable, and now still. She gritted her teeth against a fresh wave of sadness and stared at the tips of her boots until Suzanne said, "The Headmistress would have wished our work to go on without interruption. Mistress Winter, of course, will be acting Head until the Duke and the Council Lords name a successor."

Philippa hoped she was the only one who heard the slight hesitation in Suzanne's voice. Nothing was certain these days. Suzanne, like the other instructors, knew that Margareth and Philippa had brought suit in the Council against the palace and that there was hostility between Philippa and William.

Philippa looked up, and saw Kathryn Dancer's eyes meet Suzanne's. Kathryn gave a small shake of her head. The other horsemistresses, too, looked grim and a little wary. Two of the juniors whispered to each other, their eyes sliding to Philippa, then away.

Philippa felt a little spurt of anger. It gave her a sort of energy and strength, which was a respite from the dragging weight of her sadness. When Suzanne sat down, Philippa said, including all of them in her gaze, "There's no need for any of you to look worried. Clearly, the Duke will not support me. And I doubt the Council will even consider naming me Headmistress."

Suzanne said, "Philippa, no one thinks—"

Philippa put up a hand. "No, Suzanne, I understand perfectly. I'm nothing like Margareth. I'm not at all certain I want the position, in any case."

"But you're the assistant Head," Kathryn said. "It's logical."

Philippa said, "Let us concentrate on remembering Margareth, shall we?" and she knew by the tightening of Kathryn's mouth that she sounded snappish.

"But who will make assignments?" one of the junior instructors asked. She sniffled, and dabbed at her eyes. "How will we know what to do?"

"We have a schedule for the moment," Philippa said. Her throat had begun to ache again. "We'll follow that. Is that clear?"

She saw the flicker of another glance between Suzanne and Kathryn. She threw down her napkin and got up. She opened her mouth to excuse herself, but her lips trembled, and she didn't dare try to speak. She turned abruptly and stepped down from the high table to hurry out of the dining room. She was grateful there was no one in the foyer as she passed through. She went into Margareth's office, slamming the door behind her just as the helpless tears overtook her. This time, as she breathed in the familiar scents, and sat in Margareth's own high-backed chair, she wept for her old friend.

After a time, feeling spent and empty, Philippa stood up and walked to the window. The storm had eased, and only a few intermittent flurries still drifted across the courtyard. She was standing there when the mail coach arrived, its wheels cutting parallel grooves in the deep snow. Its pair of draught horses, heavily muscled blacks, wore a powdery dusting of snow on their manes and on the hames of their harness. The driver huddled beneath a wide-brimmed hat, a red muffler tied round his chin, pulled up over his nose to keep out the cold. His scarf was the only spot of color in the landscape.

Matron went out to receive the mail and carried it back up the steps to the Hall. Philippa turned away from the window and bent to put a match to the fire laid ready in the fireplace. She had seen the rolled, ribboned document on top of the letters in Matron's hands. She recognized, even at a distance, the official format of a summons to the Council of Lords. The timing could not have been worse. She would have to present her case before the Council alone.

Philippa sat down in Margareth's chair and pulled the schedule book toward her. There was a great deal to be done, and it fell to her to do it.

She had a pen in her hand, and the schedule book open, when Matron knocked on the door, brought in the summons and laid it on the big desk. She said only, "Thank you, Matron. Could you bring me a cup of tea, please, and ask Mistress Star to come in? We will have to make some changes after all."

THIRTY-TWO

THE Council had ordered the hearing of the Academy's complaint for the very next day. Philippa rose early and dressed with care. Her neck already ached with tension, and the bout of weeping the day before hadn't helped.

Her case was considerably weakened, she feared, without Margareth. Margareth's pragmatic voice, and the length and honor of her service, would have carried a lot of weight with the Council. Eduard Crisp would have stood beside her, defying the Duke without hesitation, but the new Master Breeder, the ineffectual Jinson, would be no help at all. They could have asked Eduard to come and support her cause, but she and Margareth had felt that the two of them, in their crisp black riding habits, their hair in the rider's knot and wings glittering on their collars, would make an impressive and unambiguous presence in the Rotunda. Now it was too late to reach Eduard. He had retired, after his own suit against the Duke failed, to the relative safety of his family estate in Eastreach.

Francis lay ill at Fleckham House. Margareth was gone. There was no one to speak for the bloodlines but Philippa herself.

She stood back from her mirror to survey her appearance. She had smoothed almond cream into her skin and brushed her hair thoroughly. Reflectively, she touched her rider's knot. The vivid red of her girlhood had given way to a muted auburn, softened now by streaks of gray. Lines fanned around her eyes, the toll of sun and wind aloft. Her tabard was freshly pressed by Matron, her belt cinched around her lean middle, and her boots sparkled with polish. It was the best she could do.

She wished, briefly, that she had an icon of Kalla, like the one Larkyn wore, to carry with her. It was an absurd thought. She had never placed faith in such things, and it was foolish to think she could start now.

The threat of more snow meant she could not fly into the White City as she would have preferred. Herbert had hitched the piebald pony, Pig, to the gig, and was waiting for her now outside the Domicile. Philippa put on her warmest coat and pulled on her gloves. She picked up the genealogy, which she had carefully wrapped in linen, and held it to her chest as she climbed into the gig. The genealogy might not help to persuade the Council, but its weight and its significance strengthened her own resolve.

Herbert snapped the reins and spoke to Pig, and the pony set off toward Osham through the frozen landscape.

THE white marble Rotunda sat on a low hill, its colorful pennants drooping and stiff in the cold. Carriages and phaetons waited before its grand entryway, their drivers spreading blankets over their horses, chatting together, smoking pipes under the bare branches of the ancient wych elm that dominated the plaza. They straightened and bowed to the horsemistress when they caught sight of her, and she nodded to them in return, before she bade Herbert a brief farewell and climbed the wide steps.

Today she could not pace the outer aisle of the Rotunda, as she preferred to do. Holding the genealogy in one arm, she stepped down past the tiers where the Council Lords sat in their carved chairs, their secretaries and pages arrayed behind them. She didn't look up at the balcony, but she heard the voices of the ladies as they murmured and whispered to each other. They would have heard from their lords, she supposed, that another suit was being brought against the Duke. Though this one hadn't the prurient appeal of the paternity suit, it would still command a good bit of attention and provide gossip for the Erdlin festival soon to come.

A page met Philippa, bowing, gesturing to a chair that had been set for her behind a long table with two other petitioners. She took the chair and unwrapped the genealogy to lay it on the long table. Its embossed lettering gleamed. She laid her hand upon it and waited.

William must have been awaiting her arrival so that he could make his own entrance. No more than a minute passed before the doors to the Duke's private chamber opened, and William and Duchess Constance appeared. The Duchess, looking wan and rather faded in an elaborate cloak edged with dark mink, lagged behind the Duke like a lost child. William bore himself proudly, his gilt hair shining, his high-heeled boots clicking on the marble floor.

He had worn them to make himself taller than she, Philippa thought, and was tempted to laugh. He wore a fashionable waist-coat tightly buttoned to the neck, with white fur at the collar and cuffs. It completely hid the swell of his chest.

Behind the two of them came Jinson. He avoided Philippa's eyes.

Philippa, with the Council Lords and the watchers in the gallery, stood while the Duke and Duchess made their way to the central dais and sat down. Jinson stood to one side, staring at his boots. As Philippa resumed her seat, she caught sight of a young woman in the aisle above the tiers. She was slender, and dressed in black, standing half-hidden by a pillar. Philippa narrowed her eyes, trying to see who it was, but the presider began to speak.

"My lords," he intoned, striking a tiny marble gavel on its sounding block. "Duke William of Oc is now in attendance upon the Council of Lords. Let all hear and remember."

Philippa's summons had told her that hers would be the last case to be heard today. It was the most serious, requiring delib-eration and discussion by the lords.

The first two petitioners were heard and dismissed quickly. Philippa heard not a word of their cases. She bent her head, concentrating on what she would say, what she and Margareth had discussed. She was startled when she heard the presider speak her name, and she wondered for a bad moment if he had had to say it twice.

She drew a deep breath, and stood, straightening her tabard. She lifted her head to look around at the thirty-eight Lords of the Council. Her brother Meredith was there, glaring at her. He would never forgive her for this, but there was nothing she could do about that. He should have learned by now that he could not stop her from doing her duty. It served him right, in any case. He had been eager to bond her to a winged horse solely for the purpose of ingratiating himself with the Palace. He had never once asked her about her own feelings on the matter.

She turned her face to the Duke and Duchess. Constance tilted her head to see past William's shoulder. William said something to her over his shoulder, and she shrank back again, dropping her head, toying with her great rope of pearls.

"My lords," Philippa began. She fixed her eyes on William's black ones as she spoke. "I have come before you to lodge a complaint about a breeding violation, a breaking of the law as it was set down by good Duke Francis of memory. I accuse Duke William of this crime, and by the dictates of his great-great-grandfather, of treason."

She heard the delighted hiss of indrawn breath from the balcony and a slight shifting among the lords themselves. William's face did not change, but his eyes glinted dangerously. She understood it was a warning. He had come prepared.

Philippa lifted her hand from the genealogy and pushed the book forward on the table. "This, my lords," she said, "is the genealogy of the three bloodlines of the winged horses. The ancestors of our Nobles, our Foundations, and our Ocmarins are written here, and the Master Breeder—" She let her eyes shift slightly to Jinson, but she could see only the top of his head. He stared at the floor and twisted his fingers together behind him. "The Master Breeder and the Headmistress of the Academy of the Air confer with the Duke on every breeding, in a constant effort to improve the bloodlines, to ensure that stallions and mares throw winged foals, that the distinguishing characteristics of each bloodline are kept pure."

Now she lifted her head again, to include all the lords in her gaze. "Foundations are strong and courageous," she said. "Nobles are swift and intelligent. Ocmarins are quick, agile, and have great stamina. It was Duke Francis's dream that the bloodlines would be refined so that all of these qualities would be dependable, and it was his life's work to see that the winged horses are Oc's unique resource. Duke William has violated these precepts and acted in direct opposition to the laws of the Duchy that gives him his power."

She turned her body to face William directly. He gazed at her beneath half-lowered eyelids. It was exactly that reptilian look, those sharp features and hooded eyes, that made her think of the Old Ones.

"Duke William," she said, "in collusion with his Master Breeder, has bred a winged foal in his private stable." She lifted her arm and pointed one long forefinger at him as she said in her hardest tone, "And he means to fly this foal himself."

The gallery erupted in a muffled chorus of cries and exclamations. One or two of the lords swore. Philippa looked up to see who they were.

Lord Beeth, plump and short, sat in his chair with his chin on his fist. Lady Beeth would be in the balcony, having given her husband clear instructions on how the matter should be handled. The other lords, Chatham and Daysmith and Bowles and the others, sat straight or leaned forward, frowning at the Duke . . . or frowning at Philippa. There would be some who would oppose her out of hand. She was a horsemistress, but she was still a female.

Lord Daysmith, tall and stooped, with thinning white hair, came to his feet. "What say you, Your Grace?" he asked, in the high voice of an old man. "Do you deny it?"

William looked up at him, and waved one languid hand. "Of course not, my lord," he said. His voice was almost as high in pitch as Daysmith's. "My Master Breeder and I are developing a new strain."

Another lord stood up. Philippa had to twist her head to see that it was Applewhite, a baron from Eastreach. "Why, Your Grace? What is the purpose of this new bloodline?"

William's lips curved in his crooked smile. "Why, my lord, it is exactly what Horsemistress Winter has said. We feel the time has come for a line of winged horses that will fly with men."

A stunned silence filled the Rotunda. Philippa stood very still, feeling her heart pound beneath her tabard.

And then Meredith, her brother, the youngest lord in the Council, stood. "I commend His Grace," he announced, "for looking forward and for having the courage to break with tradition."

Philippa stared at her brother. Pain laced up the back of her neck and into her skull. Her voice was tight when she said, "This has nothing to do with breaking tradition. Lord Islington is ignorant of the nature of the winged horses. Duke Francis understood it very well, as did the late Duke Frederick. Winged horses will never tolerate men as flyers, because they can't. This was not a choice made by human beings, but by whatever force created them. Duke William's interference could be the death of this foal, and perhaps many others. It's a doomed effort."

William laughed, a light, dismissive laugh. "The foal yet lives," he said. "That proves the horsemistress is mistaken."

Philippa eyed him, struck by a sudden, sickening suspicion. "How many foals have died, Your Grace?"

William's lips thinned at this, and he stiffened. He kept his eyes on her face, but he spoke loudly enough for all to hear. "We propose that Horsemistress Winter be sent down from the Academy of the Air. Horsemistress Irina Strong died at the hands of Philippa Winter a year ago, and we demand that the horsemistresses of the Academy give evidence about the enmity between the two. In fact"—he turned his head lazily toward Meredith—"we suggest that Lord Islington accept responsibility for his sister and confine her to Islington House until such time as she learns proper respect for her Duke. Perhaps this would be a good time to breed her mare, while she spends some time considering her errors."

Meredith gave Philippa a cold smile. She turned her head away, not wanting to see the triumph in his eyes. It was just what he would like, of course, and perhaps he was already in collusion with William. That it was at his sister's expense would not trouble Meredith at all. It never had. What a fool her brother was! William would turn on him without a thought if it served his purpose.

Philippa folded her arms, and squeezed her elbows tight with her fingers, trying to control her temper. "I wish the Head-mistress of the Academy were with me today. She could speak more eloquently than I on this subject. But I'm sorry to say that—" Philippa paused, horrified at the sudden stricture in her chest. She swallowed, and lifted one hand to her throat, as if the touch of her fingers might relieve the knot there. She drew a constricted breath, and her voice was rough as she said, "I'm sorry to tell you all, my lords, that Margareth Morgan, formerly Margareth Highflyer, passed away in her sleep yesterday morning. I can tell you she cared deeply about the winged horses and was appalled at this offense against the bloodlines."

As murmurs, some shocked, some sympathetic, some simply curious, sped around the Rotunda, Philippa leaned forward, placing both her hands on the genealogy. Strength seemed to radiate from it, and she felt the tightness in her throat dissolve. She thought of how calmly Margareth would have addressed the Council, how pragmatic she would have been in the face of William's counterarguments. She stood straighter, leaving her fingertips on the stamped leather covering, and waited until the presider called again for silence.

When the room quieted, Philippa drew a deliberate breath. "Duke William," she said in a loud, clear voice, "has altered his body. I don't know how, but I believe this is how he may have persuaded a winged foal to bond with him. But can it last? Will this filly be wasted because of our Duke's hubris?" She paused, tasting the heavy silence that stretched across the Rotunda. Curious eyes turned to William, and his eyes narrowed under their attention.

Lord Applewhite came to his feet. "Is this true, Your Grace?" he asked. "Have you changed your . . . have you altered yourself in some way?"

William shot Philippa a malevolent glance before he turned his face to Applewhite. Smoothly, he said, "That is a private matter, my lord."

Lord Beeth jumped up. "As a sitting Duke, Your Grace, your health and well-being are the concern of your Council."

"No, they're not," William said flatly. His eyes glittered in the light. "They are my own concern."

"But Your Grace," Applewhite pressed, "should something happen to you . . ."

Meredith stood up, also, and called, "Good for you, Duke William! It takes courage!"

Philippa laughed at that and was rewarded by a hot flush on Meredith's face. "Have a care, Philippa," he snarled, and sat down, glowering.

Lords Beeth and Applewhite still stood, staring at the Duke. After a long moment, Daysmith, too, stood up, and said, "I agree with Lord Beeth, Your Grace. The Duke's health is a matter of concern to all the Duchy."

"I am perfectly healthy," William said. Philippa saw Constance, behind him, shift a little in her chair, and her eyes found Philippa's. Something strange flickered in them, something Philippa could not decipher.

"Surely changing your body simply to fly a winged horse is unnatural, Your Grace," Applewhite said.

William's voice hardened. "I will not discuss it," he snapped. "All that needs to be said is that I have bred a winged foal, and I will fly her. Then you will see."

"And in the meantime, Duke William—"

"No more!" he roared, and Applewhite took a half step back, bumping his legs on his chair, and sat down.

Beeth and Daysmith also sat, but slowly. A speculative murmur ran through the Rotunda, until Lord Beeth put up his hand. "Let us hear the rest of Horsemistress Winter's suit."

Philippa tried to resume her argument, but there was an edge of despair in her voice. "To interfere with the bloodlines, to risk any winged horse, is a crime of high treason. Duke Francis, indeed, William's own father Duke Frederick, would have banished anyone who committed such a transgression."

William's eyes narrowed to glittering slits, but his voice was languid. "You have no right to challenge my decisions, Philippa. I am the rightful Duke of Oc."

"And I, Duke William, am a horsemistress of Oc," she responded. "We answer equally to the Lords of the Council." Though she tried to speak with authority, her voice and her words sounded hollow in her own ears.

PHILIPPA retreated to a tiny room in the rear of the Rotunda, where cloaks and boots and umbrellas were stowed, to await the

Council's deliberations. She could have gone to the ladies' reception room, but she could not have borne the avid curiosity and forced politeness she would encounter there. Instead, she paced, pleating her gloves between her fingers, feeling utterly alone. She should have asked Eduard Crisp to join her. They had not always been in agreement, but at least she and Eduard, by rights Oc's Master Breeder, were of one mind when it came to preserving and protecting the bloodlines. Eduard, like Philippa herself, had been trained by Frederick.

An hour passed, then another. Philippa went out to the privy. A maid saw her on her way back, and asked if she would like a pot of tea. She gratefully accepted, and when the maid brought her tea and a plate of decorative sandwiches, she drank the tea and ate every sandwich on the tray. The room was windowless, and she had only the vaguest idea of how much time had passed, whether the early darkness had already come on. She walked to one side of the room, hoping Pig and Herbert were staying warm. She walked back, hoping Amelia would remember to see to Sunny, as she had promised. She made another circuit, and hoped against all hope that she would not be sent to Islington House as a prisoner, riding like a chastened child beside her brother in his carriage.

She was still pacing when a knock sounded on the door of the little room. Hastily, she smoothed her tabard, and was checking her rider's knot when the door opened.

"Baron Rys!"

He bowed to her. He was modestly dressed, his hair cut short, his narrow features composed. "Mistress Winter."

"Kalla's teeth," she said, her voice tart with surprise. "You're the last person I expected to see in that doorway."

He gave her a small smile. "I should have been here sooner, but Amelia has only just found me at my lodgings."

Philippa frowned. "Amelia? Is she not—"

"She couldn't stay with me," the Baron said. "She had duties at the Academy, she told me. I believe she promised to take care of your mare."

"Ah." Philippa blew out her breath in a noisy puff. "Of course she would remember her promise. But why did she send you here, my lord?"

"Please. Call me Esmond, at least when we're alone, Philippa. We've been through too much together to stand on formality."

Philippa let her lips curve, and it was a great relief to smile, to feel that she had a friend in this dismal place. "Thank you," she said. "I do appreciate that. I think I may be in some trouble, Esmond."

"Amelia gathered that," he said.

Philippa looked at him closely. "Was she—it *was* she, then, that I saw in the balcony."

"It was. She was on her way to visit me and asked her driver to stop here. She's very perceptive, you know."

"I'm learning that about her."

"We have a small surprise for you, Philippa. I had planned it for tomorrow, but as your need is so great today, Lord Francis bestirred himself early."

"Francis!" Philippa breathed. "Is he better, then?"

In his noncommittal way, Rys shrugged. "We can say, I think, that he's no worse. Well enough to travel in a carriage, at least according to him. Come, now, let us get you out of this—this coat closet"—he made a disdainful gesture with one hand—"and go back to see what Francis may have to say to his royal brother and to the Lords of your Council."

He stood back, and held the door for Philippa to pass through. As she did, he murmured, "Your Council is unusually partisan, is it not? I find little rational argument among them."

She looked at him over her shoulder. "Politics, Esmond. A field in which I do not excel."

His smile was composed and confident. "Ah, but I do, Philippa. I have spent my life studying it."

"Bless you, then," she said with heartfelt sincerity. "I am in need of a champion."

WHEN Francis hobbled in, his face almost as white as the snow in the plaza, his eyes hollow in his thin face, Philippa could scarcely catch her breath for a moment. Surely he should not have left his bed, no matter the provocation! He leaned on a carved stick, one she remembered seeing in the umbrella stand at Fleckham House, that must have belonged to some long-ago, much older Fleckham. His pale hair was tied back with a black ribbon, accentuating the gauntness of his face. When the Council Lords saw him, they rose as one and bowed as he worked his way unsteadily down the tiered steps. One of the nurses had come with him, and stood in the aisle above with a worried expression.

William's rigid features told Philippa that no one had warned him Francis was going to appear in the Council. The presider bent to mutter an order to an aide, who dashed away to find a chair and carried it back with the help of one of the pages. It was elaborately carved, high-backed, and heavy. In fact, it was a chair to match William's, and the significance of this was not lost on the Duke. He scowled, and growled something under his breath. The Duchess shrank back in her own big chair, almost disappearing behind her fur-trimmed cloak.

The presider formally welcomed Lord Francis back to the Council after his service in Arlton. He spoke of his mission into Aeskland to save two children of Oc, and the grave wound he received there, and congratulated him upon his courage. This won a round of applause from the lords, and a much more vigorous echo from the ladies in the balcony. Philippa could understand that; Francis looked very much the pale, worn hero, leaning back in the big chair, his long, thin fingers resting on its arms. She had no doubt many a mother would be pressing her lord husband for opportunities to introduce the younger Lord Fleckham to an unwed daughter.

It was not exactly clear to Philippa what weight Francis's opinion carried with the Council Lords, but judging by William's glower, it was not inconsiderable. The presider, stumbling occasionally in his search for a polite way to state the situation, reiterated Philippa's charge against William, and his against her. Francis sat with his head lowered, his eyes on his hands, listening. He was so still, in fact, for long moments after the presider stopped speaking, that Philippa worried further about his strength.

At last he lifted his head. His dark eyes, so like William's glittered as if with a fever. He said in a clear, though slightly thin voice, "The ancestor whose name I bear would be appalled at the actions of my lord brother."

There was a hiss of indrawn breath around the tiers, and one small cry from the gallery.

William's eyes were slits of obsidian, but Francis didn't look at him. He glanced up into the circular aisle behind the tiers, where Baron Rys stood with his hands clasped behind him, watching the proceedings.

"I wondered, naturally," Francis went on, "why the Duke of Oc would disdain a mission to save two children kidnapped from a village in the Angles, or to take revenge on the barbarians who killed several citizens." He paused for breath, and Philippa bit her lip. He looked as if this effort would sap the last of his strength. The knife wound had refused to heal, and she knew the doctors worried over lingering poison in the wound. Several of the Council Lords were frowning, too, shaking their heads over Francis's weakness.

"Now," Francis went on, "I'm afraid I understand. Please forgive me, my lords, if I do not speak at length. It's true I was wounded, through my own foolishness, and I am not yet myself. But I felt compelled to tell you . . ." Again he paused, and breathed. "To tell you that my lord brother is obsessed with the winged horses to the exclusion of his rightful duties."

He let his head drop against the carved head of the chair, and his eyelids drooped.

"Theatrics!" William snapped. "How dare you? Did you not *sell* one of our winged horses, our birthright, to the Klee?" Murmurs ran around the Rotunda at this accusation. Heads leaned together, and gestures were made from one tier to another. Philippa sat very still. There was more she could say, of course. There was the incident with the oc-hound, and with Black Seraph . . . and there was the issue, the mystery, really, of the Lady Pamella. But Francis knew all of these things, and so did Rys. They would know, better than she, how much was relevant to this dispute, and how much was better, for all concerned, to keep private.

As if he had read her thoughts, the Klee Baron left the circular aisle and stepped down through the tiers, nodding to the lords as he passed them. When he reached the dais, he stopped in front of William and bowed.

William, at the sight of him, shot to his feet, his face suffused with angry color. A pulse beat visibly in his throat, and his voice grew shrill. "Rys!" he cried. "Who gave you leave to be present at Oc's Council?"

Baron Rys, with icy composure, bowed again, this time to all the Council. "My lords," he called. Silence fell, and curious glances came to rest upon him. Francis opened his eyes but did not lift his head. "I am Esmond Rys, Baron of Klee, younger brother of Viscount Richard of Klee."

Nods of recognition met this announcement. Rys allowed a small smile to curve his lips. "I acknowledge the uneasy relationship between our two lands and the reasons for it," he said in a level tone. "But Lord Francis and I, who served together at the Palace in Isamar, share a commitment to peace and the free flow of commerce between our peoples. We were one land at one time, after all."

"Commerce?" shrilled William. "You are mercenaries! Your ship and your soldiers—we know what you are!"

An embarrassed silence fell over the assembly. William threw himself back into his chair, and Philippa thought that perhaps even he knew he had gone too far.

By contrast, Rys's refined voice seemed all the more elegant. "Lord Francis risked his own safety to take action after the brutal attack on one of your villages. He needed our help, and my daughter has longed to be a horsemistress since she was tiny. She and I know this means she will be a citizen of Oc, and not of Klee. But she, Lord Francis, and I—and Horsemistress Winter—believe this exchange will strengthen the goodwill growing between our two principalities."

He bowed again, first to the Duke, then to Francis, and finally to the Council Lords. He climbed back up through the tiers, his slender figure straight and dignified.

Francis, leaning on the arms of his chair, forced his body upright once again. "This foal," he said in a trembling voice, "this winged filly William has turned to his own purposes—this filly should have been bonded to Amelia Rys. Horsemistress Winter is right. My lord brother has committed treason, and his Master Breeder should be accused with him."

A storm of shouts erupted through the Rotunda. Francis sank back into his chair, his eyes flicking once to Philippa, then closing. Through the tumult, she leaned close to the presider and begged him to send for Francis's carriage, to send him home. The presider, without asking the Duke's permission, gave the order. Then he proceeded to bang his gavel on its sounding block, over and over, without success.

Philippa saw that beyond the tall windows, darkness shrouded the White City. There would be no decision of the Council today, she felt certain. She rose, nodding to the presider. Helplessly, he shrugged, and bowed his permission for her to leave.

William glared at her as if he would happily strike her dead with his own hand. "I'm going to have you sent down," he grated. "And put away where you can no longer harm us. You have brought your own destruction on your head."

"I don't believe you have the power," she said through tight lips.

"I tell you, Philippa, you can't defy me this way."

"Stop posturing, William. I have already done so."

As she turned, her back rigid with fury, to climb up past the lords to the doors, she saw that Constance, the wan Duchess, watched her with an avid, almost greedy expression. As Philippa gathered her cloak and hat and gloves, she wondered upon which side of this great gulf Constance stood.

THIRTY-THREE

LARK spent the day cleaning tack, brushing Tup, changing the straw in the stall, even lending Erna a hand trundling barrows full of muck out of the stables. At every opportunity, she put her head out to watch for Mistress Winter. When evening came, the girls trailed across the courtyard to the Hall, their noses and cheeks pink with cold. Lark, reluctantly, went with them. The sky above them was clear and moonless, the stars like crystal flames in the blackness. Lark took one last, longing look toward the road before she went in through the big doors.

She sat down for supper with Hester on one side and Amelia on the other. As the soup was served, Hester leaned forward. "Amelia, where did you go today? I saw you climb into the hack."

Lark thought there was a slight edge to Hester's voice, but Amelia said only, "My father is in Osham," as if she hadn't noticed.

"So you went to visit him? Is that all?"

Even Lark could tell that Amelia managed to skirt the question. "He's leaving for home tomorrow. For Klee. I don't expect to see him for some time."

Lark frowned down into her bowl. She felt Hester's elbow in her side, and she knew Hester was wondering the same thing she was. She felt torn between loyalty to Hester and concern for Amelia—she was supposed to be, after all, her sponsor. But if Amelia persisted in hiding things from her . . .

Hester, with her usual directness, leaned past Lark again, and said, "Amelia, we flyers need each other. We have to trust each other."

Lark kept her head down, but she looked sideways to watch Amelia's reaction. The Klee girl hesitated for a long moment, almost too long, then she looked up at Hester. "I know, Hester," she said quietly.

"Morning," Hester corrected.

Amelia smiled. "Yes. Sorry. Morning." The smile faded, and she toyed with her soup spoon. "I have been schooled in diplomacy," she said slowly. "Since I was tiny, in truth. I was taught never to reveal anything you don't have to."

Lark touched her hand, and Amelia laid down the spoon. "I know you mean well, both of you," she said. "And I would like nothing more than to forget all of that, simply be one of you, one of the Academy students. A flyer."

"You will be," Lark said.

Amelia's eyes lifted to hers, and Lark was stunned to see that they glistened with tears. "He took my foal," Amelia said in a broken voice.

Hester said, "What?" but Lark put up her hand and hoped Hester would understand.

Amelia said, "She should have been mine, my filly, my bondmate . . . he took her, and I have to go on waiting, pretending . . ."

"It's true," Lark said, in an undertone to Hester. "I saw her. Today, the Council Lords are considering—"

"I know about that," Hester said impatiently. Amelia looked up at her, startled. Hester gave a short, subdued laugh. "You're not the only one who was brought up to diplomacy, Amelia. My father is Lord Beeth, of the Council, and everything that happens in our world has at least two meanings, sometimes three."

Amelia brought her napkin to her eyes, then to her nose, sniffling. "Sometimes," she said, "I get so tired of all of that, of trusting no one . . ."

"Then you see," Hester said firmly. "We have to depend on each other. Because otherwise we become pawns in their game. My mamá says—"

Lark interrupted to murmur to Amelia, "Hester's mamá is the most brilliant mother in the world. And very kind to boot."

Hester nodded. "She is indeed. And she says, now that I am to be a horsemistress, I must be above politics. And you, too, Amelia. You must be above politics, as much as you can."

Amelia dropped her eyes. Lark watched as two tears dripped down her cheeks and splashed into her empty bowl. At last, the Klee girl said, "I'll try, Morning. I will. It's hard."

"No, it's easy," Hester said, flashing her characteristic grin. "By comparison, anyway. You'll find out it's the Graces that are hard."

LARK invented more tasks to do in the stables so she could watch for Mistress Winter's return. The other girls, including Amelia and Hester, settled their horses for the night and crunched across the icy courtyard to go to bed, but Lark dallied. The night was bitterly cold, the stars reflecting in the frozen snow. Erna was in the tack room, keeping the close stove hot, and the Beeth watchman shivered and shifted from foot to foot outside the stables, finally moving as close to the tack-room door as he could for its warmth. Bramble, almost fully recovered now, tagged at Lark's heels as she raked the sawdust of the aisle and made unnecessary adjustments to Tup's blanket. She went to check on Winter Sunset, but Amelia had left the mare and her stall in perfect order.

She had almost decided that Mistress Winter was going to spend the night in Osham when she heard the clop-clop of Pig's hooves turning in from the main road and plodding down the lane. Lark dashed out into the courtyard.

Mistress Winter untangled herself from the heavy blankets wrapped around her legs and climbed rather awkwardly down from the gig. Herbert nodded to Lark and clucked to Pig. Lark managed to pat the pony and whisper a greeting in his ear before Herbert flicked the reins, and Pig pulled the gig on around the corner toward the back of the stables.

"Larkyn," Mistress Winter said. "You should be in bed."

"I couldn't sleep," Lark said. "Not knowing what happened."

"Well. I have no answers for you, so you might as well be off."

Lark groaned. "More waiting? At least tell me what happened, please, Mistress! I've been dancing on pins all day."

Mistress Winter sighed. "Have you seen Sunny?"

"Yes, a dozen times, I promise you! But I've been so worried."

"You're not a child, Larkyn. You must try to practice patience." Mistress Winter turned toward the Domicile. "But you can come along with me. No one will be in the Hall, but we'll go to the small kitchen and get Matron to make us a cup of tea."

Matron, they found, had also been watching for Mistress Winter's return. By the time they had shed their coats and hats and gloves and walked to the small kitchen, the kettle was singing on the five-plate stove Matron used for making late-night tea or predawn breakfasts, as she sometimes needed to. She set the table with cups and saucers, a dish of cream, and a small plate of the flat white biscuits the girls sometimes had for dessert at supper. Mistress Winter frowned at the biscuits, but Lark said, "What a good idea, Matron. Mistress Winter is thin as a cottonwood at Erdlin!"

She was rewarded by a slight quirk of Mistress Winter's thin lips and a chuckle from Matron. Lark pushed the biscuits closer to Mistress Winter, and she took one. "You're probably right, Larkyn. I doubt Sunny will notice the weight of one or two biscuits," she said. As she nibbled at it and took a sip of Matron's clear tea, her stiff spine seemed to relax and the tension around her eyes and mouth to release. She sighed. "It's been a long day," she said.

"A bad day?" Lark asked.

"Hard," Mistress Winter said shortly. She sighed again and rubbed her eyes. "Kalla's heels, I don't know how they stand it."

"Stand what?" Lark asked.

"Politics. Diplomacy. All that wrangling. What does it accomplish, after all?"

"Government?" Matron suggested.

Mistress Winter gave her usual snort, making Lark smile. "Government," Mistress Winter said sourly. "Governing gets done, I suppose. But the weaker the leadership . . ." She stopped, and looked around at Matron, apparently wondering whether she was going too far.

Matron said, "Aye, Mistress. The weaker the leadership, the more the argument. We've seen it before, haven't we?"

"Well, Matron, not I. All of my service was under Duke Frederick, and it seemed to me then—but perhaps I was young and naive—it seemed that everything ran like clockwork, issues before the Council, debate by their lordships, decisions handed down."

"Ah," Matron said. She brought her own cup to the table and sat down next to Lark, reaching for one of the biscuits. "But before His Grace's day—His old Grace, that is—I heard stories of endless disputes among the Council Lords, threats, promises, bribes, and payoffs."

"Did you, Matron?" Mistress Winter pressed her hands against her eyes. They were reddened, their lids irritated and rough as if she had been rubbing them all day. "I didn't know any of that. I was too young, I suppose, and not yet bonded."

"Oh, aye, you could ask Mistress Morgan—" Matron broke off suddenly and put a hand to her breast. "Oh, by the entwined gods, I had forgotten for a short time. We can never ask Mistress Morgan again."

Lark was appalled to see tears well up in Mistress Winter's eyes. "No," she said in a shaking voice. "No, we can't ask Margareth. The burden is all ours now."

"So," Matron said, pouring more tea into Mistress Winter's cup, "now you will be Headmistress, I suppose."

"I'm not sure about that," Mistress Winter said. Both Lark and Matron stared at her, waiting for more, but there was nothing. She said only, "I made my case, as best I could, against Duke William. The Council has not yet decided."

"But, Mistress Winter," Lark began. "Did you tell them about the foal . . . about what he did? What he's doing?"

"I did, Larkyn," Mistress Winter said wearily. "The Council is . . . well. There are some who think the Duke is right, and that men should be able to fly winged horses."

"They can't!" Lark said. "It won't work!"

"I don't believe it will, either. But the Duke has had some success with this filly—" She broke off and stared at the glow of the stove.

"But who will be Headmistress if not you?" Matron asked quietly.

Mistress Winter hesitated, opened her mouth to speak, then closed it again. Lark thought there must be more to tell, but she looked so miserable, and so exhausted, that she did not press her. Matron seemed to understand it, too.

"Come," she said to her, taking Mistress Winter's cup and the nearly untouched plate of biscuits away. "You need to sleep. It will all look better in the morning."

Mistress Winter looked doubtful about that, but she rose, said a subdued good night, and left the kitchen. Lark heard her trudging steps up the stairs to her apartment.

Lark thanked Matron for the tea and went out of the Domicile into the freezing night. She hurried past the Hall to the Dormitory, her teeth chattering as she slipped and slid on the frozen cobblestones. She pulled off her tabard and divided skirt and let them drop to the floor. She pulled her nightdress over her head, shivering mightily, and crawled into her cot. The sheets felt icy and stiff. It was a long time before they warmed enough for her to stop shivering and sink into an uneasy sleep.

PHILIPPA walked to the high table at breakfast, aware that conversation among the horsemistresses stopped as she approached. She set her jaw and took her usual chair, meeting no one's eyes, determined simply to drink her coffee, eat as much as she could manage, then go to the stables. Margareth's empty chair sat like a cold reminder that her body still waited in its coffin to be taken to its resting place. Suzanne had sent notices to the Morgan family estate in Eastreach, and they were waiting to discover what the family's wishes were. Philippa thought she would take Margareth herself, if the family wanted to bury her at home. She couldn't bear the idea of her going off in the caisson alone.

Kathryn Dancer came in a little late and sat next to Philippa. She took a thin slice of toasted bread and spread a bit of butter on it, then startled Philippa by holding it out to her. "Philippa," the younger horsemistress said. "Please eat something."

"I—" Philippa began, then realized Kathryn was right. There was nothing on her plate, not even coffee in her cup. "Oh." She accepted the toast. "Thank you. I'm so distracted."

"I know. I hear it was a terrible day yesterday."

"Matron must have told you."

Now all the instructors turned to Philippa, their faces alive with curiosity. One of the juniors, a young woman only just returned from her post in the Angles, leaned forward. "What happened?" she asked. "They're saying the Duke wants you sent down!"

A shocked silence and averted eyes followed this pronouncement, and the young woman blushed furiously. She muttered an apology, and Suzanne Star said firmly, "Let Philippa have her breakfast. If there is important news, we'll know soon enough."

Philippa cast her a grateful glance. She ate the piece of toast, and someone filled her cup with coffee. The kindness made her eyes swim again, and she pinched herself through her skirt to bring herself back under control. Idiot, she told herself. Like a first-level girl with homesickness!

She forced herself to eat a bit of bacon and was just finishing her coffee when Amelia Rys came into the dining hall, passed the long tables where the students sat, and approached the high table. She nodded to the horsemistresses, and addressed Philippa.

"Mistress Winter, I hope you'll forgive the interruption," she said. "My father is here, and would like to speak with you when you've finished your meal."

Philippa set her cup down, and stood. "I'm finished," she said. "Where is he?"

"He's waiting in the foyer."

"Thank you, Amelia."

Philippa stepped down from the high table and walked across the dining hall, being careful not to hurry. She felt every eye on her back, and it was a relief to go out into the foyer, where she found Baron Rys standing beneath one of the horse portraits. It was her favorite, a painting of the long-legged, broad-winged sorrel thought to be the founder of the Noble bloodline. Rys was standing with his hands clasped behind his back, looking up at it. Philippa walked up to stand beside him. "That's Redbird," she said quietly. "Ancestor to my own Winter Sunset."

Rys turned to her, and bowed. "He was beautiful," he said. "As your mare is."

Philippa gestured toward the Headmistress's office. "We can talk there," she said. He nodded and followed her. She pushed open the door and found the room cold and dark. With Margareth gone, she supposed no one had thought to light the fire. She hurried to light a lamp on the desk and pull the curtains to let in the weak winter sunshine. "It's so cold in here," she said. "Shall I order a fire?"

"Please don't trouble anyone," he said. "My carriage is waiting in the courtyard. I only came to tell you the news before I set out for the port."

She stiffened her spine. "Are they going to send me down, Esmond?"

"No decision has been made, Philippa. I'm sorry."

A rush of anxiety made her tremble. She swallowed, and turned to the window to hide her weakness. The blue and white landscape seemed to reproach her with its purity, the exultant quality of sunshine on snow. When she could trust her voice, she asked, "What happened?"

"The Council is at an impasse. Francis's testimony was crucial, because there are those who think Duke William is within his rights to alter the bloodlines—and himself, apparently. Francis influenced a good number who weren't certain."

"So we go on waiting."

"I'm afraid so. But I thought you should know."

"I do appreciate it," she said. She turned back from the window, composing her face carefully. "Is Francis all right?"

He shook his head. "I've seen wounds like that before. He should have recovered by now. The doctors don't know how to treat it."

"I'll go to see him soon."

"I know he'll be glad of that. Please let me know of any change."

"Of course I will."

As they walked together back toward the foyer, she said in an undertone, "I'm terribly sorry about this foal. It should have been Amelia's."

"She's heartbroken," he said flatly. The maid came forward with his coat and hat, and he put them on. "But I suppose there will be another foal."

"I will see to it," Philippa said grimly. "Surely whoever becomes Headmistress will understand that we've promised to bond Amelia, and we must keep our word."

"Everyone seems to have assumed you would be the next Headmistress," Rys said.

"Yes, I think they did," she answered. The maid opened the door and curtsied to the Baron as they passed through. Philippa squinted in the sudden glare. "But if the Duke opposes me, it won't happen. I'm not particularly well liked, I'm afraid. Too sharp of tongue."

Rys chuckled. His carriage was waiting at the bottom of the steps. A footman jumped down and held the door for him, but he stood a moment longer, staring across at the Dormitory, where some of the students were just coming out, dressed to fly. "My daughter tells me," he said, in a deceptively light tone, "that the students admire you."

Philippa cast him a sidelong glance. "Indeed?" she said. "That would surprise me."

"I've learned to trust Amelia's judgment."

"She's a remarkable girl."

A faint color tinged the Baron's cheeks. "She is, Philippa. Watch over her, will you? Sometimes she seems far too old for her years. It was our life . . . constantly on guard against mistakes, gossip, a misplaced word."

"I understand that."

Rys smiled at her then and bowed. She nodded to him and watched as he went down the steps and climbed up into the carriage.

As the pair of horses trotted swiftly out of the courtyard, Amelia came out of the Dormitory and stood alone, watching her father depart.

THIRTY-FOUR

FRANCIS lay in his childhood bedroom at Fleckham House, in the ancient post bed he had slept in since he was a small boy. The exertions of the day before had left him so weak that the short-tempered housekeeper, Paulina, had had to call for the day nurse to come and assist in carrying him up the staircase. It was humiliating, but then, there had been a string of humiliations since the foray into Aeskland.

Rys had tried to convince him that his knife wound could hardly be considered his own fault, but Francis, reliving it a thousand times in his mind, knew he had been impulsive, reckless. He remembered the warning, "Have a care, my lord," from the Klee captain, remembered it as clearly as if he had heard it only moments ago. Why had he not heeded it then? Why had he turned his back to that woman? He had stretched out his arm to the child from Onmarin, leaving himself unprotected, needlessly vulnerable.

And now he lay here, helpless as an infant.

The doctors mumbled together in the corridor when they thought he couldn't hear them, wondering why he had not yet recovered, speculating about poisons, proposing wild treatments, then rejecting them. Francis wished he could help them, but despite all the books he had read, including medical texts, he knew of nothing else they could try. The pain of the wound had lessened to a dull, persistent ache, but the lethargy and weakness remained.

He gazed out at the clear, cold, winter day, and waited to see whether he would live or die. He wanted to recover, to reclaim his life. But sometimes, especially when he woke in the small hours, he thought that it would be better to die than to live out his days as a useless invalid.

When he heard horses in the courtyard, he pulled himself up against his pillows and laid the book he had been halfheartedly reading on the bedside table. He hoped it was Philippa, though he had not caught sight of Winter Sunset making her descent over the park. It couldn't be Rys. He had sailed for Klee. Francis leaned forward from his stack of pillows, but he couldn't see the horse or its rider. He heard the tall front doors open and close, and the steward speaking with someone. It sounded like a woman's voice, so perhaps it was Philippa after all.

Francis put his feet over the side of the bed and straightened his dressing gown. He grasped the bedrail and pushed himself to his feet. He could at least sit up to receive a visitor. As the footsteps ascended the stairs, he lowered himself, with a groan of effort, into the chair beside the bed.

The door slammed open, banging against the wall with a force that made the water glass on the bedside table jump.

William stood in the doorway, one hand on the jamb, the other holding a quirt. Deep creases marked his eyes and his mouth. "Damn you, Francis," he said. His voice had grown so high that even in anger, it sounded feminine. "Have you not the slightest shred of family loyalty?"

Francis stared at his elder brother in amazement. William wore a vest so covered with embroidery it was hard to tell what fabric it was. His cheeks and chin were smooth as a girl's, and there was something odd about the shape of his hips in his close-cut trousers. "William," Francis said, ignoring the question. "Is it true? What Philippa said?"

His older brother stamped into the room and threw the door shut behind him. "Damn her, too, and all those women!" he shrilled. "It's my business and no one else's!"

"How did you do it?" Francis asked weakly. He fought an

urge to laugh. Laughing at William, when he was in a temper, was never a good idea.

William ignored the question. He stalked across the room, slapping the quirt against his thigh. "You betrayed me in my own Council—"

"*Your* Council, William? I hardly think—"

"You sat there, all wan and heroic, pretending to be so noble! You took her part, that bitch Philippa Winter, you supported her instead of your own brother, your *duke*, and you did your best to make me look like a fool!"

"I did not, William. You're managing that very well on your own."

William's face suffused, and he gripped the quirt in his fist. "You're jealous!" he said. "You covet the title, don't you? This was your revenge."

"Oh, give over," Francis said tiredly. "I've never wanted to be duke, and you know it."

"Liar!" William snapped.

Francis tipped his head back against the chair. "You've disgraced us, William. It's no longer an honor to be a Fleckham."

"Just wait. When a whole new generation of winged horses carry men into the sky, I'm the one who'll be remembered as a hero. Unlike you, getting yourself stabbed by a barbarian, and a woman at that!"

The barb found its mark. Francis dropped his eyes.

William leaped on his advantage like a hound on a hare. "What did you think, that you could go straight from your books to a war? It's a wonder the woman didn't kill you outright!"

"You're right," Francis said. "It is a wonder. And a little girl defended me, a little girl who had been beaten and abused and dragged all over Aeskland for weeks because you couldn't be troubled to go after her."

"Father was always ashamed of you," William sneered. "His womanish son."

At this, Francis couldn't help laughing, though it was a weak, breathy sound. "You're calling *me* womanish?" He took a quick breath, wincing at the pain in his back. "Your bosom swells more than Philippa's."

"It's a side effect, nothing more. I'm still a man."

"But you sound like a twelve-year-old boy."

William swiped irritably at the bedpost with his quirt. "Mind your tongue, brother, or I swear I'll whip you like a dog."

"Ah," Francis said, truly breathless now, and feeling rather faint. "I've heard how you like that. Two dead girls, is it? Or more? Perhaps I should have revealed that to your Council!"

With a cry, William lunged at him, and struck him full across the face with the quirt.

He pulled his arm back to do it again, but Francis put up a hand, and when the quirt fell, he seized it, and pulled. William yanked back, hard, and Francis's brief strength gave out. He fell from his chair, his shoulder crashing against the bedside table so that the glass and carafe went spinning to the oak floor, smashing into a dozen pieces, drenching Francis's dressing gown, and spattering William's boots.

A knock sounded immediately on the door, and the nurse put her head in. "Are you all right, my lord?" she asked, and then saw Francis sprawled on the floor. "Oh, my lord!" she said, starting toward him.

William waved her off. "An accident," he said smoothly. "I'll help my brother back to bed myself. Fetch him a fresh dressing gown, though. This one is soaked."

He bent, and lifted Francis bodily from the floor with hands that were surprisingly gentle, as if his anger had spent itself all at once. He stripped the wet dressing gown off, dropped it to the floor, and pulled back the blankets of the bed. "Really, Francis, you must be more careful," he said. "It's disturbing to see how weak you are."

Francis slipped his legs under the sheets, suppressing a groan at the pain the movement gave him. He lay back on the pillows, staring at his brother. "William," he said. "Are you mad?"

"No, no," William answered. He gave Francis the old crooked smile that had once been appealing in a young man's face. "If I were mad, I would stop you from ever telling anyone anything again." He bent over Francis, and Francis could not help but flinch away. William smiled again, and touched Francis's cheek, where the stripe from the quirt stung. "I could certainly do that. But it would not be good for the Duchy, would it? You are all the heir I have."

"William," Francis said faintly. "You must stop this—whatever you're doing to your body. You're not yourself."

"I'm not going to stop," William said. "I'm going to fly. I have a beautiful silver filly in my private stable, just there." He pointed to the window with the quirt, in the direction of the beech grove. "She's mine, Francis. Bonded to me."

"Father would be revolted," Francis whispered, "at the waste of a winged horse."

William scowled. "She won't be wasted, I promise you," he said icily. "And perhaps Father would have noticed a son who could fly."

"So," Francis said, "the jealousy is yours, isn't it? You could never forgive him."

"All he cared about were the winged horses," William said. "And the women who fly them, of course."

Francis couldn't bring himself to laugh. His brother was a cruel and selfish man, but he had never been a stupid one. As William left him, and clattered down the stairs, Francis reflected that it was a measure of how far gone William's mind was that he couldn't see the irony himself.

WILLIAM rode down the lane from Fleckham House, but turned to the left at the road to go to the small stable, where she waited for him. He slid down from the saddle, and Jinson came out to take the gelding's reins. William walked slowly as he went in through the tack-room door, savoring the anticipation of seeing her again.

He paused just outside the box stall. The mare eyed him with only casual interest. The oc-hound jumped to his feet, stiff-legged and growling. But the filly—his filly—trotted forward, her ears pricked, her delicate nostrils flaring at his familiar scent. William opened the gate and let the foal butt her head against him. He rubbed her pale, stubby mane, and ran his fingers over the faint dapples on her silvery back. Every inch of her gleamed in the winter sunlight. His own nostrils flared, tasting her fresh, oaty smell. He still felt surprise at how pleasant it was to touch her, and to feel her velvet lips nuzzle his palm, looking for treats. In the past, he had only cared about how fast a horse could carry him. He had never expected actually to like the little creature.

The oc-hound stalked past him, tail stiff, lip curled. William kicked at him, and the dog snarled, but ran off down the aisle to Jinson, who had just come in from the tack room. Jinson stroked the dog, then straightened. "Can't you get a different dog for her?" William said testily. "I don't like that one."

"There's a bond between the winged horses and the oc-hounds, my lord," Jinson said with irritating sincerity. "We're pressing our luck as it is."

William was tempted to order him, but the warmth of the filly pressing against his hip distracted him. He cradled her delicate cheek in his hand. "All right, little one," he said indulgently. "If you like him, I won't make him leave."

Jinson kept his distance, but he said, "She's growing fast, m'lord. I think we could start her on some mash."

"She's still suckling, though?"

"Aye, but the winged horses mature earlier than wingless ones. She could use more."

"Good, Jinson. See to it."

"Aye, m'lord."

"When will she fly?" William asked, still stroking the satiny hide.

"Well, m'lord—the horsemistresses say—"

William raised his head. "You're my Master Breeder," he said in a silky tone. Jinson, it seemed, understood that voice. He took a half step backward. "I don't want to hear what they do. I want to know what I can do."

Jinson cleared his throat and looked miserably unhappy. William teased the filly's forelock with his fingertips. "Well," Jinson said. "They—that is, I understand that winged horses fly at about twelve months. Then they begin to carry saddles, and sand weights to gain strength. They don't carry the girls—that is, riders—until they're about eighteen months."

"It seems a long wait."

"Aye, m'lord, but you don't want to injure your filly."

William raised his head again and fixed Jinson with a hard gaze. The man dropped his eyes to his boots, and William chuckled. "No, no, Jinson, you're right, as it happens. I don't want to injure her." He stroked her once more, and then stepped back, out of the stall. "She's perfect," he mused, looking down at her. "My little jewel."

"Aye."

"Diamond," William said.

"Beg pardon?"

"Diamond. Her name is Diamond. A single name, like the founders of the other bloodlines."

"Beautiful, m'lord. It's perfect."

"Indeed. As she is." William shut the half-gate, and nodded to Jinson. "You can let the damned dog back in now."

THIRTY-FIVE

PHILIPPA received a tersely worded invitation to Islington House for the Erdlin holiday, but she dropped it into the grate the moment she read it and crouched beside the fire to watch the card with her family's crest go up in smoke. She had received, and accepted, a more rustic invitation. It had come, in fact, with the mail coach, a carefully lettered note from Deeping Farm, the Uplands. The invitation was from all the Hamleys, inscribed on plain paper, but Philippa felt certain the hand was Brye's. She hesitated only a moment before scrawling her acceptance on a piece of the thick stationery stamped with the wings of the Academy, then she put the note into her bureau drawer, under a pile of handkerchiefs.

At luncheon that day she felt Larkyn's gaze following her. As she went out of the dining hall, the girl was waiting for her beneath the portrait of Seraph. Larkyn's dark curls were almost exactly the color the artist had chosen for Seraph's mane and tail.

Philippa stopped beside the portrait and raised her eyebrows at Larkyn. "Did you wish to ask me something?"

Larkyn's cheeks flamed. "I—I thought you might have—"

"Ah. You know, then, of the kind invitation I received from Willakeep today."

The girl was practically bouncing on her toes. "Was it—I mean, Brye asked if you would mind—we just thought, after all that happened—"

"Indeed," Philippa said. "There are no secrets here, it seems." Larkyn blushed harder.

"But you're right. It would be awkward in the extreme for me to go to Islington House. I prefer spending the holiday here, at the Academy, enjoying the solitude."

Larkyn's face fell. "Oh. Oh, aye. Of course."

Philippa relented and allowed her stern expression to soften. "Larkyn," she said. "It is the nicest invitation I have received in years. I've already written your brothers to say that it will be a great pleasure for me to spend the Erdlin holiday at Deeping Farm."

The joy that lighted Larkyn's face gave Philippa's heart a twinge of something like pain. "Oh, Mistress Winter! Lovely fine, that is! And we can fly there—together!"

"Indeed," Philippa said, composing herself. She couldn't think what it was in this child that confused her feelings so. "Indeed we can. I look forward to it." She drew her gloves from her belt and her cap. "And now. You have a flight, I believe."

"Aye." Larkyn spun about in a swirl of skirt and coat, and dashed out of the Hall. Philippa, smoothing her cap onto her hair, followed more slowly, but a smile clung to her lips, and it felt good. She would put aside her cares for a time, sleep under the Hamleys' venerable roof, eat good farm cooking. She couldn't think of a better way to spend the holiday.

THEY were fortunate in the weather. Two days before the holiday began, a dusting of snow fell in the early morning, but the sky cleared by afternoon and stayed that way. Lark and Mistress Winter, who had the longest flight to make, would depart first, while the rest of the students and instructors were still preparing. Amelia was off to Arlton to spend the festival with her father at Prince Nicolas's court. Hester and Anabel and the other second-level girls had to ride home in carriages and phaetons, their horses trotting behind. Only Lark, of her class, was allowed to fly, since Mistress Winter was going with her.

They led their horses outside, and Mistress Winter asked

Lark to keep Sunny's rein for a moment while she conferred one more time with Mistress Star. Lark stood in the chilly sunshine, feeling buoyant with anticipation at seeing her family, her goats, her cows, and her own homely bedroom once again. Little Molly bleated from the stable, making her feel just a bit guilty, but Herbert had promised to look out for her. And Bramble, of course, would keep her company.

"Very odd, if you ask me," came a voice behind Lark.

She turned to find Petra Sweet in the stable doorway, leaning against the jamb. "I didn't ask," Lark said.

Petra straightened and came out into the sunshine. Her boots squeaked on the thin layer of snow. "People are talking," she said, pursing her thin lips. "Wondering why a horsemistress— the assistant Headmistress, no less—should want to spend Erdlin at a goat farm?"

Lark turned her back on Petra and stroked Sunny's mane. It glowed scarlet in the sunshine, brushed to a silken sheen by Amelia just this morning.

"It's just strange," Petra said, coming closer. "Especially since I've heard that she's leaving the Academy. Sent down by Duke William because she killed Mistress Strong."

Lark whirled, and stamped her foot. "You don't know anything about it," she said. "Mistress Strong attacked Mistress Winter, because . . ." She stopped, remembering. She had promised never to speak of it.

"Yes?" Petra said. "Because?"

"Mind your own business, Sweet."

Petra's mouth tightened more, until her pinched face looked something like a dried apple. "Listen to me, Goat-girl," she said. She stepped very close to Lark, her chin thrust out. "You've brought nothing but grief to the Academy. I blame you for what's happened to Mistress Winter. First the crossbred colt, then you won't use a saddle—"

"I use a saddle now," Lark protested.

"You're just trouble, Black. None of this would have happened without you!"

Lark's throat closed, and her delight in the day evaporated. Tup, sensing her mood, whimpered, and Petra said scornfully, "That crybaby of yours! Can't you *do* something about that noise?"

Before Lark could even think of how to answer, Tup threw his head up, stretched his neck toward Petra, and bared his teeth a hand's breadth from her face. She jerked backward, almost losing her footing on the slippery cobblestones. Lark whispered, "Tup! No!"

Petra recovered her balance and stood with her hands on her hips, two spots of red flaming in her cheeks. "Black! Your mongrel horse tried to bite me!"

"He wouldn't have bitten you," Lark said. Her cheeks, too, were burning, and she struggled to control her temper. "But he's sensitive—"

"He's spoiled rotten!" Petra spat. "And when we have a new Headmistress, I'll make it very clear—or *His Grace* will—that the two of you need a strong hand!"

Lark drew a steadying breath. She kept her eyes on Tup as she spoke, in as steady a voice as she could manage. "Take a word of advice from the goat-girl, Sweet. Watch out for the Duke. Keep your blinkers open around him."

"What? How dare you speak of the Duke that way?"

"Just remember what I said. I know you don't like me, nor I you, but I don't want to see you end up . . . well. End up in trouble." She lifted her eyes now, and they met Petra's curious ones. "You're to be a horsemistress, and nothing should interfere with that."

Petra tipped her head to one side, considering Lark for a long moment. "You're serious," she finally said.

"Aye. I'm serious." Lark saw that the doors of the Hall had opened, and Mistress Winter, in her heavy winter flying coat and thickest gloves, was coming across the courtyard. "I know more than I ever cared to know about the Duke," Lark said in an undertone. "Believe me, for your own sake."

Petra gave a hoot of laughter. "As if I need advice from a country bumpkin!"

"Mayhap you don't," Lark said. "But now you're off my conscience."

Mistress Winter came up and took Sunny's reins. "Ready, Larkyn?"

"Yes, Mistress."

"Good. Let's go while the weather is good." Mistress Winter, with the nimbleness of a girl half her age, leaped into her saddle.

Lark mounted, too, and picked up her reins. Both horses stamped their feet, blowing, rustling their wings with eagerness to be aloft.

"Good Erdlin, Petra," Mistress Winter said.

"And to you, Mistress," Petra said.

Lark opened her mouth to offer the same courtesy, but Petra turned her back and disappeared inside the stable before she could speak. Tup shook his bridle and danced sideways, making Lark laugh. As she followed Mistress Winter into the flight paddock, and they began their canter into the wind, she forgot all about Petra Sweet and her gibes. In moments, the two horses spread their wings and launched into the brilliant blue sky, leaving the ground and its worries behind them. Lark gave Tup his head, and he surged past Winter Sunset, leading the way. Lark glanced quickly over her shoulder to see if Mistress Winter minded, but she had given Sunny her head, too, and one of her rare smiles played across her face. With a shiver of happiness, Lark turned her face toward the hills, and home.

PHILIPPA watched Seraph and Larkyn as they soared past her. The girl's seat was so much improved, she could hardly credit it. When Larkyn had managed to deceive everyone at her first Ribbon Day by flying with only a handgrip and no saddle at all, Philippa had despaired of her ever accepting the necessity of the flying saddle, but it seemed now that this, at least, she no longer need worry about. Seraph was small and neat of body, his neck muscled, his tail arched and streaming in the wind. His wings, though narrow, were strong and steady.

But what set the pair apart was not just that Larkyn's spine was erect and flexible, or that Seraph's hoof tuck was picture-perfect. It was the delight they had in flight, the accord in their movements, the evident trust each placed in the other. With a swell of emotion, Philippa put her gloved hand on Sunny's neck, feeling the heat of her body through the layers of wool and leather, the power of her wingbeats rippling up from the great muscles of her chest. They had worked together, she and Winter Sunset, for more than twenty years. They had suffered, and fought, and monitored young flyers. It was hard to think that Larkyn and Seraph might have to meet the same challenges, suffer the same tragedies, as she and Sunny had done; but they were strong enough, she felt certain, to deal with whatever their career might bring them.

She lifted her face into the sunshine, and though the cold wind brought tears to her eyes, she savored every wingbeat as her bondmate carried her on toward the Uplands.

THE last time Philippa had been at Deeping Farm she had arrived in Lady Beeth's carriage on a rainy spring day, her head and heart aching with fear for both Larkyn and Black Seraph. How lovely it was now to soar above the tiny hamlet of Willa-keep, to circle the slate roofs and slumbering winter fields of Deeping Farm, to come to ground in the snow-softened lane and canter into the barnyard to be welcomed by a chorus of cackling hens, the bleating of brown goats, and Brye Hamley's tall figure. Brye swept Larkyn into an embrace, then stepped forward to bow. "Philippa," he said in his deep voice.

She nodded to him. "Hello, Brye." She knew Larkyn glanced at the two of them with surprise at their familiar form of address. But Brye Hamley and Philippa Winter had been through three days of agony when Larkyn and her little black went missing, and a friendship had been forged. Philippa smiled at the farmer. "I have looked forward to this very much," she said.

"And we are glad you decided to come." He held out his strong, work-roughened hand.

Philippa took it, remembering the tenderness those hard fingers had shown toward Bramble. "It's good to see you again," she said quietly.

Another surprised look from Larkyn, but Philippa pretended not to notice.

The girl Peony, plump and red-cheeked in a long apron, appeared in the kitchen doorway, framed by the bare branches of the rue-tree that framed it. She curtsied to Philippa, and greeted Larkyn with more respect than she had previously. Philippa could see why.

Larkyn stood with Seraph's rein in her hand, her cheeks and nose pink from the icy winds aloft, her riding cap at a smart angle, her divided skirt brushing the toes of her boots. She looked every inch a flyer, and Seraph made an impressive sight, too, with his head high and nostrils flared to take in the familiar scents of the farm where he had been foaled. Larkyn touched the point of his wing with her quirt, and he folded his wings, rib to rib, shaking his head from side to side and snorting.

Soon the horses were settled with water warmed for them by Brye. Hay and grain was waiting for them in their stalls. Larkyn urged Philippa to go into the kitchen, promising to rub Sunny down and blanket her against the cold in the unheated barn. Philippa agreed, and Larkyn flashed her a brilliant smile. It was a day of color, Philippa thought, as she left the girl to her chores. White snow, blue sky, the red and black of the horses wings, illuminated by the sun, and the vivid violet of Larkyn's eyes. And in the kitchen there waited a pot of the Hamleys' good strong tea, no doubt a plate of the crooks for which the Uplands were famous, and a crackling fire in the close stove.

She crossed the courtyard, enjoying the crunch of crisp snow beneath her boots. She ducked beneath the branches of the rue-tree and opened the kitchen door.

A wave of warmth met her, scented with the rich smells of freshly baked bread and some kind of soup bubbling in an enormous pot. The old farmhouse was a welcome sight, with its slanting staircase and high-beamed ceiling, its mismatched chairs and rows of battered pots hanging from hooks. The curtains, she thought, were new. Everything else in the place had the air and the security of great age.

She slipped off her cap and her gloves and was folding them into her belt when Pamella came in, her young son behind her. Philippa stopped where she was, her mouth open, the cap and gloves forgotten in her hand.

She had known they would be here, of course. It had been the greatest kindness that the Hamleys had invited Pamella— formerly the Lady Pamella, Duke William's own younger sister—to stay with them. Pamella, disgraced and disowned, had come with her baby son at the same time Larkyn and Seraph had been found, at last, safe in a witchwoman's hut.

They had not even known the child's name then. Only later, as Pamella began to trust the Hamleys, did she write her son's name for Larkyn. Brandon had looked like a Fleckham, of course, with his pale hair and black eyes, nor had that surprised anyone.

But now, at nearly four, the little boy's likeness to his uncle, Duke William, almost stopped Philippa's heart.

She stared at the two of them. Pamella looked aged beyond her years, and the boy Brandon was straight and slender, tall for his age. Pamella pushed the boy forward to greet Philippa. Philippa, watching him walk across the ancient tiles of the kitchen floor, struggled for something to say.

When Larkyn came in, a few minutes later, Philippa watched her closely to judge her reaction. It was the same. The girl's eyes found hers, and they were wide with shock. Philippa nodded, briefly, and turned away. It was a matter to be dealt with at another time.

AFTER supper, a hearty meal of pottage, sliced bloodbeets, a heavy brown bread, and an abundance of freshly churned butter, Lark offered to settle both horses for the night, but Mistress Winter pushed her chair back from the table and rose. "I'll come, too, Larkyn," she said. "If your brothers will excuse me."

Nick and Edmar both nodded, their mouths still full. Brye got up, offering to help.

"Nay, Brye, there's naught for you to do," Lark said. She grinned as she picked up a lamp. "Except upset the winged horses."

"Carry hay, water," he said.

"Thank you, we can manage," Mistress Winter said. She followed Larkyn out into the chill darkness, both of them buttoning their coats as they went. She didn't say a word until they were inside the barn.

Someone had cleared the stall where the cow stanchions were so that Winter Sunset could have adequate space. Tup was in the box stall, and Sunny was comfortably settled with a fresh bed of straw. A feed box and water bucket had been neatly hung from the closed stanchions. Mistress Winter looked this over, nodding her appreciation.

Lark could hardly stand it a moment longer. "Mistress Winter," she said urgently, "Brandon looks exactly like Duke William."

"Indeed," Mistress Winter said, in a voice full of foreboding. "It is the most startling resemblance I've ever seen."

" 'Tis hardly possible," Lark said.

Mistress Winter looked at her. The lamplight made hollows

in her thin face and shadowed her eyes. "What are you thinking, Larkyn?"

"Mistress Winter, I've known breeding and birthing since I was small, and I've never seen such a likeness except between sire and son."

Mistress Winter looked away, gazing at Winter Sunset as if answers might be found in her neatly folded wings. "Nor have I, Larkyn," she mused softly. "Nor do I want to be thinking this now. Or speaking of it."

"Nay," Lark said. "Best left unspoken, I suppose."

Mistress Winter sighed. "You're wise beyond your years, Larkyn."

"I know. 'Tis what happens when you lose your parents early. You have to grow up."

"You have been lucky in your family, just the same. Your brother—"

"Oh, aye! My brother is the finest man in the world. They all are!"

It may have been the lamplight, or the cold air, but Lark thought she detected a faint shine in Mistress Winter's eyes. But as they went about their tasks, filling the water buckets, carrying a bit of muck outside, she thought she must have been mistaken. Mistress Winter spoke of this and that, made suggestions and gave orders. Her tone was as sharp as ever, and Lark found that comforting.

THIRTY-SIX

THE rhythm of farm life had a soporific effect on Philippa. She rose in darkness, but the fire already crackled in the kitchen grate when she made her way downstairs, and the strong black tea she remembered from her earlier visits was ready, waiting under a tea cozy. The table was set with thick mugs, plates of sliced bread, a wheel of cheese, a dish of yellow butter and one of homemade preserves. The brothers were there before her, and Peony was bustling between sink and stove and table. Larkyn came downstairs soon after.

Everyone ate breakfast in the typical Uplander silence. It felt companionable to Philippa, and peaceful. By the time the crowing of the rooster drew them all outside to their chores, Osham and the Council of Lords, William and his schemes, even the Academy seemed very far away. Only Francis still weighed on Philippa's mind. She wished she had been able to pay him a visit before the holiday. She had spent her only free day escorting Margareth's body home to her family, but she promised herself she would go straight to Fleckham House upon her return.

She and Larkyn put wingclips on their horses and walked them to the north pasture to cavort in the snow. As Philippa gazed into the ice-choked currents of the Black River, and listened to the winter birds chattering in the dry hedgerows, time seemed to cease flowing.

Larkyn had been tossing snowballs at Seraph to see him kick up his heels. When Seraph trotted off to nose beneath the snow for a bit of grass, she came to stand beside Philippa. She tossed her last snowball into the rushing water, and said, a little fretfully, "'Tis not the same having Peony in the house. I used to do all those things."

Philippa had to rouse herself from her reverie to answer. "Do you mind very much?"

"I don't mind when I'm not here," Larkyn said frankly. "But when I come home, I have to remind myself not to be finding fault with everything she does."

"That doesn't sound like you."

"Nay, nor should I do it," Larkyn said. "And so I keep it to myself."

"It seems to me she does quite well for your family."

Larkyn shrugged. "Aye. And it doesn't matter, does it? But everything here is so dear to me, every beast, every tree, every plant in the kitchen garden."

"It's all wonderful, Larkyn."

The girl turned her vivid eyes up to Philippa. "Is it? Does it seem so to you? I would think Islington House to be a grand place."

Philippa's lips twisted. "I think you could say that. Grand, and too big, and too cold, with a dozen servants and every room crammed with drapes and vases and uncomfortable furniture. As a girl, I preferred Fleckham House to my own. Especially when Duke Frederick still lived there, before his succession."

The horses ran up behind them, and they turned to greet them. Seraph snorted and blew, and danced away from Larkyn's hand, inviting her to play again. Even Sunny pranced, kicking up sparkling fountains of snow. As they strolled back toward the barn, the little herd of brown goats, sporting their thick winter coats, trotted out to meet them and stood staring at Seraph and Sunny, ears turning back and forth, tails twitching. Larkyn walked among them, scratching polls, rubbing their backs. They clustered around her, bleating, butting at her pockets for treats. Philippa marveled at the circumstance that had caused Black Seraph to be foaled at Deeping Farm, with this particular girl to watch over him.

PHILIPPA found Pamella alone in the coldcellar one afternoon. Brandon had gone off with Edmar, his special favorite, and Pamella was churning butter. Philippa could still hardly believe that this was the same duke's daughter she had known in Osham. Pamella, who had been such a spoiled, willful girl, worked the paddle on the churn as if she had been doing it for years.

Philippa stood at the top of the steps looking down at her. The slanting door was folded back to let in the cool sunshine, and Pamella, her hair braided and bound in a kerchief, her apron splashed with cream, bent over the churn to test the butter's consistency.

"Good morning," Philippa said.

Pamella looked up, wiping a drop of perspiration from her forehead with the back of her hand. She nodded to Philippa. Her mouth and throat worked with visible effort, but no words came, and after a moment, she shook her head apologetically and turned back to her churning, plunging the paddle into the heavy cream.

"Can I help?" Philippa asked.

Pamella shook her head and pointed to herself, then the half-churned butter.

"Yes, I can see you're good at this," Philippa said. "I wouldn't know where to begin."

Pamella gave her a brief nod without ceasing her work. Philippa said, "Larkyn and I are going to ride into the village. Can I bring you anything?"

Without looking up, Pamella shook her head.

"Perhaps something for Brandon?"

Pamella's eyes came to her then, and the expression in them startled Philippa with its fierceness. Pamella brought her forefinger to her lips, then she shook her head with deliberate meaning.

At first Philippa couldn't think what she was trying to tell her. She frowned, then said, "Ah! You're asking me not to speak of him?"

A nod.

"But surely the villagers . . . they must know by now that you're here, and that Brandon is, too."

Another nod, but Pamella pointed to her own breast and shook her head again.

"I see. The village doesn't know who you are or where you came from."

Vigorous nodding met this. Pamella's throat worked, the muscles rippling down its length. Her brow furrowed as she struggled to speak, succeeding in producing one word through a spasm of lips and tongue. "Spy."

"Ah." Philippa felt a rush of pity. "You mean William's spy, don't you?" A nod. "Oh, Pamella, I'm so sorry. I wish I could help you. I . . . I have my own troubles with your brother."

Another nod, slow, resigned.

At that moment, Seraph whinnied from the barn, and there was a rattle of hooves on wood. Philippa excused herself with some relief and hurried across the barnyard. Larkyn was saddling Sunny, it turned out, and Seraph was complaining about having to wait his turn. Philippa relieved Larkyn of Sunny's rein, and let her go to her little stallion, scolding him all the way.

Philippa tightened Sunny's cinches and checked her wing-clips, then led her out into the barnyard. The sky remained clear, as it had since they had arrived, and she thought they could perhaps take a flight up into the hills after their errand. That would settle Seraph, and the exercise would be good for Sunny, too.

She mounted, and Sunny tossed her head, eager to be off. "Wait, my girl," Philippa murmured to her. "Larkyn and Seraph are coming, too."

As she waited, Pamella came out of the coldcellar and stood beside the steps, watching her. On an impulse, Philippa rode close to her. "Pamella," she said quietly. "Perhaps you need to see a doctor. Your brother Francis is at Fleckham House for a time, and if you wanted to go there, I could make arrangements, speak to him—"

But Pamella, her eyes flooding with sudden tears, shook her head, hard, and fairly ran into the kitchen, slamming the door behind her. Philippa stared after her. She didn't realize Larkyn had come out of the barn, with Seraph at her heels, until the girl spoke.

"She hides whenever anyone comes, my brother says."

"But does she hide the boy?"

"No one in Willakeep, except me, has ever had a blink at the Duke," Larkyn said. "They wouldn't realize."

"Ah. No. I suppose not." Philippa reined Sunny around, and they started down the lane, side by side. They didn't speak of Pamella again that day, but sympathy for her, and worry for her fatherless child, nagged at Philippa all afternoon, spoiling the peace of the day.

"PAMELLA tells me that William keeps spies in the Uplands," Philippa said to Brye Hamley. They were strolling on the edges of the Erdlin Festival, which filled the town square with revelers and music and a bonfire that blazed so hotly no one could stand near it. Larkyn and Nick and Peony had gone off in search of friends, and Edmar, with Brandon on his shoulder, wandered through the dancers, dipping and twirling to make the little boy laugh.

"Duke has eyes in every part of Oc," Brye said. "Tithe-men, prefects . . . spies."

"Was it so under Duke Frederick?"

Brye shrugged. "Never noticed then. Never mattered."

"Ah. Indeed. Everything has changed for you."

He stopped in front of a booth and dropped a coin on its counter, coming away with two mugs of sweet, hot wine. She was on the point of refusing but then decided it didn't matter, this one time. Sunny and Seraph were safe in the barn at Deeping Farm, and it was Erdlin, after all. The wine was too sweet and spicy for her taste, but that didn't matter, either. She said, "There is no more talk, I hope, of confiscating your farm?"

He grunted. "No. But it's not over yet."

"No. Nor are my troubles with the Duke."

He led her a little away from the dancers and noise. She was aware that people were watching them, and in an odd way, she enjoyed it. A horsemistress in the company of one of the stalwarts of the village must be something new to Willakeep. He said, "You went before the Council."

"Yes." The warm wine, the festive air, and the comforting presence of Brye Hamley eased Philippa's reserve. "It was bad."

He waited in an easy silence as she hesitated. After a moment, she said, "I brought suit against Duke William for interfering with the bloodlines."

"That's how we got Tup, I reckon," he said.

"Evidently," Philippa said. "Though he has not admitted it." Her lips tightened. "But now, he has bred another winged foal, and kept it for himself. I—we saw it, Larkyn and I."

"Aye. She told me."

Philippa bit her lip, wondering if Larkyn had also told her brother about William's attack on her. But surely, she thought, she wouldn't have done that. She knew too well what her brother's reaction would be.

She blew out a breath, irritated at the secrets and posturing William had made necessary. She drank again from the spicy wine and forced a small laugh, as if the whole thing had no real import, as if it were not her very life at stake. "Duke William has asked for me to be sent down from the Academy, from my service. He asked that my brother take me into custody at Islington House."

Brye looked down at her, and his eyes glinted with firelight. "Daysmith and Beeth will never allow it."

She stared at him, surprised. "Do you know the Council Lords, then?"

"Aye," he said grimly. "Know who has Oc's interests at heart, and who doesn't." He looked away, to where the villagers and farmers of Willakeep danced before the bonfire, celebrating the winter holiday as if they hadn't a care in the world. "Bloodlines are important. So is broomstraw, and the bloodbeets crop, and a dozen other kinds of business."

"You're right, of course. I've been thinking of this only from my own perspective."

"'Tis natural," he said. The firelight glimmered on his cheekbones and the strong line of his jaw. Threads of gray in his hair shone silver. "But this business distracts the Council from necessary business."

They drank in silence and watched the revelers, until Edmar came up, with a sleepy Brandon now draped across one shoulder.

"Taking the lad home," he said to Brye. He nodded to Philippa. "Leave you the oxcart, though."

Philippa said quickly, "I don't mind walking."

"Nay," he said. "Not necessary. 'Tis not so far. Good Erdlin to you both." He turned, with the boy securely lodged in the crook of his arm, and headed out into the darkness.

Brye leaned back against the trunk of an ancient oak and drained his cup of wine. "Never thought to see my brother Edmar so attached to someone as he is to that boy."

"Pamella wouldn't come tonight," Philippa said.

"Nay. Doesn't like people to stare at her."

"You mean, because she doesn't speak?"

"Aye. Except to Edmar, of course."

Philippa, startled, said, "Pamella can speak to Edmar?"

Brye chuckled, a deep, rich sound that restored the sense of holiday to the evening. "Aye, Philippa. Pamella can speak to Edmar, who never speaks more than five words at once! You may be shocked to know it, but I think there may be an understanding between the two of them."

Philippa shook her head in amazement. The Lady Pamella, known far and wide for her temper tantrums, for her strings of admirers, for her dancing . . . to have an understanding with the stolid Edmar was too much to take in. "What does she say to him, Brye?"

"He won't say."

More secrets, she thought, but she kept that to herself. There were far too many secrets in the world, and she wished they could simply lay them all out in the open, like moldy sheets that needed airing in the sun. Brye went to buy more wine, and she accepted it, and drank it. They watched handsome Nick cavorting through the square with one girl after another, poor Peony trailing after him in an obvious plea to be noticed. Larkyn flitted here and there, greeting old friends. Brye and Philippa stood where they were, in the circle of the drooping oak branches, and watched the bonfire burn down to embers.

When he put his hand under hers to help her up into the oxcart, the touch, though it lasted only seconds, felt like a caress. Philippa tilted her head up to look into the glory of the icy, star-filled night, and her heart shivered with pleasure. Her body did, too, in a way she thought she had vanquished long ago.

She shook herself and wrapped her cloak tightly around her. Such foolishness, she thought. As if she were a first-level girl mooning after some youthful crush.

When they reached the farm, she went straight to the barn to check on Sunny and to lean against her warm neck for a time, reminding herself where her first loyalty lay.

THIRTY-SEVEN

SLATER delivered the girl, slightly grubby and shivering with cold, to a small room at the back of Fleckham House. It had been intended, William thought, as a parlormaid's room, sparsely furnished and tucked away under the rafters. It was empty now, dusty and abandoned. The bed had no sheets, and only a thin blanket and worn coverlet covered the straw ticking. William had trouble lighting the fire that had been laid, and sneezed at the dust. By the time Slater knocked, then opened the door, he was in a towering temper.

"This house is falling apart," he glowered, barely looking at the trembling girl, other than to notice she had dark curls, recently cut short, it appeared, and wore some sort of black tabard and skirt. "Tell Paulina if it doesn't look better the next time I'm here, she'll be out of a job!"

"M'lord," Slater said equably, "you don't want them servants knowing you're here, do you? Might lead to questions."

William slapped his thigh with his quirt and paced to the tiny window. He had to bend at the waist to look out. The scene beyond was truncated by the slope of the roof, and showed only a bit of the park, the gardens now filled with snow, the forest beyond. "Damn that Philippa," he said. "I should have made her find another place for my brother. I loathe creeping around."

"'Tis all about the foal, though, isn't it, m'lord?"

William turned on Slater, ready to snarl some insult at his devotion to the obvious, but the girl had begun to snivel, and she distracted him. "Not another weepy one, Slater, ye gods," William said.

Slater gave the girl a sharp slap on her back, and hissed, "Listen, girl, if you want to get safely home, you'd best straighten yerself up."

She choked back her sobs and tried to wipe her face with her black sleeve. The tabard was far too large for her, and when she moved her foot, William saw that her skirt was divided.

"Slater, what is this?" he demanded. "Is she wearing a riding habit?"

Slater gave him a snaggletoothed grin. "Aye, m'lord. And doesn't she look a good bit like—you know, sir." His laugh was low and suggestive. "The brat. From the Uplands."

"I don't know—lift your face, girl, so I can see you."

The girl looked up at him. She was small, like the farm brat, but her eyes were a light brown under heavy lids, and her hair was greasy and ragged-looking. In his current mood, he would have preferred to vent his rage on some drab who looked like Philippa Winter, but he would not admit that to Slater.

William shook his head, feeling suddenly weary to death of the whole thing. "Oh, you take her, Slater," he said, with a wave of his hand. "I'm not in the mood after all."

At this, the girl began to sob again, her eyes rolling to Slater and then back to William, pleading. This made him laugh. "Little fool," he said. "You'll be better off, believe me." From where he stood, he stretched out his arm to chuck her under the chin with his quirt. He hit her just hard enough to make her head snap back, and she cried out, stumbling backward to bump into Slater, then trying to step to the side to get away from the touch of Slater's dirty hands.

The sight of her fear almost made William change his mind, but his body was utterly unresponsive. He felt no craving at all, not the slightest stirring of lust. In fact, he thought, he had felt no physical desire for some time. He knew it was the potion, but he didn't dare reduce the dose, not now, not with his goal so close. Sometimes, at night, he stared at his changing body with something like revulsion. It made him feel as if he were divided into two pieces, as if his soul and his body were fighting each other. And though he had denied it to Francis, it was true that the filly was in his mind, night and day, the smell and touch and sight of her driving out all other thoughts.

He turned away to the window again. "Go on, you stupid girl! Get out of here before I have second thoughts. You're spared an hour of rather hard work, as it happens." He glanced at Slater over his shoulder, and said softly, "I'm sure Slater will be kinder than I would have been—won't you, Slater?"

Slater sniggered and pulled the girl out of the room, closing the door behind him. He came back a moment later. "I sent her on her way, m'lord. Not inclined myself, neither."

"Poor Slater," William said idly. He leaned against the window frame, tracing the sill with the quirt. "Everyone else has all the fun."

"Nay, m'lord. I have my fun."

William turned his head to eye his serving-man's unappetizing form. "Do you," he said lazily. "What fun would that be?"

Slater grinned again as he dug through the pockets of his caped greatcoat. "I meet people," he said. "And eat well." He came up with a flask and two grimy glasses. "Drink, m'lord? Brandy. Took it from that Paulina when she wasn't looking."

William sighed and turned his gaze back to the window. "No," he said. "I'm going to the stable to see Diamond."

He heard the gurgle of the brandy as Slater poured it, then slurped from the glass. The sound made William's stomach turn. "Tell me, Slater," he said. "What's in this for you?"

"Beg pardon, m'lord?"

"You can't care about the bloodlines as I do. You'll never fly, after all." William turned, and braced his shoulders against the wall. He said dryly, "I hardly think I am an inspiration to great loyalty."

Slater showed his yellow teeth. "T'be honest, m'lord, 'tis money and power. Nothing fancier than that. I likes being where the power is."

"Then you've chosen well."

"Aye. Don't I know it." He drank again.

William straightened and pulled down his vest with his

hands. "And I suppose, excellent Slater, that if I lost my power, you'd follow after it. What would I do then?"

Slater shrugged, emitting a cloud of body odor, and drained his glass. He grinned again and gave a phlegmy chuckle. "M'lord, if you lose your power, your old Slater will be the least of your problems."

THIRTY-EIGHT

AFTER Erdlin, the hand of winter passed lightly over Oc, leaving only its rain-soaked print on the paddocks and fields around the White City. Tup, who had been a winter foal, was now three years old, and Golden Morning and Take a Chance and the other horses of the second-level class would soon turn four. Spring touched the hills with a tentative green finger, and the bravest birds began to twitter in the hedgerows. At Deeping Farm, Lark thought, with a nostalgic twinge, it would be time to till the dead vines and stems from the kitchen garden and think about laying out the rows of beans and lettuces and squash. But there was little time to dwell on that at the Academy. She and her classmates had begun to worry about mastering the Graces for Ribbon Day.

They wheeled through the misty morning sky at Mistress Star's command, the horses' wings sparkling with moisture, the girls' faces damp with it. Graces could take a variety of balletic forms. For the Foundation flyers, Graces seemed a nuisance, simply a requirement to be dispensed with as soon as possible. For the Nobles, like Anabel's Take a Chance, they were meant to impress the aristocracy. But for the Ocmarins—and for Tup—Graces were the whole point.

Couriers flew in strange places sometimes. They might fly over the smooth flat fields of Isamar or the rugged peaks of

Marin. Their assignments might take them over seas or into the private estates of some of the great lords, or they might take them into the cities, where routes between towers and spires and domes could be narrow and unpredictable. Tup, with his long, narrow wings and small body, was perfect for courier work. And there would be no challenge to the Graces at all if Lark could only fly without the cumbersome saddle. But she had promised to learn to use it, and she meant to keep her promise.

Mistress Star had set the pattern before they launched. Aloft, Hester and Golden Morning took the lead, and Lark and Tup the end. It was like a great dance, the flyers ascending, tilting like swallows around a barn as they swept to the right, their wings at as sharp an angle as they could manage. Mistress Star had told them to imagine they were flying between the crenellated towers of one of the farthest castles, to come to ground in the keep, safe from attackers.

Lark saw, ahead of her, the Foundations cautiously dipping their wings as they turned. The Nobles were more daring, achieving a downward slant to the right with their riders leaning to the left, balancing their weight.

There were only two Ocmarins in the second-level. Lark grinned, watching Grace's leggy filly Sweet Spring tilt her wings and cut sharply beneath Take a Chance, just in front of her. "That's it, Tup," she called with exuberance. "We can do that, can't we?"

She felt the surge of energy in his compact body as he increased his speed, driving them higher, and then, at the shift of her weight and the slight pull of the rein, he stilled his wings and veered sharply right and down. Lark clung to her pommel and squeezed her thighs against the stirrup leathers with all her strength. It would have been so much easier, she knew, if she could simply wrap her legs right around Tup's barrel, her calves snug beneath his wings, her seat glued to his back. Instead, she had to brace her right foot in the stirrup, lean forward and to her left, and do her best not to interfere with his wingbeats.

His angle, she could see, was sharper by ten degrees even than Sweet Spring's had been. She wanted to look up, to see if Mistress Star approved, but she was afraid to move her head and afraid to release her grip on the pommel. When Tup began to tilt even more, approaching the vertical, she lost her right stirrup. The right thigh roll caught her leg, but the stirrup swung free, and her balance wavered. She crouched over the pommel, gripping it so hard her palms burned, and she exclaimed, "No more, Tup! No!"

It was doubtful he could hear her, but he knew immediately that something had changed. With a smooth movement, he straightened his flight path, neatly popping her back into the saddle. She found her stirrup, braced her rear against the high cantle, snugged her legs beneath the thigh rolls. With a wing thrust of sheer exuberance, Tup wheeled to catch up with the rest of the flight, his neck stretched long, his hooves tucked so tightly she could feel the flex of his shoulders and hindquarters. He caught the other flyers in three wingbeats, and before she could rein him in, he surged above them, swept across their line, and swooped back to resume his place at the end. Lark's tongue dried, and she realized her mouth was open, laughing. But when Tup had steadied in his proper place in the formation, she saw the thunderstorm on Mistress Star's face where she and Star Chaser hovered at Quarters, watching the flyers. Mistress Star signaled the return with a sharp movement of her quirt.

Hester obediently and efficiently led the flight in a wide descending pattern above the Academy grounds, choosing an approach, dropping toward the return paddock. They came down one at a time, first Golden Morning, then Little Duchess, Dark Lad, Sweet Spring, Sea Girl, Take a Chance, and finally Sky Heart, just in front of Tup.

Lark urged Tup, in his turn, toward the paddock. But Tup refused.

She called to him, "Tup! No! We're going in!" Tup shook his head from side to side, rattling his bridle, then, with a powerful thrust of his wings, he soared up and over the paddock, over the gambrel roofs of the stables, past the tall profile of the Hall. "Tup!" Lark cried. "What are you doing?"

For answer, he flew in a great circle, slowed, and began the Grace again, this time easing himself gently, gently into his tilt. Lark knew she was going to be scolded, would have more penance to do, but she could see what was bothering her bondmate. They had failed the exercise, and he wasn't willing to accept it. She loosened her rein, settled her boots more securely in her stirrups, and gave herself up to Tup's lead.

His change of angle was so smooth and gradual this time

that she was barely aware of it. Soon she found herself clinging easily to the saddle, her weight perfectly balanced, her right thigh secure beneath the thigh roll, her stirrups tucked close to the cinch. Tup flew this way for a half dozen wingbeats, then, as gracefully and gradually as he had come into the pattern, he leveled his flight path, and began his descending circle.

His landing was perfection, the reaching forefeet, the extended neck, the neatly tucked hind hooves that struck the ground with almost no impact at all. He cantered up the flight paddock, head high, tail arched and flying, ears stiff with pride. As he trotted to a stop before Mistress Star and Star Chaser, he gave his little whicker, questioning, asking for praise.

"Stable your horse, Larkyn," Mistress Star said through a jaw so tight Lark wondered she could even speak. "And meet me in the Head's office."

Lark nodded. She leaped down from Tup's back, tapped his wingpoint with her quirt, and waited until he folded his wings before turning toward the stables. Her step felt as heavy as lead as she walked, the exhilaration of the flight, and the newly conquered Grace, draining away. Tup sensed her mood and whimpered in his throat as she opened his stall, led him in, and began to untack him. He butted her shoulder with his nose, and his pinions drooped to the straw.

Lark finished rubbing him down and blanketed him against the still-chilly spring nights. She was about to leave the stall, to go to the Hall as she had been ordered, but she turned back to throw her arms around Tup's neck, and to bury her cheek in his silky mane. "Oh, Tup," she whispered. "My lovely fine boy! They just don't understand you!"

He whimpered again, and twisted his neck to nuzzle her cheek. She held him tighter. "They think you belong to them," she said. "They call you by the name they chose, and they tell you what to do and where to go and when! They can't understand— how *independent* you are!"

He lipped at her ear, and she laughed a little, weepily. "Maybe, Tup," she said shakily, stroking him one last time, "maybe you really are the founder of a new bloodline, a different one. And Kalla sent you to me because she knew I would understand."

At this, Tup tossed his head, and she laughed aloud. "Oh, aye, you're certain of that, aren't you? And I'll let it go this time, Tup, and take my punishment as if it were my fault. But you and I know that it was you, and you alone, that got us into trouble!"

But she kissed his broad, smooth cheek and left him an extra half measure of grain before she sighed, brushed straw and horsehair off her tabard, and headed across the courtyard to take her scolding.

IT was the same night, when Lark came late to the sleeping porch after spending two hours in the stables rubbing saddle soap into the instructors' flying saddles, that she found Amelia waiting for her. All the other girls appeared to be sleeping, but Amelia was perched cross-legged on her cot, reading with the stub of a candle held close to her book. When she saw Lark come in, she tossed her book aside and set the candle on the nightstand.

"Amelia!" Lark said softly. "Surely you should have been in your bed an hour past!"

"I was," Amelia said in a tense whisper. "But word just came from Matron . . . my foal is coming . . . I'm to go tomorrow . . . to be bonded!"

"At last!" Lark whispered, "Oh, Amelia, wonderful." Her fatigue evaporated, all at once, and she bounced on her toes with excitement. "Where? When?"

"They're coming for me in the morning," Amelia said. Her eyes shone with unshed tears. "The mare is in the stables at Beeth House. Oh, you have to come with me, Lark! You and Hester! I'm so afraid—"

Lark sat next to her. "But there's nothing to be afraid of!"

The Klee girl wound her hands together in her lap. In a voice so low it was almost inaudible, she said, "What if it doesn't go well? What if the foal dies, or doesn't have wings?"

"There's nothing for it but to wait and see, Amelia."

Amelia stared down at her hands. In an even lower voice, she said, "And what if it doesn't like me, Lark? What if it knows I'm Klee?"

Lark put a hand on Amelia's arm, and was startled to find that she was trembling like a leaf in the wind. "Beasts don't care about principalities," she said. "Tup didn't care that I wasn't a lady, nor did Bramble, nor even yon Pig, who tossed me into the dirt of the dry paddock more than once. Your foal will give you one blink and fall in love with you. And Hester and I will be right there with you."

She hoped that was true. She still had penance to do for her latest offense, but it wouldn't help to mention that now. "Now," she said, in a motherly way, though Amelia was almost two years older than she, "do you get into your bed, Amelia, and try to sleep a few hours. It could be a long day tomorrow."

LADY Beeth, in her efficient and commanding way, disposed of any obstacles to Lark's and Hester's coming to Beeth House for the foaling. The girls were excused for the entire day, and not long after breakfast, all three found themselves in the Beeth carriage, hastening to the stables. The morning was chilly and clear, and a layer of frost rimed the swelling buds of beeches and cottonwoods and the first green fuzz on the hedgerows.

Amelia looked pale, her already-colorless lips pinched tight. Hester said heartily, "Stop worrying, Klee. This is your greatest day!"

Amelia said, "I know," but she resumed staring out the window, squeezing her fingers white in her lap. Hester grinned at Lark above Amelia's head, and Lark smiled. Every bonded girl had a story like this one. There was nothing they could do to ease Amelia's anxiety.

It was, Lark mused, as the carriage rolled smoothly out of the Academy lane and into the main road, very much like giving birth yourself. There was a good bit of uncertainty, and in her case, there had been pain and cold and sorrow to add to her stunned excitement at discovering a winged foal in the barn at Deeping Farm. But everyone had to go through her own experience. There could be no surrogates in this process.

Lark had visited Beeth House on two occasions, but still she found herself in awe as the carriage trundled smartly up before the great house, and the footman leaped down to open the doors. Lady Beeth herself came out onto the wide steps to greet them, and they hurried inside with her. Her cook had cups of chocolate laid ready for them, and Hester and Lark drank greedily, hungry again even though they had breakfasted. Amelia, politely, sipped the chocolate, but soon put it down again. Lady Beeth, seeing this, said, "Come now, girls, there's Jolinda on the back step. Go along with her now."

"Are you not coming, Mamá?" Hester said.

Lady Beeth, tall and strong and composed, gave a delicate shudder. "No, dear, I leave these things to you. My own birthings were enough for a lifetime."

Hester gave a hearty laugh. "So, Mamá," she said, hugging her. "There is something, at least, you're not the master of."

Amelia said nothing. She pulled on her coat, her face pale, her mouth fixed. Lark put an arm around her shoulders as they followed the stable-girl out the back door of Beeth House and into the open door of the large, airy stables. As they walked down the sawdust-strewn aisle between high-ceilinged, roomy box stalls, Lark pulled the icon of Kalla from inside her tabard and slipped the cord over her head. She said, "Amelia, wait."

Amelia stopped, turning her eyes to Lark. Lark showed her the icon and then held up the cord, offering it to her. Amelia started to refuse, but then, with a little sigh, she took it in her hands and hung it around her own neck. "Thank you," she murmured. "It will be a comfort."

"You're welcome," Lark said. "Come now. Let's go and see if your bondmate is here!"

JOLINDA had timed Amelia's arrival perfectly. The foal had already presented when the girls reached the stall, its nose and two tiny front hooves just visible through the birth sac. The mare, a beautiful bay Noble with shining dark wings carefully clipped to protect them during the birth, grunted, and her sides contracted visibly. Amelia put both hands to her mouth, and Lark and Hester crowded close to her, supporting her with their strength.

In some ways, Lark was to think later, it was very much as if Amelia was the one in labor. She moaned at every contraction, and panted with the mare. When the foal slid smoothly out onto the fresh bed of straw, she gasped as if it were her own body doing the work. Jolinda swiftly cleared the foal's nose and mouth and then stood back.

"Winged foal, young ladies," she said shortly. "Whichever of you is the bondmate should get in here quick and give him a breath."

Amelia exhaled. "Me," she said, her voice high and thready. "That's me!" She hurried to open the gate, to cross to the foal where it lay on the straw. As if she had done it a hundred times, she cupped the foal's nose and blew gently and surely into its nostrils. Without regard for her clothes or her hands, she brushed away bits of gelatinous stuff from its eyes and cheeks and ears. The mare whickered, and stood, breaking the umbilical cord with her movement.

"Good," Jolinda said. "Now let me clean this up, and you get yon foal to nurse, Miss." She went to the corner and retrieved a stack of folded towels. Lark glanced up the aisle and saw a pitchfork and a barrow, and hurried to bring them to the stall. The stable-girl nodded approval at her assistance. Lark went in to help her scrape up the afterbirth, and together they stood over it, examining it to make certain every bit of it was intact.

"Perfect," Jolinda said.

"Aye," Lark agreed.

Jolinda squinted up at her. "Worked a few foalings, have you?"

Lark shook her head. "Only one. But goats and cows aplenty."

"Aye. Good job."

Lark followed Jolinda out and stood leaning on the half-gate, watching Amelia with her foal and its dam. All Amelia's doubts seemed to have evaporated in the face of the actual event. She guided the foal to suckle, then stood rubbing it with towels until its soft fur was dry and standing up in little waves all over its back and chest.

Now they could see that the foal was a colt. Its wings, like its dam's, were as dark as its black mane and tail. Its body was a rich red, the color of mahogany. Amelia stood back as it nursed and turned to face the other girls. Tears streamed down her face, and her mouth curved in a trembling smile.

"Isn't he magnificent?" she sobbed.

And her friends, laughing, shedding tears themselves over the marvel of the event, agreed that he was, indeed, magnificent. Another of Kalla's miracles in the flesh, fur, bone, and membrane. A brand-new winged horse, and Amelia Rys's bondmate for life.

THIRTY-NINE

PHILIPPA sat at Margareth's desk in the Head's office, with Suzanne Star and Kathryn Dancer opposite her. Together they pored over the notes that had arrived from the Ducal Palace, from Beeth House, and from two other stables where the spring foals had been born. They made a list of the students they could expect in the fall and made another list of those girls who had been disappointed, who had attended births only to find that the foals that arrived were wingless.

"I can't remember when there were so many failures," Philippa said. "The breeding program is a mess."

"Eduard would never have let this happen," Kathryn said. Eduard Crisp had spent hours poring over the genealogies with Margareth Morgan, planning, recording, comparing. Jinson had done nothing of the kind.

Philippa sighed, and all three women were silent for a long time. Finally Suzanne said, "Still no word about the Council's decision."

"Neither yea nor nay," Philippa said. "We have no Headmistress, and if this keeps up, we will have no winged horses."

"It's not quite that bad yet," Suzanne said. "Is it?"

Philippa pushed the list she had just completed across the desk so Suzanne could see it. "Only five winged foals this spring," she said. "And of five more expected, all were born wingless. Another year or two of this, and we won't have full flights."

Kathryn touched the genealogy, open to a page with the names of Noble sires and dams on it. "It would have been better simply to repeat Eduard's pairings," she said. "Eduard knows which sires throw winged foals."

"At least the Klee girl is bonded," Kathryn said.

Philippa said sharply, "We mustn't call her that, Kathryn! She's ours now. It's important to call her by her name. She feels isolated enough."

"I'm sorry," Kathryn said stiffly. "I'll address her properly in her presence of course."

Philippa put up a hand. "Forgive me," she said more gently. "I apologize for my manner of speaking. I don't meant to do it, but it just comes out that way."

"It's all right, Philippa," Suzanne said. "We understand you."

Philippa ran a hand over her face. "We need a Headmistress," she said. "Someone who is better at diplomacy than I am."

Suzanne smiled at her. "You're doing fine, Philippa. It's a hard time."

Philippa leaned back in her chair. "That's kind of you. But I wish with all my heart Margareth were here. I have never longed to sit in her chair."

"Truly?" Kathryn said, a touch of asperity still in her voice. "I thought you had planned to succeed her all along."

Philippa's lips tightened. "I only planned, all along, to serve the bloodlines and the Duke. I never expected to feel torn by my loyalties. I'm not sure I'm suited to be Headmistress."

Suzanne said, "This is not the time to be discussing this. Philippa is under terrible pressure, Kathryn."

"We all are," Kathryn said.

Suzanne put a hand on her colleague's arm. "But the Duke has threatened to send Philippa down from the Academy. You and I don't have that to contend with."

Kathryn's eyes widened. "Send her down?"

"I thought everyone knew that."

Philippa looked away, out the window to the spring day, where a sharp breeze tossed the tops of the spruce trees at the end of the flight paddock. The winter had felt like a season of suspension, of waiting for something to break. Somehow Philippa did not feel ready for spring, for buds and flowers and nesting birds. Too many issues were left unresolved—hers with William, his with her, and Francis still lying weak and ill at Fleckham House. She tapped her fingers on the desk. "Yet another reason why I should not be Head," she said, half to herself. "I am as much at odds with our current Duke as I was devoted to Duke Frederick."

"But, Philippa—on what grounds could Duke William send you down?"

"He accused me of deliberately causing Irina Strong to fall."

"That's ridiculous!"

"Yes, of course. But I brought suit against Duke William in the Council, you know that. For a breeding violation."

"Yes, of course. But I didn't hear—"

Suzanne said quickly, "Philippa didn't want the girls to be talking about it."

"Amelia Rys knows, I'm certain," Philippa said. "Her father would have told her, and he was there. But she—unlike me—knows when to hold her tongue."

"So," Kathryn said thoughtfully, "the Council Lords didn't rule on your suit against Duke William, but they also didn't rule on his against you."

"Precisely so."

"That was months ago," Kathryn said. "How could they put off a decision for so long?"

"Because Duke William has not been present in the Council in all that time," Philippa said in a flat voice.

"Then where has he been?"

"I believe," Philippa said, "that he is at Fleckham House. Or more precisely, at the small stable he built on the estate. Where he and Jinson evidently bred the winged foal."

"Diamond," Suzanne said.

"Diamond?"

"I'm told that's what he calls her. A single name."

"Like the founders," Philippa said grimly. "He is serious about this new bloodline."

Kathryn said, in a hushed tone, "Can he do that? Will it happen?"

Philippa shook her head. "Unless he finds a flight of men willing to take potions, it won't happen. They must be willing to nearly become women to do it."

"But he hates women," Suzanne said.

Surprised, Philippa asked, "Do you know the Duke, then, Suzanne?"

"When I was young," she said. "When I was bonded, he—he tried to—" Suzanne dropped her eyes, and looked away. "I hate speaking of it."

"At least you resisted him," Philippa said, sympathy softening her voice. "There are some who were not so strong."

"I was fortunate," Suzanne said. "He tried to force me, but someone interrupted him."

"According to Geraldine Prince's suit against him, he succeeded with her."

"I heard about that," Suzanne said. "But I didn't know what I should do. My family said to keep it quiet. I think William threatened them."

"Geraldine's family has paid dearly for their suit," Philippa said. "I believe the Duke confiscated some of their property in the Angles."

Kathryn Dancer had been listening to all of this, shaking her head. "And now there is this rumor," she said, "that he had something to do with Lady Pamella's disappearance."

Philippa's back stiffened, and she gazed at Kathryn. "What rumor is that?"

"I heard Erna talking with Herbert," Kathryn said. "The servants say Pamella is living somewhere away from Osham, and that—" She broke off. "It's gossip. I shouldn't repeat it."

"Probably not," Philippa snapped. Kathryn blushed, and Philippa said hastily, "I'm sorry, Kathryn. I've done it again. It's only that we have enough problems with William—Duke William, I mean—as it is. We don't need him hearing through his spies that gossip about him is coming from the Academy."

A silence fell over the office as they all considered this. At last, thinking there was nothing more to be said about it, Philippa stood up. "Well," she said, "we'll have to resign ourselves to a small class for you, Kathryn."

Suzanne stood, too. "If he tries to send you down, Philippa, we'll do something."

"There will be nothing you can do," Philippa answered. "I can fight William, but if the Council opposes me, I'm finished."

"Can he learn to fly without us?" Kathryn asked.

Philippa gave a short, mirthless laugh. "We may find out."

SUNNY had no misgivings about the advent of spring, Philippa soon knew. She had taken to visiting Francis at the end of each week, on the only day she had no flights. Winter Sunset loved these visits, flying with no younger horses to monitor, no student flyers to lead. She shook herself with pleasure as Erna brought her out into the bright morning, and danced sideways, wings lifting, when Philippa reached for her reins.

"Sunny, you rascal," Philippa said indulgently. "You're acting like one of the yearlings." She patted Sunny's neck and tapped her wingpoint to make her fold her wings.

She led her mare to the mounting block. She didn't feel so young herself this morning. She had slept poorly. She felt, as she stepped up on the mounting block and swung her leg over Sunny's back, that the weight of the world weighed on her shoulders, that every worry added to the tightness in her neck, sending needles of pain into the back of her skull. The restfulness of her Erdlin holiday was long forgotten, its energy evaporated. The memory of Brye Hamley's steady strength and surprising sensitivity stayed with her, but she already found it difficult to recall how he had looked that Erdlin night, with the firelight shining on his hair.

As she turned Sunny down the flight paddock, she found herself thinking that it might not be so bad if the Council Lords sent her down from the Academy after all. Perhaps she could find some out-of-the-way post, some distant town, where she could be the resident horsemistress. She could carry messages, be a liaison with the Academy, and do little else. She would be lonely, bored perhaps, but not under such constant, wearing pressure.

She felt a bit better as Sunny cantered easily down the paddock, her mane and tail streaming as she sped to the hand gallop and launched into the sunshine. As they rose above the grove and banked toward the White City, the Grand River shone with a sparkling exuberance, and the green sea glittered in the distance. The sky was a clear pale blue, with shreds of cloud scudding before the wind. It hardly seemed possible that such a lovely day could hide so much darkness and anxiety.

By the time she reached the park at Fleckham House, Philippa had come to a decision. Secrets and rumors and whispered stories were doing Oc no good, nor the Academy. By association, that meant they were doing the winged horses no good. She slid out of her saddle, and led Sunny into the stables, her mind clear for what seemed the first time in months—the first time since that awful winter day in the Rotunda. She was done waiting for someone else to decide her future. She was ready to take matters into her own hands.

Her improved mood faltered slightly when she saw Francis. He lay on his pillows, his features pale and drawn. She went to him and touched his hand. It felt cold under her fingers.

His voice was clear, though not strong. "Philippa," he said. "You're so good to come every week. I'm sorry I'm not able to get up and greet you properly."

"Francis," she said, trying to keep the worry from her voice. "Are you feeling worse?"

"No, no," he said, without much conviction. "I'm just a little tired today."

"Did you see the doctors this week?"

His mouth curved in a crooked smile, making him look like a younger, more benevolent version of his brother. "I did," he said. "And I sent the quacks away. All they talk of is bleeding and leeches and cupping." He held up one arm, and Philippa saw the bruising along the inside of the elbow. "Cupping, ye gods," he said, with bitterness. "Barbaric practice."

"I wish I knew what that ghastly woman had put on her knife," Philippa said.

"Never mind," he said. His eyes closed briefly, and he sighed. "I'll be better soon, I'm sure. I just need rest—and no more bleeding!"

Philippa held his hand for a moment, then stood to pour him water from a carafe on the night table. "Do you not sleep well?" She held the glass for him to drink.

When he had swallowed some of the water, he shook his head. "I don't, as it happens," he said. "I hear noises in this house, which is supposed to be empty. And hooves on the gravel of the courtyard. Everything seems . . ." He sighed.

"What, Francis?" she asked gently, sitting down beside the bed. "How does it seem?"

"Exaggerated," he said, with an empty chuckle. "I suppose because it's so quiet, and because I have nothing to do. I have nothing to do, and yet I feel exhausted."

She patted his hand, and set the glass down again. As she did so, a sudden thought struck her, and she turned to him with a smile. "Francis! I have a wonderful idea."

"What is it?"

She looked down at him, lying so thin and wasted beneath the blankets. "I had the best rest of my life over the Erdlin holiday," she said. "I was in the Uplands."

"The Uplands?" he said, his eyes brightening a bit. "How nice that sounds. Far from the Palace, the city, and the Council."

"It was perfect," Philippa said. "I spent the holiday with the Hamleys."

"Hamleys? Is there a Hamley in the Council?"

"No, Francis. You may remember that your sister, Pamella, is staying with them, with her little son."

"Pamella . . . it would be nice to see Pamella. And to meet the boy."

"Pamella is still troubled, though. She still is unable to speak. Except, as it turns out, to the middle Hamley brother, who hardly speaks himself."

Francis frowned, but listened as Philippa told him of the rumors about Pamella, the stories about William's misdeeds, about her concerns for the bloodlines and the disappointing foalings. But most of all, she told him about Deeping Farm, about the comfortable ancient farmhouse, the hearty food, the bracing air. She concluded by saying, "I've decided something else, Francis."

He smiled at her. "You look better as you say that, Philippa. Less weary."

"Ah. You're being diplomatic, Francis. You mean I look less aged."

"I should never have said such a thing."

"It doesn't matter. It would be true."

He managed a weak chuckle. "So, Philippa, tell me what decision you've reached."

She pulled her gloves from her belt to pleat them between her fingers. "I'm going back to the Council Lords," she said.

She turned her head to the window, where she could see the hills greening to the west. "The whole winter has gone by, and they have dawdled and dithered without William's guidance. I'm going to demand they appoint someone to the post of Headmistress at the Academy, and I'm going to serve poor Jinson up to their judgment. I don't blame him, really. William should have known better than to replace Eduard Crisp."

"William is insane, Philippa."

She turned to him, her brows rising. "Have you seen him?"

"He hit me," Francis said with a wry twist of his lips. "He struck me with that quirt he carries everywhere."

"While you lay in bed, he struck you?"

"Well," Francis said, with a listless gesture, "I was sitting up at the time."

Philippa dropped her gloves on the bed, and leaned forward to touch Francis's hand again. "Francis, I'm sorry. I didn't think you, of all people, needed protection from him. He wanted you to come here, after all."

"I don't need protection from my brother," Francis said, with a little flash of spirit. His color had risen a little, giving Philippa hope. "He struck me, but only once. And he hasn't come back to this room since."

"I think," Philippa said, "that he spends all his time in his private stable, beyond the beech copse. With the filly."

"The winged filly," Francis said. "I still can't believe it."

"None of us can," she said. "But you've seen him, so you know how changed he is."

"He's living in a sort of—a sort of prison. A prison he created for himself." A little color rose in Francis's face. "He is a man in a woman's body, and his mind is coming apart under the strain."

"Yet the Council won't listen."

Francis drew a shaky breath before he went on. "The Council Lords carry on a long tradition of respect for the Duke. You may have trouble standing against him."

"I don't care, Francis. This waiting will make me as mad as William. And the future of the winged horses is more important than the future of one cranky horsemistress."

He sighed, and his brief color faded again. "I will come to the Rotunda," he said. "To support you."

"You will not," she said firmly.

"But the consequences of your going alone—"

She interrupted him. "Consequences be damned. This has gone on long enough."

FORTY

FRANCIS was glad to be out of the confines of the bedroom at Fleckham House. He was thoroughly sick of being an invalid, tired of berating himself, furious about William but helpless to intervene. Lord Beeth sent his carriage, and its four matched grays drew it swiftly toward the Uplands on a glorious day, with birdsong pouring from every tree and hedgerow. The carriage was fully equipped with a driver and two footmen, all in the scarlet Beeth livery. One nurse had come along, but the blood-thirsty physicians were left behind.

From the window of the carriage, Francis caught sight of Philippa and Winter Sunset flying ahead of them. Sunny looked like a great red bird, her wings glowing in the sun like fine parchment. Philippa made a slender slash of black against the achingly blue sky. Behind Philippa came the young flyers, Larkyn and her pretty stallion, Black Seraph. Francis leaned close to the window to watch them until the scalloped roof of the carriage cut off his view.

They made one stop at a town called Dickering Park, for Francis to be helped out of the carriage by the nurse and go into a tiny, low-ceilinged inn to have a meal, use the privy, rest a bit. Philippa and Larkyn would already be at the farm, making preparations. The innkeeper bowed and fussed over the great event of having the Duke's younger brother in his establishment. Francis ate a joint of lamb and a plate of buttered blood-beets, as much to please the innkeeper as to satisfy his own hunger, and drank a bit of cider. When it was time to leave, he was embarrassed to realize that he had no money with him. It had been a long time since he needed money of his own, and he had given no thought to it.

As he touched his coat pocket, where his purse might have been, the footman stepped up quickly, and said, "Nay, Lord Francis, his lordship has taken care of everything. Don't trouble yourself." Francis was forced to nod, and thank him, and as he was helped back into the carriage, he swore to himself this dependence would soon end. One way or another.

Deeping Farm surprised him, when the carriage finally trundled out of the road and down a lane of packed dirt. The barn, though newly whitewashed, was a simple square with a slanted roof. There was no paddock. The house was tall and narrow, with a slate roof and small windows. The front door, it seemed, was completely blocked by an overgrown laurel hedge. The kitchen door, which opened as the carriage pulled into the barnyard, was shaded by a twisted rue-tree in full leaf. Everything was smaller and dingier than Francis had expected. Behind the house, a blackstone fence enclosed a kitchen garden, and all around stretched the black dirt of empty fields. What was it about this simple place that so enchanted Philippa?

Philippa and Larkyn came out through the kitchen door with a plump, rosy-cheeked girl in a long apron. Philippa greeted him, and introduced him to the aproned girl, whose unlikely name turned out to be Peony. Francis, leaning on the nurse's arm, was led into the high-ceilinged kitchen, redolent with the scents of meals long past and one, it seemed, soon to come.

Peony curtsied, and blushed even redder, and mumbled, "Oh, aye, me lord, what a—oh, my goodness—we're just so glad."

He couldn't find a proper way to respond, but he tried to smile and nod to her. He was exhausted, his muscles trembling. Philippa showed him the bed made ready for him in what was no doubt supposed to be a parlor, but he said, "Please, Philippa. I want to sit in a chair, at least to start with. My dignity is in shreds."

She squeezed his shoulder. Her fingers were strong and hard, as he might expect from a horsemistress, and he wondered if there was any strength left in his own grip. Peony pushed forward an ancient wooden armchair that looked as if it had been mended a hundred times. As he fell into it, he was surprised to find how comfortable it was, as if the wood had molded, over the years, to the human form. Soon he had a mug of strong black tea in his hand, a plate of some long, narrow biscuits before him, which Larkyn informed him were called crooks, and a padded stool for his feet. Though the day was warm, a small, cheerful fire crackled in the hearth, and something bubbled busily on a close stove. Dented pots hung everywhere, and some sort of fetish hung above the sink, with tattered skirts and a half-ruined face. Francis thought it was hideous, and he struggled against a sense of being utterly and uncomfortably out of place.

And then his sister came into the kitchen, a small boy with the ice-blond hair of the Fleckhams clinging to her skirts.

"Pamella," Francis said. He held out his hands, and she ran to him, falling to her knees beside his chair and burying her face in his shoulder. The boy, his dark eyes filling with tears, hung back, sniffling.

"Pamella, are you well? Is this your boy?"

His sister, his imperious, spoiled, willful sister, shook her head against his shoulder, and the only sounds she made were heartwrenching sobs. Francis put his arms around her and held her, but the scene only added to his sense of strangeness. Pamella had never, in all their childhood together, wept in his arms, or indeed ever cried except when she wanted something from her father. He held her and gazed at Philippa above her head. Philippa shrugged, and Larkyn took the little boy's hand while they all waited for the storm to subside.

In time, Pamella's tears dried, and Larkyn urged the little boy forward. She said, "This is Brandon, my lord."

Francis put out his hand to him. "I am your uncle Francis," he said.

The boy took his hand solemnly, squeezed it, then retreated behind his mother. Francis drank his tea, watching his sister from the corner of his eye. She had taken a seat near the fire, and the little boy stood beside her knee. Pamella was thinner than he remembered, and there was no color in her cheeks. She kept her eyes on her hands, twisted together in her lap. And the boy, Brandon—Francis found he could hardly bear to look at him, though he seemed a likely lad. He didn't know why he felt that way, but he was too weary to puzzle it out.

When everyone had finished their tea, Pamella jumped up to help Peony clear the mugs and the pot. She gave the last of the crooks to her son, then pulled on a long, worn coat, and went out the kitchen door.

This time, when Philippa urged Francis toward the bed in the parlor, he gave in. The nurse helped him out of his boots and trousers, and he lay down in a nest of pillows and old, soft linens. Beyond the curtained windows, the sky darkened to violet, then to a starry blackness. Francis watched birds flit to and fro past the window until he drowsed, lulled by the lowing of cows from the barn and the occasional bleat of a goat.

He woke to the sounds of pots clanking in the kitchen and desultory conversation. The nurse was gone, but a plain pottery cup and pitcher rested beside his bed. He poured himself water from the pitcher and drank it. By the time he had set it down again, Philippa was in the doorway. A big man stood beside her, with a broad-brimmed straw hat in his hands.

"Francis," Philippa said quietly, "are you awake? This is Brye Hamley, the owner of Deeping Farm."

"My lord," the farmer said. His voice was deep, resonating in the old parlor. He had thick, graying hair, and strong features.

Francis said awkwardly, "I'm sorry I can't get up to meet you, Master Hamley. It's kind of you to allow me to stay here."

"An honor to have you." Hamley bowed, and looked Francis over as if taking his measure but seemed to feel nothing else needed to be said. He glanced around the parlor, and evidently finding all was in order, nodded to Philippa and went back into the kitchen.

Philippa crossed to the bed, and straightened the quilt over Francis's legs.

"Philippa," Francis said. "The boy, Pamella's boy. Isn't there something about him—"

He broke off. She pursed her lips and looked behind her, as if to be certain no one could hear. "There is something about him, certainly," she said. "And both Larkyn and I have remarked upon it."

"I can't think what it means." Francis sighed, feeling slow-witted and impatient with himself. His mind shied from the implications of Brandon's face, his eyes, the cut of his chin and nose. He passed his hand over his eyes.

Philippa came to the bedside. "Do you need anything, Francis? Shall I call the nurse?"

He shook his head. "No. I just—I hate people seeing me like this."

"Give it time," she said.

"Philippa," he said, his jaw tight with frustration. "I have given it time. Too much!"

Before she could answer, the girl Larkyn appeared in the doorway to say, "Supper's almost ready, Mistress Winter." She carried a little stack of napkins in her hand. "Will Lord Francis eat with us, in the kitchen, or shall I bring a tray?"

Philippa said, "I think a tray, Larkyn, thank you."

Francis wanted to protest, but he hadn't the energy even for that. He turned his eyes again to the window, where a faint moonlight now silvered the laurel hedge. He wondered if there was truly any reason that his recovery would be quicker in this rustic place than it had been at Fleckham House. He was utterly sick of being an invalid, of spending all his time in bed, of needing help for every simple act. It might have been better if the damned Aesk woman had finished the job while she had the chance. And he couldn't help wishing, for the hundredth time, that it had been he, rather than poor Lissie, who had put an end to her cruelty.

FRANCIS slept poorly, tossing and turning in the unfamiliar bed, listening to the creaks of old timbers, the whisper of feet moving on the floor above him, the chitter of some nocturnal creature in the walls. He finally fell into a heavy sleep just as the first gray light of dawn showed through the curtains. Moments later, it seemed, a rooster crowed vigorously from his coop as if the safe arrival of day were his sole responsibility.

Francis opened his eyes, unsure for a moment where he was. He turned his head on the pillow, and found that someone, a vague figure in the semidarkness, was bending over his bed.

He was only half-awake, and he thought for a moment that

he must be dreaming. When he drew a startled breath, the unmistakable scent of horse filled his nostrils.

It was the young flyer. Larkyn. She was already dressed in her riding habit, black tabard and divided skirt. She leaned above him, with something in her hand. He squinted, trying to see what it was, wondering if he should protest.

The light grew steadily brighter outside, and now he could see her face, her smooth brow furrowed, her eyes pools of shadow, her lips pursed as she concentrated. She moved her hand across his body, and then up over his chest, and he saw that she held the fetish he had seen in the kitchen. She spun it, making its skirts swirl, blurring its distorted features into a face of nightmare. She murmured something under her breath, and repeated the motion, then, with a little smile, she touched his blankets with her fingertips and was gone, leaving Francis to lie pondering what it all meant.

He managed, with his nurse's help, to be outside in the barnyard when Philippa and Larkyn took their leave. The day was even warmer than the one before, presaging a hot summer. The air smelled of newly plowed ground, freshly turned compost, and goats. The two winged horses cantered up the lane to launch into the blue sky. Francis watched them, leaning on a staff someone had found in the barn. He didn't take his eyes off the shining red horse and the gleaming black one until they dwindled in the distance, then he turned to assess his surroundings. With a heavy heart, he admitted to himself that this had been a terrible idea. He was stuck here, on a farm in the Uplands, in a cramped, dingy farmhouse with people he didn't know and who didn't know him. The air was sweet with growing things, it was true, and the atmosphere was restful. But he had nothing in common with these people.

Common—that was the word. He moved toward the blackstone fence that separated the kitchen garden from the barnyard and sat upon it, looking out at the rows of vegetables and vines. He had spent no time at all with commoners, not in all his nearly thirty years of life. He had lived a life apart, either with his family, or with Prince Nicolas, or even, during the Aesk adventure, with the Klee Baron. He knew nothing of how common life was lived, what they spoke of, what they read—if anything—or what they cared about.

His shoulders slumped as he let his weight settle onto the old stones of the fence, and he cursed himself for letting Philippa talk him into this.

A week after her return from the Uplands, Philippa presented herself once again in the Rotunda. She had rehearsed her petition, written down every word, changed it a dozen times. She meant to be clear, but she hoped to be respectful. Many of the Council Lords thought women should never speak in the Rotunda. Indeed, Duke William was not the only one who thought horsemistresses should have no rights above other women. Philippa struggled to phrase her statement to be as inoffensive as possible, but it was no easy task. She had a great deal to say. Subtlety would not serve.

Lady Beeth sent her carriage so that Philippa would not have to worry about stabling Winter Sunset in Osham. When Philippa, attired in a fresh habit and cap, her wings pinned prominently on the collar of her tabard, climbed into the carriage, she was surprised to find her benefactress seated inside.

"Lady Beeth," she said, settling herself opposite. "It's too kind of you to accompany me."

"I wouldn't miss it," Hester's mamá said with a grin. "And you must call me Amanda."

"Then," Philippa said, "please call me Philippa. And thank you for helping us yet again. I don't know what any of us should have done without you and your husband."

"What use is a title and a position if you can't do some good with it? The Council Lords can use a bit of influence, if you ask me, and I'm only too happy to provide it!" Her hearty laugh boomed inside the confines of the carriage. Philippa managed only a smile. She was too tense to laugh.

It helped to be able to walk into the Rotunda in the company of Lady Amanda Beeth, to have little Lord Beeth bow to her, and escort her down the tiers to the petitioner's chair. She walked with her back straight, her head high. She folded her cap and gloves into her belt, but she kept her quirt under her arm as a badge of office.

There was a long wait while the Council observed its usual opening rituals. Philippa wished she could pace. Her fingers itched for something to fiddle with, but she left her gloves where they were and tried to relax her hands. She fixed her eyes on the empty chair where Duke William should have been sitting. She felt like a boiling pot with a tight lid, and she hoped she wouldn't explode before her chance came.

It was a great relief when, at last, Lord Beeth introduced her, and asked the Council to hear her petition.

She stood and clamped her quirt under her arm. "My lords," she said. Her voice echoed off the hard floors and bounced back at her from the ceiling. There was silence in the Rotunda. Even the watchers in the gallery were rapt, no doubt hoping she was about to do something outrageous.

"My lords, the Academy of the Air has been without a Headmistress for months now, ever since the death of Margareth Morgan. Our spring crop of winged foals is half what it should be. The incoming class will be the smallest in memory."

She waited for the rustle that greeted this announcement to cease, then she said, clearly and unequivocally, "Duke William sent down our rightful Master Breeder, Eduard Crisp, and replaced him with an incompetent." Grim silence met this, narrowed eyes, stiff necks.

"Without the winged horses," she went on, "Oc loses its edge over the other duchies and diminishes its bargaining position with other principalities. It's not too late to save the bloodlines. I ask you, my lords, in the continuing absence of the Duke, to appoint a Headmistress, and to restore Eduard Crisp to his rightful position as Master Breeder."

Several of the Council Lords shifted at that, and one or two began to grumble. Philippa raised her voice. "Act now, my lords. If you wish to send me down, as the Duke has asked, do so. But give us Master Crisp, and give us a Headmistress. In honor of the memory of Duke Frederick and his ancestors, I beg you take action without delay."

Amanda Beeth had advised her that when she was done speaking, it would be best if she simply excused herself. Philippa had no better advisor, and so she did as Lady Beeth had suggested. As she swept up the tiered steps to the aisle, and out to the door, she heard Lord Beeth begin to speak in his cultured voice. Someone interrupted him, and she heard her own name spoken in anger.

She stopped where she was and turned to find the speaker.

It was Meredith. Her own brother. His loud voice was like a blow, pronouncing, "My lords, this was an outrageous display of disloyalty to the Council! Let us take the horsemistress at her word. Send her down from the Academy! Make an example of her!"

And at precisely that moment, as if they had rehearsed it, the door on the opposite side of the Rotunda opened, and Duke William, his body hidden by a sweeping black cloak, appeared.

Every man of the Council jumped to his feet, and as William passed them, they bowed. Philippa felt as if her feet had grown roots right through the marble floor. Amanda Beeth came to stand beside her, and both of them stared at the Duke.

William's hair was pulled back and tied with a gleaming black ribbon. His face was nearly as pale as his hair, his chin fuller than she remembered, but his eyes were as hard as ever. He stood before his carved chair in the center of the Rotunda, lifted his arm, and pointed a long white finger at Philippa.

"My lords," he said in his high voice. "This traitoress has lost the right to wear the wings of a horsemistress. I second Lord Islington's demand that Philippa Islington be sent away from the Academy. I am the Duke of Oc, the Master of the Bloodlines, and I revoke her standing now and for always."

There was a moment of shocked silence, until Lord Chatham said, "Your Grace, don't you think—"

"We've thought about this long enough," William said. "And conferred with Lord Islington, who knows his sister better than any of us."

Lord Beeth jumped up. "Wait a moment, my lords. This rush to judgment is ill considered! If our horsemistresses think they can be treated in this way, will girls still want to bond to the winged horses?"

William sneered at the little man. "Beeth," he said rudely, "you haven't been paying attention. With my new bloodline, we won't need girls. Men will fly!"

An approving murmur swept around the Rotunda, and even some voices from the gallery acclaimed the Duke's statement.

"Come, my lords, enough delay. We gave the horsemistress months to come to her senses. Send her down and be done with it!"

"But, Your Grace!" Lord Daysmith, whose age and reputation commanded the respect of every member of the Council, tottered to his feet. "If you send Horsemistress Winter down, what will become of her mare?"

William's smile was as sinister an expression as Philippa had ever seen. "Ah, yes," he said silkily. "Her mare." He looked around at the Council Lords and their aides, and up at the gallery, waiting in breathless silence. "I have thought of this, naturally. Winter Sunset is a fine example of the Noble line. With Philippa Islington under her brother's protection at Islington House, Winter Sunset will become part of my new breeding program."

The blood drained from Philippa's face and head, and she reeled. Only the strong arm of Amanda Beeth kept her from falling. She tried to say, "Duke William—this isn't necessary—" but over the sudden uproar from the balcony, her voice faded to nothing. She saw William smiling at her, his eyes glittering like a snake's. She saw the triumphant blaze in Meredith's face, his gaze meeting hers without remorse. She heard one of the other Council Lords say, "Surely it's past time to restore ducal authority over the winged horses." A chorus of ayes greeted this.

Philippa felt, suddenly, that she couldn't catch her breath.

Voices and faces began to blur. To her horror, black spots filled her vision, and a moment later she slumped, weak and senseless, into Amanda Beeth's arms.

When she roused, she found herself once again in the Beeth carriage, rolling down the broad avenue away from the Rotunda. "Kalla's tail," she whispered. "Did I faint? I have never fainted in my life!"

"It's not surprising," Amanda said grimly. "I am as shocked as you are."

Philippa grasped her hand. "Did they decide? What happened?"

"Duke William called for a vote on the spot, Philippa," Amanda said. She looked fierce and sad, and a terrible dread gripped Philippa's heart so that she feared she might faint again.

"What, Amanda?" she whispered. "What was the vote?"

"He had the majority," was the answer. "A narrow margin, but a majority nevertheless."

Philippa sat up straight. "Take me back!" She pounded on the wall of the carriage with her hand. "I have to go back! They can't do this! It will kill her!"

Amanda shook her head. "If there's anything at all to be done, Philippa, Beeth will do it, or Daysmith. It's better you're not there."

Philippa stared at her. An awful understanding began to clear her mind, and with it, all faintness vanished. "It's his revenge," she breathed. "William's revenge. Against me. Against his father. All of it."

"Yes."

"They won't stand against him, will they?"

"Some did. Not enough."

"They don't care about Sunny."

"They care," Amanda Beeth said, every word sharp as a knife, "about power."

Philippa, her body stiff, her mouth dry, stared at the blank wall of the carriage all the way back to the Academy.

FORTY-ONE

AMELIA was allowed to bring her foal to the Academy, with its dam. It was unusual for a foal to come before it was weaned, but everything about Amelia's situation was unusual.

Lark and Hester were waiting for her in the courtyard, and when they caught sight of the little procession turning into the lane from the main road, they ran to meet it.

A single horse from the Beeth stables drew a small cart at a careful pace. Old Jolinda, grinning with delight, rode beside the driver. The foal's dam walked behind the cart, and the winged foal, wearing wingclips and a shiny new halter, trotted beside her. Amelia walked with him, one hand on his scruff of black mane. Lark and Hester slowed their pace so as not to frighten him. Bramble, pacing at their heels, went forward to sniff and be sniffed.

"Mistress Winter says Bramble can foster your colt!" Lark said by way of greeting.

Amelia gave her usual cool smile, but there was a new light in her eye, and her sallow cheeks flushed a becoming pink. "Very good," she said.

"We have your stall ready," Hester said. "The big one, back beside the dry paddock, so there's room for the mare and for your colt."

"Thank you," Amelia said. She bent to ruffle Bramble's fur. "I could hardly wait to come, though your mamá made me so comfortable at Beeth House."

"Mamá understands," Hester told her. "When it was my turn, I drove her half-mad with wanting to come to the Academy—and I had to wait until fall, with the other first-levels!"

"This is better," Lark said. "You can wean your colt bit by bit. 'Tis hard on young beasts to leave their dams all at once."

When they reached the stables, Erna came out and stood watching, her hands empty, her face blank, as Jolinda got down from the cart and untied the mare's halter lead from its ring. She shot Erna a dark glance. "You, girl," she said sharply. "Take this mare to her stall."

As Erna shuffled forward, Jolinda clicked her tongue in exasperation. "Look sharp, now!" she said, but Erna seemed not to hear. She took the lead and turned into the stables. The foal and the oc-hound followed, with Amelia hovering over them. When the whole entourage had disappeared, Jolinda turned to the girls. "Is that what you have to take poor Rosellen's job?" she demanded. "Them lords have got to do better than that!"

"I miss her," Lark said.

"We all do," Hester added.

"She was a good girl, Rosellen," Jolinda said. She brushed her hands together and said briskly, "Come, now, let's not mope about. Rosellen wouldn't want that. I'm going on to see that yon colt is nicely settled. Wouldn't trust that Erna out of my sight."

Lark and Hester watched them go, dawdling on the steps of the Hall rather than go in out of the sunshine. "What have you heard from home?" Hester asked. "How is Lord Francis?"

"I've had no news, but spring is a busy time at Deeping Farm. I have to say, he looked terrible when we left him," Lark said. "But I gave the Tarn a spin over him. If anything can help him, that will."

"Oh, Black, you goose," Hester said. "That's only superstition."

Lark grinned at her. "We'll see, Morning," she said. "We'll just see."

Hester opened her mouth to say more, then stopped. "Why—why, there's Mamá's carriage! What is she doing here?"

The girls ran across the courtyard to the foot of the Hall

steps. The carriage circled past the stables, and came to a stop, and the footman jumped down to open the door. Lady Beeth climbed out, but when Hester started toward her, she put up a hand. "Wait, dearest," she commanded.

She turned back to the carriage, and the two girls watched in confusion as Mistress Winter, moving slowly and carefully, as if she had suddenly grown old, stepped down from the carriage and started up the steps.

"Hester," Lady Beeth said. "Fetch Matron. Mistress Winter needs brandy."

PHILIPPA neither ate nor drank the next morning, but saddled Sunny herself to fly straight to the Ducal Palace. Sunny, catching her urgent mood, flew high and fast, and when Parkson, William's steward, came out onto the steps of the Palace, she laid her ears back. Parkson eyed her with distaste as he told Philippa in icy tones that His Grace was not at home to visitors.

She leaped back into the saddle, and flew on to Fleckham House, to the small stable behind the stand of beeches. Jinson came out when he heard Sunny's hooves on the gravel. He had been, Philippa felt certain, expecting her.

She glared down at him without dismounting. Sunny sniffed noisily, backing away and rattling her bridle. She closed her wings over Philippa's calves, but they rustled and flexed angrily.

"Is he here?" Philippa demanded.

"No, Mistress," Jinson said. His face reddened, and he looked at his boots. "But he said—if you came—"

"He knew I would come."

"I—uh—I'm supposed to say, you have till Estian."

Philippa snapped, "You mean, Winter Sunset—this *winged horse*—is allowed to live until Estian? Let's be clear about this."

"He won't—I mean, she won't die," Jinson mumbled. "I'll take care of her, Mistress, I swear I will."

Philippa's voice rose. "Take care of her? You fool! You can't even get near her!"

"Well, no, but His Grace—he can—"

"No, he can't!" She wanted to strike him, to scream at him. She gritted her teeth, and tried to control herself, while Sunny danced sideways, made fretful by her bondmate's fury. "Jinson, this ruling is a death sentence for my mare. Surely even you can see that."

His face darkened, and he lifted his eyes to hers. "Shouldn't have gone against him, Mistress," he said. "Nobody can go against him."

"Ridiculous! You're the Master Breeder, which is a travesty, but now you are, and you can—"

He shook his head as her voice trailed off. "You don't know," he said miserably. "The things he's done . . . you just don't know."

"Tell the Council, then, man! Have you no courage at all?"

He took a step backward, up into the protection of the doorway as if she were about to assault him. "I have a sister," he faltered. "And the Duke said—if I—"

"Idiot!" she exclaimed. "Have you seen him? He can't seduce a girl now! He looks more womanly than I do!"

"You don't know," he said. He put up a hand, and there were tears in his voice as he said, "I can't talk to you anymore, Mistress. I'm sorry, really I am. Estian. You have till Estian."

LORD Beeth and Lord Chatham, with elderly Lord Daysmith, fought hard against those who allied themselves with William in the Council. Suzanne and Kathryn and the other instructors petitioned the lords, without success. They tried appealing to Duke William, and received threats in return. They wrote pleading letters to their families, and received guarded, fearful responses. Finally, on a warm spring evening, Philippa called a halt to all of it.

She asked every horsemistress at the Academy, seniors and juniors alike, to come to the reading room in the Domicile. She stood by the window, waiting for them to assemble, and when they had taken seats, she looked into each of their faces, these devoted women who put their trust in the Duchy and in the Academy.

"I thank those of you," she said, "so many of you, who have tried to intercede for me, and for Sunny. There is nothing left to try."

Several women started to protest, but she shook her head, forestalling them. "I brought this on myself," she said. "I underestimated William's influence. Duke Frederick taught me that the power of the Council Lords was equal to his own, and I didn't understand how swiftly that could change."

Sarah, one of the junior instructors, said, "We'll keep you here, Philippa! We won't let him take you—" Her voice broke, and she began to sob.

"Sarah, you have Wind Runner to think of," Philippa said. "Just as Kathryn has Sky Dancer, and Suzanne has Star Chaser. We exist at the pleasure of the Duke, it seems. Already the bloodlines are in trouble, and if the entire Academy is at odds with him, I fear the damage may be irreparable."

Suzanne, now named the new Headmistress, said, "Everything changed when the old Duke died."

"You're not going to give Winter Sunset up?" Sarah pled. "Not really?"

"What choice do you see?"

"But after you risked yourself in Aeskland, after you helped save those children—"

"It makes no difference, Sarah. Duke William is not a forgiving man."

"Perhaps if you called upon Lord Francis—"

Philippa leaned against the window sash, gazing out into the dusk. "Lord Francis is so ill," she said. "I'm not sure he could even make the journey. And besides . . . I fear for him, too. The Duke attacked him. Struck his own brother with his quirt while Francis lay ill and helpless. The Council doesn't see it, but our Duke is no longer sane. He has—" She made a helpless gesture. "He has divided himself, and it has broken his mind."

She straightened and faced them again. "The most important thing is to protect the winged horses. What happens to me is nothing by comparison. Remember that. I am with you till Estian. Then we will do what we must."

Sarah pressed a handkerchief to her eyes, and whispered, "I would die first."

Philippa could not disagree. She said only, "Don't grieve, my friends. Please. This time will pass, and you must hold on until then."

"The students suspect something," Suzanne said.

"Don't tell them," Philippa said in a flat tone, turning her gaze back to the window. "I couldn't bear for them to look at me the way all of you are."

SPRING ripened into summer. Buds became blossoms. The yellowhammer nestlings tried their wings, and the horses grew satiny as the last of their winter coats fell away under brush and currycomb. Amelia's foal opened his wings and capered in the yearlings' pasture while his bondmate looked on with fond pride.

Tup had reached his full and final height of thirteen hands. He was small, but with his long, narrow wings, his finely cut head, his arching silken tail, he was so beautiful he hardly seemed real to Lark. The summer air was rich with the smell of timothy and alfalfa, and Lark could hardly wait for Estian to see the blood-beets growing tall in the fields around Deeping Farm and to smell the broomstraw turning gold in the sun.

Something, though, was wrong.

All through the spring, the instructors had gone about with grim faces. Tempers ran short, and the girls began to avoid the horsemistresses when they could, ducking out of their way in the stables, hanging back in the Hall so they would not have to greet them.

"Perhaps everyone is upset that Mistress Winter wasn't named Headmistress," Lark murmured to Hester. They were in Goldie's stall, repairing the support for her water bucket. They were to leave the next day for the Estian holiday, and were trying to finish every chore to perfection. It was too easy to win a scolding.

Hester shook her head. "I don't think that's it." She kept her voice low, too, as they had all taken to doing. "Everyone likes Mistress Star."

"What is it, then?" Lark asked. "I looked up at the high table last night at supper, and no one was talking at all. Not a word! It was like watching my brother Edmar at the table."

"Is Edmar so silent?"

"He is," Lark said. "Although Brye says he talks to Pamella. And her little boy."

Hester hammered the last nail, and Lark lifted the water bucket to test their work. The support held, and they left the stables to go to the Hall, where an assembly had been called. The horses were in the yearlings' pasture, wingclipped, but no longer needing blankets. The palominos and chestnuts and blacks and grays were cropping the green summer grass. Tup sensed Lark's regard and raised his head to whicker as she passed.

Hester said, "Black, look at the Head's face."

Lark followed her gaze, and saw Headmistress Star standing in the doorway, nodding to the girls as they came through. She looked as if she had aged ten years in the weeks she had been Headmistress, and today, in particular, there were lines of strain around her eyes and mouth. "I think," Lark said, with an uncomfortable twinge of intuition, "that we're about to learn what has been bothering everyone."

The girls stood behind their usual places at the long tables in the dining hall, and the instructors stood on the dais. Only Mistress Winter's place was empty. Lark looked around, but she couldn't see her coming in at the door or standing in some other spot.

Headmistress Star spoke for several minutes. Her voice sounded thin and strained. The other horsemistresses stood in a tense silence, eyes down. It was clear they already knew Mistress Star's news.

The girls gasped at her announcement. Some wept stunned tears, and clung to each other. Others whispered questions. Hester growled, "Mamá should have told me." Amelia, like the horsemistresses, stared at her boots.

Lark whirled and ran from the room.

It was not allowed for the girls to go into the Domicile unless by invitation, but Lark paid no heed to the restriction. She crashed through the front door, letting it slam behind her, and ran swiftly up the stairs to knock on the door of Mistress Winter's apartment. When there was no response, she knocked again, and again, until at last she heard a weary, "All right, all right. You can stop that banging. I'll come."

Mistress Winter opened the door, and stood stiffly, her face set and still. Lark burst out, "Why didn't you tell me? What are you going to do?"

"Larkyn. What do you think you're about?"

"Mistress Star says—she told us—you've been sent down,

and Sunny—it's too awful! You can't let this happen!" Tears flooded her eyes, blurring her sight as Mistress Winter put a hand on her shoulder and guided her into the apartment, closing the door behind her. Mistress Winter pressed her into a big stuffed chair, and when she had dried her eyes, she saw she was sitting beside the window, with a view of the courtyard and the stables. Mistress Winter stood with one hand on the window sash, her eyes fixed on the summer day beyond the glass.

A small bag, of the kind used to tie behind the cantle of a flying saddle, rested on the bed, which had been stripped of its blankets. A banded trunk waited beside the door. The wardrobe stood open and empty.

Lark took a shuddering breath. "You're really going," she choked.

"Of course, Larkyn. I can hardly stay here. The Council has ruled." Mistress Winter's voice was like a knife, hard and sharp, and it cut Lark's soul.

"But there must be something . . . surely Lord Beeth . . ." Her voice trailed off.

Mistress Winter's lips curled slightly, and her cheeks creased like those of an old woman. She was whip-thin, her cheeks hollow, her hands fleshless. "Of course," she said. "We have tried everything. Do you think we would give up without a fight?"

"Lord Francis?" Lark's voice cracked, and the tears threatened again.

"Brye will explain this to you," Mistress Winter said. "Your brother understands the world as it has come to be."

"But I thought—you're a *horsemistress*! No one can order you away!"

Mistress Winter's face softened a little, and she said in an undertone, "I thought that, too, Larkyn. It seems I was mistaken." She looked down at Lark, her eyes shadowed with sorrow. "I must go, for the sakes of all of you, girls and horsemistresses. In time, I hope . . ." She swallowed, and looked away again.

"But," Lark whispered, "what about Winter Sunset?"

Mistress Winter gave a sour laugh. "The Master Breeder assures me he will care for her."

"He can't!" Lark cried.

"So I told him."

"So the Duke means for her to die."

Mistress Winter's bitter expression was her answer. Still, Lark persisted. "You're not really going to give her up, are you? You could go to the Uplands, to Deeping Farm . . . or to Marin, or perhaps the Angles . . ."

Mistress Winter put out a hand and pulled Lark up out of the chair. "Listen to me, Larkyn," she said. "There is no place in Oc, or in all of Isamar, that I could hide. The Duke's eyes are everywhere, as you and your family have already learned." She led Lark toward the door and opened it. Lark began to sniffle again, but Mistress Winter squeezed her shoulder, hard. "You're a young woman, now, Larkyn. And you're a flyer. You must learn to accept things as they are."

A moment later, Lark found herself standing alone on the steps of the Domicile. The bright day had turned dark for her, the brilliant colors dull. Tup whinnied and cantered to the pasture fence. She went to meet him with slow, painful steps, to bury her face in his silky mane and try to comprehend the immensity of what had happened. "Never, Tup," she whispered against his warm neck. "I will never accept this."

LARK spent a sleepless night and finally rose when the sky lightened enough to see to dress. She washed her face and pulled on her tabard and skirt. She tiptoed down the stairs in her stockinged feet and sat on the Dormitory steps to pull on her boots before she hurried as quietly as she could across the dim courtyard to the stables. A lamp burned quietly in the tack room, and Lark felt certain Mistress Winter had spent the night there, with Winter Sunset. It was what she would have done.

She had only just reached the doorway when Mistress Winter appeared, leading Sunny. Jolinda, the stable-girl from the Beeth stables, was on the mare's other side. Lark quickly stepped into the shadows, hiding herself in the gloom as the two women and the winged horse emerged into the dawn.

She heard Jolinda say, in a choked voice, "I'll go to Fleckham House myself. I'll take care of her, Mistress."

Mistress Winter said, in a gentle voice Lark had never heard before, "No, please. The Duke will be there, and my brother as well, coming in a carriage to take me to Islington House. It's better they don't see you."

"But Winter Sunset—" Jolinda's voice shook, and she pressed her lips together.

"Yes." Mistress Winter bent to tighten Winter Sunset's cinch. "I know you're worried about Sunny. But I beg you, stay here, watch over these girls, especially Larkyn Black. The Duke hates her almost as much as he hates me."

"Why?"

Lark bit her lip, and watched as Mistress Winter stroked her mare's neck with a loving hand. "He's mad," she said flatly. "Drunk with power, with obsession . . . and whatever potion he's used to change his body has pushed him over the edge. Promise me, Jolinda. Promise me you'll stay here, no matter what."

"Aye, Mistress. If it's what you want."

Lark watched Mistress Winter lift her head, scanning the familiar outlines of the Hall, the Domicile, the Dormitory, the stables. The sky brightened, illuminating the emerald paddocks, the hedgerows in full bloom along the lane. She jumped up into the saddle, then said in a low voice, "Do you know, Jolinda, now that the moment is here, I can hardly bear to leave it."

Jolinda tried to answer, but sobbed instead. Mistress Winter's spine stiffened at that, and she lifted Sunny's rein. She spoke to her, and the mare started toward the gate.

"Mistress Winter! Wait!" Lark stepped out into the light. Mistress Winter twisted in her saddle, and Lark ran to her, seizing Winter Sunset's rein. "Were you not going to say goodbye?"

"Larkyn—" Mistress Winter's lean face was like marble in the cool dawn light. "Larkyn, let me go. It's time."

"But—won't you let me—or Lord Francis—"

"Let me go!" Mistress Winter snapped. She clapped her heels to Winter Sunset's ribs, and the mare burst into a quick trot. In moments they were through the gate, cantering down the flight paddock.

Lark ran after, and stood on the rails of the fence to watch as Winter Sunset, her red wings glistening, launched into the rose and blue of the dawn sky. She banked toward the White City, then north toward Fleckham House. Lark stayed where she was even when she could no longer see them, until she heard Tup calling from inside the stables. Then, with dragging steps and aching heart, she climbed down from the fence. Mistress Winter had not looked back, not once.

LARK drilled with her flight, this last day before the Estian holiday, but her heart wasn't in it. Tup seemed to know, and he was even more willful than usual, darting above the line, falling out of formation before she was ready. Only when it came to the Graces did he pay attention. At least he understood that much, that the Graces were their greatest challenge. He flew the pattern perfectly, tilting gently to keep Lark in position. He banked neatly to the left, then to the right, giving her plenty of time in between to adjust her balance.

When it was time to come to ground, she was afraid he might refuse. She put a hand on his neck and willed him to behave. She didn't think, today, that she could bear to be scolded. He soared obediently down over the hedgerow at the foot of the return paddock and galloped easily toward the stables. When she dismounted, he nosed her cheek and whimpered. She threw her arms around his neck and buried her face in his mane for long moments, letting the pain of the day wash over her, letting Tup's warmth and energy soothe her.

As she brushed him down, and cleaned and oiled his hooves, she kept thinking of Mistress Winter and Winter Sunset. They would be separated by now, Sunny whinnying desperately from that awful stable, Mistress Winter walking away, carrying herself in that stiff way she had when she was trying to hide her feelings. Her heart would be breaking. Lark remembered the perfect agony she felt when Tup went missing, and for Mistress Winter, there was no turning back. Even if the Council relented, it would be too late. No winged horse had ever recovered from being permanently separated from its bondmate. Winter Sunset would go mad, endangering herself or others, and have to be put down, or she would go into a decline and die of her own broken heart.

Lark understood that Duke William would not care. The death of Winter Sunset would be the final, triumphant conclusion to his revenge against Mistress Winter.

Lark wondered if she would ever see Philippa Winter again.

Philippa Islington, she would be now, bereft of her winged horse and her horse's name, shut up in disgrace at Islington House.

Everyone felt the same tension Lark felt, in the stables and in the Hall. Herbert snapped at the girls and complained about Jolinda. Jolinda had been silent all day, going about her tasks, and the girls spoke in hushed tones when they spoke at all. Only Amelia Rys seemed her usual calm self, but no doubt she was distracted by the first flush of being bonded.

Supper went past in a deadly silence. The horsemistresses ate almost nothing, and even the ever-hungry students had little enthusiasm for the summer salad and poached fish. They emerged from the Hall into the clear twilight, and Lark paused on the steps to look up into the lavender sky. A quarter moon had risen to ghost above the spires of the White City. Islington House was somewhere in the eastern part of Osham. Perhaps Mistress Winter and Winter Sunset were both looking up at that bit of moon, aching with longing to be together.

There were still horsemistresses and students in the courtyard, some on their way to the stables, some to the Dormitory and the Domicile, when a phaeton, with two lathered horses in the traces, came clattering onto the cobblestones. Hester and Amelia had reached the bottom step, and Lark went down to join them. Everyone turned to see who had come tearing up to the Academy at such a pace.

The driver reined in the horses with a great jangling of bits and harness. Lark didn't recognize the tall, red-haired man who stepped down from the phaeton. But she knew the lean figure of Duke William coming behind him. And she knew the look on his face, and his habit of switching at his thigh with his quirt. He was in a rage.

A little flame of hope began to burn in Lark's heart.

Hester breathed, "Kalla's heels, that's Lord Islington! Mistress Winter's brother!"

Amelia only pursed her lips in silence. Lark peered past Hester's broad shoulder to see the men striding toward the Hall. She jumped when Meredith Islington roared, "Where is she?"

Everyone gaped at him, and he demanded again, "Where is my sister?"

No one answered. No one knew.

The hopeful fire blazed up in Lark's breast. She put both

hands over her mouth to hide her smile. The Duke stalked toward the stables, and Lord Islington to the Domicile, barking orders, demanding information. For an hour they searched the Academy, looking in every corner and nook, opening every door. They found Mistress Star, and badgered her with questions, to which she could only shrug and spread her hands. They insisted on looking in Mistress Winter's apartment, in the small kitchen, in storerooms and attics. They found nothing, though Duke William threatened everyone he encountered with banishment.

It was long past dark before the two men, glowering with frustrated anger, climbed back into the phaeton and whirled away toward the White City. The horsemistresses and the students stood together in the courtyard, shoulder to shoulder, and watched them go.

PHILIPPA untied the bag from behind the cantle of her flying saddle, then unbuckled the cinches and the breast strap. She slid the saddle off Sunny's back, took a towel from the bag, and rubbed her mare thoroughly from chest to tail. She walked her back and forth on the sand, staying close to the dunes in case one of the patrols flew over, but evening was coming on, and the horsemistresses of the South Tower should be done flying for the day.

She dipped a small wooden cup into the creek that ran down the beach to the sea, and sipped from it while Sunny dropped her head and drank. While she waited for Sunny to have her fill, Philippa gazed up at the quarter moon, pallid in the summer night. A breeze blew in from the water, refreshingly cool on her hot skin. It had been a warm day, and a long flight, taking the long way into the south, skimming the coastline to avoid being seen. It would be cold before morning, she knew, but there was little she could do about that. She didn't dare build a fire, and she had only the saddle blanket to cover herself with. She had put cheese and bread in her bag, and a measure of oats for Sunny. She had managed to jam in a change of smallclothes and a hairbrush. She hadn't dared pack anything more. Her books and her clothes had all gone into the trunk, to be uselessly delivered to Islington House.

The thought of Islington House brought a bitter twist to her lips. She hoped Meredith was storming around the White City, looking for her. She hoped William's temper drove him into a fit as he badgered his spies and that ghastly Slater for information. But no one could tell him anything, because only one person— and his daughter—knew where Philippa had gone. And Duke William of Oc had no power over Baron Rys of Klee.

She led Sunny into the lee of a great boulder, where she spread the saddle blanket on the warm sand. With Sunny's nose drooping comfortably beside her shoulder, she sat cross-legged on the blanket and watched the stars appear. Their reflections sprinkled the waters of the sea, breaking apart as the waves rolled onto the beach, shining again as the water smoothed. Philippa released a great breath and began to feel more relaxed than she had in weeks.

It was not such a long flight over the sea to Klee, perhaps three hours. She and Sunny had made the journey once before. One of Rys's trusted captains would meet her on the shore.

She ate her cheese and bread, and drank more cold water from the creek. As the night enfolded her and Winter Sunset, she wrapped herself in the saddle blanket and lay down, wriggling until the sand conformed to her hips and shoulders. Sunny stayed close to her, and the rhythm of the waves soothed them both into sleep. Philippa's last thought, before she closed her eyes, was that William truly was out of his mind if he thought she would ever allow him to separate her from Sunny. Sarah Runner had been right. She would have died first.

FORTY-TWO

NICK came for Lark at midday, to carry her home in the ox-cart, with Tup trotting along behind, and Molly allowed, as a treat, to ride in the cart. Students and horsemistresses were saying farewells as they drove off in their families' carriages or phaetons. Only the third-level girls were allowed to fly home alone, after receiving stern warnings from Headmistress Star about the changeable summer weather, about flying too far or too high, about taking chances.

Everyone at the Academy was sleepy and red-eyed, having stayed up far too late the night before. They had clustered in the stables, in the library, on their cots in the Dormitory, talking, exulting, asking anyone and everyone what they knew. No one, it seemed, had suspected anything, not even Headmistress Star. No one knew that Philippa Winter had meant to disappear with Winter Sunset, but no one was surprised.

They had behaved as one united body before the Duke and Lord Islington. Even Petra Sweet had been shocked by the ruling against Mistress Winter. It helped, of course, that not one of them had the faintest idea where the fugitives had gone.

Lark, though she was as tired as everyone else, felt she must be glowing like an unshaded lamp. The sunshine that had seemed so joyless the day before now seemed almost unbearably bright.

She could hardly wait to see Deeping Farm, and Brye, and Edmar . . . she even looked forward to seeing Peony. With the weight of grief lifted from her heart, she felt so light she thought she might float right off the cart.

Nick grinned as they trundled out to the road, Molly swaying behind the high seat, Tup trotting happily behind. "Take a blink at you!" he said to Lark. "You must be that glad to get away from this place."

"Nay, nay, Nick." Lark laughed. "'Tisn't that at all! Wait till I tell you!" And as they rode toward the Uplands, with the nuthatches twittering at their passage and squirrels scolding from beneath the hedgerows, she told him all about the Council of Lords, and Mistress Winter's defiance of Duke William, and the awful decision that had come down from the Rotunda.

They reached Deeping Farm just as the sun set behind the hills to the west. Lark was nearly speechless at the sight of Lord Francis himself waiting for them in the barnyard, a pitchfork in his hands and one of Brye's battered hats on his head. He looked sun-browned and strong. In his woven shirt and trousers, he looked more like an Uplands farmer than like one of Oc's nobility.

Once Tup and Molly were stabled and fed, and everyone sat down at the long table to eat Peony's fine pottage, Lark had to recite Mistress Winter's entire story again. Brye frowned throughout, his face like a thundercloud, and though Peony and Edmar and Nick clapped at the end, at the delightful discovery that, somehow, Mistress Winter and Sunset had escaped from the Duke, Brye still scowled in rigid silence.

Lord Francis said, "She should have sent for me."

Lark answered him, "Nay, Lord Francis, she feared for your safety. Yon Duke is set upon his road, and no one can stand in his way." She blushed then, and added hastily, "Begging your pardon, my lord. I forget, at times, that he's your brother."

"Where did she go?" Brye asked.

Lark shrugged, and laughed. "No one knows, and that's the best of all! If no one knows, then no one can be forced to tell!"

"I hope she is someplace safe," Brye glowered. "He'll never have done searching."

*   *   *

BRYE'S prediction proved true when Duke William clattered into the barnyard the next day on his lathered, exhausted brown gelding. Pamella came dashing in from the barn, sweeping up Brandon on the way, and hid herself and her son in the pantry. Larkyn called for Nick, who was in the coldcellar. Francis, who had been hoeing weeds in the kitchen garden, jumped over the blackstone fence to lend his support. He kept the sharp-pointed hoe in his hand as he stood in the exact center of the barnyard to face his brother. Larkyn was in the doorway to the stables, protecting her stallion. Nick Hamley brought the paddle of the butter churn up the steps, holding it in both hands like a club.

William leaped off his horse and tossed the reins to the ground. The gelding stood with his head down, his sides heaving.

"You're going to kill that fine animal one day," Francis said coolly.

"Francis," William said. His face was red and his hair wind-whipped, but his tone was as icy as Francis's own. "I'm surprised to see you looking so well. I understood you were somewhere dying."

"I am far from death," Francis said. "Which is more than I can say for your mount."

William didn't even glance back at his horse. "You, brat," he said, pointing his quirt at Larkyn. "Cool my horse."

Larkyn came forward gingerly, a wary eye on William, and took the horse's reins. As he limped after her, Francis heard her speak to him in a tender voice. He said, "Not that you would understand, brother, but that's the way to treat a horse."

William's lip curled. "You're telling *me* how to handle horses, Francis? That's odd, in view of my recent achievement." He took a step forward, and Nick Hamley bridled at his approach, lifting the wooden paddle as if it were a bludgeon. William laughed. "Look at you, Francis! You and the farmer, prepared to do battle with your tools!"

Nick said nothing, but he didn't lower the paddle, either. Francis felt a fresh wave of shame at his brother's behavior. "What are you doing here, William? These good people have work to do. Come to that, surely you do, too."

"Ah. Now you're telling me my duty?" William slapped his

thigh with his quirt. "Since you've been shirking yours, I hardly think that's appropriate."

"I'm going back to Arlton after Estian," Francis said. "I have written to Prince Nicolas, and received a quite gracious letter in reply."

William's eyes narrowed. "He said nothing to me."

"You've been to the Palace?" Francis said lightly. "My, you are busy, aren't you. Deceiving the Council, destroying the bloodlines . . . quite an agenda."

"I have business with Nicolas. He's interested in my *new* bloodline."

"Yes, he would be," Francis said, suddenly weary of the whole exchange. "If he sees a profit in it. Is that what drives you, William? Profit?"

William took another step, close enough that Francis could smell the odd essence of his skin, that slightly sweet, slightly sour smell he had developed. "Where is she, Francis?" he whispered. "Where have you hidden her?"

Francis laughed. "I haven't hidden her anywhere!" he said. "The first I heard of the whole affair was three days ago. Apparently she's disappeared."

"I'll make these people suffer if you don't tell me."

"No, William." Francis took two long steps forward to stand face-to-face with his brother. He gripped William's arm and felt the skin give beneath his fingers. He experienced a rush of pride in the labor he had done in the past weeks, work that had made his hands hard and his shoulders stronger than they had ever been. "No, you won't," he repeated. And in a tone so low only William could hear, he said, "Because if you do, I will tell the Council, and Mother, and all of Oc—indeed, all of Isamar—what you did to Pamella."

William's eyes widened, though he quickly controlled them. He couldn't control the rush of blood to his face, though, that burned over his cheekbones in two angry red patches. "I don't know what you mean," he grated. "If our sister became a slut, it was none of my doing."

"I don't know yet," Francis said through gritted teeth, "if you forced her or seduced her. But I can see for myself who fathered the boy. And I will—I swear by our father's grave that I will—expose you if you trouble these citizens at all."

"You're mad," William said, but his protest was weak.

"Quite the contrary," Francis said. "I am the only sane one left in the family."

William sucked in a breath and wrenched his arm free of Francis's grasp. "I will call your bluff," he said. "You haven't the nerve for this sort of thing."

"No," Francis said. "You won't. And in this case, I do have the nerve, and more. I won't have our legacy besmirched any more than it already is. What will the Council think of incest, added to your other offenses?"

Larkyn had come near them as she walked the gelding to cool him. She froze, staring at William. Francis nodded to her. "Get the gelding some water, will you, Larkyn? My brother is leaving now."

William lifted his quirt, and Francis thought he might try again to strike him. But this time, with a sidelong glance at Nick Hamley, and with awareness of Francis's newly acquired health, he dropped it again. He feigned a laugh and adjusted his hat. "You will regret this one day, Francis," he said. "My memory is long."

"Yes, I know that," Francis said. "It is your character that is short."

William's eyes glittered with madness, but there was little he could do now. Larkyn was bringing his horse back, and Nick had come close enough to stand beside Francis, to hear what he had to say. William took the reins of his gelding and put his foot in the stirrup. When he was mounted, he looked down on them all, his lips pulled tight across his teeth. "Have a care, all of you," he grated. "Diamond will soon fly, and when she does, there will be no one in Oc who will dare defy me!"

He yanked the gelding's head around, making the poor animal grunt, and he put spurs to him before the horse had taken more than two steps. The exhausted gelding galloped down the lane toward the road, his pace labored and uneven.

Larkyn said sadly, "He will ruin that lovely beast."

"Aye," Nick said. "And he wants to ruin the Hamleys."

Francis sighed. "There's little enough honor left to the Fleckhams," he said, "but upon what there is, I swear to you, he won't take your farm. I won't allow it."

*   *   *

ON the eve of Estian, Francis walked with Larkyn to the river that formed the northern border of Deeping Farm. She pointed to a shallow place where the water ran as clear as crystal over the blackstones of the riverbed.

"She stood right there, my Char," she said. "Up to her hocks in the water, every bone showing. I hardly thought she would make it to the barn."

"What a shame you lost her," Francis said.

"It was terrible." She turned her eyes up to his. They were the violet of hyacinths, he thought, or delphiniums like the ones that edged the paths at the Palace. "Lovely sweet she was, Lord Francis. But Kalla brought her to me so she could live long enough to give me Tup."

They strolled along the riverbank, where long grasses dipped into the swirling water. Butterflies, gold and white and black, flitted near a willow tree. "Your family has done mine a great service," Francis said. "I owe my recuperation to your brothers. And—" he laughed, "to Peony's pottage, I think!"

"You do look strong now," Larkyn said, brightening. " 'Tis wonderful to see you working around Deeping Farm."

He chuckled. "When I first came," he said, with a little laugh, "I felt as out of place as a fish tossed out of this river."

She smiled. "Aye. 'Tis different to what you're used to."

"That it is. But I began to feel better almost immediately. And I have come to love the Uplands as you do. I think even Pamella may one day heal if she stays here."

Larkyn bit her lip, then said, in a rush, "My lord—I don't know what you'll think—but I believe Edmar means to marry her!"

Francis stopped where he was, staring at her. "What?"

Larkyn laughed a little, and the ready color surged in her cheeks. "It seems my quiet brother loves them both, Pamella and Brandon. Edmar wants to marry her, and take Brandon as his own son, but he fears—well. She's a duke's daughter, and Edmar only cuts stone in a blackstone quarry."

"And what does Pamella say?"

Larkyn shrugged. "She says naught to me, my lord. But it seems she and Edmar speak enough to come to an understanding.

And Brye approves." She grinned. "Someone of the Hamleys should marry! And though Peony tries so hard, I don't think it will be Nick!"

Francis started walking again, shaking his head. Even after all these months, he still could hardly reconcile the quiet hard-working woman Pamella was now with the flighty young sister he remembered.

"Do you disapprove, then?" Larkyn asked quietly as she walked beside him.

"No, it's not that at all!" Francis said quickly. "I am just startled by the idea."

"You're the only family she has to ask a blessing of," Larkyn said.

He smiled down at her. "It will be an honor to see my sister become a Hamley," he said firmly. "I have never known a more upstanding family."

She glowed with pleasure. "I'll tell Brye, then," she said with relish. "And he can break the news to Edmar. You must return to Willakeep for the wedding, my lord!"

"I wouldn't miss it for anything."

FORTY-THREE

RIBBON Day dawned to a perfect autumn sky. The hills to the west blazed with gold and red and rust. Puffs of white cloud floated high above the Academy, and a gentle wind carried the faint fragrance of burning leaves into the courtyard. Jittery girls hurried through breakfast in order to see to their horses. Even the horsemistresses seemed fidgety, walking through the stables to check the fit of every bridle, the length of every stirrup, the buckle of every cinch.

Lark had brushed Tup's tail until it shone, but she did it again, knowing that in flight it would flow like a banner of black silk. She had just turned to comb through his mane a third time when Headmistress Star appeared at the stall gate.

"Good morning, Larkyn," she said.

Lark inclined her head. "Good morning, Mistress."

"I'm here to make certain you're using your flying saddle," Mistress Star said.

"Oh, aye, of course."

"Good. I understand there was some—irregularity—on your first Ribbon Day."

Lark's cheeks warmed. "My saddle is right here, Mistress," she said. "I'll put it on as soon as the third-levels are done. Tup and I have worked hard on the Graces."

"I look forward to seeing them."

Mistress Star walked on to the next stall, and Lark turned back to Tup. He tossed his head, and his feet rustled the clean straw. "Easy, Tup," Lark murmured. "We have time yet. The third-levels go first. Don't fuss, or you'll be worn-out by the time the drill starts."

He lifted one gleaming back hoof as if to add to the dozens of dents he had already kicked in the wall. Lark said, "No! Tup, no! Not today. Herbert will be furious!"

Tup whickered and pushed at Lark's shoulder with his nose, making her stumble. "Stop teasing me!" It felt good to laugh, to release some of the tension in her chest. "Now you behave yourself, Tup. We have a big day ahead."

The carriages had begun to arrive, bringing the nobility to watch the trials that would make horsemistresses of the third-level girls. The ladies' jeweled caps glittered in the mild sunshine, and their long skirts pooled around the padded chairs that had been set for them in the courtyard. The lords bent their heads together, talking and joking. The very air of the Academy seemed to sparkle with anticipation.

Duke William had not appeared by the time the sun was high in the sky, but Lord Francis had come home from Arlton for the occasion, and he offered to bestow the silver wings on the graduates. Mistress Star and Mistress Dancer conferred worriedly over this, and decided, with the aid of several of the Council Lords present, that this plan would serve.

The second- and first-level girls gathered at the fence of the flight paddock to watch the third-levels fly. As the older girls and their horses passed through the gate, the younger students murmured good wishes. Lark looked up as Petra and Sweet Reason rode past her. Petra's face was pinched with nervousness, and Sweet Reason's tail switched anxiously.

"Sweet," Lark called softly. Petra looked down at her, and her neck stiffened when she saw Lark. Lark nodded to her. "You'll be perfect," she said. "Both of you. I know it."

Petra's lips parted, and for a moment Lark thought she might make some sharp retort. But as Sweet Reason carried her through the gate, she blew a breath through her lips and smiled. She said, in her own natural accent, "Thank you, Black," as Sweet Reason broke into a trot.

The third-level girls performed competently, if not perfectly. Their Arrows, that final Air that all flyers had to learn before graduating, went well, the horses diving toward the ground, pulling out at the last moment, winning applause from the assembly. Their Graces looked the slightest bit ragged to Lark, but it was understandable. It must have been hard for their flight to lose their senior instructor so close to Ribbon Day.

Lord Francis, smiling, gave each member of the flight her wings and a gracious compliment, and the brand-new horsemistresses, beaming with pride and relief, arrayed themselves behind the rows of chairs to watch their younger classmates fly.

Unlike on her first Ribbon Day, Lark brimmed with confidence. Tup felt it, too, launching into the crisp autumn sky with joyous assurance. Their place was at the end of the formation, with Hester and Goldie at the head. Their flight ran through Half Reverses, a triumphant Grand Reverse designed especially for the Foundations to show their skill, a series of Points patterns meant to show off the agility of the Ocmarins, and then, finally, the Graces. There were three required, and Mistress Star had drilled them mercilessly.

The Graces for second-level flyers included the elliptical pattern of their first Ribbon Day, then an interlocking pattern in which the horses flew one above, one below, circling the Academy courtyard. Both of these formations went flawlessly, and Lark's heart swelled, knowing how the horses' wings would look from the courtyard, a kaleidoscope of color, shifting and changing and re-forming in ever more beautiful patterns. Surely Kalla herself must regard these highly schooled creatures with pride.

And then came the final Grace. The flyers banked to the left, tilting nearly at right angles to the ground, and then, on Mistress Star's signal, reversed to the right. It was a move designed to prepare flyers to evade arrows or spears, or to dodge other flyers when necessary. It required a deep seat in the flying saddle, a perfect balance between the rider and the winged horse. Lark, as she felt Tup begin to drop his left wing, snugged her thighs beneath the knee rolls, and shifted her weight to compensate. She still would have preferred to be bareback, with only a chest strap to grip, but they had learned it, she and Tup. They flew for a dozen wingbeats, then they leveled out, and dipped to the right for a dozen more.

No formation of birds could have flown with more skill or in better synchrony than this flight of winged horses. They straightened, skimmed the trees at the end of the flight paddock, and circled back over the Academy to begin a triumphant descent. Every girl was smiling into the wind, every horse's ears turned eagerly forward, hooves tucked, wings vibrant with energy.

Lark hoped Lord Francis was watching.

The flight began to come to ground, first Golden Morning, then Duchess and Lad, Sweet Spring and Sea Girl, Sky Heart and Take a Chance. Lark and Tup were last.

Tup had already stilled his wings, preparing to soar over the hedgerow and down into the return paddock, when they suddenly began to beat again.

"Oh, no, Tup!" Lark cried. "Don't refuse now!"

Tup turned his head to the left, and Lark followed his gaze, gasping at what she saw.

She was coming fast from the north, silvery wings beating frantically, her little neck stretched, her gray hooves flailing. She must have seen the Academy flights from her paddock at Fleckham House. The sight of the winged horses lifting into the sky, creatures like herself circling and swooping through the air, must have called to her very nature. Her own wingless dam couldn't help her. Duke William wouldn't know how to help her.

It was Diamond, William's winged filly. She had launched herself for the first time, and she had no monitor to show her how it was done. She careened toward the Academy, her wingbeats growing erratic as she tired, her ears flicking forward and back as she grew fearful.

The little filly had no idea how to come to ground.

Lark called to Tup, "Hup! Hup!" but he was already ascending, his wings driving them upward. Lark knew her ribbon was at risk, and this time her punishment might be worse than mucking out stalls or mending tack, but she had no choice, and she and Tup both knew it. They couldn't let this little filly fall.

What had the Duke been thinking, or Jinson? Diamond wore no halter, no wingclips. She was too young for her first flight, just as Tup had been.

Tup flew directly above the return paddock, and ascended sharply into the sunshine. High above the roof of the stables, he banked to the left and flew north to meet the filly.

They reached her in moments, but Lark saw with alarm how her silvery hide darkened with sweat, how her immature wings trembled with fatigue. She had flown too far. Lark knew Diamond couldn't hear her above the wind of her flight, but she called out anyway. "This way, Diamond! This way, little one! Follow Tup!"

The filly's eyes rolled with panic, showing the whites. Sympathy and fear clutched at Lark's throat.

Tup whinnied then, the bugling call of a young stallion that cut through the sound of the wind. He made a perfect Half Reverse, a little ahead and above the struggling filly. The muscles across her chest were straining, but she caught his rhythm and matched her wingbeats to his. It seemed to help, as her wings steadied, and her hooves tucked a little tighter beneath her.

She was exquisite, her muzzle narrow and fine, the faint dapples across her croup gleaming like jewels in the sunshine. She was aptly named, a gem among horses. Lark prayed to Kalla that she and Tup could see her safely to ground. They had never monitored a young horse before, and Lark had only her instinct to go on. She had never longed for Mistress Winter and Winter Sunset more than she did at this moment.

But they were not here, and though she saw another horse rise from the Academy, it could not reach Diamond in time.

The return paddock was too far. The filly's strength was giving out.

Tup caught Lark's thought in an instant and began to descend. Lark scanned the ground beneath them, looking for a safe place. Especially for a young horse, they needed smooth ground, soft grass, enough room to run off the speed of landing. But where?

Tup's wings slowed as he lost altitude. The filly's wings rippled and trembled as she struggled to imitate him. And below them, Lark saw the same farmer's field where she had found the injured Bramble. There had been hay in that field, but now it was mown flat. The stubble would be stiff, but she knew the ground was even beneath it.

Tup's black wings spread wide and still, and Diamond, foam flying from her mouth and from her chest, stretched her own fragile silver wings and held them. Lark looked away from her, needing to concentrate on the landing ahead. Tup stretched out his forefeet, gathered his hindquarters, and touched the stubbled field.

The moment he began to gallop, Lark twisted her head to look over her shoulder.

Diamond's gray hooves touched. She stumbled, and her wings scraped across the stubble, but she caught herself and broke into an uneven canter, one wing higher than the other, her head weaving. It wasn't pretty, but she was down. She was safe.

They reached the end of the field, and Lark leaped from her saddle to throw her arms around Tup's neck. "Lovely, lovely boy! Brave boy! I don't care what they do to us for ruining Ribbon Day—you saved her!"

Diamond trotted up behind them and stood, sides heaving, wings drooping.

Lark approached her cautiously, holding out a hand for her to sniff, breathing into her pretty face when she was close enough. Diamond leaned against her, trembling, and Lark put her arms around the filly's slender wet neck. "You poor little thing," she said. "Poor little Diamond. Here, let me show you. Fold your wings, now."

With gentle hands, she helped the filly to fold her wings, rib to rib, the silvery membrane darkening to charcoal as it contracted. She dripped with sweat and foam, and Lark had nothing to dry her with.

"Come now, both of you," Lark said briskly. "You're both hot. Let's walk."

By the time Mistress Star reached them, Diamond was dry and cool, and beginning to recover, but she wouldn't stir a step from Tup's side. She pressed as close to him as she possibly could, her nose touching his shoulder, her shoulder tight against his folded wing.

As the Headmistress dismounted Lark blurted, "Mistress Star, I'm sorry, but she was—"

Mistress Star held up a hand. "You were quite right, Larkyn. Well done. And well done to you, too, Seraph. You did just what Star and I would have done myself."

LARK walked the two horses back to the Academy on the road. Though Diamond had no halter, they didn't need it. She clung to Tup's side while Lark led the way. Mistress Star flew back to finish the Ribbon Day ceremonies. By the time Lark and Tup and Diamond reached the stables, the first-level girls were just finishing their drills, the sun was setting in a haze of gold and scarlet, and Lord Francis was standing on the Hall steps, ready to give them their ribbons.

A few lords and ladies still sat in the courtyard, sipping cups of tea Matron had brought them. Their conversion died as Lark appeared with the two horses.

Duke William arrived moments afterward. He leaped down from a phaeton drawn by two swift-looking bays, with Jinson at the reins. Jinson climbed down more slowly, after securing the traces. He had a halter and wingclips in his hands, and a look of shame on his face.

Duke William, evidently, felt no such shame. He swept across the courtyard toward Lark, his open greatcoat swirling around his polished boots. Lark was shocked at his appearance. His face had grown fuller, and his chest, though he wore a tight vest buttoned to his neck, swelled visibly behind the lapels of his coat. He seemed to have gained weight around the hips as well, so that his narrow black trousers pulled across the middle. The angry look in his eyes was familiar, though, and the high timbre of his voice. He stalked up to Lark, causing Tup to pull back and flatten his ears. Diamond threw up her head, and stared at him.

"So, brat," the Duke said. "It's you again."

"Aye, my lord." She lifted her chin. "Yon filly was in trouble, sir."

"*My* filly," he said.

Lark glanced at Diamond, who shrank back against Tup, watching the Duke with wide eyes. As the Duke stepped close to her, one hand out, Tup bared his teeth. The little filly's ears drooped, and flicked confusedly from Tup to the Duke.

"Diamond," the Duke said. Lark blinked in surprise at the gentleness in his tone. "Come to me, my little Diamond. Let's get you home."

"She must have seen the flights, sir," Lark said. "You'll need to wingclip her now, and you'll need a monitor. She shouldn't fly alone."

"A monitor." He shot a look of fury over her head at Jinson. "Find me one, Jinson."

"M'lord, I don't know . . ."

"I'll take the brat, then," William said. "Now that she's already done it."

"You won't take her anywhere," Francis said. Lark caught a swift breath and turned to find that Lord Francis had come up behind them, and stood now at a comfortable distance from Tup and Diamond, but close enough to give his lord brother a steady stare. "Larkyn is now a third-level Academy student, finalizing her training to be a horsemistress. This is hardly a time to take her away from her studies."

William's face reddened. "Must I remind you, Francis, that I'm the Duke, and you're not? If I command one of my flyers to do something, she does it. She can come and stay at Fleckham House—with her little black, of course—and teach my Diamond to fly. In fact, I order it."

"No, you don't," Francis said. Lark felt that her eyes must be stretched as wide as Diamond's. It didn't seem possible that Lord Francis, gentle, kind Francis, could stand against the violence and madness of his brother. Duke William began to turn his quirt in his fingers, and his eyes hardened. Lark looked around for someone to help, but the lords and ladies kept their distance, though they looked on with avid expressions. The horsemistresses watched from the steps of the Hall. Mistress Star, it seemed, was poised to act if necessary, but Mistress Star was a slight woman, only barely taller than Lark herself.

Lark clung to Tup's rein. She kept her chin thrust out, but she trembled inside. She struggled for something to say that would forestall such a disaster. If she were forced to go to Fleckham House—this madman would kill her! He would find an opportunity, catch her alone, and there would be no one to protect her.

But Francis, in a mild tone, said, "William. Let's talk a moment." To Lark's surprise, Francis put a hand under William's arm and led him across the courtyard. It seemed to her that the Duke resisted, but briefly. When they were out of earshot, Francis began to speak. He kept his hand on the Duke's arm, and Lark remembered how hard that hand had grown, doing a farmer's work. Francis spoke, and William pulled back, glaring at him. Francis spoke again, his free hand making a sharp movement, his face intent. The two brothers stared at each other for long moments as Lark held her breath.

And then William gave a short, humorless laugh that carried across the courtyard in the dusk. He turned his back on Francis and strode back to Tup and the filly.

Jinson handed him the halter and lead, and William went to the filly and buckled it on. She tolerated this, but Tup backed away, making Diamond whicker longingly at him. William tugged on her lead, and she followed him, her wings flexing, her ears turning back to Tup. To Lark, every line of her body spelled reluctance, spoke of her longing to be close to another winged horse.

The Duke gave Lark one last, malevolent look over his shoulder. He didn't speak, but the glitter in his black eyes made her blood run cold.

She shivered and turned to Jinson, forcing herself to speak in a level voice. "Does the little one have an oc-hound to foster her?"

"She did, but the dog didn't like the Duke," he said. "So he sent him away. Her dam is breeding again, so she's off at the Ducal Palace. The filly just has His Grace for a companion."

"She's sad," Lark said.

"Aye, Miss. I fear so."

"You should find her a wingless horse, at least, something for company."

Jinson glanced down at her. "Young or old?"

Lark shrugged. "That doesn't matter so much as that they like each other. Some horses take to each other, and some don't."

Jinson sighed and started after the Duke, who was tying the filly's halter lead to a ring behind the phaeton.

"Oh, and Jinson," Lark said, trotting after him. "She's tired. She flew much too far for such a young horse, and on her first flight. Keep a gentle pace as you go back."

"I'll try, Miss. But His Grace likes to take the reins."

Moments later, they were gone, the Duke whipping up the bays, the little silver filly trotting prettily behind the phaeton. Tup whickered as she left the courtyard, and she whinnied a response.

Lark stood with one hand on Tup's neck, frowning. When

Lord Francis came up to her, to hand her the ribbon she had earned that day, she dropped Tup's reins and stepped away to meet him. Francis smiled at her as he pinned the ribbon on her tabard.

"Lord Francis," she said. "What did you say to the Duke?"

"I warned him," Francis said quietly. "That I would tell these lords and ladies in the courtyard all about Pamella. It's the only real threat I have to control him."

"Aye," Lark said, nodding. "He would not want that to come out."

"No. He hasn't admitted anything, but he knows there is too much talk already." Francis looked after the Duke's phaeton as it turned into the road. "I think I will ask the Prince to release me from his service so that I can come home to Osham. Someone must prevent William from further madness."

"Lord Francis," Lark asked. "Do you know where she's gone?"

He knew, it seemed, who was on her mind at that moment. "No, Larkyn. I don't. But I can guess."

"Will you tell me?"

"It's better you don't know. Better for you, and safer for Philippa."

She released a long breath, full of the excitement and the fear and the tension of the day. "I wish she could have seen me," she said. "Winning my second-level ribbon."

"I'm sure she feels the same, Larkyn." He smiled. "Let us hope that one day, William and the Council Lords will reconsider, come to their senses."

"Could she return then? Come back to the Academy?"

"Amnesty could be granted. But William would have to agree." Lark shook her head. "I don't think he ever will."

"Anything can happen, Larkyn, if an Uplands farm girl can become a horsemistress."

She flashed him a grin. "Oh, aye. Miracles! We'd best put Mistress Winter in Kalla's hand and see what happens."

Tup whickered at her, and she turned to speak to him. "Aye, Tup, I know. Excuse me, Lord Francis. Tup here wants his supper."

"Go, then. I'll see you in the Hall. Your Headmistress invited me to celebrate this great day with all of you."

"Aye, my lord. A lovely great day indeed."

As Lark turned into the stables, where the other girls had already untacked and fed their horses, she was still thinking of Mistress Winter. She wondered if, wherever she might be, Philippa would know that she and Tup had passed their Airs and Graces.

At Tup's stall, Amelia Rys was waiting for her, holding the gate open, a faint smile on her narrow face. It occurred to Lark that there might be one person, after all, who knew where Philippa had gone.

As Lark led Tup in out of the cooling evening air, Amelia said, "Congratulations, Black! I watched everything. You and Seraph were marvelous."

"Thank you," Lark said. "It was mostly Tup."

"I'll help you rub him down."

They went into Tup's stall and rubbed him dry. Amelia filled his water bucket while Lark measured grain and buckled his blanket over him. The nights were drawing in, and soon there would be frost on the grass in the mornings.

"Your class will be arriving before long, Amelia," Lark said. "You'll be flying before you know it."

"I can hardly wait."

As they left the stables and climbed the steps to the Hall for the festive supper awaiting them, Lark looked hard into Amelia's eyes, trying to guess if she knew something.

Amelia smiled as if she understood perfectly, but she said not a word.